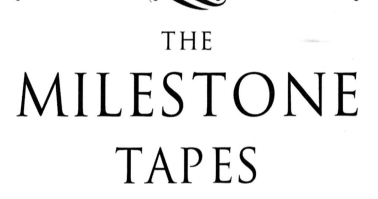

THE
MILESTONE
TAPES

Copyright: The Milestone Tapes copyright 2011 Ashley Mackler-Paternostro

ISBN-10: 1468150065
ISBN-13: 978-1468150063

Contact Information:
    Website: www.ashleymacklerpaternostro.com
    E-mail: ashley@ashleymacklerpaternostro.com

Cover Designer:
    Scarlett Rugers of Chick Lit Book Covers www.chicklitbookcovers.com

To Susan,
There is so much to thank you for...
like, absolutely everything.
Love you always.

THE END - THE PROLOGUE

AUGUST 18, 1999

"Dr. Vaughn seemed hopeful. I took that as a good sign," Gabe said as rested his hand on Jenna's leg and the plane lurched forward, beginning its taxi towards the end of the run way and the open air beyond. Beneath her seat Jenna could feel the rotations of the wheels cease, the underbelly unlatching to cradle them. The plane picked up speed as it launched itself into the sky and Jenna held her breath, waiting on the brief, sweet moment of weightlessness that followed.

She turned towards her husband and forced a smile for him. *Stage three, stage three, stage three.* The diagnosis echoed. But it was not *the diagnosis*, it was *hers, her diagnosis.* She had begun to singsong it in her mind as if, somehow, set to a melody cancer became less frightening, lighter, more digestible and manageable. *Lymph nodes and muscles and breast tissue.*

"I was thinking we could get a place in the city. Then we wouldn't have to travel back and forth. A place like we had before. Maybe even in the same building. I could call and see what's available. What do you think?" he continue to speak, as the air pressure around them changed and her ears popped as they entered into the new atmosphere.

She tried to grab hold of his words and his voice, but she couldn't. She blinked, her mind spinning as she listened to Gabe carve out a plan while his fingers stroked her leg. *Stage three, stage three, stage three.*

"Or we could buy a place. Sell it when this is behind us. Whatever you want."

"I don't want to upset Mia's life." Jenna answered softly, "I want to keep everything as close to normal as possible for the duration."

"She's three. She doesn't know. It's important that we're close to hospital. That's what the doctor said."

"They have a hospital in Port Angeles." Jenna answered.

"Not the sort you need."

The hospital would become a hive, she would become a worker bee. Shuttling back and forth for treatment. *Chemo and radiation and a radical mastectomy.*

What she wanted was her mother.

Since the moment the lump had been located, Jenna had obsessed over her mother, Elizabeth. Ached for her in new and foreign ways. She tried to imagine what Elizabeth would have said, tried to hear her mother's voice in the silent moments of worry and fear Jenna felt when she was alone. But she was long gone, and with her, all the answers to the endless loop of questions Jenna had now.

"I read an article about a woman who left letters for her daughter. She had Alzheimer's disease, I believe. Early onset. She just wrote out everything she wouldn't remember to say. I think she wrote them in birthday cards. One for each year. That's nice, don't you think?" Jenna whispered.

She could feel Gabe still beside her. The lazy, invisible circles he'd been drawing on her leg were left unfinished, like a long, winding life snuffed out before the natural end.

The recycled air of the plane hummed between them. "I'm not saying I'm dying." Jenna spoke softly, "I'm thinking about my mom. I've been doing that a lot lately. And I'm just saying, the cards, that's a nice thing to do. I would have loved something like." *Especially now,* she thought, though she didn't say that to him.

"All you need to focus on," Gabe cleared his throat and continued, "Is figuring out how you want to work the treatment schedule. First things first."

Jenna turned towards the window and the wide, beautiful world below. The incision in her left breast ached. Hovering over heart. The place where her oncologist's needle punctured her pale flesh had flowered with a dusky bruise and throbbed exquisitely behind the lifting veil of numbness.

BOOK ONE

Because I can no longer ignore death,
I will pay more attention to life.

—Treya Wilber—

CHAPTER ONE

MAY 9, 2002

THE SKY, HEAVY AND THREATENING, was an ominous beast brewing overheard. *The perfect beginning,* Jenna thought as she lay wholly still in her bed, her arms crossed against her chest, her eyes open and unblinking, she stared up, watching the way the clouds undulated through the pitch of the glass paneled roof above her. Thick waves of grey brought in from the west, carried on the winds stirred up by the sea. She studied them as they crossed, low-slung and hulking with the promise of heavy rain, interspersed with thready wisps that raced against each other like long-tailed ghosts. She admired the way the faint spittle of mist that fell collected on the glass, beading and drooling, creating an abstract work of art. The lush green wilderness beyond the enclave of her home sprawled out and over into the docile bay, through an opened window she could smell the earth alive and well — the green sweetness of the flora, the brine of the Pacific waters that filled the Salish Sea, the rot of the soft ground. In the hush of morning, Jenna ached to take it all in for a long moment before the day unleashed itself upon her.

Today she would untie herself from the last filament of hope that had kept her tethered to the fight. She would watch silently as it floated away like a balloon slipped from between her fingertips. Today would be what some called the beginning of the end, others called it long goodbye.

Gabe. She could feel his back, long and warm, through the thin cotton of his undershirt pressed against her upper-arm as he slept beside her. He was where the story of her began, where the chapters of her life had started to matter. Of course she wouldn't untangle herself from motherhood now, given the chance; it was same as imaging herself suddenly without her sight or another comfortable, almost given, attribute. Life without Mia was entirely unimaginable. But those childless years they'd once had still made her heart flutter. The lilt of it, the way it had been so simple, so easy. Now that she was facing the end, she'd become a necromancer of the past, dredging it up just to delight in what she saw.

They had managed the first years of their marriage with something that resembled hope; they had been young and crazy with love, and their conviction in what could be had been the sustaining force of their relationship, a sustenance as real as any other, something that had nourished them in times of less as Jenna pounded away on her secondhand typewriter chasing a dream and as Gabe wore paths on his drafting table with the tip of a pencil. Then, one day, it simply clicked. It clicked so completely that if anyone had been listening, they could have heard it.

From the outside looking in, it would have

appeared to have happened overnight. From one day to the next, Jenna was no longer a struggling author, her third book had found a home with a literary agent, gone to auction and secured a multi-book deal with a prominent New York publishing house in what the industry write-ups had called a *very nice deal*. Gabe was no longer overworked and underpaid, and the plaque on his desk declared him creative director of the start-up architectural firm which had just begun to flourish. They had celebrated the windfall by renting a handsome apartment in the Belltown neighborhood of Seattle. It had been the sort of pre-war affair Jenna had always romanticized. There, beyond her smog splotched windows, were endless views of the congested, rain-soaked city. The sound of shuffling feet was a soundtrack of their new life and could be heard above and below at all hours of the day or night. The thick plaster walls they'd repainted in shades of sea-glass divided all twelve-hundred square feet into happy spaces warmed by faulty radiators.

It was only the ticking clock that changed things for them. Jenna had awoken to her thirty-seventh year and knew that the time had come for the hard decisions she'd been meaning to make for years, and the change that was coming, as it so often did, had begotten bigger change.

Convincing Gabe to leave Seattle behind had been more of a challenge than she had anticipated. Gabe loved the culture and the steady drone of life in the city. It was from all of that around him that he drew the inspiration for his work. He could look at the skyline and see what was missing the same way a painter could look a blank canvas and conceptualize a masterpiece. He had put forth a valiant effort trying to sell her on staying. He had taken her to see the large Victorian brownstones that lined the quiet streets of Queen Anne and promised her any one she wanted; he could give her space and a home right there, he said, making a point of taking her to the most versed shows, the cleanest parks, the most culturally diverse districts and shops, reintroducing her to the place they called home. But Jenna hadn't be budged.

To be fair, they had always been city folk, they hadn't know small town life, or even if they could adjust to it. Having converged on Seattle for different reasons—Jenna because of her love for all things artistic in nature, and Gabe simply because of a job offering—they had gotten to know each other during lunchtime strolls at Pike Place Market, sipping Starbucks coffee from the famed original storefront, dining over fresh-catch at the top of the Space Needle, and infusing themselves into the din. Seattle was as much a part of their love story as they, themselves, were and in many ways it was their home there that had defined them or, at least, defined the things that defined them. They'd have to reinvent themselves away from a city that offered the ability to be local or be lost. They'd have to become small town people with small town lives. The thought of leaving everything behind had left them an intersection of bitter and sweet.

Build me a home, she'd whispered to Gabe one night as they walked hand and hand back to Belltown from an impressive showing at an art gallery. She'd watched Gabe all night weave around the room, shaking hands and studying the instillations with the keen eye of an artist in his own right. *Not a house. Anyone can build a house. But a home. Let us leave here and build a life. Let us grow old together in a place that speaks of us—the people we are and the people we're meant to become. And, for that, Mr. Chamberland, I will write us a happy ending.*

What she had really asked when she purposed the home was this: Design it, execute it, live in it with her and their baby.

To the west, the Olympic Peninsula offered life by the mile. An entire coastline of bedroom communities and harbor towns with small airports and ferries that would give Gabe what he needed to continue to grow in his career and give Jenna what she knew she wanted most: A quaint town where their baby could feel the Pacific Ocean waters rush between the spaces of her fingers and sand beneath her bare feet, see the snowcapped mountains from any room in their home, hike the Hoh rainforest to marvel at the amount of the green, and, in equal measure, take in the culture of the big city. In the bargain, Jenna saw something that would be a beautiful balance.

As summer set in they took meandering drives each weekend, looking for a place to lay down their roots. Once they had reached Port Angeles, they had stopped driving. The town was picturesque and flush with possibilities. The main street was lined with locally owned specialty stores and boutiques offering antiquities, arts, practicalities, and necessities. The plots of land still available for developing offered spectacular views of the Salish Sea, and through the almost constant cover of clouds, the crown of Hurricane Ridge. All of that appealed to Jenna, while Gabe took comfort in the ease of access to both the ferries and the small airport, which boasted several charter flights in and out of SeaTac daily, any one of which could deposit him in the heart of Seattle within an hour.

Once they had decided on the *where*, they were tasked with creating the *what*. The home. Something that would anchor them, something large without being pretentious, something unusual without being overly eccentric.

Jenna had sat up at night making her plans. Design magazines cluttered the tables where she worked and the wish-boards she'd taped to the walls were tacked with fabric samples and paint colors. They made trips to the wild coast of Rialto Beach and gathered stones of various shapes and colors, which Jenna laid by hand in all the bathrooms. Weekends were spent ordering copper-foil glass from local artists, evaluating the particulars of exotic woods, mulling over paint samples and all the other trivial yet defining bits that would equal their home. It was an exhausting labor of love.

The completion had signified a dream realized and two more years of their lives with it. In the end, the Chamberland home stood high above Port Angeles, slopping downward to the water's edge, nestled on a large plot of land rimmed with lush gardens, and, beyond them, the natural forest. Thick craftsman pillars dotted the wraparound porch, and leaded glass windows were in abundance, set neatly into the ocean-blue shaker siding. The home was wide and long, a series of rooms that flowed from one to another. The ceiling of their bedroom was a pyramid of glass, letting the sky inside. The rear wall, which faced the untouched wilderness and dropped down towards the bustling port below, was a series of floor to ceiling windows that could be folded inward, opening seamlessly onto a stone patio that ran the length of the home. The kitchen was central, the heart, just as Jenna had wanted, with plenty of cabinet space, thick soapstone counters and double butcher-block islands.

Jenna sighed deeply and rolled over, curving herself around her husband. Today would be a long day for them both; she could feel that settle into her bones and tears prick her eyes as everything piled upon her in one fell swoop. The looming charter flight to Seattle, the meeting, the final decisions she would be asked to make, and then the last flight home. But none of that felt as daunting or exhausting as what would await their return: Mia.

Mia, her miracle baby. Once life was settled, they had agreed to start trying. Jenna had been creeping ever closer to forty, and understood getting pregnant wouldn't be easy, that those days were long gone. She knew that by having waited past her peak, it could be years before the blessing of a baby would grace them. She'd done research on adoption and surrogacy, but life worked in mysterious ways. Almost as though Mia had been waiting patiently in the wings, within a few short weeks of ceremoniously pitching her birth control, Jenna discovered, much to her joy, that she was pregnant.

For the first handful of years after Mia joined them, life was bliss. Jenna doted on her baby, loving the changes motherhood had brought her more than she ever thought possible. Even the sleepless nights and long stretches of days never displeased her. Parenthood had realigned Gabe's focus in equal measure. He commuted to Seattle for a few months after Mia was born before tiring of the grind, but more so, he tired of missing his daughter and wife. He left his firm and opened a local custom home construction company to meet the booming demands of the area. It grew slowly, but soon became steady and dependable work.

Measures of time came to mean something new as Jenna published, Gabe built, Mia grew. They had a full life, leaving no room to miss the before; the present was so rewarding and enveloped them so entirely.

Then the clouds rolled in.

Jenna turned over in their bed and pressed her back against Gabe, facing the wide expanse of yard. The stone patio was dark with the morning rain, the blades of grass beyond it glittered with raindrops and dew. It had happened right there.

When Mia was a jubilant three-year-old, speaking and walking and engaging the world around her with opinions and imaginative play and friends, Jenna first found the lump.

An unleashed hose in the back yard on a warm summer's day had been to Mia's afternoon companion. She'd taken up a game where the hose was not just a hose, but untamed, dangerous green snake which had broken free from its cage and Mia's job was to wrangle the reptile. Jenna had watched as that rubber hose flipped and twisted wildly and listened to Mia scream with laugher and delight, skipping back and falling to her knees when she got splashed with an errant flood of that reckless water. That was all it had taken to make Jenna want it again. The pregnancy and the baby and the toddler. She'd never imagined Mia as an only children, pictured her having a sibling; but now she wanted another child for herself. She was hedging on forty-four, but to have another one, it would be worth anything it took—they could try she reasoned, and if all else failed, she would freeze her eggs if she could and find a surrogate, and if not that, then adoption. As her mind wove webs around the idea, her family had grown before her eyes, and she could see it so clearly.

But that time would be different: there would be no twin-pink lines and toasts of apple cider in chilled champagne flutes. They had found it then, the irregular mass in her left breast, growing silently over her heart, deep within the tissue. It felt like a golf ball beneath her fingers, pitted and pebbly and surprisingly hard. Her doctor made no more mention of trying to have another baby once her fingers fell upon it; she only pushed Jenna towards an oncologist for further testing with a regretful smile, watery eyes, and best wishes.

"This message is for Mrs. Chamberland. Mrs. Chamberland, hi, this is Lisa from the Pacific Oncology and Treatment Center. We received the results of your test this morning, and the doctor would like to speak with you in person at your earliest opportunity. Please call us back so we can make arrangements. Thank you."

That was it—all that it took. The long. The short. The whole story. The message that effectively changed her life. Took the axis the Chamberland world had so effectively spun on for years and reduced it to dust.

Jenna had stood in her kitchen, at the intersection of

hope and death, doubled over at the waist, feeling light headed, pressing her hands against the cool expanse of her countertops to steady herself. The anger she had felt had eventually crumpled her to the floor, she had pulled her knees up to her chest and curled inward. She told herself now, looking back, it was because she knew. She hadn't been being dramatic, or pessimistic. She had simply known. Cancer, a predestined thing, like blue eyes or blond hair. Something that was born into a child. A genetic lasso that tangled her up. In someways, she'd been waiting on that call for years. She was incensed, she was terrified, but not surprised. After all, Jenna had been down this road when she was eighteen years old, with her own mother, with the same lump and the same phone call and the same heartbreak.

Now, three years from that message and that visit that followed—the same outcome. She was dying.

Stage four, stage four, stage four. The voice that had taunted her from the beginning began barbing at her as she grit her teeth and tried not to cry. It wasn't just her breast that betrayed her any more, but her bones. Her liver. Her brain. Her lungs. *Riddled* was the word she'd first thought when she saw her most recent scans. The nooks and hollow spaces of her body lit up, her tumors glowing white in the grey fog.

Jenna rolled over, "Gabe?" She brushed her husband's shoulder lightly. "Are you awake?"

"Yeah." His voice sounded hoarse, exhausted, and beaten.

"We should get moving. Ginny will be here soon and our flight leaves in two hours..." Jenna let her voice trail off. She didn't want to get moving, she didn't want to face the nanny or board the flight or see the doctor or give up. What she wanted was to sink back into sleep, back into her memories of a life that was no more complicated than juggling a baby, a book, and an impending grocery store visit.

"Jenna." His voice was full of the pleas he'd imposed on her over the past few days since she'd leveled her decision down upon him and left him no say in the matter. She'd been ice and stone, an unmovable glacier of righteousness and because of that, he didn't make more entreatments now; he just let the weight of what was left unsaid hang in the air.

"When you say my name like that, it just makes it harder for me." Jenna lifted her chin and closed her eyes. *The long goodbye,* the voice inside her head murmured.

Gabe threw the covers off and slipped out of bed, padding towards the bathroom without another word.

Their marriage, more than twenty-years old, had gifted her with ability to feel what he'd felt. She knew him so completely that she could read all his errant thoughts simply by looking into his eyes, could sense and touch what he reckoned as though emotions and silent wants were tactile things and this morning, the anger and despair that radiated from him was thick. So thick she couldn't breathe with it in the room. Jenna opened her eyes to the sky above her again as the tears of frustration and disappointment she'd tried to temper slipped from her eyes, rolled down the rise of cheeks, wetting the pillow beneath her. The early morning clouds rolling in from the sea were no longer pieces and parts, no longer abstract and lovely, but a smothering blanket of grief.

This cancer was killing them all. It had killed them

over the years by inches, little by little, with each moment it stole and each day it progressed. Her cancer had become their cancer, each of them sick with it in their own way. If the first three years of their lives here had been a practiced bliss, the last three years had been learned heartbreak.

After the doctors had found—and subsequently confirmed—the lump, she had rallied. She saw the right doctors, she sipped the right tea, she lay perfectly still while the medical tattoo artist marked her breast for radiation, pinpoint black dots that would hone in and hopefully kill their target. She swallowed the pills dutifully with bottles of entirely pure water; she had willingly removed her breasts, nipples, lymph nodes, and glands, praying all the while that the last surgery would get it all. *Take everything*, she had bargained. *Leave me with my life.*

When it spread, she smiled blithely and bravely as the nurse slipped the needle into her shunt and opened the trickle of healing poison through her veins. Throughout it all, she endured and prayed and hoped. Time had slipped and faded into scenes of Jenna crumbled on the cool stone floor of the bathroom, retching hollowly into the toilet, brushing her hair out in patches when the chemotherapy stole that from her, too, nursing her radiation burns with medicinal ointment, withstanding it all stoically.

There was never a moment of motherhood that wasn't subject to the precursor of treatment or disease. Birthday parties were postponed or canceled entirely because Jenna was sick or was feeling better. God forbid one of Mia's friends had a cold and attended and sent Jenna into a spiral, her immune system was so compromised and fragile. Holidays were thrown together at the last minute for the sake of Mia because Jenna couldn't muster more than that. And her marriage, what sacrifices hadn't she made there, as well? The intimacy, spontaneity, and humor had all changed. Looking back now, she saw it for what it had been, a mile-long tally of losses without a single win.

Because of—or, in spite of—that, Jenna tried harder. Cultivated a world that would make sense of the senseless for Mia. On not so good days, Jenna would encourage Mia to crawl into bed with her, and, snuggling together, they would read stories or play with Mia's menagerie of stuffed animals, giving them voices and characters with faults and flaws and redeeming value. It was here, between the quilts and pillows piled high on a king-sized bed, that Jenna tried to teach Mia about the world at large, about human nature and the importance of understanding and forgiveness. On good days, Jenna would rise and help Mia with her homework, encouraging the budding creativity she saw in her little girl, make the most of those precious hours before she'd tuck Mia into bed at night.

But more often than not, there were really bad days. It was then that Jenna was physically pained more so by the limitations imposed by her disease than the disease itself. She would sit by the bedroom door, her ear pressed against the solid wood panes, listening to her little girl play make-believe with the nanny, running through the halls as a princess or ballerina or magical pony, telling Ginny about school, her friends and teachers. It was only then that Jenna would allow herself to break and shatter under the disappointment. That should have been her, she'd obsess, her hands balled at her sides, her nails chiseling quarter-moon slivers into her palm and tears running uninterrupted down her sallow cheeks. She should be the one huddled over homework, or knee deep in Barbie clothes, or chasing after Mia, cackling like a wicked witch enthralled by a game of pretend. She shouldn't be sidelined while hired help raised her baby. But she was, and the further the tentacles of the disease spread, grabbing the remaining bits and pieces of her life and swallowing them whole, the more removed she had to become.

But on those nights, at the end of those bad days, Jenna would sneak into Mia's room long after she'd fallen under the lull of sleep. She would gather her daughter's plump, dimpled hands in her own, and then Jenna would sink beside the bed on her knees and pray her own prayers.

She'd spend what felt like hours silently talking to God. Promising and pleading, appealing and eventually bartering, offering anything for more time and restored health—*if not both, then please just one*. She'd stare at her daughter's heart-shaped lips, parted and slack with sleep, dreams running wild in her head, and Jenna would sweep Mia's curly brown hair from her forward, pressing her hand against it, as if she were trying to feel those dreams with the palm of her hand.

God had answered her prayers. Jenna was visiting her primary Seattle oncologist alone when he had leveled the blow. *"The cancer has spread. Breast, brain, bone, blood. Lung...muscle"* Dr. Vaughn had said morosely. They could continue the fight, he explained compassionately, but they wouldn't win. Winning was lost to them now.

Jenna had sobbed, screamed, and implored him for something more — a clinical trial, a holistic shot-in-the-dark, a new drug, anything at all. She couldn't believe that there was nothing left for her, not after they had come so far in the past three years. There was no way she could simply roll over in defeat, there had to be something more she could do. But, as Jenna had learned, tears didn't change anything.

"Jenna, honey, you in there? You okay?" The knock and calling voice at the door was so sweet, soft, and nurturing that it made Jenna's heart seize up.

"Hey Gin, I'm here and I'm okay. We'll be leaving shortly. Can you get Mia up? I laid out an outfit for her." Jenna sat up slowly, planting her feet on the floor. Time, more time, had slipped past her.

"Okay, sugar, and I'll fix you and Gabe something to eat for the road." And with that, Ginny's heavy footfalls retreated down the hallway towards the kitchen.

Jenna tapped lightly on the door of the bathroom and turned the handle in the same moment. She found him sitting on the rim of the bathtub. His hands shielding his face and his shoulders hunched forward, elbows planted squarely on his thighs.

"Gabe…" Jenna sunk down beside in him, curling her arm around his waist, she rested her chin on his shoulder. "Please."

"I'm just…just not ready. I wish I could be, you know—for you." He looked up; his eyes were raw and red.

"I know." She looked at him then without

blinking, willing him to believe her; it was a look of sheer honesty, one they had traded so many times in their marriage.

When Jenna had closed her eyes on the plane as it lifted off back to Port Angeles last week, the envelope of fresh scans tucked inside her bag, a wash of calm had swallowed her. The decision that she had fought against, one that seemed entirely inconceivable just hours before was suddenly her harbor of peace. *Stop fighting, let what will be, be.*

She wasn't quitting on him, or them, or their responsibilities. She was giving everyone the only sort of chance she could. An ending come much too soon, but she'd be damned if it would be anything short of happy or the closest thing to happy that she could make it. That's when she decided. Chose the only thing left worth choosing. By stopping her treatments, they'd have time. Would that time be three weeks or three months or a year? No one knew, and no one could tell her, at best she'd get a rough estimate. But whatever it was, they'd at least have some of that, and it would count. However long or short, she would take the time they were given and make it matter.

Jenna stood up and moved in front of Gabe, taking his hand in her own, she gently tugged him, urging him to stand. She rose up on her toes and kissed him hard on the lips. Sighing deeply into his mouth. He felt so good. He had always felt so good to her, like home, like a place she undoubtably belonged and a place she could return to time and again. The passion of their relationship had ebbed and flowed over the years and had dipped off significantly when she had gotten sick, but she still loved him like crazy and that had never changed. Never would. She lifted his shirt over his head, pressing herself against his bare chest, she felt the shift of his taut muscles under his skin. She backed away, her fingers undid the buttons of her nightshirt, one at a time, slowly. Once, not so long ago, she had shied away from these moments of raw exposure, her chest a plate of slashes and scars that wrapped around her back and upward into the crook of her armpit. After her radical mastectomy, she had never felt less like a woman; the breasts that had filled her dresses and fed her baby had been removed, leaving behind a complex circuit of drains and staples, which eventually healed into a web of cicatrix, telling the story of what she had endured. But in that moment, she lost the ability feel even the slightest hitch of modesty. She felt him move away from her, twisting the handle of the shower on, and, as steam filled the stall, they stepped inside together, lost to the outside world entirely.

"Ginny?" Jenna called as she made her way down the long hall towards the kitchen, dressed in a soft cashmere sweater dress and black leggings with casual leather flats. The smell of warm blueberry toast and coffee wafted through the bright, large space. Ginny never failed to make the house feel good just by walking through the door, and made it feel even better when she set herself in the kitchen, whipping her way around a meal.

"Well look at you—you look good!" Ginny smiled from across the kitchen table, sipping a cup of coffee. The table was set for a party of one, awaiting the presence of Mia, who would devour her breakfast and scamper off to play for a few precious moments before school.

"You flatter me." Jenna bent down, giving Ginny a strong hug.

"You hungry, honey?" Ginny asked her as Jenna released her.

"I'll just grab something at the airport in Seattle."

Jenna had always wished she could be the one to say she'd found Ginny. That when she knew the time had come for help she'd searched high and low to find the best. But the truth was: Ginny had found Jenna.

For the first few months after the initial diagnosis Jenna had tried to do it all. She cared for Mia and tended the house during the day, balancing that with her treatments and appointments, and wrote her stories at night. It worked for a while but had wore Jenna down fast; the neighborhood mothers had pushed for her to entertain the thought of *help*. The idea had horrified Jenna at the time. Things were bad enough; she knew children of cancer patients needed different things emotionally than other children and she couldn't imagine leaving Mia to someone who wouldn't love her entirely and care for her compassionately.

Then Ginny had shown up. Simple as that. Jenna had answered the door wrapped in a robe, a ghostly pallor to her face and the deep purple bruises of exhaustion under her eyes. Ginny had taken one look at Jenna and Mia toddling behind her and said *I heard you might be in need of some help.*

It was the first time Jenna realized that a small town, with its rumor-mills and gossip-mongering, could be a gift. Ginny and Jenna had sat down at the kitchen table that day and talked. Ginny was a recent widow from the West End — *down on by Ruby, you know* — she had explained and Jenna had nodded, though, in truth, she hadn't has the slightest idea. Ginny told that she had three children spread out across the country in various states of living their own lives now, and being alone didn't sit well with her. She and her husband — *may he rest his soul*— had visited Port Angeles the way others visited Disneyland or Las Vegas; this sleepy town had been their place for relaxation and enjoyment. When he passed, she had sold their home and moved here for good. Her sister joined her shortly thereafter and together they owned a small shoebox prefab home that fit their needs perfectly. She'd been asking around about work when Jenna's name was mentioned and she'd come right on over because, as she put it, she was still *able bodied and able minded.* She didn't have marketable skills, she had mused, using finger quotations around *marketable* but she had raised three children into adulthood and knew her way around a kitchen and a laundry room.

Jenna had liked her. She'd felt the warmth Ginny exuded and the fact that Mia took to her instantly, didn't hurt either, so when Ginny sent Jenna off for a good long nap, she didn't argue. Hours later, when Jenna emerged from the room to find Ginny and Mia coloring pictures at the kitchen table, she had given herself permission to exhale.

In the years since then, Jenna had grown to love and, surprisingly, at times resent Ginny. Love was the more fierce affection of the two, but resentment bubbled just beneath and roared up only on occasion. Jealousy. Jenna had named it long ago and battled it back regularly with reminders of how good Ginny was to all of them. Ginny had the time and space with Mia that Jenna herself wasn't able to have. Ginny could sit beside Mia and not speak; she didn't need to fill their every second together to the brim like Jenna did, because for Jenna, every single second was so precious and fragile. Ginny could comfort Mia when she was sick and visit her school without fear of catching something that would land her in the hospital for long stretches of time. Ginny knew Mia's friends and had rooted opinions of them which she wasn't shy about sharing, often bending Jenna's ear to who was bad and who was good, who was too bossy for her liking and who just followed along.

"Seattle today?" Ginny looked over the rims of her glasses at Jenna.

"Yes and I wanted to talk to you about that." Jenna hung by the table, trying to string the words together in her head so that they would make sense. These were words she knew she would be saying over and over again today and then for a while after, and there was no one better to practice them on than Ginny.

Ginny set her mug down and pulled off her glasses, a worried expression pinching her features.

"They say I'm stage four now."

Ginny exhaled, low and slow, and reached for Jenna's hand, squeezed it tightly, reassuringly, and waited for her to go on.

"We've done all we can do," Jenna added softly, squeezing Ginny's hand back. "I can either choose now to live the rest of my life making these trips to Seattle and end up with an extra few weeks, maybe. Or I can stop all that now and enjoy what's left. I can be home with Mia, and we can all have just a little bit of how it should've been. I guess what I'm saying is, I'm choosing the *or*."

Ginny was quiet for a moment. Hard lines gathered around her lips as she pursed them thoughtfully. She dropped Jenna's hand and placed her palms flat on the dark wooden table, as if bracing herself for what would come next.

"I have prayed for you since the moment we met and you know, after all this time, Lord knows I love you like you were one of my own. I can't say you're doing the virtuous thing or the wrong thing, but I trust that you're doing the right thing for you." Her eyes welled with tears as she finished her thought. Slowly rising from her seat, she reached out and cupped Jenna's face with her hands, so gently it was as if Jenna's bones were glass. "Now, if you'll excuse me, I have a sweet little girl to go check on." Ginny pivoted towards Mia's room and walked away.

Gabe paced into the kitchen, his hair still wet from the long shower that morning. He looked devastatingly handsome, Jenna thought, in his casual jeans and cable knit zip up. So handsome and all hers, for just a little bit longer. She stared at him as he poured his coffee, sugared and creamed it.

From the moment Jenna had laid eyes on Gabe, she had been hooked. Hinged tight by his beautiful eyes, easy smile, and effortlessly mussed hair. He was so handsome and so unaware of the fact. But, if possible, he was better on the inside.

When Jenna had been writing fast and furious, crafting novels with an archetypal male love interest, she had had a peculiar habit of brainstorming her characters in one word; it helped her fit them into the novel and eventually it was as if all their other traits bloomed from that one word, like a flower. Jenna had once played that game with Gabe to see if, in fact, her methods were practical, if she could deduce an entire person down to one lonely word, and if that person would still be who they were when she was done dissembling them. She'd made a long list of all the things she was certain Gabe was and she had worked backwards from the petals to the core and in the center, in one word, what remained and truly who he was. Gabe was good. He was a good man, a good husband, a good father, a good friend, a good boss. She wasn't objective, of course, but her Gabe, as she knew him, was just a good person.

"J, you ready?" Gabe had wandered over, draping an arm across her thin shoulders.

"Let me say goodbye to Mia and then we can go." Gabe leaned down, pressed his lips to her head, and released her.

He was trying, she'd give him that.

Six months. That was the answer they had gone for, and the answer they had gotten. Six months without treatment before Jenna would need pain management and hospice. Eight months with treatment, at most, before she'd face the same inevitable fate. Two months' difference. Eight weeks. Sixty days. One-thousand, four-hundred and eighty-eight hours. Eighty-six-thousand, two-hundred and eighty minutes. Five-million, three-hundred-and-fifty-six-thousand, eight-hundred seconds. But how much of that would be spent enjoying the time? She would, as Dr. Vaughn explained, be required to be in Seattle four days a week if things went well, possibly more if things went poorly. Subtracting the time she'd spend shuttling back and forth, she'd actually be left with less time by trying for more.

Jenna had clung to Gabe's hand. She knew that numbers would change things for him; numbers were real things in his world of measurements and sums. He'd look at that as a countdown, but she looked at it as a count-up. This was tangible time she could fill doing things she loved. A crest of hope rose up in chest thinking of it, and she wondered if this was how most woman felt when they woke each morning, without a guillotine hovering, feeling impossible amounts of both optimism and peace with their husband beside them and their child down the hall.

"We're home!" Jenna called out. Lights glowed from every room and the air was layered with the scent of something spicy and warm simmering on the stove.

"Momma!" Mia trilled from the family room. Her voice was melodic, and Jenna loved the sound of Mia's bare feet slapping the hardwood as she rushed towards her arms.

Jenna dropped to her knees and wrapped her daughter up, squeezing tightly until Mia squirmed to free herself. Jenna inhaled the sweet scent of Mia's strawberry shampoo before releasing her to Gabe, who picked her up and flung her around in circles. Ginny walked into the foyer, gathering her purse and rain slicker from the hall-tree.

"Mia had a wonderful day at school, homework is all done. Dinner is on the stove keeping warm; figured you'd be hungry when you got back, so I just went ahead and made some sauce and noodles. Mia already ate, didn't you honey?" Ginny reached up and tickled Mia's cheek eliciting a giggle as Mia turned away playfully. "I'm gonna see myself out and I'll be back in morning, bright and early."

"Why don't you go ahead and take tomorrow off. I've got Mia covered." Jenna reached out and gently brushed Ginny's arm in silent thanks.

"I'll be home, though, so if plans change, you just give me a holler, okay?" Ginny smiled weakly and mussed Mia's hair before slipping out the leaded glass door into the dark hush of the evening.

It suddenly struck Jenna: this was her brave new world. At least for a little while. Ginny would still have her place in their lives, of course. Again at the corner of bitter and sweet where change begot bigger change. When the time came, Jenna knew Ginny would once again swoop in and save them all. But until then—and she wouldn't focus or dwell on that—she would be the parent she had intended to be before life had made other plans.

"Mia, would you like to help me set the table while Mom goes to get changed?" Gabe lifted up their little girl in his arms again without waiting for a reply, and he tossed her carefully over his shoulder and disappeared into the kitchen a second later.

Jenna twisted her bedroom doorknob open and slipped inside quietly. Stripping out of her clothes and into comfortable loungewear, she sunk onto the down duvet, flopped backwards, and breathed deeply.

She and Gabe had discussed in hushed whispers on the plane ride back to Port Angeles how best to explain to Mia what was happening.

Ever the logical one, Gabe thought a therapist or counselor would best relay the message and help make an easy transition. And while it made sense, of course, Jenna had resisted the notion entirely. Mia had had enough of the heavy laid on her in counselors' offices over the years of art therapy and play therapy. She was still only a six-year-old, and half of her childhood—the stuff she would remember—had all been bad. Jenna had reasoned that, if only for a little while, what harm would it do to let Mia have time with her mom without an expiration date looming on the horizon. *Just let it be simple,* she'd whispered to him.

In the end, Gabe thrown his hands up in surrender and turned away from her. He didn't understand, she knew that. He couldn't understand. He'd have all the time in the world with Mia; six months would be no more than the changing of two seasons in the Olympic Peninsula. A semester of life. He'd have all that time in multiples. But six months was all Jenna would ever have.

"Do you think I'm selfish?" she asked, rolling away onto her back. The night sky above was an inkblot, a deep, velvety navy, sprinkled with incandescent stars. The clouds of the morning had moved on, leaving behind a whole moon. Beside her, she could feel him move, the whisper-shift of the sheet, the sigh of the mattress beneath him.

"Selfish? What do you mean?" He'd propped his head up on his hand, with his other, he traced a long line from the hallow of her collar bone to her naval, on the flat plane of her belly he drew invisible words and symbols with his finger tip.

"To want what I want now. I know it bothers you and you know I tune you out," she curled onto her side to face him, to study his eyes, she brushed a curl of hair from his forehead. "But, tell me...am I selfish?"

"Selfish is subjective," Gabe sighed.

"Explain..."

"I look at you and I see the woman I love. You're here with me, alive. Pink cheeks." His hand moving to graze her face. "Soft skin. I can't imagine life without you. For me, I wish you wouldn't give up. But for yourself? I can't imagine how tired you are. I know you want to just *be.*"

"I think that's the very definition of selfishness."

"Like I said." Gabe sighed and collapsed onto his back, his eyes closing, "It's subjective. Because I know you, I know you want what you want for us, too."

Long after he'd had drifted off and the house was serenely quiet, Jenna allowed herself to really think about the matter of time, consider it the way Gabe did, not in moments she could fill with happiness, but the hours and days themselves. There was good, certainly, and as the crest of hope she'd felt before rose up again she smiled, feeling the way it swelled and undulated as she imagined what her life would be like without treatment. But what she'd never said out loud was the fact that the amount of time she left on earth beat in her chest like a tight drum. For every choice, a consequence. Wasn't that what she taught Mia? There was still the matter of what would come next. After the six months had passed. There was that to consider, and all that would come after she was gone.

Jenna slipped from bed and threw on her robe. Creeping down the hallway, she quietly let herself into her office. This haven had been a gift from Gabe when they designed the house. She had fussed over not needing such a large space to work, said she could work at the kitchen table or in bed, but in the end, she'd relented and let him build a dream for her. The room was full of tranquility, done up in the shades of watery greens and icy blues, outfitted with romantically-lined furniture, and artifacts from her travels. She ran her hands over the spines of her novels; each had been more successful than the last as her following grew. She'd miss that, the feeling of creation under her finger tips. Each one, a world that had gifted her a dozen second lives. Every novel had allowed her to make different choices then ones she'd made in her real life and follow those choices through to the natural end. Some were bitterly sad, others were love stories with quintessential happy endings, but each was beautiful in their own way. She had actually made money as an author. She had toured the country and thrived in a circle where many others failed. She had left her mark on the literary world, small though it might be, and she would be remembered by those who had indulged and even purchased her wild dream.

Jenna sunk to the floor and alone in her office, she allowed herself to think about the decision she had made and what the ricochet effect of that would be. Gabe would be left alone when it was all said and done; for the first time in nearly twenty-two years, he'd be on his own. But not really alone or carefree or able to move on: he'd be solely responsible for the nurturing of a child. *What a heavy thing that must be,*

ASHLEY MACKLER-PATERNOSTRO

she thought. He would have to have all the answers and make all the choices for Mia. She couldn't picture it, simply could not understand how that would feel. If the situations were reversed, and this was Gabe leaving their life together unfinished, she wasn't sure she could have survived it, wasn't sure who she'd be when she surfaced from the loss.

Determined—she had been so determined. Mia, Mia, Mia. Her only concern, her only reason. Gabe's loss had failed to resonate with her like Mia's loss did. He'd be a widower at forty-seven. He'd bear the teenage years without a comrade in arms, someone to understand and lessen the load. He'd host the sleepovers, correct the papers, mull over the impending decisions of which college Mia should attend or what car she should have or what curfew was fair. The passage of time would come to mean different and new things in the challenges and triumphs he'd embrace and endure all alone. Or maybe not alone, but with someone new, someone who was not her.

Just once, right after Jenna had first been diagnosed, she had attended a local support group. It was held in the basement of the old Methodist church in the heart of town, open to everyone. The flyer announced that the group gathered monthly, but even before she'd gone, Jenna had known sitting in a circle discussing the weight of breast cancer and the fallout wasn't ever going to be her thing. Even after she forced herself to go, even as she sat amongst them she still believed she didn't belong there. Those ghostly women, with their terry cloth turbans and oversized t-shirts terrified her, she saw them as specters of both the future and the less fortunate. But it was there she met her, the first and only time Jenna ever saw the woman who would go on to haunt her for years.

Jenna had watched as the woman climbed from the passenger seat of an ancient car and as a man, Jenna assumed was her husband, rushed around from the driver's seat to carefully escorted her to the top of the stairs. Jenna had followed behind them as they descended into the belly of the church, and observed the heedful way he helped her into an empty seat.

She had seemed so small and sick, her bald head swaddled in a frayed silk scarf, her sweater hanging loose from her fading shape, barely concealing knobby bones beneath. Jenna had wanted to look away, but couldn't. And her hands, Jenna could remember them so clearly, the skin like tissue-paper, nearly translucent, her engorged blue veins visible, running circuits below. Her eyes, watery pools of grey that flittered about —*chemo brain*, Jenna had thought — as every glance exposed the jaundiced scleras. Her breath came in slow pulls, gargled and congested, and a faint continuous thrum came from somewhere deep in her chest.

It was her turn to speak that evening, the kindred greetings that bounced off the cinderblock walls of the basement hushed as the host of group went and stood behind the woman's chair, resting her arms on the slight shoulders of woman who sat before her. And when the woman finally spoke, her voice had been thready and thin, but commanding.

"I have five children," she began, her clouded eyes brightened. *"All boys, all under the age of ten, handsome young men,"* she had said with a hitch of pride that every mother knows to envy. She was only

thirty-five. Her husband was a logger who made daily trips to the West End and was forced to leave her alone for the better part of the day, and now that she wasn't able to work, their money was stretched tight, they couldn't afford much, and his company's insurance hardly covered her treatments. They struggled to support their family; it was a place she'd never dreamed they'd be, and, like so many of the other obstacles they faced now, it was never something she planned on. *"We didn't save. We didn't have time to save. We were setting up our lives for the here and now, trying to have the things a young family is supposed to have. We just figured whatever came next we'd sort all that out then."*

She'd gone to college, fallen in love, became an educator, put in her years teaching others to appreciate the English language and the nuances of it the way she did. She had only just begun to raise her own children when she was diagnosed. She was dying now, and everything her family had had the potential to become together was thwarted. She didn't talk about her treatments, or the heinous side effects, or how cheated she felt. *"I'm not a cautionary tale."* she'd smiled before continuing, *"I am a survivor. How could I not be? I've been dropped off at death's door too many times to count and been told to walk home. I have a better understanding of what they mean when they say 'uphill both ways.' After that, whether I beat this or not, I am a survivor. I'm here to tell my story. My name is Susanna Taft."*

Susanna spoke of responsibility, which was her message for the night. The insight into which was something she credited her years in education for.

She'd always realized that a parent's work was never really done, but she understood it better now. That no matter how big, smart, or steady the child—they would always need their mother. Her death, she reasoned, didn't change that or negate that, but only stood to make it more important.

She had begun recording tapes for her sons. Five tapes for each one of her boys. *"These are my milestone tapes,"* she said as she pulled a small plastic bag from the pocket of her purse. Inside were small cassette tapes with names and events scrolled across the labels. It wasn't easy, she admitted, acknowledging she wouldn't be around for them, but it was the truth. She wasn't going to see them graduate high school, or go off to college; she'd never meet their future wives or bounce her grandchildren on her knee. But that didn't mean she couldn't be useful when the time came for those things.

"Being a mother," she reasoned, *"means figuring out how best to fit into your child's life and how to best be what they need—a friend, an authority figure, a confidante, or a touchstone. I'll never leave my boys, even after I'm long gone. And maybe I'm wrong, but even as a grown woman I still want for my mother, and I suspect they'll feel much the same."*

"This tape, though, it's for my husband." She lifted a single tape from all the others. *"These are my wishes for him. He's not ready to hear them now, he can be pretty stubborn. But I know he is going to be left with an incredible responsibility. We forged this family together and I'm leaving it incomplete. I have wishes for him, too. I pray now that someday he'll meet someone. Someone good and kind and accepting of the*

life my husband and I created when we were together. Someone who doesn't mind a ready-made family and will look at my boys and see them as I do—the way a mother does. Someone who will be willing to pick up where I left off."

Jenna remembered walking out of the meeting that night feeling for the first time since her diagnosis that cancer was the worst thing in the world. She was angry, furious. But those feelings were not for herself, she harbored them solely for Susanna Taft, her husband, and her boys. Jenna drove away as quickly as possible, back to her comfortable house, stripped off her jeans, sweater, and boots, turned the shower on as hot as it would go, and stood under the spray of water until her skin was red and tender. Inside, safely locked away, Jenna had cried for the woman, for her sons, her husband, and their countless struggles. She prayed that night, as always, but not for herself.

In the obituary that came out on December twenty-third of that same year Jenna learned that Susanna had taught at Sequim High. A quick note had been published in the local paper, along with a picture taken on the first day of school the last year she taught. Susanna's hair had been long, pretty waves cascading over her shoulders, across her breasts, her arm was casually draped on the shoulders of a smiling student in a classroom that looked both inviting and well-tended. In health, Susanna had been plump and womanly, with wide hips, her complexion was peaches and cream, a faint flush colored the apples of her full cheeks. The article mentioned the strides she'd made as a teacher, encouraging a love of literature with books and poetry and field trips, made mention that she someone who believed learning shouldn't be confined only to the classics or the classroom.

When she died, her students came out in force to mourn her, a testimony to how many lives she touched. She had left more than tapes behind; she had left a legacy, and Jenna had fiercely hoped that her boys and husband knew that. The students asked for donations so they could plant lavender bushes around the property of the school in her memory. Jenna had asked Ginny to drop off a check with a note thanking the students for their effort.

This must have been how Susan felt, Jenna considered, sitting on the floor of her office now. The hopeless realization that life would go on without her and there so much she'd be leaving left undone and unsaid. She dabbed her eyes with the sleeve of her robe and climbed to her feet. Life going on, moving forward—those were good things, the way it should be. Jenna had often wondered if Mr Taft had ever remarried, if he'd ever met that someone Susanna had prayed he'd find and fallen in love again. If he'd loved that new someone enough to bring her into his family, to help him raise the sons he'd had with Susanna. She wondered if he was happy again—a different type of happy, changed, but still happy nonetheless.

Could she be brave enough to want that for Gabe? Her Gabe.

It felt like the worst sort of infidelity; they loved each other so completely. Never in their marriage had he looked at another woman; even when Jenna closed herself off to him and retreated inwards, he still told her she was beautiful, funny, and brilliant. He still reached for her and he was still everything she needed him to be. Thinking of him feeling that way about someone else stole her breath. But would it hurt her more to know that, in time, he would grow lonely? That'd he'd never have someone worry about his day, or fix his meal, or celebrate the holidays with him? For a man who knew how to give himself wholly to love, there was simply no middle ground.

Mia would grow up; she'd get on with her life and leave. Maybe those new found things would take her across the country or across the world. Maybe she'd only be able to call every so often, but not nearly enough. She'd do the right thing—the normal thing: she'd start her own family, and gather all the distractions that came along with that. And then there'd be Gabe, alone. He wouldn't grow up, he'd grow old. Eating his meals, watching his shows, washing his dishes.

The truth was that, below the pain of the idea, was the realization that she didn't want him to spend the rest of his years by himself. Somehow, picturing a life that found Gabe on his own hurt her more than imagining him with someone new. She loved him enough to know that she'd want for him whatever it is he wanted for himself. She balled her hands into tight knots of fury, pressing them into her legs, soundless sobs found no purchase; she gasped for air between the wracking. It was guttural. Her marriage was ending, and not because they didn't love each other but because with death, as their vows promised, they would part.

CHAPTER TWO

MAY 17, 2002

"GABE, HONEY, CAN WE TALK for a few minutes?" Jenna peeked her head into Gabe's office. The bright drafting light bounced off the white blueprints he was hunched over.

"What's up?" Gabe took off his glasses, rubbing his eyes and pushing away from the desk.

Jenna slipped into the office and sank into the chair across from his desk. Through the window she could see Ginny pushing Mia on the tire swing Gabe had strung from a low branch of a live oak the year before. Mia wanted nothing more than to kiss the sky that summer, and Jenna could still remember the hours spent on this side of the glass, watching as either Gabe or Ginny pushed Mia towards the Heavens, Mia's back arched, her hair so long it brushed the ground as she swung, all while she cried out to go higher and higher.

"I just want to talk to you about a few things."

"You feeling okay? We could ask Ginny to come back more regularly, just to help," Gabe offered, trying to read her.

"I don't think we need that, do you? I think we're

doing okay." Jenna gnawed on her lip.

"I think we're doing pretty good, all things considered." Gabe smiled and tilted his head.

"I was just thinking about a few things—one thing, actually—and I wanted to discuss it with you."

"Okay..." Gabe hesitated, picking up his pencil and rubbing it between the palms of his hands, leaning back and rocking in his chair.

"Life after life...when I'm gone. I think we need to start considering it." Jenna began, worrying a loose thread on the hem of her shirt, keeping her eyes lowered.

"Jenna—" Gabe folded his arms across his chest and narrowed his eyes.

"We can't put everything off until there is no time and then have to be worried because we didn't say what we had to..." Jenna sighed, climbing from her chair and wandering over to the thick bookshelves. They were a mirror image of her own, only his held the domicile masterpieces he'd designed since going to work only for himself.

"Okay, I'm listening," Gabe sighed, dropping his pencil on the desk.

Jenna didn't turn around; she felt the prick of tears threaten behind her eyes. She knew if she turned to him, she'd lose all the nerve she'd worked up. "I'm concerned for you. I want you to be happy again..."

"Jen." Gabe's voice seeped heavy with compassion.

"This is as hard for me to say as it will be for you to hear, but we both know that—that your life is going to have to go on. And I just...I want you to know that I want that for you." Jenna focused in on a tiny balcony on one of his models. A *Juliet balcony* he'd called it and Jenna had imagined the owners calling to each other from it, romancing their beloved with sweet words.

"I don't even want to think about that...I don't want you to think about that."

"How can I not?" Jenna asked. "You and Mia, you're my whole life. I just want you to know that I want your happiness more than anything else, so that one day—when it doesn't hurt as much—you can know that you moving on, that's what I wanted for you."

She heard the scrape of his chair against the floor and felt his arms around her waist, his lips on the side of her throat. Her heart broke.

"J," he breathed into her ear, spinning her around so that their eyes met, "I love you. You. That's it. And whatever else may or may not happen someday, this is right now, focus on this—don't worry about anything else."

"What if you meet someone?" Jenna leaned into him, resting her head against his chest. Gabe ran his fingers down her spine soothingly. "Don't you want to know that I'm okay if you do?"

Gabe pulled back, holding Jenna's arms in his hands, meeting her eyes. "That's what this is about?"

"I thought you understood."

"Really? That's sick, Jenna, really. It's pretty screwed up."

"Gabe..." Jenna yanked herself free.

"No, don't do that. Don't get mad and turn this around on me. I don't want to talk about other women or moving on." His eyes burned into hers, and he sighed heavily before continuing, "You want to tie this life up with a big, neat bow but that's not how losing someone you love works—and you know it."

"Please." Jenna extended her hand, trying to reach him.

"Jenna..." Gabe lifted his eyebrows, his arms still crossing his chest.

"I just need to know that you understand how I feel about this. I'm not asking you to do anything until the time is right for you, obviously...but I...I guess I don't want you to feel like you're betraying me. You wouldn't be."

"What if that isn't what I want? Did you ever think of that?"

"You aren't built that way, Gabe. That's what I thought about."

Jenna could still remember the way he'd looked at her on their third date. They'd met at a restaurant, dined on five courses, sharing petite appetizers and chocolate-death desserts, they'd talked about their childhoods, his in Las Vegas, hers in Chicago. Near the end he'd looked up and at her with a jarring intensity and told her that he was the marrying sort. He wanted a wife, a family, a life with someone. Sitting with him, she'd realized suddenly that despite what she'd always believed, with him, she wanted those things too.

"And here I was, thinking you'd want to talk about dinner tonight." Gabe pulled Jenna to him again, holding her against his chest so she could feel the pulse of his heart racing through his thin t-shirt.

Jenna rolled her eyes and wrapped her arms around him. "Dinner. There is that."

"And it's very, very serious," Gabe whispered in her ear, "Nothing could ever be more pressing."

"Nothing. Ever." Jenna pulled back, looking into

his eyes.

"Pizza?" his lips pulled into a thin smile.

"Are you a mindreader, Mr. Chamberland?"

"I moonlight as one from time to time, yes. So answer me this: thin crust or deep-dish?"

"Thin?"

"Ugh! I was reading you as more of a deep-dish kind of girl."

"Hand-tossed?"

"This must be the compromises of a marriage everyone speaks of."

Jenna swatted at him playfully, grateful for his teasing. "I'll go gather the child, if you order."

"Deal." Gabe winked and pulled her close again, his voice lowering, the sharper edges of his words softening, "I love you J, more than you'll ever know. I loved you yesterday and I'll love you always."

As Jenna slipped out the door she turned back and watched as Gabe settled into his chair, lifted his pencil, he studied it for a moment before letting it drop, bowing his head he covered his face, his shoulders rising and falling. He'd heard her, of that she was certain.

He can be pretty stubborn at times. But I know he is going to be left with an incredible responsibility. We forged this family together and I'm leaving it incomplete, Susanna Taft whispered from Jenna's memory.

———— ❦ ————

Jenna leaned against the jamb of the door, watching as Ginny stood with her eyes shielded from the sun by her hand.

"What's she doing?" Jenna asked and Ginny spun around.

"Goodness, you scared me!" she laughed, and motioned for Jenna to join her. "That, right there, is what we call climbin'."

Jenna watched as Mia tried to wrap her arms around the wide trunk of the tree, tried to find purchase with her feet which slipped off the bark and stomped back on the ground, and marveled at her girl who was so undeterred by her own faltering she tried to grab hold that tree once again.

"She's failing miserably," Jenna shook her head, biting her lip to keep from smiling.

"But the magic is," Ginny whispered and looked towards the tree, "she keeps right on tryin'."

"Mia!" Jenna called out, "can I climb with you?"

Mia spun on her heels and dropped her arms by her side. "Mommas don't climb trees!" she said, her brow furrowing.

"Says who?" Jenna planted her hands on her hips, an indignant, mystified look crossed her face as if what Mia was saying were heresy of the worst kind.

"Everyone!" Mia giggled, shaking her head.

"Then everyone must not know about me." Jenna started across the yard towards the tree, walking slowly, her arms swinging by her sides. "Because this momma, she loves to climb trees." Jenna reached up for the lowest branch, sucked in a deep breath and using the trunk for leverage, she hoisted herself up, swinging herself until her belly was flat against the bark. Pushing up she crawled to her knees and let herself drop with a guttural groan, straddling the branch.

Mia's mouth dropped open as she looked up at Jenna who had perched herself on the limb of the tree, her legs swaying, making circles in the air. Jenna tilted her chin towards the sun that slipped through the leaves. Her heart raced in her chest, pumping wildly as her breath came up short.

"It's so pretty up here!" Jenna called out, "I wish someone would join me..."

"Me, me! Up!" Mia called to her from the ground.

"Ginny, why don't you give our girl a boost?" Jenna asked.

Ginny lifted Mia from her middle and with outstretched arms, Jenna grabbed hold of her daughter and hoisted her up until she was seated beside her.

"You *do* climb trees!" Mia gave her a shocked look before glancing around at the world above ground.

"I did when I was little," Jenna confessed, thinking of her childhood home and backyard where she'd play. The narrow patch of sunbaked earth; dry, crackled dirt and yellow grass that poked at her feet through the holes in her jelly-sandals. The best part had been the stand of trees just beyond. Hundreds of them, a gateway into the dark midwestern woods where the air was cool and the hours of play had seemed inexhaustible. That had been magical.

Maybe that's why Jenna picked this lot after all, though she'd never thought of that until now that she was settled in, a dozen feet above the ground, beside her daughter. Perhaps something in the cloister of madrone and oak trees and the towering pines that hadn't been cleared that first time they'd driven up had reminded of her the *way back when*. It had been a different time. A different world, some said. As a child, Jenna would disappear after breakfast and not return until the streetlights flickered on at twilight, the universal signal that it was time to go home. Maybe that's what she'd wanted for the children she'd thought she'd have and for herself, too. That in the echo of something familiar, she'd find a way to go home again. Then, when she couldn't help it any longer, she thought of Sophia.

"Aunt Sophia was a much better climber than me," Jenna whispered. It was true. Sophia had always had a reckless, adventurous spirit, though to know her now, one would have a hard time picturing it. "She could make it to the top of almost any tree. The kids in the neighborhood, they didn't believe she was the best climber, they would dare her go higher just to see if she could. She always did."

Born five years apart; Sophia had always been the little girl running around after her, a hindrance and an annoyance, and Jenna had always been the big sister, irritated and tired of babysitting. But that wasn't their problem now, the things that kept them apart as children did not divide them now as grown women. What stood between them was something much deeper and darker than benign sibling rivalry.

When Jenna had left home at eighteen, bound for Seattle, she'd left behind a happy family. Her mother had stood at the curb at the airport, stuffing a few small bills into her pocket with teary eyes and encouraging words. Her father had patted her back, told her he was proud of her. Sophia had shuffled her feet and swatted away a swarm of summer bugs, whining that it was too hot to stand around all day.

When Jenna returned, only a few months later,

everything had changed. Her mother had become bedridden and worn as the cancer nibbled away holes inside her. Her father spent most of his nights at the bottom of a whiskey bottle, yelling, cussing, and stumbling around. Sophia had grown quiet. Her eyes were deadened and her smiles, when they came, were forced and sour. Jenna had taken one look at that and done the wrong thing. She had run.

She'd made excuses—school, work, or both—to keep herself safely away. And eventually, it was too late. Her mother was dead and her father had already gone off to places unknown. And Sophia was alone, shuttled off to live with their cankerous grandmother on a downtrodden farm in the backwoods of Southern Illinois.

Jenna had been only twenty then with nothing of worth to offer Sophia, but she had tried. She wrote, called, and when she'd managed to scrape enough money together to rent a shabby apartment on the wrong side of town, she'd given Sophia the option to come west if she wanted. But Sophia hadn't wanted that, or anything else that involved Jenna. While Jenna had been running, Sophia had been building. Walls, so thick and unbreakable around her heart and her life that nothing touched her.

Make nice with your sister, Jenna, she looks up to you. She loves you. Jenna could hear her mother's voice on the breeze that blew all around her.

"Could we call Aunt Sophia?" Mia asked, her hands holding tight to the branch.

"We could." Jenna nodded, closing her eyes. "I think that's a very good idea."

There was an art to dying slowly Jenna decided, shuffling through the glossy brochures she'd picked up at the hospital. When a life is lost in the throes of living — an accident, an act of violence, a stupefaction — as terrible as it is, it simplified things considerably. But when one is in a time of dying, when every day leads one closer to the end, there are measureless amounts of choices to make.

Did she want to pass at home surrounded by those she loved? Or perhaps in a hospice facility where she could arrive and wait out the end with those who'd soon take the journey with her? Did she want a funeral? A wake? A private service? A memorial? A burial or cremation?

A burial required a plot of land, a casket, a headstone, while a cremation required a simply urn. Every decision demanded further decisions from her. The pamphlets laid out before her were graphic-designer ideals of the hereafter; soft, cotton-puff clouds set against powder blue skies, doves ringed in halos of ethereal light, hands cupped, holding the brilliant gateway to Heaven and the ever after. She wondered, running her thumb across the spread wings of dove, if it would really be like what everyone imagined.

If any of what was pictured was what awaited her, she couldn't say she minded. The idea of returned health, freedom from pain, being reunited with the ones she'd loved and lost, all the things the afterlife promised her were all the things she'd wanted in this one.

Jenna closed her eyes and shuffled the brochures like a deck of playing cards. When she opened her eyes, *A Compassionate End - Dying with Dignity*, stared back at her. She turned over the cover and read.

> *The final act of compassion is the greatest show of love we can give those in the throes of great suffering. We offer our patients the alternative to pass with peace, dignity and choice.*

Doctor assisted suicide. She'd heard of this on the news, read about it in the papers. A courtroom war that pit the terminally ill fighting for the right to die on their own terms against those that believed only nature and God should have the final say. It existed in Oregon and critically patients in Washington and other surrounding states could find their way into an angel network where the drugs were shuttled across state lines. She'd never paid much attention but Gabe had scoffed at the idea. *It's euthanasia*, he'd said, pointing the television, *they don't want to call it that because it's an ugly word, but that's what it is. These people, they just want to alleviate their own guilt. Taking a life is taking a life, no matter how you word it.*

Jenna had nodded and agreed, but what did she really know about any of it when she'd leapt to judgement. Death was never without guilt, but was it so wrong to wish for a peaceful end, even if that meant going before the worst of it came? Was it so horrible to want to die with a modicum of dignity and without pain?

"Let those in glass houses," she whispered, closing the pamphlet and setting it aside.

She and Gabe had never discussed what any of

this would look like for them. When they were young, death had been a notion, a theoretical idea, something that happened at the end of years upon years. There were things that came first — homes, and children, and dream jobs, and happiness. To discuss it felt morbid and contrite, like chewing over divorce on one's honeymoon.

Jenna couldn't decide, it wasn't the sort of thing that came together easily and she slipped the brochures into her nightstand and ambled off into the kitchen. She spotted Mia singing along to a movie, standing on the sofa, twirling about to the dancing scene on the screen, pulling the hem of her skirt into an awkward circle as she spun, stumbling over the rise of the cushions.

"Mia?" she asked over the music and watched Mia plopped quickly onto the cushion, fixing Jenna with an innocent gaze.

"You know you're not supposed to stand on the furniture." Jenna walked to the television and clicked it off, leaving them in sudden silence.

"But *they* were dancing in clouds!" Mia protested, pointing towards the blackened screen.

"That doesn't give *you* permission to jump on the couch."

"Turn it back on!" Mia whined, her lower lip poking out as she pointed to the television.

"It's almost dinner time. You can watch more later."

"I'm hungry." Mia climbed off the couch and followed Jenna from the room, quick on her heels.

"I know, honey. Daddy is finishing up his work and then we're going to order pizza. Would you like to help me make some dessert?" Jenna asked, wetting a towel to brush off the counter.

"Yes, please!" Mia smiled, climbing onto a tall barstool, resting her elbows on the counter she cupped her chin and waited as Jenna went to the fridge.

"Ah! Blackberry cobbler." Jenna smiled, pulling a container of plump, juicy berries from the fridge.

"I don't like that!" Mia's face scrunched up in disgust.

"You should hold off on making that face until you've had a bite. This was your Grandma Elizabeth's recipe, and it's very, very good." Jenna smiled, taking jars of sugar and flour from the cabinet.

"I don't care! I don't want that! I don't like it!" Mia's lower lip jutted out, her eyes narrowing to slants of anger.

"How do you know that when you've never had it?" Jenna asked and sifted flour into the bowl the way her mother had done.

"Can you make something else?" Mia whined.

"Maybe tomorrow."

"You're mean!" Mia screamed, her voice petulant and angry.

"I'm not mean, I'm just not giving in." Jenna slipped a stick of butter from its wax-paper wrapper and set it in the microwave to melt.

"I don't want stupid cobbler!" Mia scooted from the chair, stomping her feet on the floor, she crossed her arms against her chest.

"Then have nothing, it's your choice. But I'd like it if you'd at least take one bite." Jenna pinched a little salt into the batter. "Would you like to stir?" Jenna held out the spoon but Mia turned away.

"I want my daddy, he's nice, he lets me have what

I want and he doesn't make me eat stupid things!"

"Daddy's working, so we're not going to bother him."

"I hate you, you're mean!" Mia stomped her foot again, screaming.

Jenna stopped. The words slashed at her, and she felt her heart seize up. "Mia, it's not nice to say things like that. You don't hate me, you're angry with me, and you need to watch what you say to people and be mindful of your tone."

"I hate you!" Mia repeated, her voice loud and high, quivering with tears.

"Really? All of this drama over cobbler? Over a dessert you don't even have to eat, just something I want you to try?" Jenna asked incredulously, wide-eyed and stunned.

"What's going on out here?" Gabe opened his office door and walked into the kitchen.

"She's mean and she's making me eat things I don't like." Mia broke into a run to Gabe's side, linking her arms around his thigh, her hands clasped and holding tight.

"Jenna?" Gabe said as he glanced between her and Mia.

"It's nothing. she doesn't like what I'm making for dessert, so, naturally, she claims to hate me." Jenna shook her head and rested one hand on her hip and the other on the counter.

"Mia." Gabe twisted away from Mia's grip and lowered himself to her level. "You can't say things like that, we've talked about this."

"She's so mean." Mia's eyes welled up with tears, her nose running, and she thrust herself into

Gabe's arms, burrowing her head into the crook of his shoulder.

"She's not mean," Gabe repeated patiently.

"It's fine. Go back to work. I'll handle this," Jenna offered, moving from behind the counter towards them.

"I don't want you! I want my daddy!" Mia screamed, breaking into frenzied tears, sobbing hard, holding tighter to Gabe.

"Why don't we go wash your face and you can work on calming down." Gabe picked Mia up and carried her toward her room.

"Fine. But I'm not eating any gross cobbler, I don't care what Momma says," Mia whined.

Jenna watched the butter cool and congeal in the measuring cup as she contemplated Mia's temper-tantrum. Dumping the butter into the bowl she whisked until her forearms burned.

Gabe reemerged a moment later, shaking his head as he closed the door behind himself.

"What was that?" Jenna asked, dropping the whisk into the bowl, turning towards him, openmouthed, fixing him with her eyes.

"That was a six year old, Mia at her finest—I think she gets the dramatics from you," he replied easily, popping a fat blackberry into his mouth. "Usually Ginny and I tag team her, whichever one she doesn't claim to loathe in the moment is the one to take over. She's on her best behavior around you."

"She does that to Ginny?" Jenna was horrified.

"Sometimes. Gin handles it better than I do. She ignores it, lets Mia burn herself out."

"That's awful!" Jenna put both hands on the counter, steadying herself.

"She's a six year old, Jenna. You can't take it seriously. Tropical storm Mia: Comes in quick, blows over fast."

"I should go talk to her—she can't be that way, so angry and nasty over nothing. It's not right." Jenna started towards Mia's room but Gabe blocked her path.

"Give her a few minutes. Finish dessert and then go in, she'll be calmed down. If you go in now, she'll just pick up where she left off."

"Have you spoken to the counselor about this?" Jenna chewed on her lip for a moment, glancing between Gabe, who nodded, and the closed door. "And he said?" Jenna pressed on.

"He said kids will be kids." Gabe shrugged, which, if anything, bothered Jenna more.

Jenna spun on her heels and walked back into the kitchen as Gabe moved back into his office. Of course temper tantrums were normal for children, but she always knew that in homes where a parent was sick, they could be worse and mean more. And to think that Mia behaved like that towards Ginny caused a warm flush to creep up Jenna's neck.

"May I come in?" Jenna knocked softly on the door to her room before pushing it open. Mia was sprawled across the bed, a blanket tucked up under her chin. "I'd like to talk to you for a minute."

Jenna walked across the room sat on the edge of the bed beside Mia as she pulled herself up to a sitting position and nodded slightly.

"Do you want to tell me why you acted up like that?" Jenna asked softly.

Mia shook her head no, and Jenna sighed.

"Well then, I guess I'll start...what you did in the kitchen — the way you behaved and the things you said. That's unacceptable. Daddy told me that you act that way towards Ginny, too, and that embarrasses me and makes me very sad. Words have a lot of power, they can make people feel things—good things and bad. When you say you hate someone, even if you don't mean it, even if you're just saying it because you're upset, it's not okay. You can't talk or act that way towards me, or Daddy or Ginny...but especially Ginny. She's here to help us, and I know you love her."

"Momma—" Mia began, but Jenna held up her hand so she could continue.

"I'm not finished, you'll have your turn. I know you know better than that. But in case you've forgotten, that word *hate*..." Jenna tilted her head, shaking it slowly side to side, "hate—it isn't a good thing. It hurts you, Mia, it doesn't hurt the other person. You're a little girl, so things like hate and anger are almost the same to you...but when you say them to someone else, they mean a lot more." Jenna rubbed her hand against Mia's back soothingly.

"I'm sorry, Momma," Mia whispered, leaning into Jenna.

"I know you're sorry, but you need to promise me that you're going to think about the things you say *before* you say them."

"Okay." Mia sniffed and leaned against Jenna.

"Promise me," Jenna repeated.

"I promise."

"Next time I hear you do something like that, there will be a consequence. Do you know what a consequence is?"

"Yes."

"Tell me what it is…"

"A consequence is when you do something bad and then someone takes your toys taken away."

"Or you don't get to go outside to play, or you miss out on other fun things because you're learning a lesson." Jenna nodded, watching Mia scrunch up her forehead. "Do you understand?" She waited a moment until Mia's head bobbed. "Okay, good. How about you help me in the kitchen?" Jenna pulled Mia into a tight hug.

"Sure," Mia said and crawled off the bed.

"Oh, and one more thing. Try everything once. Be open to new things. What you end up liking might just surprise you," Jenna added carefully, placing her hand on Mia's head, steering her out of the room.

Jenna stood at the counter, sprinkling a bowl of tomatoes with salt before dumping them into the salad bowl, watching her family. Gabe was leaned forward, reaching for his beer. Mia was giggling, animately waving her hands around, telling Gabe about her day. Jenna would miss this most of all. The quiet, ordinary moments of this life were the most beautiful of all.

"I was thinking," Jenna said, moving towards the table and setting down the salad before sliding into her seat, "I might like to get out of here this weekend. Take a drive down the coast."

"Do you think you'll be up for something like that?" Gabe asked setting his beer down and forking the salad onto his plate.

"Probably," Jenna replied between bites of her pizza, wiping her mouth. "We haven't been anywhere in so long. Maybe we could head down to La Push. We could hike Rialto like we used to."

"I don't want you overdoing it," Gabe cautioned, reaching across the table for the dressing.

"I'll be okay. Just to Ellen Creek and back. That's what? A mile or so? I could manage that."

"Momma climbed a tree today," Mia said, picking at her pizza.

"She did?" Gabe turned and faced Jenna, his brows raising.

"I did." Jenna held her palms up for Gabe to see where the wood had scuffed her skin, "and, let me just say, it felt incredible."

"It felt incredible..." Gabe laughed, shaking his head side to side. "So, you think you're up for Rialto then?"

Jenna nodded, "I say yes."

"What's Rialto like?" Mia asked, chewing loudly, her lips slick with grease and tomato sauce.

"It's beautiful." Jenna smiled, picturing the way it used to look; the sea-salt deadened trees, the miles of black sand interspersed with lively, thriving tide-pools full of lethargic purple and orange sea-stars.

"Can I bring my bathing suit?" Mia asked.

"It's not a swimming beach, kiddo," Gabe answered. "The waves are way too dangerous."

"Oh." Mia shrugged, reaching for her glass of milk.

"We'll have fun, swimming or not." Jenna tousled Mia's hair lightly and gathered her plate and headed towards the sink. "So we'll leave early tomorrow morning?"

"Yeah, it's a good two hours to the coast, so the earlier the better." Gabe picked up his plate and followed her to the sink. "I'll call tonight, get us a room."

"I'll pack so we can get on the road first thing." Jenna pulled the bubbling cobbler from the oven and set it on the waiting hot pad. The crust was a glittery golden brown with melted sugar, and bubbles of blackberry juice peeked out along the edges of the stoneware plate. The smell of warm fruit filled the room reminding Jenna suddenly of her mother. Elizabeth had taught Jenna to make the dessert from sight and intuition alone. A pinch of that, a cup of this. Elizabeth had always had a sixth sense when it came to baking.

"Anyone want cobbler?" Jenna asked, opening the freezer and pulling out a tub of vanilla ice cream.

"I do." Gabe yawned loudly, reaching for a stack of bowls Jenna had set out before.

"Me, too." Mia followed Gabe's lead, moving her plate a little to the left.

"Good girl, Mia." Jenna heaped the hot dessert into two bowls, plopping large scoops of ice cream on top.

"Thanks, babe," Gabe patted her bottom as she placed the bowl in front of him.

"If you don't like it, you don't have to eat it," Jenna pressed her lips to the crown Mia's head, placing hers on the placemat. "Just take one bite."

Mia took a small, timid spoonful, her eyes lighting up as the flavors washed over her tongue. "That's good." Mia dove in for another bite, licking the spoon in earnest.

"Your grandma used to make this for Aunt Sophia

and me when we were little girls. It was always my favorite. There was a wild blackberry bramble behind our house, so in the summer we'd pick berries all day, and at night we'd feast." Jenna settled back into her seat with a bowl.

Jenna could remember the way the blackberry juice had stained her mouth and the tips of her fingers purple on those long, hot summer days. The lush skin of the berries breaking between her teeth, the flesh and juice slipping down her throat, filling her up.

"I never met Grandma Elizabeth, right?" Mia asked, pushing around a lump of melted ice cream.

"No. She passed away before you were born, but she would have loved you. You look a lot like her." Jenna took a small bite of her cobbler, thinking about her mother and how true that was. Elizabeth would have adored Mia.

"Was she sick like you?" Mia asked innocently.

"Yes...she got sick when I was older." Jenna stumbled over the words.

"Are you gonna die, too?" Mia asked, pressing further, her eyes wide with sudden curiosity.

The spoon slipped from Jenna's hand and clattered against the bowl. Her heart skipped as she looked at Mia, who had gone back to poking her dessert.

"Finish your dessert, Mia," Gabe interjected, glancing at Jenna.

You could tell her, Jenna's thoughts whispered and she imagined the motions of telling Mia in her mind. Pictured herself lifting Mia onto her lap and nuzzling into her neck, telling her yes, but that death was nothing to fear. That she'd soon be with her mother again. An angel, with a golden halo and snow-white wings watching over her as she grew up. But she couldn't, *not now*, her thoughts bucked wildly against the truth.

"Mia, have you given any thought to what you want to do this summer?" Gabe managed to stutter out, watching Jenna closely, trying to read her mind while changing the subject.

"Sarah is going to summer camp." Mia's eyes brightened and a little smile pulled at the corner of her lips.

"Would you like to go to camp?" Jenna asked, taking a small bite.

"Can I?" Her smile bloomed, and her eyes grew wide with excitement.

"I would have to look into it." Jenna leaned back in her chair.

"It's not sleep away camp, Momma. And it's just for girls. Sarah said they make friendship bracelets and stuff with clay, and they go swimming at the YMCA and learn about animals. She went last year and her sister is a counselor."

"That sounds like lots of fun. I'll call Sarah's mom on Monday and find out where she's going. If they still have room, I'll sign you up." Jenna nodded, smiling back at Mia from across the table.

Camp would be good, Jenna decided. Mornings of play, crafts, secret handshakes, and easy laughter. Jenna could run errands and make her plans without feeling guilty about dragging Mia along. Mia would return, her skin kissed by the sun, ready to spend the afternoons snuggled together on the couch right around the time Jenna would need to rest.

"All right, Mia, a bath and then time for bed. We've

got an early morning and a long day ahead." Gabe stood up, pushing his chair back noisily against the floor. He gathered bowls and dishes in his hand and dropped them loudly into the sink.

"Can Momma read me my story tonight?" Mia turned to Jenna, who was gathering the placemats.

"Of course I can." Jenna smiled.

"*The Giving Tree?*" Mia suggested, carrying her bowl to the sink. "Ginny brought me a copy because I love trees."

"That was sure sweet of her, and I think that sounds like the best book to read tonight. Daddy will get your bath ready and I'll set out your pajamas, after you brush your teeth, and climb into bed, I'll be right behind you."

Mia ran towards her room, and Jenna stood by the sink watching her go.

"Camp?" Gabe asked once Mia was out of ear shot.

"Yeah, you know, it would be good for her. A change of pace. She's a kid, kids go to summer camp." Jenna brushed his shoulder with her hand lightly and walked off towards the laundry room.

"*There once was a tree, and she loved a little boy...*" Jenna began softly, reading by the dim light the lamp beside Mia's bed cast.

"Like our tree and how it loves me," Mia sighed. She was tucked in tight, curled beneath the layers of bedding, her sleepy eyes fought to stay open.

Gabe had retired back to work, making up for the hours he'd miss tomorrow. The washing machine thrummed in the distance, turning around the dirty wears of the day. Mia's clothes for the their trip were folded neatly on a slipper chair tucked in the corner, ready to be packed into the suitcase Jenna would fill after Mia had given up the fight of staying awake.

Mia yawned loudly and rolled over. Jenna ran her fingers over the length of her back softly, through her silky curls, and down her bare arms, lulling her to sleep with ease as she read.

"Well, I'm an old stump, good for sitting and resting. Come, Boy, sit down and rest. And the boy did. And the tree was happy."

Jenna closed the book and snapped the light off. A stifled sigh slipped past Mia's lips and she curled away, inwards. Only then did Jenna answer the question Mia asked. "No, baby. Not like how the tree loves, but like me. Like how I love you." She whispered, leaning over to kiss Mia's cheek.

CHAPTER THREE

MAY 18, 2002

T HEY DROVE ALONG THE WINDING road towards Rialto, taking the one-oh-one until it dropped them on Mora Road where they followed the narrow avenues of the Reservation towards the wild coastline. Jenna had leaned her head against the window of the car, her eyes catching sight of everything as they drove by. The day had broken through beautifully, cooler towards the coast, but dry with a crystalline blue sky that stretched for miles.

"Momma?" Mia chirped from the back, pushing her finger against the glass of the window, "What's that?"

Jenna turned and saw the intricately carved eagle atop the tower of wood just as it drifted past. "That's a totem," she said before launching into the magical traditions of the Quileute people. They were fishermen, she explained, out in the wilds of the Pacific Ocean. "The totems they carve stand as a testimony to both their appreciation of the gifts the world has given them and the Gods they believe in. It tells the story of their life."

"I believe in God," Mia said, leaning forward.

"I do too, Mia." Jenna pivoted in her seat and smiled, cupping Mia's cheek in her hand.

"Here we are," Gabe said as he pulled into the deserted parking lot at the head of the trail.

Rialto hadn't changed, and seeing it as it had always been gave Jenna a sense of comfort; time doesn't change everything. The stand of trees were still bark-barren and bone-white from the years they'd spent braving the salty winds. Beyond them was the familiar stretch of water-washed boulders, pebbles, and black granite sand, littered with blanched driftwood that gave way to the violent sea of white-capped waves.

"Wow." Mia scaled a log and stood close to Gabe, taking it all in.

"Now Mia," Gabe cautioned, dropping down to her level and zipping up her sweatshirt, slipped gloves onto her hands, "This is a dangerous beach. You stay with Mom and me at all times. You can collect shells but you are not to run ahead. Stay close to the trees and if you do get too close to the ocean and the water touches you, stand still—do not move an inch."

Here the laws of ocean reigned supreme above those created by man. Whether one was granted safe passage or not was decided by the tides and churning undertow.

"Okay." Mia bobbed her head in agreement, entranced, watching the grey waves batter the shore. Jenna could remember the first time she'd bore witness to the magic there was to be found there, standing exactly where Mia stood, captivated, just the same, by the feral nature of the lawless water and majesty of the Olympic forest.

Jenna pulled out her camera, snapping photos of Mia atop Gabe's shoulders as he stood beside a fallen tree as wide and tall as a small house before they trudged towards Ellen Creek and the Hole in the Wall just beyond. Mia stripped off her gloves and dipped her fingers in the sea foam that had been left in the retreat of the waves, the bubbles were oil-slick iridescent under the spring sun.

"It's gritty! Like sand!" Mia screamed, pushing a finger back into froth.

"Do you see that?" Jenna asked, dropping down beside Mia and pointing towards the barely visible curve of the beach still many miles ahead.

Through a break in the fog, the Hole rose from the shore like a secret doorway, a passage to a real life otherworld. Mia squinted, "I think so."

"That is Hole in the Wall. It's a very long walk and I don't think we'll make it there today. But someday, when you do, you'll see the most beautiful tide pools. Hundreds of starfish and crabs and even, every so often, an octopus!"

They slowly walked towards the break where a the creek bisected the beach, listening to gulls scream as they swooped against the sky, watching as Mia discovered the wonders of the coast.

"Momma, look!" Mia cried suddenly, slipping her hand from Jenna's and charging forward.

"Mia, wait!" Jenna ran after her, stumbling over the uneven ground, losing her footing and catching herself, the palms of her hands breaking her fall. The air burned her lungs and her legs protested in vain as she tried to keep up.

"What's that?" Mia called back to her, but her voice was lost on the wind that whipped against her as she raced ahead.

Nestled amongst a patch of overgrown sea grass sat a frosted turquoise ball inside a thick brown hemp net.

"Mia! Don't you dare do that—Oh my God, Gabe...she found a glass float!" Jenna called back breathlessly, sinking to her knees beside her daughter.

Jenna lifted the float up and turned it over in her hands, giving herself a moment to let her breath catch and slow before she spoke again.

"Momma?" Mia touched the glass curiously. "What is it?"

"A Japanese glass float. They're very, very rare. I can't believe you found one." Jenna held the glass ball in her hands, raising it up for Gabe to see. No bigger than a orange, she closed her fingers around it.

"It's pretty." Mia put her arm around Jenna's shoulder, peeking at the glass ball.

"This, Mia, is very special. Do you see how the glass looks frosted?" Jenna pointed the places between the ropes where the glass has been turned sugary from its years at sea. "It's because the ocean water, and sand, and salt, it turns it into sea glass. This has come a long way...all the way from Japan. A long time ago the fishermen use these to secure their nets. But once in a while, one gets lost. It takes years and years, and it travels hundreds miles lost as sea—surviving everything—to land here."

"Wow..." Mia sighed softly, stretching her hands out for the ball again.

"People say that the spirit of the glass blower lives inside. That, because his breathe created it, a part of him remains." Jenna handed the ball back to Mia, who held it up to the light, letting the sun glint off the dingy surface.

"Mia!" Gabe thundered, catching up to them. "I told you—do not run off!" His breath came in jagged gulps and whooshes, his face was rosy from a mixture of wind and anger.

"She got excited, that's all," Jenna calmed him, standing up slowly, stretching her legs.

"That's no excuse." Gabe's face was set in frustration, his hands resting on his hips.

"Sorry, Daddy." Mia looked down, kicking a few rocks.

"Sorry, nothing. If you can't listen to what we tell you, you're going to get hurt. You need to stop and think before you do stuff, Mia. Jesus..." Gabe sighed, his breath flattening out.

"I was with her the whole time," Jenna added softly, patting Gabe's arm. "She was never in any danger."

"You look pale, Jenna."

Standing still, Jenna had to admit that her body ached, that her skin felt ice cold and clammy under the layers of clothing. "I'm fine, Mia's fine, we're all fine."

"Why don't we head back, get some lunch? We can take a drive to the rainforest if you girls want," Gabe turned away, back towards the way they'd come, brushing her off.

Jenna pulled back the blanket of the bed and fluffed the pillows, smoothing their cotton cases against the down inners. She could hear Mia in the bath splashing the water while Gabe scrolled through the television menu.

"I should call Sophia," Jenna blurted out and

watched as the news settled over him for a long
moment before he nodded his head in agreement. "But
I keep thinking, what if she doesn't care?"

Gabe turned towards her, and he leaned his head
against the cushion of the couch where he'd sprawled
himself. "Call her. That's all you can do."

"She hates me," Jenna moaned, cupping her face
in her hands, crawling onto the bed and sitting cross-
legged atop the quilt.

"She doesn't hate you, J, she doesn't know you."

In someways, that was true. They exchanged
holiday and birthday cards, and gifts for the children,
but they didn't know each other beyond those stilted
pleasantries. Sophia was a notion, a name at the bottom
of a card, but she was not a real person to Jenna, and
she imagined, in reverse, Sophia considered her just
the same. But, in the ways the mattered, Jenna knew
Sophia knew her best of all, a keen awareness and
staunch conclusion drawn by having observed all
of Jenna's weaknesses and fears, shortcomings and
failures. Sophia had suffered directly because of
those things.

"That's the thing, though. She knows me, maybe
better then anyone knows me and she doesn't like me.
It's our—" Jenna held her arms out in wide, an empty
observance of the divide that existed between them.

"Your mother," Gabe cut her off; he knew the story.
"But still. She's your sister. She's going to care. She's
going to want to know. So give her that chance."

Jenna gnawed her lip. What she feared wasn't the
call, it was the retribution that might await. That her
sister would treat her with the same disconcerting
distance she'd watched Jenna dole out onto their own

mother in her time of need. If that were the case, and what was awaiting her on the other end of the phone call, Jenna wouldn't fault Sophia because Jenna knew she deserved nothing more.

"It's not like I blame her. I left her alone to deal with all of that, to take everything on...she was just a kid!"

"But she turned out okay."

"I don't know if how someone turns out is ever a justification for what happened to them in the past," Jenna said softly and turned towards the ajar bathroom door, "Mia, you have one more minute in there. Can you deal with her? I need to get some air." Jenna climbed off the bed and without waiting for a reply she opened the sliding door and stepped onto the porch.

Night on the coast was different, a saturated richness that wasn't diffused by the high-beams of cars or the neon-lights of buildings. Here everything was undomesticated and organic and she found that she could think clearly with clean air moving steadily in and out of her lungs.

Sophia had left their Grandmother's home the week she turned eighteen, fled to South Carolina without a dollar to her name and without a single reason to ever return. She'd found work as a transient crafter along the boardwalks of sleepy towns near the Atlantic, joining up with weekend markets to sell the home goods she toiled over, building a niche that catered to those who had an affinity for the eclectic and unusual. It was there where she eventually would met Alex Fledger.

He had been a budding family practitioner when they'd been introduced. Fresh from an Ivy League medical school, heir of a good, solid family that had not only money, but eloquence, and roots that ran both deep and wide. He was straight-laced and quiet with southern manners, and a dry, brittle personality. They married shortly after meeting and in short order Alex had set Sophia up with a store, and together they'd had three beautiful sons. Sophia was upper crust now, a boutique owner, a doctor's wife, and a mother, who traveled in the prim and educated circles of the south.

Maybe Gabe was right. Maybe what she wanted now was to tie this life up neat and tidy. Maybe she wanted what she left behind to make sense, so that people who were individual parts could somehow become a whole.

Jenna cinched her robe against, breathed in the cool Pacific Northwestern breeze that blew in off the water, she turned and walked back inside.

CHAPTER FOUR

MAY 20, 2002

"BYE, MIA. I LOVE YOU. I'll see you after school!" Jenna bounced on the soles of her feet, waving as the school bus pulled out of their drive and onto the main road.

The weekend had been blissful. They had cooked out on an old barbecue beside the rental cabin, watching carefully for stray bears and admiring the elk that grazed in the empty field beside them. They had explored the rainforest, and shopped the local gallery for a trinket to bring back home for Ginny. It was wonderful, the time together, just their little family.

Jenna padded back into the entryway, hanging her sweater on a waiting hook. She had a few errands to run, but none of the stores opened for hours. She poured herself a cup of coffee before she jotted a few more groceries down on the list. She cleared the table, wiping the wide, polished planks with a soapy towel, changed their weekend laundry over to the dryer, and swept the floor in the mudroom. When she couldn't put it off any longer, she reached for the phone and dialed.

"Casa Bella," Sophia's sweet southern

voice answered.

Sophia had assimilated herself quite nicely into the milieu of southern society, even acquiring the particular drawl that spoke to both her southern sensibility and midwestern roots. Jenna could see Sophia, just by hearing her voice: the blonde highlighted and perfectly coiffed bob, the red lacquered lips, the long, manicured nails with blunt white tips and pink cuticles.

"Sophia, hi," Jenna answered.

"Oh, Jenna." The ice that crept into Sophia's voice made Jenna feel ill.

"I was just calling to say hi…is this a bad time?" Jenna twisted the cord of the phone around her finger nervously.

"No. It's fine. Let me take this in the back room." Jenna could hear Sophia place the receiver on the counter and instruct someone to hang it up. Sophia sighed as she lifted the connection, "Sorry about that. So what's going on?"

"I'm just calling to touch base, you know. How are the boys?"

"Good, busy. And Mia?" Sophia's tone was polite and Jenna took this as a good thing.

"Good, busy," she allowed before laughing. "She's why I'm calling. We were climbing a tree the other day and I remembered how you would…"

"Is there something you needed, Jenna?" Sophia cut her off quickly.

"I just wanted to call. Catch up. See how things are. You know." Jenna stuttered wishing this were easier.

Sophia let loose a rip of unnerving laughter in the phone, "Jenna, you don't call to catch up. What's going on?"

Jenna sighed and closed her eyes. "I wanted to let you know that the cancer came back. Stage four. Same as Mom."

The line between them crackled and popped.

"Are you seeing that oncologist in Seattle still?" Sophia finally asked with a hint of urgency.

"Dr. Vaughn? Yes, but, Soph…I've stopped treatment."

"Why?" Jenna could hear the air rush from Sophia's lungs along with her question.

"The cancer's spread. Brain, bone, blood, lung. I'm terminal. Either way." Jenna closed her eyes against the truth and waited.

"What does that even mean, Jenna?" Sophia whispered.

"It means I have six months."

"Oh." The chill of Sophia's tone returned in earnest, brittle and formal and Jenna felt a warm blush radiate up her throat. All of her self-doubt and worst fears crashed upon her. Why had she called Sophia at work? Why hadn't she waited until the evening? What had she expected besides a stilted *oh*.

"I'm sorry to call you at work. I just thought— maybe—you'd want to know…"

"Mia and Gabe…" Hitched to her voice was an unbridled sadness that made Jenna want to cry.

Jenna knew where Sophia's mind was. Far and away, back in Chicago in the little bungalow, a little girl again facing the same daunting things Mia was facing now, probably wondering if Gabe was teetering on the same fine line their father had tottered on before falling off into a great abyss.

"They're okay. We're managing," Jenna answered

honestly. She wanted to tell Sophia that Gabe was good man, a solid father, nothing like their own dad, that Mia was going to be fine and loved.

"I'm very sorry, I'm sure this is...very hard."

"Yeah, well—"

"Listen, I'm swamped. Can I call you later?"

"Of course. Sorry. I just wanted to know if maybe, over the summer, you wanted to come here, I'd come to you, but traveling so far might be...isn't...I thought it might be nice if we could—"

Sophia exhaled loudly, "I really can't discuss that right now."

"Sorry." Jenna found herself apologizing again, tripping over her words.

"It's no problem. Really. Thank you for telling me."

"Soph?" Jenna asked into the silence of the line. "I also called to say that I love you."

She had needed to say it, let it be heard, let the words mean whatever they'd mean. *All a person can do is try,* isn't that what Gabe had said? With the rest of her life, she'd commit to trying.

Jenna held the phone close to her ear; the other end cut off with an audible *click*. The tears silently slipped down her cheeks.

As her disappointment dwindled down to dejection, she realized suddenly that behind the false bravado of embracing whatever came, she had been hoping for things. Compassion, kindness—maybe something more. Jenna sat at the counter for a long time, her coffee growing tepid in the cup beside her, her list of groceries left untouched, the damp clothes in the washer waited while the dry clothes in the dryer became wrinkled. She couldn't move; it was as though she were suddenly rooted in place. She wanted to hear Sophia say, *This is where you come from, this is where you were first loved, this is where you're still loved, you will be okay.* That's what she had wanted.

Jenna climbed woodenly from the stool and wandered into her room. The blinds were snapped shut from last night and the bed had been left unmade. Gabe's boxers and t-shirt lay in a forgotten pile by the bathroom; her robe was draped across the chaise at the foot of the bed where she'd left it. The television was on, loops of the seven-day forecast replaying. She lay down in her bed, pulling the heavy comforter over herself, shielding herself from all signs of life.

Mia bounded off the bus hours later, running towards the house with her lower lip quivering.

"Mia?" Jenna held the door open as Mia burst through.

Mia tore her rain jacket off, threw her book bag down and rushed Jenna's arms as the tears came, loud and shocking, her body vibrating with them.

Jenna wrapped her arms around Mia tightly.

"Baby, what's wrong?" As Jenna rocked Mia, Mia wrapped her arms and legs around her, clinging to her the way she had when she was a baby, as if trying to crawl back inside Jenna's skin.

"The kids on the bus…made…made…" Her voice got lost in fresh sobs.

"Shh, it's okay, it's okay," Jenna soothed, patting her back gently.

"They said…they said…I'm…I'm…stupid." Mia cried harder into Jenna's shoulder, hiccuping and gasping as she tried to explain.

"Oh, Mia."

"They said they can't be my friend anymore because I'm dumb."

"Who said that?"

"McKenna and Hailey."

Jenna pulled Mia back and looked at her. "Mia Elizabeth Chamberland, you look at me and you believe me when I say this: You are not dumb. Now, tell me, why would they say that?" Jenna carried Mia into the family room and sat down on the couch, spinning Mia so that she was on her lap, still draped across her.

Jenna waited while Mia calmed down, her sobs thawing into heavy breathing and soft, quick sighs, she rubbed at her eyes with her tiny fists.

"Ms. Field asked me to read out loud in front of the class, and I didn't know a couple words. Everyone laughed, but Ms. Field told them to stop it and be nice; she was real angry. And at lunch, McKenna and Hailey said I couldn't sit with them because I got them in trouble by being dumb."

"Oh." Jenna breathed out a heavy moan, hugging Mia closer. She felt furious, hurt for her little girl who was obviously wounded by words. She wanted to call their mothers, to wring little necks and teach them the value of being kind. But she wouldn't.

"I tried not to cry, Momma. I did. Just like Ginny told me to do. But they were whispering and laughing at me. I had to sit alone and no one played with me at recess."

"Baby girl." Jenna rocked her daughter slowly. "I'm sorry you had a bad day."

"I'm not going to school anymore," Mia decided,

clinging to Jenna.

"Oh, you don't want to quit. You like school and you like your teacher."

"No, I don't!"

"Mia, listen to me, what happened today—it happens, and it's an awful thing, but sweetheart, you can't just quit school. People, especially little girls, can be unkind. Sometimes, people are mean because they think it's funny, and sometimes people are mean just to be mean because it makes them feel tough and cool or they're jealous of you, and saying hurtful things makes them feel better about themselves. But when you give them power over you, when you stop being yourself so that they will like you, or you run away because it's tough, they win and they don't deserve to win."

Mia rested her chin her mother's shoulder, her breath was warm and sweet against Jenna's neck as she sighed heavily.

"What you need to do is be brave. If McKenna and Hailey don't want to sit with you at lunch or play with you at recess, you make new friends. It's just like Ginny said, what they want from you, honey, is a reaction. They want you to get upset and cry and feel bad...so when you're strong, they learn that the mean things they say and the nasty things they do—none of that can touch you or change you."

"It hurt my feelings." Mia started to whimper again, the memory of her pain almost as strong as the pain itself.

"I know, baby, I know. If I could take your hurt feelings and make them my own, I would. But I can't. So, we'll just sit here together for a while and I'll hold you until you feel better."

Jenna held onto Mia until she pulled away.

"Hey girls." Gabe walked through the door, dropping his briefcase and hanging up his coat.

"Hey hon, dinner's almost ready—you have time to get changed," Jenna called from behind the stove.

"How was your day?" He walked up behind her, wrapping his arms around her waist, kissing her neck.

"Long." Jenna spun around, holding him close.

"Did you call Sophia?"

"Yes."

"How'd that go?" he murmured in her ear quietly.

"We'll talk about it later, okay?" Jenna pulled back kissed his lips quickly. "I think you should go talk to Mia, *she* had a tough day, too."

"I'll change after we eat. How 'bout I help set the table." He wandered over to Mia who was working on her homework at the breakfast bar, and gave her a kiss.

"You had a rough day?" he asked, sitting down beside her, rubbing the top of her head.

Mia nodded but didn't look up at him. "Some kids were mean," she whispered.

"And what did you do?"

"I tried to be brave, but when I got home I cried," Mia said.

"You want me to teach you how to deal with bullies? Give 'em the old one two." He shadow boxed the space between them and then tickled her side until she let loose a peel of laughter.

"Gabe!" Jenna cried, "Don't you dare teach her

that! Mia, ignore your father."

"Fine," Gabe laughed standing up. "Just do whatever Mom said."

"Mia, honey, dinner's almost ready, can you get your work picked up?" Jenna asked, spooning a summer mix of vegetables into a bowl as Gabe grabbed a stack of plates from the cabinet.

"So how was work?" Jenna asked, cutting Mia's chicken into bite-sized pieces.

"Good. The house is fantastic." Gabe sipped his glass of wine. "We should take a drive out, let me give you the nickel-tour."

"You know I'd love that."

"Momma? Did you call Sarah's mom? About camp?" Mia asked.

"I did and then I signed you up for the morning session." Jenna nodded, passing Mia her plate.

"Cool." Mia speared a piece of meat, blowing on it before popping it into her mouth.

"So you called Soph?" Gabe asked casually, placing a roll on his plate.

Jenna looked down, nodded and then shook her head. Gabe let a long breath out and set his fork down. "I'm sorry, babe."

"No. It's okay. I called her at work, she was busy," Jenna dismissed, motioning for Gabe to eat. "We can talk about it later." She glanced at Mia, who was busy munching on her salad.

"She's a real piece of work," Gabe began.

"Stop. Not now. We will talk about it later, okay?" Jenna fixed him with a meaningful stare. Whatever her problems with Sophia were, Sophia was good to Mia, and Mia loved her aunt. It wasn't the sort of conversation that they should have in front of her.

"Fine." Gabe went back to his dinner.

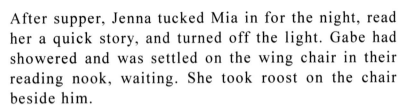

After supper, Jenna tucked Mia in for the night, read her a quick story, and turned off the light. Gabe had showered and was settled on the wing chair in their reading nook, waiting. She took roost on the chair beside him.

"It didn't go...well," Jenna began slowly, folding her legs under her.

Gabe nodded patiently and waited for her to continue.

"She was busy. The conversation was forced. I asked to her visit." Jenna gnawed her lower lip, imagining how desperate she must have sounded.

"Is she coming here?" Gabe's eyes opened wide, and he looked almost hopeful.

"No. I don't know. She was too busy to discuss it." Jenna wiped a tear from under her eye.

"She was too busy for this?" Gabe raised his brows in curiosity, a hard edge to his voice.

"I kept apologizing and tripping over my words."

"Jen..."

"I don't know what I'm doing anymore." She put her hands over her face, shaking her head slowly back and forth.

"You're doing the best you can, and you have to stop beating yourself up over everything that doesn't come easily."

"I just wanted her to care."

"I'm sure, in her own way, she does. But this is close to home; she lived through this once, it has to be very hard for her."

"And I ran away." Jenna dropped her hands and locked eyes with Gabe.

"No. That's not what I'm implying, Jenna. I'm saying, just think about it: Mia's not much younger than she was—only a few years. And the whole thing really fucked her life up; she's probably scared."

"But she's my sister. She's where I came from. She's my family. I need her," Jenna whispered softly. "I just wish—"

"It doesn't always look like what you'd imagine." Gabe reached over and gathered Jenna's hands in his. "But we're where you came from, too. We're your family, we love you."

"I know that—but it's not the same."

"Sometimes you can move things with your will... and sometimes...you just can't."

"You know what the hardest part is? It's all the stuff I'll never have, all the things I'll never see or do or be. Watching Mia grow up, growing old with you, being close to my sister...the things I want most in this world, the things I thought I'd have. It's admitting that this is it and I'm scared." Jenna wept. Gabe stood up and went to her, kneeled in front of her and rested his forehead against hers.

"You have to be strong, Jenna, you have to be brave." Tears ran down Gabe's face as he held her hands over his heart.

"That sounds like what I tell Mia." Jenna laughed lightly.

"It's good advice." Gabe wiped his face on the sleeve of his shirt.

"You once accused me of wanting to tie this life up

with a bow. And I did. I do. I want that. I know how losing someone can change everything. I'm scared for you, Gabe, I can't imagine raising Mia, being alone—it's not what you signed up for, we were supposed to do this together. I thought if Sophia would come around, then between her, and Ginny, and you...you'd all make it for Mia."

"Jenna, I need you to believe what I'm about to tell you, okay? Because I'm not sure about a lot of things, but I do know this for certain: I'm not scared—not about the same things you are." He steadied his voice. "Whatever it takes, that's what I'm going to do. She's my little girl, and you never, ever have to worry about her, not for a minute."

"And what about you? When do you get what you deserve?"

"What if it were me?" Gabe asked gently. "If it was me, what would you do?"

Jenna inhaled sharply. She'd thought of it a hundred times and for each time, she'd imagined different things. A life where, without him, she fractured. A life where, without him, she moved on, rising every morning only to raise Mia. A life where, without him, she was a shell of who should could have been, where colors were muted and days were long, where heartbreak was not simply a feeling, but air and water. "I don't know," she admitted solemnly.

"I think you do. You'd look at Mia and you'd see me, and all the things we wanted would still be things you'd want, for her and for yourself, so you'd find a way. I don't know what my life will look like without you. But I think about it like this: I had you for twenty-two years. The years and what we've done with them—how lucky have I been? And after, life after life, isn't that what you called it? I'm going to raise our little girl and do what's best for her. I can't see beyond just being a good dad."

"Gabe." Jenna reached out her hand, encircling her arms around his neck, pulling him close.

"I love you Jenna, so much, and I'm sorry, so sorry, we can't..." Gabe's voice drifted off.

"Me, too," Jenna cut him off.

"I wish—"

"I know." Jenna pulled back and took his face in her hands, looking into his eyes.

She studied him, looking closely at the way his eyes held hers, steady and sure, despite all the doubt and fear.

She'd loved him for most her life. She'd watched his hair turn grey around the temples and the skin around his eyes go soft as it webbed with the faint beginning of wrinkles. She'd watched him hold their daughter in his arms while he paced slowly around their home, speaking in hushed tones that lulled and soothed Mia to sleep when she was colicky. She had watched him worry over the sharp corners of the table and the slick floors when Mia was starting to toddle about, so afraid that something might hurt her. And that day on the beach, when Mia ran off ahead, the fear that—for one moment—Mia was beyond his reach. Jenna didn't know for certain what the future held for her family without her, but she did know that they would be okay; it wasn't something she had to force herself to believe, she felt it in her bones now watching him watch her.

CHAPTER FIVE

JUNE 27, 2002

S UMMER SNUCK UP AND THREW the Chamberlands into a whirlwind of activity. Mia got her wish and was off at day camp. She came home each afternoon tired and suntanned. Beaming, she'd offered up new, intricately woven friendship bracelets, pottery trinkets, and beaded lanyards she called *boondoggles*. Jenna hung the new drawings on the front of the fridge, set the soft-clay ashtrays and vases on the windowsill to harden, wrapped her wrists in the thinly threaded bracelets and fawned over each as though they were the most lovely things she owned. But more than anything, it was a comfort to Jenna. Being endlessly busy left no time for her to worry about the passage of time.

She had spent the first days wandering aimlessly around her house, looking for something to occupy her. She invented laundry, pulling their sturdy and warm winter clothes from their closets, washing and packing away would serve them next season and donating the things Mia will have outgrown by the time the winds turned cool and the leaves that grew on the trees fell to the earth. She scrubbed the already-polished countertops, swept the floors, and changed linens. She straighten up hall closets and wiped down the all cupboards in the kitchen. When there was nothing more to do, she finally wandered into her office, gravitating to the library.

The niche was home to all the books Jenna loved and had collected over the years, full of all the first editions and leather bound volumes she'd searched for. She loved the smell of old ink on soft paper and the subtle intimacy that came with turning a page. Anticipated the feeling of being an invited voyeur into the life of a protagonist. Savored the feeling of the binding crack open between her hands. She ran her fingers over the spines tenderly, lifting books from the shelves, thumbing through the first pages, she hoped to be pulled into the adventures of a novel, only to find that the all the works she owned were all still familiar, their words unforgotten. She wanted something new. A distraction. A world unknown and fresh. She decided to head into town for a few hours, stop by Port News and Book, choose some novels for herself and a few stories for Mia. She just finished gathering her things when the doorbell chimed.

Standing at the front steps of her home, looking travel-worn, was Sophia, with her three boys in tow.

"Sophia?" Jenna asked, incredulous, hardly believing her eyes, pulling the door open.

"Jenna," Sophia greeted her, shifting her weight from one foot to the other.

"Oh my God, come inside." Jenna stepped to the side, opening the door wide, waving for them to come in.

"Thank you," Sophia answered politely, ushering the children inside, where they immediately dropped to the ground, taking off their shoes.

Jenna was stunned. Sophia had never called back; Jenna had never expected her to. After the phone call and the conversation with Gabe, her mind had branched off elsewhere. But here her sister stood, in front of her. She had shown up after all.

"Oh, Caleb, Harlen, Thomas—I am so, so glad you all are here!" Jenna's face broke into a wide, welcoming smile. She sunk to her knees, gathering her nephews up in her arms and squeezing them tightly.

Jenna mentally ran down the sleeping arrangements in her mind, she could put Sophia and Thomas in the guest room and the older boys, they could bunk in the basement on the pull-out couches.

"Let me show you all to your room..." Jenna began, standing up.

"Oh, no. We're at the Red Lion Hotel, we didn't want to impose." Sophia bent down and gathered Thomas in her arms and walked deeper into the house. Jenna watched as Sophia glanced around, knowing her sister appreciated good design and good decor. She had never seen Jenna's home, Gabe's creation, with its exotic woods, leaded glass, muted walls, and thick moldings.

"The Red Lion? Are you sure? You're welcome to stay here, we'd all love to have you." Jenna smiled at her sister tentatively.

"Our stay is rather...indefinite...and being here would be quite an imposition." Sophia wandered towards the great room, taking in the vast views of the bay swaddled in lush greenery. Jenna followed her sister into the family room, where Sophia had settled down on the couch.

"Boys?" Sophia lowered Thomas to the floor and snapped her fingers, and all three of the boys immediately looked towards their mother. "Aunt Jenna and I have to speak privately. Is there somewhere they could play?" Sophia turned to face Jenna.

"Um, the basement?" Jenna answered, unsure if Sophia would allow her children to play that far from her sight. Jenna would have never allowed Mia to wander off in an unfamiliar house; she felt guilty even suggesting it, wondering if she should have directed them to Mia's room.

"That'll work. Boys, take your brother, please. And remember, play nicely." Jenna pointed to the doorless frame off the kitchen, from which stairs descended to the lower level. The boys dutifully trudged down the stairs towards the basement.

"So..." Jenna began, looking at her sister.

"So..." Sophia mimicked, folding her hands across her lap and squaring her shoulders, her body language rigid and tense.

"Indefinitely?" Jenna asked curiously.

"I just felt like I should be here, and Lord knows I can't leave the boys with Alex. So we're all here, for as long or for as short as you wish," Sophia summed up her presence and plans succinctly.

"And Alex, he's fine with that?" Jenna asked.

"Of course!" Sophia snorted, her eyes opening wide. "Why wouldn't he be?" Her mouth pinching up as she asked.

"Well, I don't know..." Jenna trailed off.

"He knows I'm here. He knows I'll be here for

a while, maybe even all summer," Sophia said, a hint of defiance seeping through her hardened voice, surprising Jenna further.

"And the store?" Jenna couldn't help but worry about all the things Sophia had left behind.

"It will be just fine. Actually, I've heard wonderful things about the artists here, and I may just take some time to make a few connections."

Jenna had seen pictures of the neighborhood boutique Sophia owned and she had read reviews of the decadence. Casa Bella was touted as the place where a shopper could indulge herself on the finer home appointments and splurges. Jenna tired to imagine how the bead crafts and grain-sack pillows found in town would mesh with Sophia's refined style of gold-leaf mirrors and citrine-hued mercury-glass candlesticks.

"How are you feeling?" Sophia asked, narrowing her eyes, looking Jenna up and down.

"Pretty good actually."

"You look good," Sophia nodded, "Color in your cheeks, up and moving."

"I'm happy you're here, Soph. Gabe and Mia will so excited." Jenna smiled, longing to hug her sister, but knowing she wouldn't.

Sophia smoothed her hand over the duck-cotton material of the couch. "Do you have any coffee or tea or something? I am absolutely beat from the travel; you'd never believe what time we had to leave to get here!"

"I'll put some coffee on. Are the boys hungry—can I make them a late lunch? I have some peanut butter and honey spread, bananas, jelly...whatever" Jenna stood up and started towards the kitchen.

"I fed them at the airport, they'll be fine until supper. Just a bit longer, and we can check into the hotel." Sophia followed Jenna, swiping her hands across the counter. "So tell me, I'm curious to know, why stop?"

"Stop what?" Jenna glanced over her shoulder as she flipped the sink faucet on and filled the coffee carafe with water.

"Treatment. What else?"

Jenna pulled two cups from the cupboard and filled a filter with grounds before she flipped on the pot to brew. "I don't know. It felt like the right thing to do?" Jenna kept her back turned to Sophia.

"I just think that you're being short-sighted. I've been doing some reading, you know, since you called. Things are changing. Rapidly changing. New drugs, new trials. If you'd just give yourself more time by *trying* there might be something soon that could—"

"Can we not do this now?" Jenna asked, spinning around. "Can we just enjoy each other's company? I don't want to get into an argument fifteen minutes after you show up. I want you here, I do, but you don't know everything."

Sophia stilled for a long moment before she straightened her back and nodded. "That's why I'm asking."

"I'm sorry," Jenna sighed heavily pouring the coffee into two mugs.

"It's fine, really."

"How do you take it?" Jenna gestured to the mugs.

"Black."

Jenna set Sophia's cup before her and leaned against the counter, "Why don't you just stay here at the house?"

"I appreciate the offer, I really do. But I think we'd all feel more comfortable at the hotel. Where's Mia?"

"She was going over to her friend Sarah's this afternoon, she won't be back until later. I could pick her up—"

"Jen? You home?" The front door clicked open and Gabe trudged into the entryway, calling out to Jenna as he did every day.

"The kitchen!" Jenna called out, thankful for the interruption.

"Whose car is that in the driveway?" Gabe asked as he loped into the kitchen, stopping short when he saw Sophia perched at the counter.

"Gabe," Sophia greeted him, rising to give him a hurried hug.

"Sophia!" Gabe wrapped his arms around her and kissed her cheek, "This is a surprise!" He walked over to Jenna and kissed her lightly on the forehead.

"Yes." Sophia painted a smile across her face, drumming her fingers on the counter.

"Isn't it nice? The boys are playing in the basement. I was just as stunned as you were."

"Caleb, Harlen, Thomas! Uncle Gabe is here, please come say hello!" Sophia called out loudly for the boys.

"Hi, boys. Caleb—man, you have gotten big. Harlen—you, too. You've gotta be like, what? Eight and nine now? And you must be Thomas." Gabe smiled, giving them high fives and mussing their hair as they emerged from the basement. The boys awkwardly smiled at Gabe.

"Well, we should be going." Sophia rose to her feet

and herded the boys toward the door.

"Will you come back for dinner? After you get checked in and settled?" Jenna followed them out towards the door.

"Not tonight, but thank you. I'm tired, and these guys are going to need to get to bed soon, it's almost seven o'clock at home—still on South Carolina time." Sophia smiled and squeezed Gabe's arm in goodbye.

The boys shoved their feet into their shoes and ran from the house toward the waiting minivan. Sophia hustled after them, turning to wave as she slid into the driver's seat.

Jenna waved and smiled, watching as Sophia pulled from driveway, thinking the whole while how surreal this felt to her.

"That was weird." Gabe came up behind her, wrapping his arms around her waist and resting his chin her shoulder.

"Very," Jenna agreed, wrapping her arms around his as she watched the van pull out of their long driveway and onto the main road.

"How long are they staying?" Gabe wondered out loud.

"Indefinitely." Jenna continued to stare after the car, now long gone. "It'll be good, though." Jenna nodded once, pulling the door closed.

"You think?" Gabe asked, making his way back to their bedroom to change.

"I hope so." Jenna shrugged, following behind him.

"Is Alex here?" Gabe asked, pulling his jeans off and tossing them into the hamper.

"No."

"And she's not staying here?"

"I offered, but she was pretty set on The Red Lion."

"We have the room."

"That's what I said!." Jenna flopped back against the pillow.

"Well, I'm glad," Gabe decided, laying down next to Jenna. "This is going to be a good thing, Jen. It's what you wanted."

CHAPTER SIX

JULY 31, 2002

"A UNT SOPHIA!" MIA CALLED, HOLDING up a palm-sized oyster shell for her aunt to see before racing back towards the boys as they ran down the brief bay of Hollywood Beach.

Jenna had always loved the stump where she and Sophia sat together now. Once, years ago, she'd counted all the rings, wondering how long the tree had lived in full bloom. The art of dendrochronology, Gabe had told her as she worked from center on outward. She loved the way the rings of had names, the rate of growth and years measured in *summer wood* and *spring, late wood* and *early*. She had ran her hand over the petrified surface, smooth as glass, wondering who had downed it and why.

Sophia had been in town for almost three weeks. The awkwardness of that first day still lingered between them, but with four children underfoot and the summer stretching out before them, they'd made a unspoken pact to not dwell, to let the past stay where it belonged and try to be better than they'd been before.

Mia had fallen in love with Sophia all over again.

She latched onto her aunt with a sort of vigor, and it warmed Jenna's heart to see that Sophia had the same affection for the little girl in return, never forgetting that one day soon, Mia would need to lean heavily on Sophia for comfort. Together, they had spent hours collecting shells, packaging them, and mailing them off to Casa Bella as vase fillers. Sophia embraced Barbie and read stories to all the children before bed, even speaking in different voices to vary the characters. She was a powerhouse mother, and such a warm, giving aunt. It was a different side to her sister—a softer side.

After Mia had pestered and pleaded and wore Sophia down, unable to refuse her niece a moment longer, she'd checked out of the Red Lion and moved their camp to the main house. Being under one roof, sharing meals, and casual conversation had seemingly relaxed Sophia, but the new arrangement had also betrayed the things Jenna imagined that Sophia would have wanted to keep private. Alex never called, and to Jenna's knowledge, Sophia never called him. Jenna longed to ask more, but it was hard to think of disrupting the peace that finally existed between them so she let it be.

Ginny had seamlessly fit into the new, expanded dynamic. Wrangling four children didn't faze her, and she continued her rule unchallenged. She busied herself around the house, preparing meals and laying down laws about toys, sharing, picking up messes, and being kind.

The house was full of family, laughter, love, conversation, and suddenly Jenna's sickness wasn't the foremost thing that hovered over them—it was happiness.

"I'm worried." Sophia pushed her sunglasses up on her head and turned her face upwards towards the faint light of the early afternoon sun, closing her eyes.

"About what?" Jenna asked, picking at a pebble that lodged in a pock of the stump.

"You," Sophia said simply. This was the conversation—Jenna could feel it—that they had been skirting around since Sophia's arrival all those weeks ago. The reason for her visit, the reason for her extended stay.

"I'm okay. Really," Jenna tried to reassure her sister. But, if she were being honest, lately her level of energy had dipped. By five o'clock, she was ready for bed, and mornings were harder than before.

"Don't you dare lie to me." Sophia slipped into the tone Jenna had learned to associate with Sophia's mothering style. Firm, honest, and no-nonsense.

Jenna looked down the beach at the hoard of children playing in the shallow tide. Ginny hovered nearby, lugging a paper sack full of shells they'd pulled from the shallow surf.

"I can't stay here forever, Jenna, so I need you to be straight with me so I can make some choices on my end of things." Sophia turned away from the sun and gathered Jenna's hands in her own, squeezing them tightly. "I am here to help you, comfort you, love you and those things are easier for me to do when I know the whole truth." Sophia squeezed harder.

Jenna inhaled deep and pushed the air out of her lungs hard. It was uncomfortable to talk about things like this, especially in this moment, when there was so much good all around them.

"Today, I'm okay. That wasn't a lie," Jenna started, biting down hard on her lip. "But yesterday, I was exhausted. Only, the kind of tired I feel is different. It's not like the 'I'm beat because I chased after kids all day' tired. Mentally, I go on for miles, but physically I hit a wall and my whole body hurts."

"Why didn't you tell me?" Sophia's voice rose with concern.

"Do you remember when you asked me why I stopped treatment and I said you didn't know everything? Well, this is why. This is the whole the point. Of all of this. What I've been trying to do, and why I made the choices I did. I'm dying. Either way, I am going to die." Sophia sucked in a sharp breath and Jenna placed her hand atop Sophia's, "It's scary to say out loud, because then I have to acknowledge it and accept it. But I did…and I have. I did the acknowledging and I have started in on the accepting. I knew there would be days I'd hurt, days I'd have to literally drag myself from bed. But it's a trade-off. A pretty fair trade for days like this." Jenna gestured down the beach towards the children busily burying their bare feet in the granite sand. "I could focus on death, or I could focus on life. I chose life."

Sophia nodded her head reflectively and Jenna continued on.

"I was absent for a long time. I watched Mia grow up in pictures and on the outskirts of her life. She was on her very best behavior around me like I was guest in her life, not her mother. And the truth is, I couldn't be a real mother, not the sort I wanted be anyway, because I couldn't even be a real person half the time. I was sick from the chemo and treatments, and when I wasn't sick, I was getting ready to be sick or getting over being sick. I didn't want that to be her only memory of me.

"So when the doctor told me I could have some time, some real time, without treatments and trips to Seattle and banishment to my bedroom, I grabbed hold of it. What else could I do? It didn't make sense to waste what was left. And now, I'm not ready to let go. I may be tired, and I may have aches and pains... but I've also had way worse. And, for as tired as I may be at the end of the day, at least I have this." Jenna wiped under her eyes with the sleeve of her sweatshirt and looked out across the Pacific Bay. "This is what I prayed for."

Sophia laced her fingers through Jenna's but said nothing.

"I'm going to get worse. The bad days will become more frequent. Eventually I'll be on medication to control the pain and keep me comfortable. Each day I have is my last best day—yesterday was better and tomorrow will be worse, that's the way the long goodbye works." Jenna smiled sadly. She had finally said the words she'd needed to say to her sister, given her the reasoning and logic, and she hoped Sophia understood.

"Truth for truth?" Sophia asked.

"Yes."

Sophia sat, quietly reflective, beside her. "I think you're very brave."

Jenna held her sister's hand tighter. It shocked her, thinking of Sophia understanding Jenna after all she'd experienced, but maybe that's why Sophia did understand.

"I think we're going to stay until the end of the summer, if that's all right with you and Gabe. Then we'll go home." Sophia smiled. "But I'll come back as often as I can. I'll be here, I promise." Sophia leaned into Jenna's shoulder.

"Mama?" Caleb ran up the beach, his thin, spindly legs dripping with salt water and frosted with sand.

"Yes, baby?" Sophia answered, climbing to her feet and stretching her back.

"I'm hungry." It had been hours since they'd devoured Ginny's blueberry pancakes, and it was nearing lunchtime.

"Why don't you go wash off your legs and feet, put your shoes back on and then we'll grab some sandwiches?" Sophia suggested, gesturing towards the Landing Strip mall across the parking lot. "Tell your brothers and Mia to do the same—no sandy legs in the restaurant!" she called after him as he loped back towards the water's edge.

"Enough with the heavy; let's feed these monsters." Sophia turned to Jenna, smiling brightly, holding out her hand to help Jenna to her feet.

That's how it was done, Jenna mused as she watched Sophia switch from being a woman talking about the coming death of her sister to being a mother able to organize and take action. The transition between being introspective and being present. Prioritizing. There was time for everything, room for everything, but it took peace of mind to allow that balance.

"Sounds good to me. I could eat. There is this amazing sandwich shop—the food's really good." Jenna slipped on her sandals, gathering her straw market tote.

"Those kids, I swear!" Ginny smiled as she trudged towards Sophia and Jenna, lugging the heavy sack of shells behind her. "Think they cleaned out the beach today."

"Oh, Ginny, you are so tolerant. Here, let me take that for you." Sophia reached for the bag.

"We're going to go grab some lunch if you're hungry, Ginny," Jenna offered, dusting off the seat of her pants.

"Thank you, but actually, if you don't mind, I'm gonna head into town for a bit. Errands and whatnot. I can come by later if you need me," Ginny offered.

"Oh no. Go, enjoy your day!" Jenna hugged Ginny.

"All right, then, I'll see y'all later. Boys, Mia... you be good for your mamas, otherwise we won't be doin' anything fun tomorrow!" she teasingly hollered over her shoulder as she made her way to the rusted out truck in the gravel parking lot.

The kids waved animatedly and screamed their goodbyes as Ginny's truck rumbled away.

"You are so lucky to have her. She's wonderful." Sophia smiled at Jenna as they strolled across the parking lot towards the mall.

"Oh, I know, believe me. Ginny's been a blessing, helps me out so much—honestly, I couldn't do any of this without her. But sometimes I do feel really jealous." Jenna felt the blush creeping across her chest. No one but Gabe knew that.

"But all things considered, you are still lucky," Sophia chided, bumping Jenna teasingly.

"It's just hard, you know? Watching someone else raise your kid, doing all the things you want to do, reaping all the rewards. It's the hardest thing in the world." Jenna held her hands up in defeat.

"Yes, that would be really...trying. It's a balance, and you're doing just fine."

"Do you ever miss Mom?" Jenna started, unprompted, as she speared bits of lettuce with her fork.

Sophia nodded, "Every single day."

"What do you think she'd say to me now?" Jenna asked softly.

Sophia placed her elbows on the table and rested her chin in the palm of her hand, considering for a long moment, her lashes fluttering. "I think she'd tell you that she loved you and that you've raised an amazing girl, and that, although this hard, she knows you're doing the best you can and she wouldn't want you to be afraid."

"Was she angry with me? At the end, when I wasn't there?" Jenna met her sister's eyes and stared at them.

She'd always wondered if her mother felt her absence. If when she'd had a lucid moment on those last days when the morphine haze lifted, she ached for Jenna and felt the ebb of disappointment when she realized she wasn't there.

"Never. Not once." Sophia shook her head, "She was proud of you. I was the angry one. She'd say to me, *Sophia, you listen here, I raised you girls so that you'd fly away someday. A mother helps her children find their wings, then it's her job to push them from the nest. Jenna is flying.*"

"I should have been there."

"What difference would it have made?" Sophia's shoulders rose and fell.

Jenna chewed quietly for moment, thinking over what Sophia had asked.

"Maybe it wouldn't have...but maybe—"

"Maybe we shouldn't talk about it?" Sophia sighed, cutting Jenna off and wiped her mouth before placing her napkin on her plate. "You weren't there. That's what happened, that's how it went."

"Do you want to talk to me about Alex then?" Jenna eyed Sophia cautiously.

Sophia looked towards her sons, they were huddled over a paper placement, their lunches pushed aside, playing a game of tic-tac-toe.

"We aren't happy. We try to be, for the boys, but I can't wait for him to leave for work in the morning, and I find myself trying to drag my day out at the store to avoid seeing too much of him at home. Isn't that awful? That's not a marriage." Sophia sipped her sugary iced tea and looked at Jenna meaningfully.

Jenna thought of Gabe. She still loved him madly, couldn't wait to be around him, hated to be away from him. Even now that their marriage was older and they were older and so much had changed, she still couldn't imagine not being with him, not loving him.

"That must be so hard." Jenna spoke in hushed tones, pursing her lips.

"I think this summer apart has been good for us," Sophia confessed.

Jenna nodded in understanding. Sophia and Alex were small town society people, public people. She owned the local boutique; he was a family practitioner, successful and respected with a practice in full bloom. They had three handsome sons and a beautiful, stately home. The shell of their relationship was perfection;

it must have been very hard to admit that the inside wasn't as good, was slowly rotting away.

"What will you do when you get home?" Jenna pushed on. The candid nature of their conversation had bolstered her courage to pry a little deeper into Sophia's long-term plans.

"I'll move forward, I suppose." Sophia shrugged her shoulders in defeat. "What else can I do? Alex wants out, he's said as much. He doesn't love me anymore. I'm just catching up to feeling the same about him. A bad marriage changes people, it can turn the whole world inside out if you'll let it. I won't let it be that way. Not for my boys, and not for me." Her voice was shallow, allowing the hurt that lingered below the break through the surface.

"You're going to be just fine."

"Of course. We all will. The boys will still get the best of us—I'll make sure of that. I will have the store, and Alex will have his practice, and hopefully, in time, we'll be able to be friends."

Jenna longed to offer her sister more. Whatever she needed but mostly a safe harbor if things at home in South Carolina were too hard.

"I don't mean to put this on you, Jenna. As if you don't have enough to worry about."

"It's not like I didn't notice, it's why I asked. I worry about you; I want you to be able to tell me anything."

"But still, you have more than enough to deal with without me adding to the heap. I'm sorry."

"Soph, you're my sister."

"This is why I didn't want to tell you!" Sophia closed her eyes, pushing her fingers into her temples. "You, Jenna, no matter what you say, have a lot—more than enough—on your own end. That's why I'm here, to help you, not give you more worries."

"Even if everything was fine, I'd worry. I've always worried. When you were living with Mom and Dad, I worried; living with Grandma, I worried; when you left Illinois and went south, I worried. I worry about you because I love you. Because no matter how old we get, I'm always going to be the big sister."

Sophia patted Jenna's hand lightly and waved to the waitress for their check.

The children were exhausted as Jenna guided them through the door. Mia's eyes were sliding closed, and she had already wedged her plump, pink thumb between her lips.

"I'm going to put Mia down for a rest, guys," Jenna called over her shoulder to the three boys, who were making their way to the overstuffed couches in the family room. She scooped Mia up and made her way towards the bedroom.

Everyone would be asleep in moments, she was sure. Their tired eyes had betrayed them on the drive back from town, leaning against each other in companionable silence. Sophia had dropped them off before rushing back out to make an appointment she'd arranged in town with a glass artist.

If Jenna and Mia had been alone, she would have pulled her little girl into bed with her, snuggled deep beneath the soft, down comforter, and taken a long nap. But with Caleb, Harlen, and Thomas there, such a luxury was not possible.

She settled Mia under the covers, smoothing her

fine, curly hair against the pillow before drawing the shades and tiptoeing from the room. The house was cool and dark; the sun had slipped back behind its cover of clouds and the afternoon stretched out before her. Checking on the boys, she found them huddled in quiet slumber against the overstuffed pillows of her couch, so she silently pulled a throw blanket off the back of the couch and covered them. She snapped the plantation shutters closed, darkening the room even further, and made her way to her office.

Picking up her finely bound leather journal, Jenna pulled a pen from the recesses of her desk. It had be a long time since she had sat in here, behind her desk, with any real purpose. She flipped open the journal and began to think.

She wrote quickly, crossing off and underlining, as thoughts flashed in her mind, some overruling others, as she highlighted the pivotal moments of her daughter's coming life.

Her...
Becoming A Mother
Father Getting Remarried
College Graduation
First Love
Wedding Day
High School Graduation
First Broken Heart
Leaving Home
First Time
Cancer

Ten tapes, ten corresponding milestones her

daughter would pass in her absence. *You raise your children to fly*, Elizabeth had said, *but a mother's work, even in death, is never really done,* Susanna whispered from behind.

CHAPTER SEVEN

AUGUST 16, 2002

"Jenna?" Gabe called out to her as he did every day.

"In the bedroom!"

She could hear him greeting the children, who screeched in laughter; she could imagine him hoisting them over his shoulders, tickling them into surrender.

The warm scent of stew bubbling on the stove wafted down the hall.

"Babe?" Gabe wandered into the room, the thick carpet swallowing his footfalls.

"Getting dressed, give me one minute! How was work? Good?" Jenna slid the sheath of her black dress over her trim figure, fluffing her hair and straightening the hem. She felt sexy, the thin fabric hugging her hips and falling lightly just above her knees. She'd slipped her prosthetics in her bras. In the palm of her hand they looked like raw chicken cutlets, but tucked into the hidden pockets of her bra, they filled her out, gave the illusion that what was missing, wasn't.

"We're going out?" Gabe mused, leaning heavily against the doorframe, looking her up and down appreciatively.

"Soph told you?" Jenna feigned a pout before wrapping her arms around his middle.

"More or less. She had a pile of videos on the counter and kid-friendly food on the stove, and you're all fancy...I came to the conclusion on my own. So, what's the plan?" He smiled.

"We're going out. On a date. Bella Italia. I am craving some of their bruschetta. Soph offered to watch Mia, and I figured we'd take full advantage of the free babysitting." She looked over to the bed. She had laid out an overnight bag, clothing draped across, ready for packing.

He raised his brows subtly, gesturing to the luggage.

"The *whole* weekend. So, please, go, get cleaned up. We have reservations in an hour." She glanced at the bedside clock.

Jenna listened as the shower turned on, followed by the sound of his clothes hitting the floor, and his soft, off-key humming. She was thrilled to be escaping for the weekend. She had arranged for Sophia to watch over Mia while she kidnapped Gabe for a two days of rest and relaxation in Port Townsend. She hadn't visited the quaint harbor town with its bed and breakfasts in a number of years, but she remembered loving the tiny main street and all of the beautiful antique shops and trendsetting boutiques.

Summer in the Olympic Peninsula was designed for weekend excursions. Not stiflingly warm, but comfortable, the inhabitants of the small towns converging, soaking up the congested tourist season with markets and festivals. The summer had raced by; August was beginning its steady decline into the cooler fall months. Sophia would be leaving soon, and this was the only opportunity to take Gabe away, something Jenna had been meaning to do. She could picture it, the two of them, hand in hand, lightly buzzed on good wine, retracing the steps they'd taken when they were younger.

"Momma, you look so pretty!" Mia gushed from the living room floor, where she was sprawled beside her cousins watching one of the dozen or so movies Sophia had picked up.

"Thank you, baby," Jenna cooed, sinking to the floor beside her, kissing her head and rubbing small circles on her back. "You're going to have so much fun with Aunt Sophia, and we'll be home Sunday night, okay?"

"Okay," Mia agreed easily, turning back towards the vivid colors on the screen.

Climbing to her feet, Jenna joined Sophia in the kitchen, watching her sister stir a spoon around the boiling pot as steam seeped upwards.

"Thank you for this, Soph." Jenna settled on a stool to wait for Gabe.

"Not a problem. It'll be nice; I'm excited to see this rainforest I keep hearing about." Sophia smiled, tapping the spoon once before returning it to the rest.

"We'll be back Sunday, probably late. But I've left all the important numbers on the fridge, and I've left money in the top drawer of my office. Ginny will come by, probably Sunday morning, to help, so feel free to run errands or sneak in a nap." Despite wanting to get away with her husband, she felt uncertainty bubbling in her chest.

Most parents could leave without a backwards

glance, grateful for the time away. But looking at Mia, Jenna couldn't seem to bring herself to feel that sort of relief. She loved her home, more so now that it was overflowing with all the people she loved and she was able to enjoy it. But still, she knew this trip was of great importance; she needed to speak with Gabe alone.

"I know what you're thinking and yes, we're going to be fine." Sophia rolled her eyes as she opened the fridge to pull out a fruit salad and jug of punch.

"Hey girls." Gabe emerged from the bedroom, lugging the suitcase behind him. "Ready to go, J?"

"Sure. Bye guys, bye Mia. Love you all, be good!" Jenna called from the kitchen.

"Bye Mia, love you. See you later, guys, have fun!" Gabe thanked Sophia with a hasty kiss on the cheek and a one-armed hug.

"You two have fun. See you Sunday!" Sophia walked towards the door with them and waved them off, smiling brightly the whole while.

The restaurant was quant, a series of vinyl-wrapped booths and small gatherings of tables crowded the dining area and red glass luminaries held flickering candles beside bud-vases that overflowed with deeply lobed peonies. The hostess skillfully weaved through the clusters of diners, guiding Gabe and Jenna to a secluded back booth.

"Wine?" She flashed a pretty smile, offering the drink menu to Gabe.

"Malbec?" Gabe smiled, handing the list back.

"Good choice, your server will be with you in a

few." She pivoted on her high stilettos and disappeared towards the bar.

"So, this is a surprise." Gabe looked around the cozy dining area and back at Jenna who smiled and took his hand in her own from across the table.

"I thought it would be nice. Fun to get away, just the two of us."

"And where are we going?" Gabe asked, flipping open the heavy leather-bound menu.

"It's a surprise."

"A surprise..."

"I promise you'll like it."

The waiter arrived with a bottle of wine already uncorked and poured two neat ounces into each large goblets before taking their appetizer order.

"Actually, I did want to talk to you," Jenna began quietly, her fingers drumming on the laminated front of her menu.

"About?" Gabe asked, setting his menu aside and folding his hands together on the table.

"I've made arrangements."

"For?"

Jenna sighed deeply. "For me."

"What do you mean?" Gabe's brows creased together, pinching the delicate skin between his eyes.

"When I'm...gone...there are things that will need...attention...stuff that's important, the details," Jenna began. "I know this sounds morbid, but, Gabe, I really don't want you to worry about anything at all—just Mia—when the time comes."

"Jenna." Something that resembled horror crossed his face quickly.

"Please, just listen, okay? And be open-minded.

What I remember most about the time after my mom died was all the running around. No one had thought to order a casket, or select flowers, or buy a burial plot— forget about getting her only good dress cleaned and pressed."

Gabe nodded once, curt and formal, but offered nothing.

"We had so much to do, and it was overwhelming and exhausting and everything was so much worse because of it. I don't want that for you; I want you to be able to be there for Mia. So, I took care of myself and most of the plans."

"I would have done it, Jen. I'm your husband, it's not..."

"I know that." She raised her wine glass to her lips and paused. "But that wasn't the point, it's not that you couldn't or wouldn't, it's that now you don't have to. Mia is going to need you, probably more in the first few months than ever before or ever again—that is the main thing I want you to focus on, not the other stuff. Can you understand that?"

"You're not a burden."

"And I don't feel like I am; that's really not what this was about. But if there is any blessing in knowing, and maybe this is my way of accepting things, it's that I can help."

"Okay." Gabe nodded, listening.

"And I've made arrangements with my money, the book money we never used and set aside for a rainy day. I set a trust up for Mia, and the remaining parts of my royalties will be directly deposited into it. The rest, of course, is yours, so I don't think I need a will, and you have power of attorney and health...but

I want Mia to go to college and to have a nest egg, something she can pull from to help her start her life."

"Jenna..."

"It will be easier. You'll see. Having it all taken care of, arranged for, it's going to be...uncomplicated. Mia is going to need you, and you're not going to want to be anywhere but with her."

"I don't really know what to say..."

"You don't have to say anything. This was my wish, something I wanted to do—for all of us."

"That was so good." Gabe rubbed his distended stomach as they strolled out of the restaurant onto the quiet, rain-splattered streets of downtown, in the late evening the heart of the town was darkened and desolate.

"I've always loved their bruschetta," Jenna agreed, pulling her thin cashmere wrap tighter around her shoulders, blocking the misty, rain-whipped wind from touching her skin.

"You don't think it's the slightest bit ridiculous to spend the night in a hotel down the street from our house?" Gabe asked, opening the door for Jenna as she slipped inside.

"All part of my plan! And besides, it's just for tonight. Tomorrow, we're escaping this place," she laughed wickedly.

As the evening had passed, Gabe had drilled her for information, but she was firm, not budging an inch.

"And you won't tell me where we're going, correct?" Gabe pressed, turning the engine over and pulling smoothly from the parking spot.

"What happened to your adventurous spirit?" she teased as they made the short drive to the only nice hotel in town.

"I'm just curious, that's all," Gabe added quietly between the swishing of the wiper blades.

"We're only staying here one night—that's it. Tomorrow, we're gone. So, please, try to enjoy this." Jenna pivoted in her seat, looking at him.

"Okay, okay. You win," Gabe relented with a heavy sigh, pulling into The Red Lion parking lot.

Inside the lobby was quiet; Jenna had dropped in earlier to collect the room key, and the girl behind the desk smiled at them as they passed through on the way upstairs. The room was well appointed for a hotel in a small town and provided stunning views of Victoria, Canada from across the waterway.

Jenna wandered towards the windows, pulling back the sheers. She could hear Gabe drift towards her slowly, and when his lips pressed against the side of throat, she shivered.

Away from the ever-present company and tiny ears, they enjoyed each other slowly. His lips worked themselves against her skin, igniting her, and her body arched to meet his. Their words were tender whispers in the dark, the only light was that of the moon, hung high in the sky, reflected on the shimmying waters of the bay below. Afterwards, she lay against him, their breathes evening out as the tendrils of sleep crept ever closer.

"Jenna?" Gabe stroked her arm lightly as she dozed, snuggled into him.

"Mmhmm."

"Thank you for this." He kissed the top of her head.

"It's been a while, huh?" She moved slightly, draping her arm across his bare stomach.

"Too long."

"I could do this forever."

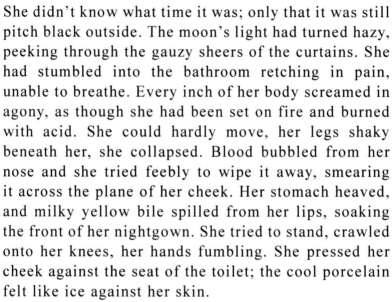

She didn't know what time it was; only that it was still pitch black outside. The moon's light had turned hazy, peeking through the gauzy sheers of the curtains. She had stumbled into the bathroom retching in pain, unable to breathe. Every inch of her body screamed in agony, as though she had been set on fire and burned with acid. She could hardly move, her legs shaky beneath her, she collapsed. Blood bubbled from her nose and she tried feebly to wipe it away, smearing it across the plane of her cheek. Her stomach heaved, and milky yellow bile spilled from her lips, soaking the front of her nightgown. She tried to stand, crawled onto her knees, her hands fumbling. She pressed her cheek against the seat of the toilet; the cool porcelain felt like ice against her skin.

"Gabe?" she whispered, trying to pull herself up to the rim of the toilet. "Gabe," she moaned louder, managing to lift her head up.

"What? What's wrong? Are you hurt? What happened?" Gabe ran into the bathroom, his eyes unfocused and blurry with sleep, sinking down beside Jenna, going white with horror.

"I think...something is wrong. Please, help me." Jenna tried to grab onto him, finding her arms useless and dead.

Gabe was up in an instant. Running from the bathroom back into the bedroom, Jenna heard the phone snatched from the cradle and Gabe pleading with someone on the other end to send help. He spoke in quick, panicked tones and Jenna tried to grab hold of his words, *blood, vomiting, pale, fever...terminal cancer,* before her eyes slid closed as she gave herself over to the darkness.

CHAPTER EIGHT

AUGUST 17, 2002

"J ENNA? JENNA, CAN YOU HEAR me? Please squeeze my hand if you can," Sophia's soft voice pleaded with her. "What happened to her? She was fine when you left!"

"I don't know. We went to bed…and next thing I knew, she was on the floor of the bathroom, screaming. She was saying that everything hurt; she was bleeding and she was burning up with a fever." Gabe's voice pitched with stress.

"And the doctors…?"

"They'll watch her and run some tests in the morning. They're talking about skilled care, night nurses, hospice."

Jenna opened her eyes slowly, blinking at the harshness of the fluorescent lights of the hospital room.

"Gabe?" Jenna tried to sit up, pushing against the bed rails. She knew where she was; the air inside these rooms felt different to her.

"Hey baby. I'm here." Gabe leaned down to brush the damp, matted hair from her forehead, pressing his lips to her skin. "You really gave us a scare."

"I don't...remember."

A television mounted to the wall was flashing news scenes of early morning Seattle, and a steady thrum of machines kept time beside her. Benign pictures of seascapes dotted the wall. The room was sparsely furnished: a few well-worn chairs for visitors, and a two-person dinette. Looking around, she knew: this was a long-term care room; this was the sort of place you came and stayed for a good, long while.

"You got sick. You're okay now, everything is going to be okay," he spoke gently into her ear.

Jenna caught Sophia's eyes as she stood at the foot of the bed. The look on her face betrayed the pacifying words Gabe whispered. The tender skin below her eyes were stained with the bruises of sleeplessness and real worry.

"Soph, where is Mia—is she here?" Jenna leaned back, her head crunching against the plastic hospital pillow beneath her.

"Ginny's with her. She came over when I called her after Gabe reached me. Mia is just fine, honey, just fine." Sophia exhaled, forcing a smile that looked more like she was gritting her teeth against something painful.

"Good, okay, good." Jenna nodded solemnly. Ginny was there, everything would seem normal for Mia when she woke up, she wouldn't even know about this. Jenna exhaled, if there was anything good about it happening when Jenna was away it was that Mia would never need to know. So she'd gotten sick. That had happened before; this was nothing new. She'd stayed over nights in the hospital before, too. This was all okay. Well, not okay, but not the end of the world.

"You should get some sleep. We'll be here when you wake up, but you need some rest." Gabe switched off the bedside light.

"I'm not tired. I would like to go home." Jenna tried again to pull herself up into a sitting position.

"You can't, not yet. Your doctor wants to run some tests in the morning. No one is going to release you at this hour," Sophia reasoned, settling into a worn chair by the small dinette in the corner of the room, pulling her knees up into her chest.

"I can just come back in the morning. I'll sleep better at home, anyway," Jenna protested weakly.

"Jenna." Gabe spoke her name softly, subtly pushing a red button beside the bed, calling for the nurse.

"I *want* to go home, this is just silly." Jenna tried again to sit up, and Gabe laid his hand on her shoulder, keeping her in place, rebuking her efforts.

"They want to observe you for a while. That's all. We need to understand what happened and...what it means." Gabe voice had a raw edge to it, and she felt the tears building in the back of her throat.

The squeaking of medical shoes on linoleum broke the conversation off as a plump, sweet-faced, elderly nurse walked into the room.

"Mrs. Chamberland, it's good to see that you're awake." She smiled jovially at Jenna, checking the fluid bags and subtly placing a cool hand on her forehead, on her wrist. This nurse was practiced; the caress was no more than a whisper of a touch, but effective and deliberate.

"Call me Jenna, please," Jenna answered automatically. She hated the formality of the hospital almost as much as she hated the hospital itself.

"Okay then, Jenna. And I'm Peg. You gave everyone quite a scare. Tell me, sweetheart, how are you feeling?" She clicked a pen in her hand as she scanned a metal tablet over the rims of her reading glasses.

"Good, actually. Just wondering when I can go home."

"I'm going to page the doctor, let him know you're up. I'll be back shortly. Try to get some rest." She smiled once before she pivoted and left.

"Ugh!" Jenna groaned.

"It's still really early. There is no sense in going home, anyway; you'd just have to come right back." Gabe sat down in the chair across from Sophia, who was pulling on the tattered cuffs of her sweater, tugging them over her balled fists.

Jenna watched him carefully. His shoulders were hunched forward, his elbows rested on his knees, and his thin fingers raked through his hair. She gave an annoyed sigh and admitted defeat, she could argue, but she wasn't going to get her away and settled back into the hospital bed.

"Go home, Gabe. Soph, can you drive him, please?" Jenna asked.

Both of their heads snapped up, looking at her.

"I mean it, go home. You need rest, too. I'll be good, I'll get some sleep...but only if you two go back to the house and try to unwind. Seriously, I bet the two of you look worse than I do!" Jenna made shooing motions with her hands, careful not to disrupt the IV tube tacked into her hand.

"I can stay," Gabe protested exhaustedly.

"Oh, look at us, such a matched pair! I don't want to stay, you don't want to leave!" Jenna weakly laughed out loud at the irony. "Now, go—get out of here. I need my rest!" She feigned a yawn.

Sophia looked at Jenna meaningfully, watching for any hint of uncertainty. She wouldn't find any. Jenna had learned long ago how to fool everyone into believing what she wanted them to believe.

"Okay, okay. Come on, let's let Jenna sleep in peace. I'll bring you back here in a few hours, but you do really look like you're going to pass out at any minute." Climbing to her feet, she walked over and kissed Jenna softly on the cheek. "You really, really scared the shit out of me. We are going to talk about what happened later," she whispered quietly in Jenna's ear, too low for Gabe for hear.

"I love you. Call if you need anything. I'll come right back." Gabe kissed Jenna sweetly on the lips, his morning stubble scratching at her cheeks and chin. His eyes were so conflicted, it broke her heart, but she wanted him to learn how to take care of himself first, make that a priority.

"I love you, too. The both of you. Very, very much," she said, taking his face between her hands and kissing him again, unhurried.

Jenna listened closely as the sounds of their retreat faded and when she could no longer hear them she sighed deeply and leaned back against the pillow and closed her eyes. Rest offered nothing to her now; she wasn't tired, she was frustrated.

The evening had been so perfect. The meal was delicious, the wine was bold and noted, she'd had three glass, more than she should have, but with each sip her insides warmed and relaxed her mind, she found herself letting go to all the worries she'd clutched on to and with the worries gone, the atmosphere around them had lightened. They'd discussed the end of summer, the back to school shopping that would need to be done soon, who would go to school and register Mia, what extracurricular activities they should sign her up for. They had talked about Jenna's plans, the funeral and casket and burial plot, her freshly laundered black dress that hung in the back of the closet in a dry cleaner's plastic. They talked about their weekend away, and he had tried to tease her into telling him more, but she'd stood her ground. They'd talked about work, the couple that had hired him to build a vacation home and how amazing it was going to be. Normal, average, everyday stuff, balanced with the things that should never need to be talked about.

She recalled how Gabe had teasingly resisted the hotel, but once inside the room, how he had easily been won over by the privacy it allowed them. She remembered that they had made love, engaging and slow. She remembered his lips running over the scars where her breasts had once been, kissing the hollow of her neck, the sweet spot behind her ear, lying on top of her, holding her close, telling her how deeply he loved her, needed her, begging her to stay. She remembered knowing that this would be the first of the last times they'd be that way. That with beginning of fall, she'd enter into the tedious time of dying, not in months, but in weeks and days. She remembered the way he'd looked at her, the way he saw her and the way his eyes filled with tears. The way the silk of her nightgown had caressed her body, how perfectly happy she'd been, how Gabe had lulled her to sleep with his fingertips and how, if she could, she would have frozen time in that exact moment.

But that was all. Nothing more until she awoke in this place. Dressed not in her pretty nightgown, but an over-washed hospital gown, thin and thread-barren. Not asleep beside her husband, pressed against him safe and warm, but rather alone, in a sterile single bed, attached to machines under the watchful eye of hospital staff. She still felt the dull ache of her muscles under her thin skin.

Her eyes snapped open as she felt the soft tug of someone adjusting her bedside IV.

"Sorry, I didn't mean to wake you," Peg whispered quietly, backing away from her.

"I wasn't asleep, just thinking."

"All the same, sorry. But since you're awake, I did speak with Dr. Vaughn. He should be coming by to see you soon." Peg smiled, jotting a note on Jenna's chart.

"Can I ask you something?" Jenna implored.

"Of course." Peg hovered.

"What happened? I can't remember anything, and I'm just...confused." Jenna searched Peg's face, hoping she would have answers.

"The doctor will be here soon, I'm sure he'll be able to help answer—" Peg began reasonably. Jenna understood Peg's hesitance, and she hated it. The humanity always seemed to be faltering in the lines certain professionals wouldn't cross. "Would you like a sedative? Something to help you rest?"

"No, I'm good. Thank you." Jenna returned the smile.

Turning to the clock, she saw the red blazing numbers. Only four in the morning. Hours to go before the normal business day, before Gabe would come back or Sophia would call or the doctor would grace them all with his presence. Yawning, Jenna closed her eyes once more. Maybe she could rest, just for a bit.

Dr. Vaughn sat beside the Jenna in the hospital room, Gabe at her other side, clutching her hand. "We have noted substantial growth in your tumors, and blood work shows decreased levels of red blood cells, which accounts for last night's episode—the lightheadedness, fainting, the hemorrhaging." he said softly.

When they'd first met, Jenna had thought Burgess Vaughn looked too young to be a doctor. Yet, he was the best oncologist in Seattle, highly sought after, regarded in glowing terms by the patients his practice saw and medical journals alike. Young, educated, tirelessly dedicated, his smile was easy, his bedside manner unmatched. Jenna had liked him instantly, and she'd gone on to trust him entirely with her life, a decision she'd never regretted. Even now, she knew he hadn't failed her.

"What does that mean?" Gabe asked, searching Dr. Vaughn's face for any hint of something positive beneath his serious demeanor.

"It means a few things, but most importantly, Jenna," Vaughn continued, "we're going to let you go home today. I'm sure you're anxious to get back to Mia." He smiled then, patting Jenna's hand softly. He knew her well; he knew she'd be clamoring to go home, she hated hospitals and had told him as much on countless occasions. He had always made a conscious effort to respect her feelings, sending her home whenever he could.

"We're going to give you a new prescription: Epoetine Alfa. It's going help stabilize your red blood cell count. But, I think now is the time you have to start considering the care we discussed a few months back." He took his glasses off and rubbed the tender spot between his eyes. "I think we should seriously discuss pain management and some fashion of home health care." He looked between Jenna and Gabe, studying them, appraising their reactions.

"I thought I had six months; it's only been three— it's only August," Jenna objected.

"Yes, and at the time I really believed that that was what we were looking at. But sometimes the medications and treatments are more effective than we believe. Sometimes the best they can do is to keep symptoms at bay and that's what they were doing for you." He splayed his fingers across the thick folder on his lap, uncrossing and then recrossing his legs.

"The cocktail you were on, Jenna, should have entirely killed your cancer—you should have gone into remission. When you didn't, and the cancer continued to grow, we agreed that what we were dealing with was no longer treatable. The science of oncology is an imperfect thing. We assumed, at the time, that your cancer was slow-growing and that even as it spread, you'd have significant time. We didn't know how much the treatments were helping you." The straightforwardness of his answer hung loosely in the air of the small room.

"And now?" Jenna pressed.

Please say something, Jenna prayed. *Give me something to hope for, don't let be this simple and done.*

"Now..." Dr. Vaughn sighed and opened his folder,

reading briefly through the text before continuing, "we keep you comfortable, we treat the symptoms." A sad look crossed his face, like clouds rolling over a beautiful day.

"This is the end?" Jenna felt the tears thicken in her throat and she closed her eyes.

"Jenna." Vaughn placed his hand on his.

"Can I have a moment please?" she asked from between gritted teeth.

"Honey." Jenna felt the weight of the bed shift as Gabe moved to sit beside her. His arms wrapping around her.

"Please? I just want to be alone." Jenna turned away from him.

"Why don't we step into the hall for a moment, Gabe," Vaughn suggested, and Jenna could hear the shuffling of paper as he stood up.

"I'll be right outside," Gabe pressed his lips to the top of her head before standing up.

Jenna waited until she heard the click of the door close behind them before she opened her eyes. She stood slowly, without the tubes of the IV stuck in her hands she could move freely and she walked towards the window. Below her, she the watched the cars moving on the street, above her, the sky stretched out for an eternity. A heavy rain fell, purifying everything, washing the world clean. Beautiful and heartbreaking.

Jenna knew she had been putting it off, pretending death wasn't lurking, all black and evil, counting the minutes of her life and every breath she took. She'd gone through the motions, but she'd detached herself from the truth, convincing herself of her good days, even when they weren't so good. She only had herself to blame for ignoring it all along. She had felt sore, worn out; there had been signals and warning signs. She just hadn't paid attention. She had skillfully ignored the way her muscles screamed out in protest in the morning, and the way she felt overcome with vertigo only to find her nose dripping with the tiniest droplets of crimson blood. She had just wanted the time so badly that as it passed, she never acknowledged it. But the end would come for her, she'd known that all along. Six months had always been the best case, the most she'd get and now, for what was left of her life, she'd decline slowly, steadily into the grave.

<hr />

She felt better in her own clothes; the softness of the worn sweats made her feel more human. Gabe had excused himself to find Sophia so they could go home. Jenna gathered the few belongings scattered about the room. She couldn't find her beautiful nightgown, the one she'd splurged on for their weekend away, French hand-painted silk and Chantilly lace. It had been so unlike her to gravitate towards the silky shift of the floral haze, but she loved the way the pastel blooms scattered, as though tossed down the length of the gown. It must have been beyond saving; she shuddered at the thought. Gabe, Sophia, or a well meaning nurse must have simply disposed of it, taking away the tactile evidence of her body's breakdown. It was just as well, Jenna knew there were certain clothes one wore for a certain time that one could just never wear again, like a wedding dress or a christening gown.

Sophia knocked softly at the door, poking her head in through a narrow opening.

"I'm almost ready." Jenna spun, surveying the room, mentally tabulating her belongings, checking for anything she might have overlooked.

"No rush." She pushed the door open further and crossed the distance between them. "Gabe's signing you out and pulling the car around, so you have some time."

"Oh, okay." Jenna sat on the edge of the bed, pulling the weekender onto her lap.

"How are you feeling?" Sophia asked, sitting down beside her.

Jenna looked at her sister with wide eyes; she wasn't sure how she felt. "How did Mom do it?"

"I don't know." Sophia shook her head slowly. "She had her faith, and I think she found lots of comfort in that. I never saw her cry—did you know that?"

"Do you think she knew, you know, that the end was coming?"

"I do. But she didn't let that hold her, you know? Things were different then, she didn't have all the things you have, but I think she tried."

"What was it like?" Jenna wondered out loud.

"It was peaceful. After Daddy left, the church brought in that nurse from the local hospice chapter. She stayed with Mom and helped her…and me. Mom talked a lot during those days. I'd sit in bed with her and we'd just have these long conversations." Sophia's voice was wistful, her eyes unfocused, like she was miles away.

"I miss her." Jenna wiped a stray tear from her cheek with the back of her hand.

"Have you decided what you're going to do about Mia now?" Sophia asked quietly. "I think you have to tell her, now."

Jenna sighed. "I just wanted her to have a normal childhood, at least for a little while. I didn't want her to have to deal with this. It's not fair, she's just a baby."

Sophia nodded in agreement beside her.

"I keep thinking of when I got pregnant with her, and how it was the best time of my life. I had all of these plans. I'd be the heavy, but I'd listen and I'd be a good mom and then, one day, she and I'd be best friends." Jenna looked up at the drop-ceiling and shook her head. "I waited so long to have a child because I wanted her to have a good life. I didn't want her to know anything about struggle...and it was all for nothing, because now she'll know everything about struggle and pain and loss."

"It wasn't for nothing, Jenna." Sophia patted her hand softly.

"Really? Do you believe that? What kills me is that if we'd done this earlier, I would have had time. Mom was my age when she died...do you realize that? Fourty-six and three months old. If I'd had Mia younger, if I'd just said to myself *do it now because who knows what's ahead...we'd* have had twenty years together."

"It's not about how much time you have, it's what you do with that time that matters."

"How do I tell her? Look into her little face and say *Mommy is dying*?"

"I don't know." Sophia answered honestly.

"How did Mom...tell you?" Jenna turned towards Sophia.

Sophia chewed her lower lip thoughtfully,

"She didn't."

"What do you mean *she didn't*?"

"She went to bed one day and she never really got up again. It took me a while to figure it out, but one day it was like I just knew without knowing, like she'd told me without telling me and I understood without really understanding. She just sort of faded away. Don't do that to Mia. Be honest with her. That's what she needs from you. Death is scary, but it's the silence that makes it terrifying."

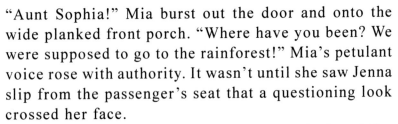

"Aunt Sophia!" Mia burst out the door and onto the wide planked front porch. "Where have you been? We were supposed to go to the rainforest!" Mia's petulant voice rose with authority. It wasn't until she saw Jenna slip from the passenger's seat that a questioning look crossed her face.

"Mia," Jenna dropped to her knees before Mia, straightening the hem of Mia's shirt, pulling her in close. Jenna buried her face in Mia's hair, capturing the scent of her innocence, memorizing the way her little body felt in her arms, committing it all to memory.

"Momma? I thought you were going away this weekend?"

"Oh, Mia." Jenna cupped Mia's face with her hand, "Something came up instead. I was wondering if you'd like to take a walk with me?" Jenna looked closely at Mia's face, her long lashes and lovely eyes, the faint peppering of freckles that crossed the bridge of her nose, spilling across her full, berry-pink cheeks. *What a beautiful daughter I have*, she thought wistfully.

"Aunt Sophia, are we still going to the rainforest?"

Mia looked past Jenna to Sophia, who was standing solemnly beside the bumper of the minivan, waiting patiently.

"Maybe tomorrow," Sophia answered quietly, adverting her eyes, looking down at the driveway.

"Okay, I'll go for a walk." Mia gave in with an easy shrug, reaching out to take Jenna's hand.

"Not far," Sophia whispered.

Grasping Mia's small hand in her own, Jenna headed towards the small path that led into the thicket of woods. Under in a canopy of leafy green, the wilderness pressing in around them, they walked slowly, the earth was damp below their feet, soft with the fallen pine needles and moss, and air smelled of rotting wood, rain and sea brine. Jenna led Mia towards the steep row of stone stairs that descended down to the dash of beach below. Slowly, they approached the landing. Sitting down on the first step, atop the sea cliff, Jenna opened her arms and Mia settled onto her lap.

"Did you have a nice day, honey?" Jenna brushed Mia's hair back, her fingers smoothing down the unruly waves before pulling her closer, tucking Mia's head under the crook of her chin, tightening her arms around her.

"Yeah. We played a game and watched some TV and Ginny made us lunch." Mia relaxed her arms. It was as if she were a baby again, the way it used to be, when they would snuggle together with a book, rocking in the wooden chair by the window.

"That's good."

"Did you have a good day, Momma?"

"It's better now that I'm home...with you." Jenna

pressed her lips to Mia's head, and breathed in deeply, her eyes scanning the distance of horizon. "I have something very important to tell you, and you're going to need to be very brave," Jenna began, searching for the words, for something that would help make sense of all of this. "I had to go to the hospital last night because I'm sick."

"Oh, Mommy, I know. You've been sick for a long time." Mia turned her face toward Jenna, snuggling deeper into her chest.

"Yes, but this time, it's different. I'm not getting better, honey; it might seem that way to you, because I'm not sick like I was, but I'm not getting better." Jenna ran her fingers through her daughter's hair, looking out over the bay, watching the ferries pull into the harbor, the gulls that swooped over the coastline, the flickering of lights turning on as dusk began to turn the day to night.

"What do you mean?" Mia asked, puzzled.

"In just a little while." Jenna pointed up, and Mia looked towards the sky, a darkening abyss, the few needlepoint stars just beginning to twinkle, "I'm going to go to Heaven, and I'll watch over you from there." Jenna shoved her face into the curly mass of unruliness that crowned Mia's head, hiding her tears, trying to be strong.

"Heaven where Grandma Elizabeth is." Mia said.

"That's right."

Jenna knew where Mia was going with this, they'd talked about Heaven and death before when she'd asked questions about Elizabeth.

"Are you gonna die?" Mia's eyes went wide with fear. She looked away from the sky and back towards Jenna.

"I don't want you to be afraid."

Mia's chin began to shake, and Jenna held on to her tighter.

"It's okay, everything is going to be okay." Jenna rocked Mia slowly, holding her closer. Jenna could feel Mia give herself up to the tears, the weight of her words settling in, heavy tremors rocking Mia.

"If you're in Heaven," Mia hiccupped between sobs, "I won't see you anymore."

"I'll be with you always, even if you can't see me," Jenna lulled.

Mia wailed, screaming wildly against Jenna's chest.

"It's okay, it's okay," Jenna soothed, wishing for the right words, for the motherly insight it would take to calm her baby down, appease her, heal her heart. But she was lost.

The sun was setting over the sea, the evening mist rolled in, swirling, disappearing before it reached the ground. Jenna and Mia sat, locked together in misery and pain and panic. Mia sobbing silently, inexhaustible, in the temporary safe haven of her mother's arms, Jenna rocking her, soothing her, as she had done when Mia was still her tiny baby, innocent and unbroken.

The crunching sound of leaves broke through the clearing before Ginny did. She appeared, a heavy quilt in her arms.

"Jenna?" she whispered against the wind, holding out the blanket, an offering. "I don't mean to interrupt, but figured you girls might be cold."

Jenna looked toward her home, visible through a break in the trees. The lights shining through the windows made the house look warm, she could see her nephews splayed across the couch, the flashing of the television cast bright colors and deep shadows across their faces. Mia should be in there with them, not out here in the middle of the woods. She needed to take Mia home.

"Mia, baby, we need to go now. It's getting dark, and you're going to catch a cold." She patted slow circles on the plane of Mia's shuddering back; the tears had calmed some time ago, and she just remained huddled, throbbing, in Jenna's arms.

The sounds of woodland nightlife hummed in her ears as, the ocean roared with high tide, the swells lapping at the shore. Snuggling Mia closer to her chest, she carefully pushed herself from the ground, cradling her child closer. Ginny stepped forward, opening her arms, silently offering to take Mia from Jenna, to carry her home. Jenna shook her head no, clutching her baby closer. She wasn't ready to hand Mia over just yet.

Ginny nodded and draped the quilt across Jenna's hunched shoulders. She walked slowly beside Jenna, keeping her hand anchored to the small of her back.

As they reached the manicured lawn of the side yard, Jenna saw Gabe, resting on the white rocking chair on the wide front porch, waiting.

"He's been out here the whole while you were gone," Ginny murmured softly in Jenna's ear.

Jenna's heart seized up. Memories flooded over her all at once: the first time they had taken the turn off the 101 to find this hidden, massive lot of land that would be theirs; the first time they had pulled into the driveway when the house was newly finished, staring up at the beautiful home they had dreamt of; the first time they had taken these steps with a baby, pink and fresh, swaddled in Jenna's arms, changing everything about them.

Gabe opened the door to the house as Jenna approached, gradually climbing the steps and crossing the wide porch. The smell of roasted tomatoes, steamed peppers, meat, and warm bread wafted forward, greeting her.

Sophia popped her head out of the kitchen, looking Jenna over, appraising the situation and the condition of her sister. The boys scrambled off the couches, lining up biggest to smallest, staring at her with sad, curious eyes.

Ginny closed her arm around Jenna, encouraging her forward.

Mia lifted her head from the crook of Jenna's neck, blinking her eyes.

"Momma, I'm hungry." Mia pushed free of Jenna's arms for the first time in hours and she set Mia carefully to the ground.

"I made some chili, honey. Can I get you a bowl?" Sophia spoke, the encouraging smile that broke across her face failed to reach her eyes.

"I don't want chili," Mia said, turning her eyes up to Jenna.

"Pizza?" Sophia offered.

"Maybe." Mia shrugged listlessly.

"Okay, well, I'll order a pizza...and if that's not what you want, I can make you a grilled cheese or whatever else." Sophia walked over to the take-out menu box, flipping through the neatly organized pamphlets to find a place that would deliver.

"Can I watch some TV?" Mia asked.

"Of course, honey. Sure you can." Jenna stroked the top of Mia's head affectionately.

"Come on, Mia, we can watch something you want," Caleb offered from the family room, shoving Harlen with his shoulder, Harlen catching the unsubtle cue and nodding eagerly in agreement.

"Jenna, how about a bath?" Gabe walked up behind her.

"That actually sounds really nice," Jenna placed her hand on his chest, felt his heartbeat.

Gabe guided Jenna into the room, clicking the door shut behind them. He pulled opened drawers and lifted out fresh clothes for Jenna. Watching him go through the motion, she found that she couldn't move, she felt as though she had floated away from her body, with nothing to hold her in place anymore.

Gabe placed a neat pile of soft pajamas on the foot of the bed and walked into the bathroom. The sudden sound of rushing water filled the room as the tub turned on, and she heard the sound of bath salts pinging against the porcelain of the footed tub, and a minty sweet smell the followed.

She followed it, encouraged by the promise of warmth and rest. Steam billowed like land- bound clouds across the marble and stone.

She peeled the clothes away from her skin, leaving them in a muddy pile on the floor. She hurried into the tub. The stifling heat of the water instantly burned her cold skin; it felt like a million needles were poking into her ruthlessly, but it felt good all the same. She sunk down, submerged her head under the water.

She exhaled and watched the bubbles surface. The world above the water shimmied, a blurry wash of blues and greens. She broke the surface slowly, leaned against the back of the tub and exhaled.

Gabe sat patiently on the teak stool, a clean white towel waiting on his lap. She turned her hand over and studied the purple smear of a bruise, the scabbed center when there the IV has pricked her pale skin. It would be the last time the surface of her skin was painted with the watercolors of intravenous salvation. In hospice, there would be none of that. Jenna pulled the plug, listening to slurping sound as the proof of her bad day washed itself down the drain.

Gabe stood, opening the towel wide. She climbed from the tub, the bathwater rolled off her body and puddled on the floor. He toweled off her hair, her arms, her back and front, then ran it over the length of her legs. He picked up a brush, smoothing it through her short hair carefully, slicking it neatly down. He guided Jenna to the chair and helped her sit. He opened her bottle of lotion and kneaded the white balm into her skin: her arms, legs, neck, face, shoulders, feet, and hands. It smelled like gardenias. He wrapped her in a freshly laundered silk robe, guiding her gently into the bedroom.

Jenna collapsed on the bed. Her eyes slid shut effortlessly, the pillow soaking through under her damp hair. Gabe lowered the blinds, closing their room off to the world, shuttering the bedside lights, and then removed his jeans and t-shirt, sliding into place beside her above the covers. He moved his fingers carefully through her hair, along her arms, across her face. Finally worming his way beside her, snuggling close, taking her in his arms.

"I love you, Jenna," he murmured over and over again until as she fell into sleep.

CHAPTER NINE

AUGUST 24, 2002

THE SMELL OF THE DENSE, sweet smoke snuck through the open window of Jenna's office. Peering through the glass pane, she saw Sophia, settled on a rocking chair looking out towards the bay.

Jenna cinched her robe around her waist and walked out the door. It was nearly three in the morning. Sophia was leaving in only a few hours, homebound for South Carolina just in time for the boys to go back to school. Jenna thought she'd be asleep.

"Sophia?" Jenna hissed crossing the damp lawn quickly, her bare feet slipping on the neatly-trimmed grass. "What are you doing?"

Sophia turned, startled by Jenna's quick approach, and curved her wrist, hiding her hand attempting to tuck the joint from Jenna's view.

"Are you smoking pot?"

"No!" Sophia tried to protested.

"Don't you lie to me! I can smell it! I can see it." Jenna's planted her hands on her hips, challenging her sister, thrusting her head in the direction of the faint whirl of bluish smoke drifting upwards.

"Oh, sweet Jesus, stop being such a hall monitor! Yes, I'm smoking, and I'm also an adult and I also consent to this." Sophia produced the joint, lifting her chin, she took a long drag, causing the butt to erupt in fiery red, burning away the paper and releasing the pungent scent into the early morning air.

"Well, at least you're honest," Jenna relented, sitting down beside her sister in the matching chair. "Is it good?"

"The best." The corners of Sophia's mouth turned upwards.

"What are you doing out here?"

"I couldn't sleep." Sophia pulled on the end of the joint, holding her breath before blowing out a series of smoke-rings.

"Is everything okay?" Jenna asked.

Sophia had been nothing short of wonderful to Jenna, Gabe, and, most of all, Mia. The rocky plane of their relationship seemed to have smoothed considerably over the expanse of the summer.

"I can't turn my mind off," Sophia answered dismissively.

"Alex?"

"Yes and no, but primarily yes," Sophia allowed.

Alex was nearly a forbidden topic of conversation, an unwritten rule, but set in stone nonetheless. After Sophia had allowed for the candid honestly, she'd locked the door. She had claimed she only wanted to focus on Jenna, and that nothing was as important as that. But just below the surface Jenna could tell Sophia was reeling from the dissolution of her marriage.

"Do you want to talk about it?" Jenna asked, reaching for the joint.

"You really shouldn't be smoking, Jenna." Sophia pulled back, keeping the blunt out Jenna's reach.

"It's my prescription, I think it's only right that you share," Jenna retorted easily, "so quit bogarting it."

"That's not even remotely funny!" Sophia glared at Jenna, before she handed it over.

"No, it's not," Jenna replied evenly, pulling in a short drag and looking the smoldering blunt held between her fingers before breathing out.

"He has a girlfriend." She spat the words like they were poison.

"No!" Jenna gasped in horror, turning to her sister but Sophia's face remained impassive.

"Yes. For some time now, actually. Years, maybe. I don't really know." Jenna passed her the joint. "I've allowed it to go on because I didn't want to hurt the boys; the boys need their father. I figured that if I pretended he wasn't screwing around on me, kept my head down, went on about my business, we'd all just be okay. I thought that if I didn't make it hard on him, he'd never feel the need to choose between us and her, but Alex has decided he wants to start a life with this woman, so, naturally, he needs a divorce." She snorted out a bitter laugh. "I guess he's enjoyed his *summer off.* A sabbatical from our marriage and he's decided not to return to it in the fall."

It explained his ongoing absence over the summer—not so much as a phone call, even to speak to his sons. He was off playing house with another woman, and Sophia and the boys fell into the *out of sight, out of mind* category. Jenna felt her temper flared wickedly.

"I worry how it will affect the boys. I'm going to be fine, but they're just children." Sophia shook her head sadly.

"Children are resilient." Jenna couldn't think of anything more to say, any way to comfort her sister. Her words sounded false and brittle, even to her. But she had nothing else to offer; her sister's fears were her own. How did children rebound after the loss of a parent? This was something that had haunted her for years now.

"That's what they say, anyway." Sophia lifted her joint to her lips as a small smirk tugged at the corners of her mouth in humorless mockery. "But let me tell you, the end of marriage can screw a kid up six ways to Sunday, too. Some kids fair better than other."

Jenna turned away, blinking hard.

Sophia dropped the joint on the grass and stubbed it out with the toe of her shoe. "Oh Jesus, oh Jenna... I'm sorry. I didn't think, I didn't mean that, shit! I'm sorry—Mia will be fine—this is different, not the same," Sophia chastised herself, as if the conversation were playing on a loop in her head, the words about a parentless child sinking in.

"It's okay. I know what you meant." Jenna pacified her sister. Jenna knew her sister hadn't meant anything malicious about it. She was simply sharing her fears, which were, of course, every bit as valid and real as Jenna's own. But marriages dissolved in a dozen ways, the only commonality was that the children who were left, were left to a life that was beyond their control.

"I'm sorry, that was so thoughtless," said Sophia, grimacing in the dark, fishing in the pocket of her robe for a pack of cigarettes. "What I should have said was...when a parent *chooses* to leave." She stretched the word *chooses* out, placing emphasis on it.

"I think it's all sort of the same," Jenna challenged. "It's varying degrees of being left—by choice or by force, children have a hard time seeing the difference when all they want is their parent."

"Maybe you're right, maybe it's all different degrees of feeling alone," Sophia allowed softly, clicking the lighter.

"And, to be honest, I have no clue how kids deal with it. But I look at how we were, with Mom. Sure, we were older, but it was still hard. But I like to think we did okay, we managed." Jenna took her sister's hand, squeezing it.

"I resented you," Sophia admitted, the words hanging in the air.

"I know that," Jenna murmured.

"Not because I didn't love you, but because I did. You were out there in the world, off at college with your friends, living your life, and I was stuck at home in that house with her, taking care of her. Taking care of Dad. He was like a sinking ship. A total a wreck. I just didn't know where to put that sort of anger."

All summer they'd tiptoed around this conversation. The one where Sophia would let all pretense slip and Jenna would be forced to face the truth. They'd been patching a hole with putty, but not addressing the reason the hole existed in the first place.

"I'm so sorry, Soph." Jenna wished she could say more, but she couldn't.

The truth was, Jenna had known what was going on back then. She could have transferred to a local college or taken time off, but she hadn't. She had chosen to stay her own course. Even now, she wasn't sure that she would do things a different way, given the chance.

Her life's path had brought her here. Her apology wasn't for what she could have done differently, but for what her choices had cost her sister.

"I know that," Sophia sighed, a tone of acceptance in her voice. "I stopped being angry about that a while ago, honestly. Once I got out and was on my own, I understood why you'd done the same thing."

"I just want you to know that I love you very, very much. I'm sorry if I've ever hurt you or made you feel alone. And I am so grateful you came out here for the summer—really, I am." Jenna brushed away a few stray tears, trying not to think about the fact that in a few hours, Sophia and her boys would be on a flight home, and she might never see her sister again. At least not in this way, not where they could talk and laugh. This would be their last real conversation of substance.

Sophia shook a cigarette from the pack, pursing it between her lips and holding the small flame from the lighter up to the end.

"Soph, I need to ask something of you now and I just want you to promise me you'll think about it. If you say no, I understand, but just swear you'll think on it for a while and not decide either way right now."

Sophia rested her hand of Jenna's and searched her face.

"When I was at the doctor that last time, when I got my scans and we knew that it was only a matter of time, a social worker gave me some pamphlets. They're the sort that help you make plans for the end. I didn't know what I'd want, and it took me a while to make myself right with the decision, but I know now."

"Jen?" Sophia tilted her head.

"I want you to help me when the times I comes. I want to go with dignity and grace. If I have to go, I want it to be on my terms."

"Jenna, if you scared of the pain…"

"I'm not scared of the pain. I just want the pain to stop. I've had enough. I want to say my goodbyes and make peace with this life and let go, not linger in some place between here and there, doped up on drugs. I know nothing if not that life, on your own terms, is better and I'm guessing death might be just the same."

"I don't know if I can do that…"

"It's not as terrible as it sounds. After the medicine, I'll close my eyes, I'll slip into a coma, and then I'll be gone." Jenna shook a cigarette free from Sophia's pack and put it between her lips. "Did you see Gabe in the hospital? How he looked? How I'd hurt him? He doesn't need to see me in the sort of pain he can't take away. And Mia, she's so scared. I don't want her last memories of me to be the ones where my body is failing, where I can't see her and I can't hear her because I'm in between life and death, because I'm gone but not letting go. She won't understand that. I'm asking you to help me, but mostly, I'm asking you to help them."

"Jenna…"

"I know it's a lot to ask."

"I need to think about it."

"Of course." Jenna placed her hand over her heart; it felt lighter in her chest, like she could breathe.

They sat in silence.

"I wish I could stay longer." Sophia stomped out the butt of her cigarette and took Jenna's hand. "As

soon as I get the boys situated, I'm coming back."
Sophia brushed away a few tears before, digging her
heels into the soft earth. "It really is beautiful here,
Jenna, like a picture or something, almost perfection."

"It is, isn't it? We're lucky to have all of this."
Jenna followed suit, settling deeper in. "Do you want
to go to the front of the house? Watch the sun rise over
the mountains?"

"Here's good." Sophia held Jenna's hand tightly in
her own, squeezing it.

"Jenna? Sophia?" Gabe appeared at the sliding
door, looking disheveled and half-asleep.

"Over here, babe," Jenna whispered, holding up
her hand.

"Everything okay?"

"Everything's just fine." Jenna sighed.

"Okay, 'cause it's early." Gabe padded across
the yard.

"We're just hanging out, talking, no big deal. Are
you up now for the day?" Jenna asked, leaning slightly
backwards, turning to face him.

"Yeah, early morning. Do you girls want coffee
or something?" Gabe came to stand behind Jenna,
rubbing her shoulders tenderly.

"I'd love some. Soph?"

"Sure." Sophia smiled towards Gabe.

"Were you smoking?" Gabe sniffed Jenna's hair
subtly, spotting the pack sitting obviously on the
side table.

"Guilty as charged." Jenna raised her hands.

"Nice," Gabe laughed, as he turned back towards
the house. "Two coffees, coming right up."

Jenna watched him go.

"He loves you a lot." Sophia smiled and closed her eyes. "You're lucky."

"Very lucky. Are you packed up?" Jenna leaned back in her chair.

"Yes, got everything done and laundered yesterday." Sophia nodded, tapping another cigarette from the dwindling pack.

"Can I do anything?"

"Nothing. I think we're pretty much ready. We need to leave for the airport in a few hours."

"I don't mean do anything just now—I meant in more general terms. What can I do?"

"Honestly? I'm better prepared for this than you'd think. I've already hired an attorney, did it before I left for the summer. The house and business will remain mine, and he'll keep what's his. I think the word for this is *amicable*—we're amicably ending our marriage."

"I imagine it makes things easier for you."

"In many ways, yes. But it also makes it sadder, more surreal. A marriage that bore three children, a medical practice, a store, a beautiful home…it can be taken apart like *that*." Sophia snapped her fingers. "It takes so long to acquire those things, and so little time to deconstruct them. It's hard to wrap your mind around how quickly you can just pull that single thread and unravel it all. It makes me think about Dad. I wonder how he could do what he did—you know, just leave and never look back."

"I look at Gabe. He's so strong, brave and steady, and sometimes I want to ask him *aren't you tired yet? Tired of being so solid and selfless?* It's hard to watch someone you love die, and yet he does it, every single day. I think it must have been that way for Dad. He chose differently. What he did, that was wrong, though."

"Do you ever wonder what happened to him? After he left? He's never tried to contact me." Sophia's eyes were closed and her cheeks with wet with tears.

"No. I really don't. When Mia was first born, I thought about looking him up—hiring a private investigator and finding him—but I never did. Whatever his reasons for going, he stayed gone. I don't know how you do that or how broken you have to be to think that's the better way, but I figured he had his reasons. He wasn't my father anymore—not the man I remember, at least—and I decided that rather than dig him up, I'd respect his wishes and let him go. For me, our dad died when Mom did."

Sophia nodded slowly. "I still needed him."

"I know."

"I'm going to be okay," Sophia whispered, more to herself than to Jenna.

"Yes, Soph, you really are. It's like Mom always said: Find your wings and fly."

"Coffee?" Gabe emerged from the house, two steaming mugs in hand. He'd already showered and changed into a pair of faded blue jeans and a soft flannel button up; his hair was still damp, glistening in the rising sun.

"Thank you, kind sir." Jenna kissed him lightly on the cheek, aware that she probably tasted like an ashtray.

"All right, I have to run to the site. I'll be back before you guys take off so I can say bye." Gabe waved as he turned back towards the house.

Jenna wrapped her hands around the warm cup, taking a long sip.

"I'm going to go get dressed, get the boys moving. I'd love to feed them before it's too late so they can eat lunch at Sea Tac. We have a long flight home." Sophia stood up, and bent to pick up the discarded cigarette butts littering the yard.

Jenna nodded in agreement and watched her sister tiptoe carefully across the yard. The sun was up now—such as it was—covered by thick threatening clouds, but the morning was a hopeful one. It looked different to her now.

CHAPTER TEN

SEPTEMBER 12, 2002

MIA CLAMBERED INTO THE KITCHEN, dumping a large bucket of colored pencils on the table from the craft corner. Jenna bent over the table, reading the instructions Mia's teacher had sent home regarding the self-expression picture. She had been asked to draw a picture of her family and write a few lines about them to share out loud with her class in the morning.

Summer had wound down expectantly, and Mia had been overjoyed to return to school. The thrill of free days had run its course, and Mia seemed particularly taken with her new teacher. Excited about experimenting with homework, being seven now, and starting second grade boosted Mia's confidence.

Jenna had, predictably, gone all out for Mia's birthday party, celebrating the passing of time. The last birthday party she'd ever have with her daughter had been bittersweet. Gabe had roped off the yard and Jenna had hired a petting zoo. They supervised roasting marshmallows in the fire pit, pitched tents in the patch of land off the back, and hosted an epic sleepover, complete with Ginny's homemade apple cider donuts for breakfast. Jenna loved the sound of the children running wild in the back yard, squealing with delight as the goats scarfed feed from their hands.

"Mia, you have to draw a picture of your family, and then you have to write a short story about us," Jenna explained, pointing to the assignment.

"I know!" Mia sifted through the rainbow on the table, picking out colors and laying them neatly in a line.

"Do you want me to help you?" Jenna asked, handing a crisp sheet of white craft paper to her daughter.

"No." Mia chewed on her lip, weighing the merits of light blue versus navy blue.

"Okay, baby, I'm going to be in the kitchen, then. Do you want pasta for dinner tonight?" Jenna shoved away from the table, heading towards the pantry to pull out ingredients.

"Sure, that sounds good," Mia said before pressing a black pencil to the paper.

"Daddy will be home soon and that mess will have to be cleaned up before dinner, so work hard and finish up, all right?"

"Okay," Mia mumbled, fully focused on the task at hand.

Jenna put a large pot of water on the stove to boil and removed a Tupperware container from the freezer that contained leftover sauce. As it spun in the microwave, thawing, Jenna poured herself a glass of water and shook two tiny pills from an orange plastic container.

"So you like your teacher?" Jenna posed the question to Mia, cracking the pasta in half and setting the noodles aside for boiling.

Mia nodded her head. "She's really pretty."

"She seems like a really fun teacher," Jenna continued, grabbing a loaf of soft French bread and slicing it into small, round pieces.

"Today, we went on a nature walk. And in music class, I got to play a recorder!" Mia beamed, still coloring fiercely. "Later, after lunch, we went to the library and had story time. It was a fun day!"

"Wow, busy, busy. Are any of your friends in your class this year?" Jenna whisked melted butter, garlic, oregano, and paprika together in a small bowl, dipping the slice of bed in the gritty mixture before placing it on a baking tray and sprinkling cheese on top.

"Sarah and Kelly are, but Geneva isn't, so we just get to play at recess," Mia summarized, not looking up.

"Oh, that's too bad." Jenna set the oven to 'bake' and walked over to table, where Mia was finishing her picture. "Maybe we can have Geneva over this weekend for a play date?"

The crisp white sheet was now covered with rolling hills, thick clouds, and a cluster of detailed people, all easily recognizable.

"That's you, me, and Daddy." Mia pointed to a small grouping of three people, beaming proudly in front of a house. "Ginny, Aunt Sophia, Thomas, Caleb, and Harlen." She pointed to another group. "That's my family." Mia smiled proudly at her drawing.

"That most certainly is your family." Jenna kissed Mia on her head. "That's a very lovely picture. You're a good artist."

"When I finish showing it at school, you can frame it if you want," Mia offered, a proud smile stretching across her face.

"I'd really love that." Jenna held up the drawing,

looking closer at the detail Mia had included—the wide house, the thick nest of forest, the way everyone looked so happy. This was the way the world looked to Mia, Jenna realized. Her heart swelled with love and pride and joy. This was how she saw her family.

"Ladies?" a voice boomed from the entryway as Gabe walked in, dripping beads of water over the entryway rug.

"In the kitchen!" Jenna called out. "Mia, can you pick up the pencils and help me set the table?" She gestured towards the mess scattered about.

Mia went about grabbing handfuls of brightly colored pencils, shoving them back into the bucket.

"Dinner in thirty, Gabe. You have time to get changed!" Jenna called out, hearing Gabe shuck off the excess water from his raincoat. The door closing behind him.

"Smells good," he commented, walking in, planting a kiss on a Jenna and mussing Mia's hair.

"How was work?" Jenna asked, ladling the thawed sauce from the Tupperware to a waiting pot on the stove.

"Good, it's going to be a great house." Gabe grabbed a beer from the fridge.

"That's great. I'd love to see it." Jenna spun the sauce around in the pan.

"All right, I need a quick shower. You good, J?" Gabe asked, leaning against the counter, his pants splattered with a dusting of mud, soaked entirely near the hem of the pants.

"I'm good, go shower." Jenna stepped up on her tiptoes to kiss him lightly on the lips. He tasted of beer.

"See ya." Gabe reached down to kiss her again, a

little longer, subtly grabbing her butt and giving it a playful squeeze. Jenna shooed him away with her hands, laughing.

"What's funny, Momma?" Mia asked, running back into the kitchen after putting her things away.

"Your daddy is just being silly." Jenna rolled her and slid the tray of garlic bread into the oven, setting the timer.

"Momma?" Mia asked, gathering the small stack of plates Jenna had set out.

"Hmm?" Jenna answered, sliding the noodles into the boiling pot.

"You were an author, right?" Mia wouldn't remember her mother writing, she had been just a toddler the last time Jenna was published. It wasn't something Gabe or Jenna talked about much anymore.

"Yes, I was." Jenna stirred the noodles thoughtfully.

"Are your books in my library at school?" Mia wondered as she clanked the silverware down.

"No, I wrote books for grownups. They are in libraries, but not elementary school libraries," Jenna patiently explained.

"Can I say you wrote books in my story about my family?" Mia asked

"Of course you can.." Jenna smiled at her daughter, pinching her cheek playfully.

"Can I read one of your books?" Mia finished setting the table and wandered over to look in the oven at the toasting bread.

"When you're older, of course you can. Right now though, they are a little bit too old for you to understand."

"What do you mean 'old'?"

"Well, the books I wrote were about adults, living adult lives, making adult choices. They weren't for children, a lot of the stuff I talked about, you wouldn't understand just yet."

"You could write a kids book, you know."

"Oh, I don't know about that. That's a special kind of writer," Jenna explained.

"I could help you," Mia offered. "I know lots of stuff about kids, and it would be easy."

"I don't know, baby, let's talk about it later." Jenna tried to change the topic of conversation. It broke her heart to say no, knowing she'd love nothing more than to write a book with her daughter.

"It could be about princesses and knights and castles," Mia triumphed, breaking Jenna's heart, knowing she'd have to dash those hopes if the topic was brought up again. She simply didn't have the energy.

"We'll see. Hey, could you fill the glasses up with ice for me?" Jenna handed Mia three glass goblets and pointed the freezer.

As Jenna drained the pasta, Mia ran off to get Gabe for dinner. The shared the meal, bantering over the trivial aspects of their day. Mia's school took center focus for most of the conversation, Gabe asking her about her friends, teacher, and homework assignments. Jenna spooned small bites of food into her mouth, realizing that her appetite was fading. Like a child, she scuttled the majority of her meal around her plate, hoping to conceal that fact that she wasn't really eating. Diminished hunger, she'd been warned, was a sign of the worst.

With the table cleared and the dishwasher splashing wetly in the background, Mia returned to her place at the table. She pulled a lined piece of paper from her bedazzled folder and sharpened a fresh pencil. Jenna warmed herself a cup of tea, dipping the bag into the steaming water, sweetening it with a hint of honey and a splash of milk. Gabe had retired to the family room, some sports show animatedly recapping the highlights of various events.

"Are you going to write your story now?" Jenna asked, consulting the clock above the table, sipping her tea. Only an hour remained before Mia's regular bedtime, and she hoped Mia could truncate the assignment into the time remaining.

"Want to help?" Mia asked, neatly writing her name in pretty script at the top of the page.

"Sure, of course." Jenna settled down beside Mia. "But, I'm only going to help. This is your story, I want you to tell it."

"I know that! It's not hard! It's about my family," Mia rebuked, rolling her eyes.

"Nice attitude, Mia," Jenna scolded. She wasn't amused by the eye rolling, even in jest.

Mia quietly went to work, her pencil deliberately moving across the page. Jenna sat beside her, answering questions as Mia posed them. Gabe designed homes, Jenna wrote fiction books, Ginny was her babysitter for four years now and also like a grandma, her Aunt Sophia lived in South Carolina in a big city by the ocean and owned a store. Finally, Mia lowered her pencil in victory. Jenna appraised the clock. It was definitely time for bed.

"All right Ms. Mia, ready for bed?" Jenna asked, taking the paper and placing it on Mia's folder. She'd pack her up for a school in a minute, and make sure the picture and story found its way to the correct spot.

"Aren't you going to read my story?" Mia's brows furrowed in confusion.

"Of course I am!." Jenna said tickling Mia's tummy.

"I'll take her," Gabe groaned, shoving himself off the couch.

"You sure?" Jenna asked.

"Yep. She's all mine!" Gabe tossed Mia easily over his should, stalking off towards her bedroom.

Jenna followed close behind. Gabe flopped Mia down on the bed, and she collapsed in fits of giggles.

"Alright, alright you" Jenna sat down beside Mia, running her hand over Mia's face, cupping her cheek. "I'll see you in the morning. Have the sweetest dreams." She yanked back the covers as Mia scrambled in, kissing her on the forehead.

"Love you Mommy," Mia said, snuggling deep under the blanket.

"Love you more, Mia," Jenna whispered as she blew her another kiss.

Jenna listened outside the door for a moment longer as Gabe read to Mia, The Giving Tree, for the hundredth time, it had been one of Jenna's favorite children's books, too. She listened closely to the way the words rolled off of Gabe's tongue, filling the silence of the house with goodness. He's a good dad, Jenna thought. Mia would always have that.

The kitchen was oddly quiet as Jenna strolled back in. Gabe had switched off the television and the dishwasher was humming now. She settled herself back at the kitchen table, lifted the sheet of paper Mia had worked so hard on, and began reading.

My Family - By: Mia Chamberland

I have a Mom and Dad. They are really nice to me. But I also have a lot of other family members, and they are great, too.

My Dad is really funny, his name is Gabe. He designs houses for people who live here in Port Angeles. He used to work in Seattle before I was born, and he designed some buildings there, too. He built the house I live in, and my bedroom is pretty cool.

My Mom is really pretty and nice. Her name is Jenna. She's sick, so we can't do a lot of stuff together, but that's okay, because I love her and the stuff we do do is lots of fun. She used to write books, but not the kind of books we have at school, books for grown-ups. When I asked if I could read one, she said they were too old for me, but I will read them all when I get bigger. She and I might write a book together one day, that would be lots of fun. So, I really need to learn to write this year.

I have a babysitter named Ginny. Ginny is like a grandma to me since my real grandma is in heaven. She is a really good cook, and makes all sorts of good stuff with things she grows herself. Sometimes I help her plant, and I like that.

I have an Aunt named Sophia and she had three boys named Harlen, Thomas and Caleb. We hung out all summer and had so much fun, I was going to camp, but when they came I decided to hang out with them instead. We played on the beach and we went to the rain forest. My Aunt owns a store in South Carolina, so I helped her pick up shells on the beach that she brought all the way back to South Carolina and then she sells them in store because people like to put shells in vases and bowls.

I have a great family, we love each other very much. I am very lucky. That's my family.

Jenna rubbed tears from her eyes as she laid the paper back down on top of the folder. What a beautiful, smart child she and Gabe were raising. She picked a piece of fresh paper out of the folder and began to write ...

Dear Mia,

I read your story after you went to bed last night, just like I promised. You're a really good writer. I'm so proud of you. Your story is awesome.

And yes, our family is great...because of you.

Love,
Mom.

Jenna slipped the paper behind the assignment where Mia would find it in class tomorrow. She hoped the note would booster Mia's confidence as she stood before a class, reading out loud.

"God, almost put myself to sleep with that book." Gabe ambled down the hallway rubbing his eyes.

"You should go to bed, babe, you look exhausted," Jenna commented, pushing her chair back into the table.

"I will, just wanted to say good night first ... Are you going to be up much longer?" Gabe stopped.

"Just a few minutes, I want to clean the kitchen up and pack Mia's lunch still." Jenna opened the fridge, pulling out turkey, cheese, lettuce and tomato slices.

"Okay. Love you," Gabe yawned loudly, waving behind his back as he walked towards the master bedroom.

Jenna assembled the sandwich quickly, scooping a handful of chips in to a plastic baggie, slicing an apple and pinching off a cluster of hothouse grapes, two cookies and a string cheese. Placing everything in the tiny lunchbox Mia loved, Jenna closed the fridge and turned off the lights.

CHAPTER ELEVEN

SEPTEMBER 13, 2002

"W HAT ARE YOUR PLANS TODAY?" Gabe asked, filling a thermos of coffee before heading out the door to his job site.

Jenna consulted the calendar that hung by the phone in the kitchen. "Absolutely nothing. I think I'd like to go shopping in town."

"Anything in particular?" Gabe shoved a few papers into his briefcase, snapping the brass locks closed.

"Not really. Mia needs a few things, and I'd like to get a jump on Christmas shopping. How about you?"

"I'll be in Sequim all day. We're going to try to pound this house out in the last few weeks of good weather. I'm thinking about taking the winter off, but we'll see."

"Will you be home for dinner?" Jenna ran her fingers through her hair.

"I'll try; no promises though. You should just order in either way, but I'll call you later and let you know for sure," Gabe kissed her briefly on the lips and trudged out the door.

"See you." Jenna waved from the doorway as Gabe

walked around to his car, blowing her a kiss before climbing in and turning the engine over.

Mia had boarded the bus for school an hour before, and with nothing to do, Jenna strolled back into the kitchen, pulling the phone off its cradle.

"Casa Bella," a familiar voice chirped on the other end of the line.

"Hey Soph," Jenna greeted her sister, sipping her coffee and sitting down on a barstool.

"Jenna! I was just thinking about you! Hold on, let me take this in the back room." Sophia quickly gave instructions to someone waiting nearby, and a moment later picked up another connection. "God gosh, we're swamped! How are you? I miss you!" Her cheerful laugh filled the line.

Jenna laughed at her sister's monolog, running a mile a minute, her usual style. "I'm good, just killing some time before I head into town, thought I'd check in. How are you?" Jenna knew bits and pieces of what was going on with Sophia back home, but she always felt like it was only part of the story.

"The store is so busy, everything I brought back with me is selling like you wouldn't believe, everyone just wants the stuff!" Sophia laughed lightly again. "Good thing, though. Keeps me in house and home."

"How are the boys? I miss them," Jenna pressed.

"Well, Thomas is running amuck around here today; half day preschool is a curse for working parents, Caleb and Harlen are doing really well in school. We're all in a place of transition," she allowed, and a slightly sad tone flitted into her voice.

"You're welcome to come out for a long weekend, you know." Jenna encouraged.

"Oh, I'd love that. More than you know. But the boys are just starting to ... adjust ... if that's the right word. Alex moved in with *her*, and the boys hate it. Can't trust them to stay there more than an hour before they start calling to come home, forget about a weekend or longer." Acid dripped from her voice like syrup.

"Bring the boys!" Jenna offered.

"We'll see ... let me think about it," Sophia answered softly.

"Okay, do that. So, what else is new?" Jenna looked towards the clock; she had thirty minutes before the town opened for business.

"Eh, nothing really. Same old, same old," Sophia dismissed Jenna's concern, which only stood to concern her more. "How are things there?" Jenna caught the implication in her tone.

"Not bad. Mia's in love with her teacher." Jenna tapped her fingers on the counter. "Gabe's building this huge house in Sequim, so he's gone a lot trying to finish it all before winter, but he really loves the creative freedom this couple has given him. Apparently, they're some big deal in Seattle; this is their second home. It's a monstrosity, absolutely huge and stunning."

Gabe had finally, after much pestering, driven Jenna out to the job site. The house was glorious, and Jenna felt house-envy as she wandered about the palatial home.

"That's great!" Sophia chimed. "Did you ask if they need a designer or maybe a few knick knacks?" Sophia laughed lightly, her voice like sweet bells.

"I'll be sure to put in a good word," Jenna mused,

snickering softly.

"And how are you feeling Jen? No bullshit." Sophia's voice darkened a note.

"The pain medication is keeping a lot of things at bay, which I'm grateful for." She hated talking about her symptoms, knowing it only upset everyone, worried them.

"As long as you're comfortable." Sophia murmured. "Just don't do too much running around."

"Speaking of which, do you know if the boys want anything in particular for Christmas?"

"You're not being serious! It's only September!"

"I most certainly am! I love the holidays, and who knows what shape I'll be in when they roll up this year. But Santa Claus comes whether I feel good or not, that's the way it's always been—the way it always will be."

"No one would think badly if you wanted to defer that this year ... " Sophia's voice was soft, cautioning.

"I know that. But this is loaded. I can put it off—and then what? Mia has no Christmas? I have to admit that no matter what, these will be the last holidays I can prepare for Mia, the last time I can pretend to be Santa and wrap her gifts. Even if I don't make it to see Christmas morning, I want her to have happy memories. Life goes on you know."

"Jenna..." Sophia's voice mellowed. "I could shop for you. I could do that."

"No. I mean, yeah, you could, but you won't. This is what I have left in my life—this little patch of room to be a good Mom, and doing these things, it makes me happy. It might seem like I'm worrying about the wrong stuff, but it doesn't feel that way to me.

What else can I do? Crawl into bed? That's not me, that's never been me. I'm a mother and this is what mothers do."

Sophia sighed heavily on the other end.

"Listen, I know you're busy, I just called to say *hi*. Give the boys a kiss for me, okay?" Jenna twirled the cord around her finger.

"I will."

"Okay, we'll talk soon, I promise."

"Good. Well, call me later, please. Let me know how things go?"

"As always."

"Okay, good. I love you Jenna."

"Love you too, Soph." Jenna replaced the receiver with a slight click.

She grabbed her fall jacket off the hook by the door, then, grabbing her keys and purse, she headed out.

"Excuse me, could I please see that jewelry box?" Jenna pointed across the wide counter of the antique store to a beautiful vintage jewelry box set on the high shelf.

"Of course." The faded shopkeeper reached up and removed it from its post, setting it softly down on the counter for Jenna to look over.

It was perfect. Exactly what Jenna had been looking for. She ran her hand across the white chippy-paint, studied the hand-painted rose buds in shades of pink adoring the exterior. Lifting the lid, Jenna smiled, inside was a raw silk the color of orchids and pristine, a series of rolled cushions and tiny holes waiting to be filled with treasures.

"How much?" Jenna asked, closing the lid and admiring the intricate detailing again.

"Two hundred." the shop owner.

Jenna exhaled loudly. Two hundred dollars, for a small jewelry box, seemed awfully steep. "Are you firm on that?" Jenna asked.

"It's not actually mine to sell, it's a commission piece. Owner's had it since it was new, hard to part with it without getting the right price, I suppose." He shrugged and tapped a calloused fingertip on delicate lid.

Jenna gnawed the inside of her lip thoughtfully. It was perfect, exactly what she had been looking for, very rare and so beautiful. "I'll take it." Jenna decided.

"Is it for you?" the old man asked, wrapping the box neatly in tissue.

"My daughter." Jenna beamed.

"Lucky little girl," the owner eyed Jenna as he moved towards the register. "Must a special occasion to receive such a lovely jewelry box."

"It is, a very big deal," Jenna agreed, handing over her credit card.

"Birthday?" the owner pressed, clearly wondering what a child would do with such an expensive jewelry box.

"She just turned seven," Jenna smiled, "I want her to have something special, from me, and this is really perfect," Jenna allowed, signing her name in the appropriate place.

"Would you like it gift-wrapped?"

"No, thank you."

"I hope she enjoys it," the shop owner shrugged,

slipping the box into a paper bag before he handed the package to Jenna.

"Me too. Thank you for your help." Jenna waved goodbye and drifted out the door.

The box was perfect, exactly what Jenna had hoped to find. The idea to give Mia a jewelry box crossed her mind as she was cleaning out her closet. Over the years of her life she'd aquired beautiful pieces of jewelry from Gabe. She had her engagement ring, a rose cut diamond chip bezel set into a thin, etched gold band, the matching wedding ring she'd never taken off until it no longer fit and slipped free of her finger all on its own, a pair of diamond earrings he'd given her for their tenth wedding anniversary, a strand of pearls she had splurged on in New York while touring for her first book. Then there were the things that even predated Gabe, the charm bracelet she had worn as a little girl, a butterfly broach that had belonged to her mother. All of it would go to Mia, and she would, of course, need a safe place to keep her inherited treasures until she was old enough to wear them.

Jenna spent the remaining hours wandering around the sleepy streets of the town, collecting bags and presents as she went. Toys and books for Mia, sweaters and a handsome watch for Gabe, warm boots and coat for Ginny, games for her nephews, a pair of gold and emerald earrings for Sophia. She sipped a coffee in the local bookstore, wandering the aisles, filling her basket with everything that looked interesting.

Jenna glanced at the clock in her car as she pulled out of the spot onto the main street, still a few hours before Mia got out of school, but the weather was becoming treacherous. Rain pelted her windshield faster than the blades could sweep it away. She was no more than a few minutes from Ginny's house. She wanted to finish as much business today as possible.

CHAPTER TWELVE

SEPTEMBER 14, 2002

Jenna watched the tide roll over the bay below her. She stood at the end of her land, feeling like it was end of the world. Mia was playing a few strides back, and Gabe was lounged on a lawn chair. It was early, Ginny would be collecting Mia soon, and Gabe would leave for work with an apologetic smile. But before any of that, after breakfast, for a few stolen moments, they'd taken to the yard. It was the sort of morning that called them outside: the wind was mild and abiding off the coast, the clouds holding the rain at bay, and though there was no sun, the fall rarely offered a escape so inviting.

"I don't have school today, Daddy," Mia grinned.

"I know, that must be nice."

"I'm going out with Ginny, we're going to the movies!" Mia twirled about in the soft grass, spinning pirouettes, her skirt swirling out in a parachute of soft fabric. "And the beach!"

"That'll be fun," Gabe agreed, glancing at Jenna with questioning eyes, silently questioning why. "You feeling okay, babe?" he asked, folding his newspaper and setting it aside.

"Oh, I'm fine. Just a bunch of things to do, Mia would be bored to tears." Jenna brushed off his concern, not bothering to turn around, pretending to be bewitched by the sight of the ships going out to sea.

"Want company?" Gabe pressed.

"You'll be thinking about work all day if you're here, so you might as well just be there," Jenna laughed, knowing that the truth in that rang true.

"Probably right," Gabe sighed deeply in defeat. "Speaking of, I should be heading out," Gabe groaned as he hefted himself from the seat.

"Bye Daddy, have a fun day!" Mia jovially waved, sprinting across the short distance to his side, latching her arms around his thigh.

"Bye Mia baby, have a fun day, too." Gabe lifted Mia up, smothering her cheeks with kisses until she caved with fits of squirmy, joyful laughter.

Jenna turned, pacing across the lawn to the little klatch of love. She wrapped her arms around Gabe from behind. She pressed her face between his shoulder blades, breathing in deeply, committing his scent to memory.

"All right, all right, I've gotta go." Gabe finally gave up, placing Mia on the ground gently.

"I'll miss you today." Jenna released him as he turned to face her.

"I'll stay," Gabe answered, meaning it. He'd stay with her ignore all the distractions if she'd asked him to.

"No, you go. Make beautiful houses," Jenna teased lightly, stepping up on her toes to kiss him, tasting the his coffee on his lips.

"You sure?" He pulled back, a pensive look causing his eyes to squint in speculation.

"Scout's honor." Jenna held up her hand in innocence, lying to him. She hated it, wishing she could cross her fingers to absolve her guilt, but it was childish and she'd own her deception.

In another life, with another set of circumstances, she'd have begged him to stay. She would have devoured a day of nothingness with him alone. But that luxury would require time, something she didn't have, something she hadn't had in a long while.

"Okay," he drawled, stretching out the word to let his hesitance to seep through.

"Bye, I love you," Jenna murmured, kissing his cheek again, giving him a playful shove back towards the house.

"Bye." He grabbed her again, pulling her in close, kissing her again.

She loved him. The feeling of that was a high tide, swallowing everything else. Nothing was untouched by how she felt.

Ginny's truck rumbled up the long drive, dividing the silence with its forceful protest.

"Ginny!" Mia screamed with delight, breaking into a barefooted run towards the house.

Gabe plowed after her, and Jenna stood still, rooted in place, watching the people she loved moving away from her. Silence was left in their wake, a soft breeze whipped at her sweater coat, and she pulled it closer around her, holding herself together. She started after them, still watching the place where they disappeared, into the deep recesses of their home. It was longing she felt now, for all of them. She knew then, that she'd always want the most what she could never have. She wanted to keep pace with them, stay with them forever, latch herself to their sides.

Inside, Ginny was already busying herself, putting sacks of fresh vegetables and fruit into the crisper, stocking the freezer with Tupperware full with sauces and casseroles and soups. Tarts and muffins rested on thin paper plates spread across the butcher block island.

"Momma! Look at what Ginny brought! Isn't it so pretty!" Mia held up an ornately carved box, "She said it's my hope chest!" Mia ran her chubby fingers over the beautiful detailed carvings.

"That's lovely. Did you thank Ginny?" Jenna rested her hands on her hips, leaning over Mia to study the box.

It was crafted from dark, burled wood. Native American detailing etched each side, tribal fish swam across the raw wood panels. A bronze latch secured the top, and inside smelt of planed-wood and oil.

"Of course, not saying thank you is rude!" Mia replied, still enthralled. "But she said I can't have it yet, that I have to give it to you first, 'cause that's how a hope chest works. That Momma's fill up the hope chest for daughters. She said that it's still mine, but not until I'm older." Mia held up the box, offering it to Jenna.

Jenna looked at Ginny, who was busying herself, placing the packaged items in the fridge.

"Ginny?" Jenna asked curiously.

"Just a place for you to keep things for Mia, for when she's older." the implication dripped from her cryptic message. A house for the tapes, a place for her hopes.

"Thank you, it's perfect." Jenna wandered over, wrapping Ginny up in a big hug, kissing her on the cheek.

Ginny waved her away. "It's nothing. Just came across it up at the Makah reservation, and thought you'd get some use out of it."

"It was very thoughtful of you, and you know I will." she pulled Ginny in again, and this time Ginny hugged her back.

"Ginny?" Mia interrupted.

"Yes, baby girl?" Ginny asked over Jenna's shoulder.

"What time does the movie start?" Mia asked, still stroking the wooden box, running a curious finger over the swimming fish.

"The theater doesn't open till 'round three, honey. But, if you're up for it, I've got some apple trees in my yard gettin' ready to drop fruit. We could go pick some and make a pie?" Ginny winked at Jenna, knowing the promise would enchant Mia.

"Really?" Mia asked. "Can I eat the whole thing by myself?"

Ginny's laughter filled the vast kitchen, bouncing off the walls. "Think you can?"

"Yes, ma'am!" Mia flashed a toothy grin, running to gather her shoes and coat by the front door.

"Please don't let her eat the whole thing," Jenna pleaded, imagining the tummy ache that would come after the gluttony.

"That girl couldn't eat the whole pie no matter what I said," Ginny laughed, and patted Jenna's shoulder lightly as she passed by.

"Bye, Mia, love you!" Jenna called from the open

door, balancing against the frame as Mia sprinted towards the passenger side of Ginny's truck.

"Love you more, Momma!" Mia called back, throwing her a quick kiss before climbing into the cab. Ginny waved and slipped into the truck, off to start their adventure.

Jenna watched as the truck rumbled out of the driveway until they were long gone from sight. Turning away, she quietly closed the door, locking it behind herself.

There was no more putting off the inevitable. No lingering hope. Jenna lifted the box Ginny had brought, tucking it under her arm, turning off the lights in the kitchen as she made her way down the hall to her office.

The room was darkened and depressed, a small Tiffany lamp glowed from the corner of her desk, a beacon. It reminded Jenna of her first three years here, the small sliver of light casting a glow over her workspace, a baby monitor resting beside it, the wall above her desk tacked with notecards and plot points. She would write, create perfect worlds, knowing the whole while that her life was better than any book she'd ever written. She remembered the way she would press the monitor to her ear, listening to Mia's hushed, dreamy breath on the other end.

Jenna set the box on her desk before sinking into her chair. She studied the carvings, the sculpted peaks of the waves, running her fingers across the grooves of the fishes scales and the planed-wood, she thought of Mia's wonder when Ginny had handed it her. Usually hope chests were much larger, full of rag-quilts and lace dollies, but all of Jenna's hopes, they could be held inside something small.

She pulled the slim tape recorder from the desk drawer. The man at the office supply store had promised this was his best model. She popped the deck over and slipped the first little cassette inside.

With much determination, Jenna willed her fingers to press the record button. She couldn't allow herself to think about how silly she felt speaking the paramount words to only herself and a small tape recorder in the dark of her office, years and years before they'd even harbor an inkling of truth. Or how heartbreaking it felt to know that eventually she would be finished recording and the silence left behind would speak volumes.

She had no notes, and no way of knowing exactly what her daughter would need to hear when she finally, in time, came about pressing *play*. All she had was a list—a list of milestones—and a corresponding blank tape.

The fear and utter sadness of what she was about to do enveloped her like an inferno, burning her, buckling her heart and breaking her in a million ways that would remain unseen, as so many other breaks did. She would never really know if she got it right, of course. She'd. Never. Know.

Hadn't that knowledge pinged her so many months ago, in quiet and dark of her home? Hadn't that been the reason Susanna Taft whispered to her from her memory the night?

She would only be left with the unknown. All of the things that couldn't possibly be known. It was no longer a question of science, medicine, and time. Now it was a matter of fate, faith, and the natural unfolding of things. But she could plan and prepare and hedge her bets like a mother would. With these tapes, she would bet on her daughter, and leave behind her voice.

Jenna thought of the girl her daughter was now. Seven years old, curious of the world at large. She knew the determined expression that crossed Mia's face when they worked together side by side in, Jenna curating Mia's creativity like precious gems and treasures. She knew the telltale face of a fib or half-truth, Mia's mouth dropping open just enough as she tried not to smile and tried harder to convince Jenna of the story she wanted believe. She knew the way Mia's lower lip would tremble as she departed the bus when the kids had been less than kind, running for the security of home and the comfort of her mom, running to the place that would nurture and welcome her budding individualism rather than shy away from it.

Jenna knew Mia better than she knew herself in every single way possible and she loved her more than she loved her own life. From the very beginning, her baby girl had been the epitome of a miracle in Jenna's eyes, and remained steadfast in that role forever after. Mia was reason and logic, hope and heartbreak; she was Jenna's dream personified.

But who would Mia be when these tapes became relevant?

Suddenly the unknown crept in again, playing around, twisting two or five or a million different landscapes, different paths, different outcomes. A lifetime of experiences Jenna would be absent for, but things that would change her daughter, things that would define her and hurt her, inspire her and humble her. Would Mia be analytical and thoughtful, living a life of logic and reason, a breathing echo of her father? Would her love of words bloom into a love of numbers? Or would she hold fast, stay true to her dreamy and creative nature? Would Mia grow up into the sort of girl who had tattoos running the length of her arms and a tiny stud her nose? Would Mia be a wanderer, with a only a backpack to keep all her worldly possessions and a ticket for her next adventure? Or would Mia want to lay down roots, build a family, build a home?

Would some of these tapes be left, unheard, in their little plastic casings because they didn't apply to Mia? And if they didn't pertain, why not? But, if they did, and Mia needed them, and Jenna failed to push the worry aside, then what? What if Mia carried the responsibility, all the joys and all the burdens of life alone? What if, someday, Mia ached for her mother the way Jenna ached for her own?

Jenna pressed her finger firmly against the flat button with the red circle. She thought about the laughter and tears, the piles of homework, the family trips, the snuggles and hugs and kisses and fights. She thought about her husband, trying to understand the enigma that was a teenage girl. She pictured her daughter, grown up with a life of her choosing, whatever that meant and whomever she'd become and imagining that, Jenna felt courage. These tapes were not expectations, they were hopes— her hopes. And with all of that floating around in her head, she began.

"Mia...I love you."

Placing the final tape in the hope chest, Jenna turned off the lamp, allowing her head to loll back. She was emotionally exhausted. She had climbed all the mountains of motherhood in the short expanse of one afternoon. She wiped the tears that slipped onto her cheeks away with the back of her hand; she had tried to hard not to cry when she was recording and, at times, failed miserably. There was joy—imagining Mia marrying a man she loved, imagining her as a new mom with a perfect baby in her arms, but she couldn't picture the man Mia would marry or whether the swaddling blanket would be pink or blue. There was the irrefutable uncertainty of telling Mia to chase her wild dreams — what those dreams might be had lit Jenna up with hope and terrified her in equal measure. Then there was the sadness, the last tape, the one she, herself, had wanted most of all. What if, in the middle of a perfectly extraordinary life, the cancer came for Mia? What if, on a routine visit, a lump was found? But even then, Jenna found there was hope. Hope that her words would be archaic, that there would be a cure and beyond that, long life for Mia. The most important tape Jenna recorded was the one she prayed Mia would never need.

The clock on the wall chimed, six trills, signifying that the day had slipped into evening. She should go make dinner, she should go turn on the lights, she should do a lot of things, but her body refused to move. She wanted to rest for a while longer. It was a surreal thing, to travel to the future, to a different time where different things were important, to have conversations with her child about parenting, love, sex, marriage, heartbreak, college and then prepare to watch that same child come bouncing through the door, a tiny seven year old with slick, buttery fingers and sugar coursing through her veins. She wasn't sure how to reconcile the two realities into the run of only a single day.

Headlights cut across the slats of the plantation blinds. Jenna willed herself to move, but still she couldn't. She closed her eyes; she wanted to just be for awhile longer.

"Jenna? Jenna, are you here?" Gabe's voice called to her through the home, his lightly frenzied tone stirred her.

"In the office," Jenna called back.

"Honey?" Gabe cracked the door open, light pooled through the as he leaned in. "Why are you sitting here, in the dark. Where's Mia?"

"Mia is still with Ginny. They went to the movies. I was working."

"In the dark?" Gabe opened the door wider, appraising his wife.

She could tell she'd frazzled him. He wasn't used to coming home to dark, silent home. What had he pictured finding, she wondered, but somewhere inside, she knew.

"It just got dark. I had the light on."

"Are you tired? You sound tired." With worry folded into his tone as he crossed the carpet to her.

"Very," Jenna sighed heavily.

"You should go to bed."

"Mia will be home soon. I need to fix dinner."

"I can do the Mia shift tonight. You need to rest."

"Are you sure? You worked all day."

"Very sure. You're done for the day, I can tell."

"She's going to be sugared up, this is your fair warning, she made apple pie and went to the movies.

You're entering stomachache territory. It could be a very long night," Jenna warned him seriously.

"I can manage." Gabe pulled on Jenna's arm, towing her from her chair. "Come on, let's go."

Jenna paused briefly, taking the box, now full and heavy with her hopes, from her desktop.

"What's that?" Gabe asked, offering to carry to box for her.

"Mia's hope chest, my hopes for her." Jenna handed over the box to Gabe. "Please keep it for her, until after ... " Jenna's voice trailed off, realizing that this was it, the handing off process. She was officially giving the future to Gabe, but this was willingly and on her own terms. Her heart cinched around that.

"The milestone tapes. You finally recorded them." Gabe pressed his lips to Jenna's forehead, pulling her in close with his free arm. Jenna linked herself to Gabe's waist, and in tandem, they began walking the short distance to the door.

Jenna turned, looking back at the room she had loved so much, with its thick bookcases and plush carpet, refined woodwork, her desk, the room that allowed her to work in peace, to live her dream of being an author, and she closed the door knowing she'd never go back to that place. The end was growing closer, she could feel that now. It was almost time.

CHAPTER THIRTEEN

NOVEMBER 2, 2002

Sophia had flown into Port Angeles early that morning. Gabe, as he had promised, let her know when Jenna's condition turned for the worse.

"I don't understand," Sophia murmured to Ginny, sitting at the kitchen table. "I just spoke to her two, three weeks ago, and she was fine, she was fine. What happened? How is this happening?" her voice pitched in protest.

"No one knows for sure, honey, no one knows." Ginny's tone was clipped as the hospice nurse walked into the kitchen, filling a cup with ice from the freezer before she turned quietly, leaving the ladies to resume their conversation. "It just happens, sometimes fast, sometimes slow."

Sophia's head bowed under the weight of Ginny's words. "Sometimes fast," she repeated. "How's Mia?" Sophia asked, looking at her niece, who was stumbling around the back yard, kicking at a small ball. Ginny had bundled her up against the cold autumn wind, laced her neck with a thick scarf and covered her fingers in wool mittens. Planters full of rusty mums dotted the patio and pumpkins of every size lay on the steps leading down towards the yard.

"Bad." Ginny shook her head sadly.

"Gabe?"

"Hasn't left the room in two days for more than a minute, been by her side the whole time those nurses have been here, round the clock."

Sophia has desperately wanted to see Jenna, but she was sleeping, as she did most of time now.

"How long?" Sophia gulped out the question, tears welling in her eyes.

Ginny simply shook her head.

"What can I do?" Sophia asked helplessly.

"Pray," Ginny suggested, then turning towards the windows, she added, lifting her chin towards the small little girl, "and comfort Mia."

"Oh Mia." Sophia lowered her head to the table, tears slipping down her cheeks. She knew what that little girl needed more than anything in the world, and it was the one thing Sophia couldn't give her.

Sophia walked towards the sliding glass door and slipped outside. Her stocking feet froze instantly as she padded across the grass and the mid autumn wind whipped around her violently, she wished she'd remembered her coat.

"Mia?" She wandered towards her niece, not wanting to startle her.

"Aunt Sophia!" Mia crossed the yard, meeting Sophia half way. Her lower lip poked out, trembling with hidden tears.

"Oh, baby." Sophia opened her arms wide and Mia threw herself inside them. Sophia knelt in the soggy grass, letting the dampness soak through the knees of her jeans, holding Mia close while the little girl heaved heavy sobs against her chest.

"I ... I ... I ... want my momma," Mia wailed against the wool of Sophia's sweater

"Shh, it's okay, I know," Sophia soothed, smoothing her hair, rubbing her back, rocking her.

"I want my mommy, I want to see my mommy!" Mia struggled against Sophia, pushing away, defiant with grief. Sophia held her tighter. "Let me see my mommy!"

"Honey." Sophia didn't know what to say, but she knew, she remembered, that feeling of longing, the innocent belief that if you could just see them, you could heal them.

"Please, please," Mia begged, breaking Sophia's heart in new ways.

"We can't see your mommy right now, baby, she's sleeping, and she needs to rest." Sophia put her hands on Mia's shoulders, meeting her eyes, trying to break through the will of a seven year old who felt alone in her frustration and grief.

"I miss my mom." Mia calmed, self-soothing; only the slightest hitch to her breath remained.

"I know you do baby, I miss your mom, too. But she wouldn't want you to be sad, she wouldn't want you to cry." Sophia sat down on the grass, pulling Mia onto her lap, tucking her head under her chin, rocking her slowly..

"Can I see her later, when she wakes up?" Mia pressed, needing a promise from Sophia she couldn't make.

"We'll see what your daddy says, okay?" Sophia owed her honesty; it was truly Gabe's decision.

Mia nodded in her chest, sniffing.

"Are you hungry? You must have been out here forever, you're cheeks are pink, you're freezing." Sophia pressed her hand against Mia's face. Mia shrugged lithely. "Let's get you warmed up and see what we can scrounge up." Sophia planted Mia on her feet and offered her a hand. She felt relief bubble up inside her chest when Mia took it.

Ginny was propped against the opening of the door, watching with watery eyes.

"Can I make you lunch?" she asked, stepping aside to let them in.

"I should go get changed." Sophia gestured to her ruined clothes "but Mia is hungry."

Ginny easily slid her arm around Mia's thin shoulders, guiding her towards the kitchen while Sophia disappeared into the guest room to change.

The room was familiar to Sophia now, having spent almost the entire summer there. Jenna had done a lovely job making this room a haven a place that embodied the comforts of home. Sunny yellow walls, paisley bedding in shades of blue and red, crisp white plantation shutters, leaded glass windows looking out to the green forest. It felt safe and comfortable, well lived in.

Sophia striped off her sodden jeans, tossing them carelessly aside into a heap by the bathroom, exchanging them for a fresh pair. Slipping into them, Sophia sank to the ground. Maybe it was the travel catching up to her or maybe it was world that was crashing down, but she gave herself up to it. Burying her face in her hands, she silently sobbed, hard painful jags. She cried for Mia, for Gabe and selfishly, for herself. She cried for the time she had lost being angry, for the time she'd never have to make it right. She cried for her sister, for the pain Jenna must feel and for the heartbreak Jenna's family was enduring. Sophia balled her hands into fists, shoving them hard into her eyes, wanting the scream out, rage, but knowing on the other side of door was a vulnerable little girl who needed strength and reassurance.

A soft tap at door brought her back, pulling her from the swirl of misery she was giving up to.

"Sophia? Can I come in?" Gabe's broken voice questioned from the other side.

"Of course." Sophia smudged the back of her hand against her eyes, pulling herself together.

"Hey, sorry to interrupt you. Ginny said you were changing." Gabe stared hard at the carpet, his hands clasped behind his back.

"It's okay, I was just finishing up. Is everything okay?" Sophia stood up slowly and reached out to touch his arm, which was just beyond her reach.

"Jenna's the same. Asleep." He seemed to relax a little, losing up, he ran his hands over his face. He looked beaten. His eyes were rimmed with red, blurry and bloodshot; days' worth of stubble spread across his cheeks and chin and down his long neck. His hair was a mess, disheveled and oily, his clothing was wrinkled and creased, Sophia wondered idly when the last time he showered and changed was.

"Can I see her soon?" Sophia asked, running her fingers through her hair.

"When she's awake," Gabe mumbled, not promising if or when that would be.

"Mia really wants to see her, Gabe," Sophia

implored, begging him.

"I know that." Gabe looked down again, wiping the palms of his hands across the front of his pants. He was so far from the composed, funny, dedicated man she spent time with this summer; he was scared and lost, just as Jenna had promised he would be. "But she can't, not like this." Gabe took long strides past Sophia towards the small sitting area off the rear of the room.

Sophia followed after him, watching him sink into the overstuffed wing chair, burying his face in his hands.

"Gabe, she needs to see her mother. She's scared and confused." Sophia sat in the chair beside him, resting her hands on her knees.

"It would make things worse, Jenna's not ... Jenna's not Jenna anymore," Gabe whimpered more to himself than to Sophia.

"Mia needs to see her mother, Jenna is still her mother." Sophia spoke calmly. She remembered how this moment felt, being the scared little girl on the other side of the door.

"I know she's still her mother, Jesus Christ, I'm just fucking protecting her. Isn't it better for Mia to remember Jenna as vibrant, not some shell, lying there totally out of it? Do you know her bones are breaking? For no reason. The cancer's just eaten them whole, and sometimes they just snap. Mia shouldn't ... she's just a kid." Gabe glared at Sophia.

"Maybe, but maybe not." Sophia held her hands up in surrender. She didn't want to upset him more, she just wanted him to see both sides of the issue.

"I'm sorry, that was out of line." Gabe's

anger evaporated, and the rage that flowered so quickly disappeared.

"When was the last you slept, Gabe?"

"I sleep. When Jenna does, in the chair beside the bed." He grated his fingers over his face again, leaving white streaks of pressure, letting his head fall backwards.

"That's not sleeping. You need to take care of yourself. I'm here now, so let me help. Why don't you go to sleep? I'll sit with Jenna, and if anything happens, I'll come get you." Sophia gestured to the wide bedside, soft and inviting with its swirly down bedding and perfectly pilled sheets.

"I can't," Gabe sighed.

"You have too. You have to take care of yourself, for Jenna and for Mia." Sophia stood up and walked to the bed. Pulling the bedding back, she patted the mattress, as she did for her boys when luring them to nap. "Just for an hour, and I promise, if anything changes, I'll run right here, promise."

"One hour?" Gabe looked at the bed, supple and tempting, a longing flashed in his eyes.

"I won't wake you up if nothing is wrong, you need your sleep," Sophia sighed.

"But you will wake me if something's wrong?"

"Of course I will," Sophia nodded and placed her hand on Gabe's shoulder. "I'm going to go sit with Jenna, she'll never be alone, I promise." Sophia passed her, closing the door silently behind herself.

"Aunt Sophia?" Mia called to her as Sophia crossed the kitchen on her way to the master bedroom.

"Yes, honey?" Sophia paused, walking over to kiss Mia on the top of her head, running her fingers through the tangling curls.

"Is Daddy okay?" Worry scrunched her face, making her look like she was about to cry.

"He's just sad and tired, that's all," Sophia tried to explain.

"Is he mad at me? He looked angry." Mia pushed a small pile of peas around with the tip of her fork.

"Not at all, not even a little. He loves you so much." Sophia hugged Mia close, pulling her into her chest, resting her cheek on the little girl's head.

"I don't want him to be mad at me." Mia took a jagged breath.

"Don't you worry about that. Okay?" Sophia gave Mia another tender squeeze and released her. "I have to go sit with your Momma for a bit. Would you like me to ask Ginny to put on a video for you?"

"Can I come with you?" Mia's eyes widened with hope.

"No, baby, not right now. Your Momma is asleep; I'm just going to sit by the bed."

"She's always asleep." Mia face fell, her hopes dashed.

"It seems that way, huh?" Sophia nodded in agreement.

"When she's awake, can I see her? Did you ask Daddy?" Hope bubbled up again.

"Let's wait and see, okay sweetheart?" Sophia kissed Mia's head again, waved lightly to Ginny, and then she padded towards the bedroom.

The smell hit her first, pulling her back to being ten years old again, in the small bungalow in Chicago. She was there again, holding her mother's wasted hand, singing softly in the dark room while her mother lay motionless in her death bed. It assaulted now; every step closer to the room, the smell of sickness and dying hung stale in the air.

The room was dark, nearly blacked out, all of the shutters pulled tight keeping the outside out, only small spots of light glowed from lamps dotted about the room. The hospice nurse sat quietly in the reading nook, a light shining down on the crosswords pamphlet that rested on her lap and a pencil was squeezed between her fingers. She smiled politely and nodded towards Sophia.

Sophia sat softly beside the bed where Jenna lay. Her sister, so full of life just weeks ago, burrowing her toes in the black granite sand, fixing dinner in the kitchen, playing on the floor with all the children squirming over her, worrying about Christmas shopping, and the loading the trunk of her car with pumpkins, so full of life.

Jenna was withered now. Gabe had been right, she was a shell. Her breathing came fast, in shallow gulps of air, the rise and fall of her ribs keeping an uneven time. Her skin had faded, sallower in the low light, and it looked yellow and waxy. A fine skim of sweat beaded her brow. Her lips were chapped, and bone white, and her hair was damp, secured from her face by a wide band of cloth. Beside the bed sat a crystal bowl full of ice, melting and pooling. Sophia picked up a small sliver, running it gently over Jenna's lips.

"That's good for her." The hospice nurse quietly approached the bed, running her hand over Jenna's wrist, measuring the life in her thready pulse.

"What else can I do?" Sophia blinked back tears.

"When she's asleep? You can rub her feet and

her hands, it keeps the circulation going." The nurse suggested, placing a thin hand of Jenna's clammy forehead.

"Gabe said her bones were breaking?" Sophia glanced up.

"Hairline fractures." The nurse nodded, "But the morphine is keeping her comfortable."

Sophia moved to the foot of the bed, pulling back the covers. Jenna's feet were a pale, lifeless blue even in the diminished light. Sophia started rubbing slow, smooth circles on the balls of each foot, humming a peaceful tune, working towards her toes.

"Can I paint her nails?" Sophia asked the nurse who had again roosted herself under the low light.

"Sure," the nurse said before lowering her eyes.

Sophia crept towards the master bathroom and plucked a glossy pale pink bottle from the cluster on the marble counter. She turned the hourglass shaped bottle over in hands, running her fingers over the embossed print of the brand. It was like her mother would have wanted, it had always been their thing, polishing each others toes and having some of the best conversations. They'd done it for their whole childhood and into the older years before Elizabeth got sick and Jenna left for college, perched on the edge of the bathroom vanity, their feet nestled in their mother's lap, they'd laugh and joke and share secrets in hushed tones. This was something she could do for Jenna, something only Jenna would understand the importance of.

Sophia wandered back to the bed and sat down at the bottom, raising Jenna's foot in one hand carefully. She unscrewed the dainty brush and slowly, methodically began dragging slow steady strokes over the nail.

"Jenna," Sophia began softly, "I want you to know that I love you, and that ... I'm sorry ... sorry we wasted so many years. I wish I could take all of that back now. I always knew you loved me ... and I love you so much. You're just like Mom; so brave and so strong and so loving. You're a good mother, Jen, I hope you know that. I look at Mia and see how much you love her and I hope you know that you have nothing to regret, that you lived your life the best you could and that you did really, really well," Sophia moved from nail to nail without thinking, lost in her own mind, saying all the things she'd held back.

"Do you remember what asked me last summer before I went home?" Sophia waited and watched as Jenna's eye lids fluttered, "I've thought about it a lot. I never said no because I know you needed me to say yes. But I couldn't. I couldn't imagining it getting to that place. I don't know why I couldn't, but I couldn't. But if it's what you want..." Sophia felt Jenna stir, just a little, a silent acknowledgement. "Then you will have your dignity and your grace."

Sophia recapped the polish and blew lightly on Jenna's toes.

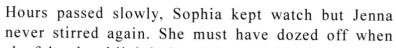

Hours passed slowly, Sophia kept watch but Jenna never stirred again. She must have dozed off when she felt a hand lightly brush her shoulder.

"Sorry, didn't mean to you wake you." Gabe spoke softly. "Can I talk to you, in the hallway?" He tilted his head towards the dark hall and motioned for her to join him.

Sophia couldn't help but think he looked better, rested. He was still sloppy and needed a shower and shave, but she could see that the hours of unconsciousness that done him some good.

"Did you sleep well?" Sophia asked, following him out and slumping to the floor in the hallway. She could hear Ginny and Mia chattering in the kitchen, along with the smell of something cooking on the stove. Her stomach rolled, almost painfully empty she hadn't had anything to eat since Gabe had called her early yesterday morning.

"Yeah, thanks." Gabe also sank to the floor across from her, his knees pulled up and arms resting slightly askew on them.

"Is this shift change?" Sophia asked casually, craving a hot shower, warm meal and soft bed, in that order.

"In a minute. I just wanted to ask you something... Jenna told me that when your mom was sick, you took care of her."

Sophia nodded.

"You were just a kid..." Gabe voiced trailed off as his gaze followed the voices in the kitchen.

"She was my Mother, she needed me." Sophia leaned her head against the wall and looked at the ceiling, wishing there something else to say.

Gabe nodded once before continuing. "Did it hurt you? Like now, do you wish you hadn't had to be there, to see her like that?"

"Sometimes. But, I can't imagine it any other way. I think, if I hadn't been there, it would bother me more." Sophia looked towards the bedroom, remembering the way Jenna carried her guilt around for the rest of her life. Sophia didn't share the same burden, and for that, she was grateful.

"Is that how you remember her?"

Sophia closed her eyes and thought of her mother. Maybe it was the moment she'd shared with Jenna or maybe it was genuinely how she remember Elizabeth, but the first thing she remembered was how Elizabeth used to paint her toenails when Sophia was just a little girl. After a warm bath, she was tell Sophia to prop her toes up on her lap, and her mother would skillfully sweep the tiny brush coated in a shiny lacquer over her tiny shell pink nails. Sophia smiled. Her toes always looked like tiny pink sugar coated gumdrops.

"No, Gabe, that's not how I remember her." And that was the truth, she needed to be sure, but it was the truth. "I remember her being sick, of course I do, but I remember all the good stuff first."

"Hmm," Gabe sighed.

"And to answer your other question, no, I don't regret it, not for a single minute. I'm happy I was there. Happy I got to hold her hand and tell her how much I loved her. It brought me peace," Sophia continued. "Actually, I think I found a deeper peace with Mom passing than Jenna did. I was able to help her pass on. Jenna, I know, regrets not being able to be there ... She told me that, Gabe. She'd want Mia there, not for the scary stuff, but for Mia's own everlasting peace."

"Are you sure?" Gabe asked, searching Sophia's face.

"I am Gabe, one hundred percent sure." She climbed to her feet, stretching her back, which felt stiff and brittle, patted him once on the hand and wandered towards the kitchen.

"Momma?" Mia walked slowly towards Jenna's bedside. Each footfall tentative. Gabe and Sophia stood nearby, gently encouraging her forward.

"Hi, baby," Jenna said, her voice splintering over each word, the sound of labored breathing filling the room. She'd saved all her strength for this.

"Hi." Mia sat on the edge of the small chair beside the bed, looking at her mother.

"I've missed you." Jenna reached for Mia's hand, and Mia, meeting her halfway, smiled.

"I miss you, too, Momma." Tears slid down Mia's cheeks. Sophia turned away, biting hard on her lip.

"How's school?"

"Daddy is letting me stay home."

"That's fun, it's always nice to play hooky." Jenna smiled at her daughter. Her lips spread into a feeble smile, the most she could muster.

Mia stared at Jenna, her eyes wide and uncertain, scared.

"Gabe, Sophia...I'm okay. Can I have a minute alone with Mia, please?" Jenna asked softly.

"I don't—" Gabe began, taking a small step forward.

"It's fine, Gabe, really. I just want to talk to Mia for a moment, it won't take long." Jenna halted him, and an urgency in voice told him to let her win this one.

"We'll be right outside," Gabe cautioned.

"I'm counting on that," Jenna chuckled softly, ever aware of the protectiveness Gabe felt for his girls.

Jenna waited until she heard the knob click quietly closed before she continued. "Scary, huh?" She turned to Mia, looking into her eyes.

"Kind of," Mia conceded, looking embarrassed, a

rosy blush creeping over her cheeks.

"This is scary, and it's okay to be afraid, you're just a little girl," Jenna soothed, stroking the top of Mia's hand lightly with her thumb.

"I don't want to be scared," Mia said, trying to be strong, always so brave.

"Sometimes life is scary, and when it is, it's brave to say you're scared."

Mia nodded softly, trying to understand the message behind Jenna's words. "Are you going to get better again soon?" Mia asked.

Jenna shook her head *no,* but she couldn't bring herself to talk about death and dying and what would come next. She didn't want to spend this precious time with so little left on that. "Do you know I love you, Mia?"

Mia nodded again.

"And do you know that you are the best thing that I've ever done, the greatest gift I've ever been given, that you're everything to me?" Jenna affirmed. She needed to know that Mia knew that, felt it, understood that she was the reason for Jenna's whole life.

"Yes, Momma, I know." Mia's little lip trembled with unshed tears.

"Come lay down with me." Jenna lifted back the corner of the blanket for Mia to crawl in beside her. Mia snuggled down on Jenna's side, resting her head on Jenna's shoulder.

"When I first found out you were coming, that you were this tiny little being, warm and safe inside me, I thought that was the happiest day of my life. I had wanted you so badly, for so long, I thought nothing could be better," Jenna began, her voice no more than a hushed whisper in the cool, dark room.

"And then you were born, and I thought, *no, this was the happiest day of my life.* And then one day, you called me Momma, and I realized I'd been wrong all along—that this must be the happiest day of my life. And then one day I realized that there is no one singular happiest day of motherhood, that every single day is the best day. You taught me that." Jenna leaned down and kissed the top of Mia's head.

"I love you so much, Mia, and I want you to have the most beautiful life. I want you to chase your dreams, and dream big. I want you to have every opportunity and set this world on fire. You are an amazing little girl, and I have been so blessed—beyond words—to be your Momma." Tears slid down Jenna's face, and in her arms she felt Mia shake with quiet tears.

"And soon, I won't be able to be with you anymore, I have to go be with the angels in Heaven. But I promise, I will always be watching over you, I will always be your Momma, and even if you can't see me, you can trust that I'm nearby, with you always."

"Please don't go, Momma," Mia begged.

"Oh, baby, I don't want to go, but I have to." Jenna wept; it broke her heart to know that the words were true, and that she would give anything to stay, but how could she possibly explain this to a child in a way that would make sense when it hardly made sense to her?

"My heart hurts." Mia fussed in her arms, her cheeks wet with tears.

"I know baby, mine, too." Jenna held Mia close, letting the quiet settle over them like a warm blanket.

Hours later, Gabe slipped into the room. The nurse had come to get him, a panicked look spread across her face.

"Mr. Chamberland, you need to come get Mia—quickly!" She turned and rushed back down the hall, Gabe and Sophia close on her heels.

Jenna's breath came in short, frenzied spasms. Mia sat beside her, holding her hand, her eyes wide with horror.

"Mia, baby, come with me," Sophia coaxed sweetly to her niece, prying her hand away from Jenna. "Ginny!" she screamed down the hall as Ginny ran towards the room. "Take Mia, please!" Sophia transferred Mia's hand into Ginny's and hurried back to Jenna's side.

"What's going on? What's happening?" Gabe pleaded with the nurse to answer him, but she was fixated entirely on Jenna, rolling her slowly on her side, rubbing tenderly at her hand.

"She's having trouble breathing," the nurse said softly.

"Jenna, Jenna," Gabe repeated, kneeling close to her face, smoothing his hand through her hair. "It's okay, baby, I'm here, I'm here, you're going to be okay. Please be okay."

"Mr. Chamberland, please," the nurse implored. "Can someone page her doctor?" She turned to Sophia, knowing Gabe couldn't be moved.

"Of course." Sophia sprinted from the room.

Jenna's breathing slowly calmed, ratcheting her chest, but the gasping subsided. Gabe collapsed into himself, his face hitting the soft mattress.

"What the fuck was that?" he managed to ask.

"She was on her back for too long. Her system is depressed." the nurse explained sympathetically, pressing a stethoscope to Jenna's back, listening to the gurgling breaths.

"She's suffocating? She's going to strangle to death?" Gabe's adrenaline melted into pure fury, locked only on the nurse.

"I will try to keep her as comfortable as possible." The nurse pulled the sheet up around Jenna.

"Dr. Vaughn is on the phone." Sophia returned, holding the portable phone out as an offering.

"I'll take it in the kitchen." The nurse reached for the phone, walking smoothly out towards the common area before pressing it to her ear.

"Should you be leaving her?" Gabe yelled out to her, concerned that, without the nurse, things would escalate again.

"Keep her on her side and talk to her, she can hear you," the nurse called over her shoulder.

Gabe slowly pulled himself into the chair, and only then did he look at Jenna and see her, her eyes wide with panic, horror, and pain.

"It's okay, J, you're okay, it's over now, you're okay," Gabe murmured, but Jenna remained locked in her silent agony.

"Gabe, you should go be with Mia, she's really shaken," Sophia whispered to him. "I'll stay with Jenna."

"I can't..." He looked at Sophia, shaking his head, his eyes filled with tears.

"But you have to. She needs you very much right now."

Gabe looked between Sophia and Jenna with

uncertainty, but slowly stood up. He knew what Jenna would want: she'd want him to go to Mia, comfort and protect her.

Sophia waited until she was certain no one could hear her.

"Jenna?" Sophia leaned down close to Jenna's face, brushing her lips against Jenna's cheek. "Is it time? Do you want to go Mom?"

Jenna's eyes welled and her fingers inched along finding Sophia's arm, she nodded once, a thin smile pulled on her lips. She pointed towards the nightstand. Sophia reached over and pulled open the drawer. Inside Jenna had place vial of liquid and a silver spoon beside the notes from a doctor.

"Okay," Sophia pulled the contents from the drawn and read the instructions quickly. One tablespoon and Jenna would slip painlessly into a coma. She would linger long enough for *goodbye* and then she'd be free. Free from the pain, and the terror.

Sophia pressed down on the safety cap and poured the medicine until it filled the spoon. She wedged her arm behind Jenna's back and helped her sit up, slipping the spoon between Jenna's lips, she tilted it and let the liquid spill into Jenna's mouth. She stroked Jenna's throat softly, helping her to swallow, dabbing at the corners of Jenna's mouth before she laid her back down, and fell to her knees beside the bed, gathering Jenna's hand in her own.

"Thank you," Jenna mouthed silently and Sophia, pointed up, towards the pitched roof above them.

"Look at the sky, isn't it beautiful? Mom is waiting for you up there." Sophia whispered, gritting her teeth and sniffling. She wouldn't cry. Not now. There would time enough for that later.

Jenna stared up at the sky above her unblinking. An endless wash of rose gold as dusk settled. This was the end of the end, the last moments of the long goodbye.

"You can go now. We're all going to be okay. I promise you. Find your wings, Jenna, fly home. You're free and it's okay. I love you. You can go now, you can go. Let go." Sophia whispered, pressing her lips to Jenna's ear. As Jenna's eyes slipped closed, Sophia began to hum, climbing into the bed beside her sister and wrapping her arms around her. The song she hummed was one that their mother had used to sing to them when they were little, holding Jenna close, rocking her slowly.

Gabe wandered woodenly down the hallway, following the sounds of Mia's jagged cries. *A matter of hours, maybe days,* the nurse had said to him, holding his hand.

There wasn't anything left he could do. He could rub her feet, her hands, brush ice over her lips, hold her hand, love her—tell her that he loved her every moment of every day left. But then there would be nothing.

Only Mia.

Mia would remain. Their daughter would stand to remind him of what was shared between them. The love that built this house, and then built this family. Jenna would be inside of Mia, in her wavy hair and sweet smile. She would remind him that Jenna had existed, that all of her goodness hadn't been imagined, hadn't been a dream that had been dashed by the unforgiving morning light. That Jenna, for a time, had been his wife, his lover, and his best friend. And that though he'd miss her, he would carry on for his—for their—little girl.

He had a job to do now, a purpose, like he'd swore to Jenna: He had to be a father.

Gabe saw Ginny holding Mia. They sat together in the comfortable recliner, Ginny's arms cradling Mia, her voice low and methodic, soothingly slow and steady, like a song.

"Let me," Gabe interrupted, reaching out for Mia.

"Daddy, I'm sorry," Mia whimpered, leaning in closer to Ginny for comfort.

"You did nothing wrong." Gabe lifted Mia from Ginny's lap.

"I hurt Mommy," Mia cried, taking her share of responsibility innocently, wrongfully.

"No, you did not, Mia, you did not hurt your mommy...you made Mommy happy, baby." Gabe carried Mia around the room, cradling her in his arms, like he had when she was an infant, pacing the floor. He had paced this room with her at night, lulling her to sleep.

"She couldn't breathe," Mia sobbed into Gabe chest, tears wetting his shirt.

"That wasn't your fault."

"I was scared. Mommy said it was brave to say when I'm scared. Mommy said she wasn't getting better."

Gabe said nothing, the words clinging to the walls of his throat. He knew she wasn't getting better, but he couldn't say the words out loud, couldn't stand to hear them echo off the walls. He'd known this would happen all those months ago, sitting stoically beside his wife as she decided to take herself out of this life. He'd thought about what it would mean to be without her while driving the empty roads of this sleepy town. He'd tried to imagine what *after* would be like, the adjustments and changes, but still, he had never really let himself believe she'd be *gone*.

"But I want her to get better," Mia pleaded softly.

"I want her to get better, too, sweetheart." Gabe could say that much; he had prayed those exact words for years now.

"I miss my Momma."

Even if he was only half of the whole he'd when Jenna was gone, he'd have Mia and he'd look at her and see the love he and Jenna had had for all those years. She would die and he would be without her, but even gone, Jenna's dreams would linger behind.

"I'm scared, too," Gabe admitted as he paced the floor with Mia secure in his arms. "But we will be okay, I promise you. We will be okay."

BOOK TWO
Death ends life, not a relationship.

—Jack Lemmon—

CHAPTER FOURTEEN

NOVEMBER 3, 2011

Hey Mia, sweetheart, it's time to wake up...I know, your warm in bed and probably would be just fine staying where you are, but embrace it. Every day is an important one, you never know what can happen.

Mia SNAPPED THE 'STOP' BUTTON on her tiny silver tape recorder and snuggled deeper into her soft pillow. It was her ritual, to listen to her mother's tape every morning; it gave her a suspension of normalcy, if only for a brief moment. If she closed her eyes and just listened, Mia could almost believe her mother could be alive and well and encouraging her out of her warm bed. Her father had given the tape recorder to her a few weeks after her mother had died, pulled it from the box Ginny had given her. The only words scrawled across this tape were "Good Morning." She had listened to it every day since. She liked hearing her mother's voice fill up her room before she even managed to crawl out of bed. She liked the way it was familiar and predictable; the words were comforting, and in a small way, it allowed her mother to remain a part of her everyday life.

Mia had managed to remember a lot about her mom—or at least she tried to. In the years that had passed, she could recall the way, when her mother laughed, how she would throw her head back and let the sound overtake her, her eyes crinkling and her shoulders shaking. Sometimes Mia believed she could still hear it if she closed her eyes and listened really hard, as though it had seeped into the walls or blended into the furnishings of this old house. Mia remembered Jenna cooking, how she used to throw things together and it was always so good, haphazard recipes and the sort of homegrown talent that allowed every meal and every bite to be savory and sweet and rich and delicious. She remembered how her mother would hold her hand when they went into town, not just when they crossed the street like other mothers did, but as they wandered the aisles of a store or sat on a park-bench. How they'd eat ice cream cones at the ice cream shop—even in the winter, because why not?—that's what her mom used to say with a wicked, defiant smile, licking the side of her drippy cone. She could remember how her mom would play with her hair and rub her back when they watched television— she missed that a lot. She missed her mom a lot. Every single day.

But she also didn't remember a lot of things. Grey, fuzzy areas of her memory that time and space had stolen. Aside from pictures, Mia couldn't remember her mother's eyes or the exact color of her hair or the particular shade of lipstick she wore. Gabe had been good about keeping pictures around the house, hung on the walls, dotted about on shelves and the fireplace mantel, but Mia couldn't remember any of that in real life. Almost as though Jenna only existed in print. She couldn't remember the way her hugs felt, how tight they had been, or if Jenna had kissed her a lot, but Ginny told Mia all the time that she was a gravitational pull for her mother; she couldn't get enough of her.

"Mia!" Gabe yelled from down the hall like he did every morning. Making sure she was up and dressed and ready to take on the day.

She was not.

There was something about waking up to clouds and overcast skies that never really encouraged Mia to rise from bed with determination. She felt safe here in her room, surrounded by the things that mattered to her, pictures and books and soft bedding, the small recorder and the precious tape. High school was an unavoidable thing, and eventually she'd have to pull herself from the warm bed and take on the day, but she couldn't force herself into that just yet.

"I'm up, Dad!" Mia hollered back, buying herself more time before Gabe would knock on the door and ask if she wanted breakfast, and, if so, what. He wasn't a hoverer; his work took him away every day, and his return was often late at night. But when he was around, he tried. Mia could hear Ginny puttering about the kitchen, unstacking bowls and clanking the silverware down on the wooden table. It was comforting, knowing that Ginny would wrap her up in a good morning hug, feed her something homemade, warm, and delicious, and sit beside her, sipping coffee and talking to her about her friends, teachers, and homework.

Holding the recorder close to her ear, Mia pressed the 'rewind' button and listened to the whir of the tape going back in time, back to the beginning. Mia worried that one day the tape would break, that the thin film would snap, stealing her mother away. But it hadn't. Not in nine years, and today, like every morning, she crossed her fingers this wouldn't be the day it failed.

"Mia?" Ginny called to her from outside the door, tapping her knuckles against the panels of whitewashed wood.

"I'm up!" Mia pushed off the heavy winter-weight comforter and dropped her feet on the rug beside her bed, stretching and rubbing her eyes.

"May I come in?" Ginny hesitated. Over the years since Mia had grown into a teenager, Ginny had respected her privacy in the mornings.

"Um, sure." Mia grabbed the robe draped over the foot of her bed, wrapping it around herself.

"How you doing, sweetness?" Ginny asked, crossing the distance to put her arms around Mia.

"Good." Mia melted into the hug without really trying; Ginny was so warm.

"You sure?" Ginny pulled back, keeping her hands on Mia's upper arms, looking at her speculatively.

"Yeah. Is something wrong?"

"Just wondering, that's all." Ginny glanced over Mia's shoulder to the wall calendar hanging beside her desk. Mia followed her eyes, pivoting slowly.

"Oh." The realization settled over Mia like a heavy fog. Today. The third of November the annual occasion for concern. "I forgot—not forgot, but didn't know today was..." Mia let her voice trail off, sitting back on the edge of the bed with a heavy sigh.

Ginny sat beside her and gathered Mia in her arms again, drumming her hands over Mia's back in comfort. "Wanna stay home today?"

"Dad wouldn't like that," Mia answered quickly, but the thought of staying nestled in her bed was tempting. Gabe had worked hard at creating a life for Mia that wasn't defined by the death of her mother; he wanted her to have a good childhood, a normal childhood. He didn't approve of Mia wallowing in misery, and the therapist she'd seen off and on since she was a little girl agreed.

Ginny waved her hands in the air, dismissing Mia's reserve. "You worry about you; let me worry about him."

"Okay..." Mia relented with a breathy sigh.

"All right, honey. You crawl back in bed or jump in the shower, whatever you want." Ginny cupped Mia's cheek fleetingly before standing up slowly, her joints protesting with small groans.

"Ginny?" Mia asked, stopping her.

Ginny turned to look at Mia, tilting her head just slightly.

"Thanks." Mia half-smiled, crawling back beneath the shelter of her down comforter, letting her long dark waves fall against the crisp pillowcase, she exhaled.

Ginny nodded once before softly shutting the door behind her.

Jenna had died on a beautiful fall day the morning after she'd fallen into a coma. The day had been so unlike the average start to November in Port Angeles. The wind blew coolly against the house, but the sun bleached the land with a warm glow. Mia had been at her side, holding her hand, Gabe holding tight to her other, when the final shaky breath finally released itself from her mother, and then, after death erased all the suffering, she was finally at peace.

Mia could remember that moment with vivid clarity. The way the room had smelled ill, the way her mother had looked waxy and faded, laying on the fresh sheets with only slivers of light passing through the plantation shutters. She remembered the way her aunt had gathered her in her arms, holding her, rocking her, whispering promises and words of comfort. The way her father hadn't let her mother's hand go until the people from the funeral home, in their black suits and polished shoes, arrived. The way Ginny had tended to Mia after Aunt Sophia had gone back home.

Mia remembered the funeral, the way the church had overflowed with friends of her mother's and father's, people she'd never met, never heard mentioned. She could still smell the flowers—death flowers, not the pretty ones that flourished in the small tended gardens around her home, but the ones that had spilled over her mother's lacquered casket, fluted blooms of white and deep purple. The way the glossy wood pews were hard and unrelenting beneath her. She could taste the butter cookies that overflowed from the silver platters that were set around the receiving room. Mia had greedily shoved them in her mouth when no one was looking, pressing the stale, yellow cookies to the roof of her mouth until they turned into a mush of saliva and sugary dough. Even now, nine years later, she couldn't look at butter cookies without wanting to cry. She could remember the strange rattling in her chest, and the way her whole body vibrated with soundless sobs as they lowered her mother into the ground under a shower of white roses. The way people would touch her shoulder in comfort or whisper their condolences; all the nameless, faceless people.

She remembered the blanket of blackness that had swallowed her father when they finally went home. The blackness had lingered for months and months, as he rarely smiled and never laughed and her visceral fear that he might never surface.

But he had, and slowly their lives had begun to heal, their world began to spin again. And now, nine years later, she could hear her father's soft voice reasoning the virtues of not wallowing to Ginny on the other side of her wall.

"She shouldn't skip school, Ginny."

"If she wants a day, she should take it. That's all. It ain't much, whatever she misses, she can make up."

"It's not about what she's missing, Ginny. It's about her not...giving in. It's not good for her."

"It's one day, Gabe, and she's sixteen. She hasn't missed a single day of school all year."

Mia could hear Gabe mutter and then, give in. He rarely went up against Ginny and won.

"Just make sure she gets her work done today, okay? Have her ask Sarah to bring her schoolwork; she can't afford to get behind. She's going to be applying to colleges in the next couple of weeks. Her grades matter. I'll be home late; I'm going to Seattle for a client meeting," Gabe sighed in defeat. He should have known better; Ginny, with her reason, was a dangerous thing.

She heard him approach. "Mia, honey, can I come in for a minute?"

"Sure, Dad." Mia pulled herself up to a

sitting position.

"You feeling all right, honey?" Gabe stood in the doorway, leaning heavily against the frame.

"It's just a mental health day." Mia smiled weakly at him.

"Of course. Mental health." Gabe nodded in agreement, as if he understood entirely what she meant, but she knew he didn't.

When Gabe had pulled himself out of the depths of his loss, he'd reentered life with purpose. He'd signed a contract with a new developer looking to make tract homes in the area to design the optional floor plans. He left every morning at nine and returned every evening at five. He built a new routine, and, for a while, it worked. When Mia had turned twelve and ached for independence, he closed his private firm and took a job in Seattle with his old company.

"So..." Mia awkwardly pressed, wondering what he needed.

"I have something for you," Gabe began. "Do you have a minute? I could go get it."

"Yeah, sure." Mia nodded.

"Why don't you meet me in the kitchen? We can discuss this over breakfast," Gabe offered before turning on his heel to leave.

Mia wandered to her closet, pulled on a ratty old sweatshirt over her pajama bottoms, and padded into the kitchen. Ginny was sliding an eggy mixture around in the large cast iron skillet, sprinkling chopped vegetables and finely-shredded cheese atop the scamble. The aroma wafted at Mia, making her stomach tighten with hunger.

"Hungry, honey?" Ginny continued to cook.

"There's some biscuits and jam on the table, the eggs will be ready in a minute." She gestured to the white bowl on the table; a blue and cream napkin lay at the bottom, nestling plump, airy biscuits, still warm, and two small ramekins filled with blackberry jam and softened butter were set off to the side.

"Thanks." Mia smiled and slid into the dark wooden chair to wait, helping herself to a biscuit, smothering it in jam and butter. "This is really good," Mia offered between healthy bites.

"Made the jam yesterday, blackberries like you wouldn't believe in my freezer." Ginny spooned the scramble onto a large platter and crossed the room to the table, setting it carefully down by Mia.

Mia took a small serving on her plate, nibbling carefully.

"Ginny?" Mia asked between bites.

"Yes, hon?" Ginny lowered her cup mid-sip.

"Do you know what this thing is, what my dad's getting?" Mia asked, her fork spearing bits of pepper and onion.

Ginny lifted the hand-thrown mug that Mia had made for her in fifth grade to her lips, taking a small sip of the strong black coffee before continuing, "I could guess, maybe, but don't know for sure."

Gabe crossed the distance of the kitchen at just that moment, setting a carved box down beside Mia before taking his place at the table, heaping mounds of eggs onto his plate and smoothing his napkin across his lap, reaching for a biscuit.

"I remember this box!" Mia wiped her mouth and reached for the box, pulling her back to the day that Ginny had given it to her, her hope chest. She ran her fingers carefully across the carvings, appraising its beauty.

"Mom filled it with things that might be important to you. I figured now that you were old enough to take care of it—and follow her wishes," Gabe explained, splattering hot sauce on his eggs.

Lifting the intricate lid, Mia looked inside. Tapes— ten of them—just like the one she listened to every morning, and a thin envelope addressed to Mia in her mother's neat handwriting.

"I don't understand..." Mia trailed off, flipping through the contents carefully.

"Read the letter. It's all there" Gabe gestured.

"Okay." Mia turned the thin white envelope over in her hands, wanting to bury her nose in the paper, to catch any scent her mother may have left behind once upon a time when she had touched this paper.

"Seriously, read the letter first before you do anything else, okay? That's the way she planned it," Gabe continued.

"Got it." Mia picked up her plate and carried it to the sink, turning on the faucet. She let rivers of water push the remains of her meal down the drain. "Dad?"

"Yes, honey?" Gabe pushed away from the table, the bottom of his chair scraping noisily against the polished hardwood floor.

"Are you coming home for dinner?" Mia placed her plate in the dishwasher and leaned against the counter, waiting.

It was an uncomfortable thing between them, Gabe's comings and goings, and Mia always thought it was ironic that in a different world it would be the other way around, that Gabe would be the one asking the questions.

"Mia…" Gabe sighed with exhaustion at her question. This was nearly the same conversation they had every day, and Gabe couldn't understand how it failed to root with Mia. "Work's busy right now…I have meetings all day and client dinners at night."

Mia shuffled her feet, looking downwards. She knew Gabe had to work to keep them in their home, had to work to keep their lifestyle as comfortable as it was. But, under it all, Mia could ignore her suspicion that there was something more that kept him in Seattle long after the sun fell and she'd gone to bed.

"Why don't you go read the letter?" Ginny intercepted the conversation, holding the box out for Mia, an offering.

Mia shoved off the counter and wove her way around the island to the table.

"Let me know if you need anything, honey. I'll be in and out all day." Ginny squeezed Mia's shoulder lightly.

"Thanks," Mia slipped out of the room. The box in her hands felt heavy with possibilities.

Mia closed the door behind herself quietly, and Ginny waited a moment before she leveled him with her eyes and shook her head slowly.

"You're gonna have to tell her sometime. You can't keep carrying on like this forever. It's not right and it's not fair!" Ginny placed her knotty hands on her hips and waited. This a conversation they'd had many times, usually right on the heels of Gabe dismissing Mia's worries.

"I know," Gabe sighed, "but there is never a right time, it's not an easy thing. Am I just supposed to spring this on her? How is that even fair to her?"

"I think Mia deserves to know, that's all I'm saying. She's a smart girl. Perceptive. Give her the credit she deserves and then let her decide for herself how she'll feel about it."

Gabe sighed heavily, letting Ginny continue.

"Mia is sixteen, not six and she worries about you," Ginny concluded.

"I know, it's just never the right time..." Gabe began and trailed off, Ginny raising her hand to stop him.

"This isn't what Jenna would've wanted, either."

And there it was, the fact Gabe couldn't bring himself to admit. It wasn't that he didn't want Mia to get to know Kris. Kris was an outstanding woman: smart, loving, caring, funny. It was that Gabe didn't want Kris in this part of his life. Gabe wanted Kris—so bad it buckled his knees—but that didn't change anything. This home was Jenna's home. This child was Jenna's child. How could he possibly open all of this up to another? He couldn't, he wasn't ready.

"So what do you suggest I do, then?" Gabe prodded. Ginny seemed to have most of the answers for life's riddles; she was his anchor.

"I suggest you bring Kris over for supper or take Mia to Seattle, put both of those women together and let them sort it out." Ginny swept a smattering of crumbs into her palm and locked eyes with Gabe, making it seem so impossibly simple.

"What if I told you I feel like I'm cheating on Jenna? That the thought of bringing another woman into the life she built still feels like a betrayal?"

Ginny nodded, but carried on. "Then I'd say you're only cheating yourself out of happiness. And that's a real shame, 'specially after all these years, and 'specially knowing what Jenna wanted."

That was truth. Jenna had told Gabe that she wanted him to have a full life, one that wasn't defined only by her and her death. She wanted him to be happy again. She didn't—above all else she had said—want him to be lonely. At the time, Gabe had been disgusted. He loved Jenna; no one else would be for him what she was, and considering settling for anything, at the time she'd suggested it, had been physically painful. But now, after all the years of being alone, he felt differently. It wasn't that he loved Jenna any less, but rather that he'd found that he needed more, just as Jenna had once suspected he would. She'd told him once that he was a man without a middle ground when it came to love. The sort of man who knew how to give himself away completely and wholly. The sort of man who wanted to love and be loved in return; it was figuring out how to do that which gave him pause.

"I'll think about it and I'll talk to Kris," Gabe conceded, but knowing Kris, he knew she would consider it an honor, something she'd do with joy. She'd wanted to meet Mia for months now, had even asked several times and had hinted at not understanding why the walls around his life were so hard to take down when together, they were so happy. His excuses were wearing thin, he knew as much, but what he could never tell her was that, the moment she stepped into his life, it would be like removing Jenna just a little bit more.

Gabe looked towards Mia's room, the door shut tightly, keeping everyone out. He had wondered over the years if he'd done right by Mia, if keeping her there, in this house, had been right thing. If maybe it wouldn't have been easier, more natural, if they'd started moving on before.

"Have her call Soph today, please?" Gabe asked as he pulled his briefcase from the chair and shrugged on his trench coat.

"Of course," Ginny agreed.

"Make sure she figures out what she's missing at school today. She can't fall behind, no matter what. It only takes one assignment," Gabe cautioned.

"Sometimes you worry about the wrong things," Ginny muttered quietly.

———————❧———————

Mia flipped the plantation shutters open and looked out over the calm bay. The box felt like it weighed a thousand pounds in her hands, and she set it safely on the corner of her desk, pulling out only the thin white envelope with her name neatly printed in the center.

Mia.

She slipped her finger under the seal. It felt brittle and stiff with time, but it cracked open easily. Inside was a single sheet of stationery, linen-white with a fern leaf border. Mia gasped; she remembered this paper. It had sat in a little tray on top of her mother's desk. It was thick and expensive, and Mia could remember how she used to sneak into the office to steal pieces to paint with watercolors on. It had been her favorite. Looking at it now made her miss her mother more than she had in a great while.

Dear Mia,

Do you remember this box? You were so excited the day Ginny brought it to the house for you, so now that it's yours, please remember to thank her again for it...and tell her 'thank you' from me, as well.

Do you remember what we called this box? A hope chest. As you'll probably figure out some day, they are typically much larger. Usually, mothers fill them for their daughters with quilts, frames, pictures, trinkets, tablecloths, and candlesticks. They are intended to be stuffed with things that a mother hopes her daughter will use when she gets old enough to appreciate what's inside. Useful things, things to help start a daughter start her independent life.

This is your hope chest. My hopes for you. Inside I have left ten tapes, one for each important occasion of your life. These, Mia, are your milestone tapes.

When I found out that I was dying, that our time together was coming to a close, I wasn't ready. I wasn't sure how to relinquish the hold that motherhood had put on me, or how to trust your life to anyone else. I love your father and I know he'll do right by you, guide you, encourage and inspire you, but there are some things only a mother can offer; it's not something you can replace or substitute, no matter how many other people love you. I don't think anyone is ever truly ready to let go of their child, but you were just a little girl—my little girl—and that, Mia, was the hardest part for me to come to terms with.

Because I knew I was leaving you much too soon and you were still much too young to have the important conversations, mother to daughter, I made these tapes for you for if or when you find yourself in that place and want to hear my take on things. I promise you'll find honesty and stories, and you'll probably hear things you won't like—typical, of course: I am your mother. But here's the deal—you can only listen to them when they become relevant to your life, not before.

These tapes are my hopes...but they are not my expectations. The truth is, I have no idea who you'll grow up to be...a lawyer, a doctor, a poet, an artist...but I do know that your options are limitless. Maybe you'll get married, or maybe you won't. Maybe you'll go to college, or maybe you won't. I was never very good with numbers, but I'm guessing there are millions of paths you can take and millions of choices down each individual one. I'm sure I've missed some milestones, I'm sure the world you live in now is much different than the world I lived in...but none of that matters because I've always wanted only one thing for you and that is true, regardless of space or time: I just want you to be the best version of Mia Elizabeth Chamberland you can be.

I'm sure that once these tapes make

their way to you, you'll want to listen to them all right away. Over the years, after your grandmother passed away, I longed for her voice, so I can understand how you're probably feeling. But please don't; please try to wait. The truth is, listening to these tapes now wouldn't make sense—the context is wrong. We could have had many of these talks when you were a little girl. We could have talked about being in love, choosing a path in life, making your way in the world, but I knew you weren't ready for those sort of conversations. You were seven years old and these sort of life lessons were more than what you could understand, and probably even now you're not ready for some of them. These were made with moments in mind, times when you'd take away something important, so even if you're tempted, wait—it will be worth it. Listen to them at the time for which they were intended for—they'll mean more to you.

Love, Mom

Folding the note up, she slipped it back inside the envelope. The tapes were small and labeled. There were ten, like Jenna had promised. They were disorganized and in no particular order, so pulling each one out, Mia read the labels.

Your Wedding Day
Becoming a Mother
College Graduation

Your First Love
Your First Broken Heart
Your First Time (the sex talk)
Your Father Getting Remarried
High School Graduation
Leaving Home
If You're Ever In My Position

Mia closed her eyes, trying to envision her mother writing the note, recording the tapes. She couldn't. The silver recorder beside her bed tempted her; she wanted to listen to each word right now, skip the waiting. She wanted to have all those moments now. She wanted to hear her mom's stories and her voice, her soft inflections and the way her voice rolled over certain words. But she wouldn't. She would listen to her mother and respect her wishes, trust her logic and wait. The thought almost made her giddy.

Often at school or in social settings, she would watch her friends roll their mascara-rimmed eyes over the rules their mothers laid down, groaning over how unfair it was to be leashed by their parental laws. Mia had always wished her mother was around to give her those sorts of boundaries; it was an odd thing to miss, but Mia always knew that behind the curfews, consequences, and limits was love. She wanted that, missed that.

Collecting the little tapes, she placed them neatly back in the box along with the envelope and tucked it high up on a shelf, wondering when the first milestone would come.

The silver phone beside her bed trilled and Mia grabbed it quickly, checking the caller ID.

"Hey Sarah, what's up?" Mia chirped into the phone.

"Where are you?" Sarah whispered aggressively on the other end.

"Home. I'm playing hooky." Mia looked at the box atop her desk.

"Well...Bryan has been asking everyone where you are," Sarah laughed. "I told him I would call you and figure it out."

Mia felt herself blush, the warmth creeping up her cheeks and she chewed her lip, embarrassed, even in the privacy of her room.

Bryan was older, a senior, and dangerously good looking, with dark brown hair frosted with blonde tips—which was the trend—chocolatey eyes, a wide inviting smile, a broad chest, and well-defined arms. They had started hanging out a few weeks ago when Sarah had started dating his best friend, Griff. Mia liked Bryan for the obvious reasons: he was good looking, popular, intelligent, and funny. As she got to know him over games of bowling and red cups filled with lightly spiked punch, she peeled back the surface and discovered he was even better underneath the superficial stuff. He wanted to be a teacher, an unusual dream for a high school football star, but that made him interesting. He wanted to go to college in Seattle, just like as his parents had, and then come back to Port Angeles to start his life. He was one of the few local kids who actually appreciated the raw beauty of this place and wanted to stay here forever. He liked to read, loved music, and worked the weekend day camp at the local YMCA for spending money.

"Really?" Mia pretended to be indifferent, but inside she was tingling, bubbling. Bryan Devon was asking about her.

"Yes, really!" Sarah hissed. "He was worried! Can you believe it? *Worried*! I think he likes you, like, a lot!"

"Well, I don't know, just tell him I'm home."

"Can we come over after school?" Sarah pressed. Mia's house was the perfect place for lounging around: minimal supervision, wide-open, comfortable spaces, a huge fire pit in the back yard, and plenty of food in the fridge.

"Ginny's here, but yeah, sure that's cool—you can all come over," Mia agreed, excited.

"Okay, perfect. Call you later!" The phone clicked off.

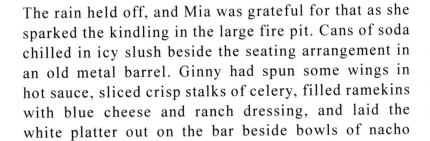

The rain held off, and Mia was grateful for that as she sparked the kindling in the large fire pit. Cans of soda chilled in icy slush beside the seating arrangement in an old metal barrel. Ginny had spun some wings in hot sauce, sliced crisp stalks of celery, filled ramekins with blue cheese and ranch dressing, and laid the white platter out on the bar beside bowls of nacho chips, candies, and freshly-baked cupcakes.

"So, this Bryan boy, he's coming here to see you?" Ginny asked as she filled another bowl with tortilla chips.

"I think so; he was asking about me today." Mia felt the same heat rush of her throat and she looked away.

"He's a good-lookin' boy." Ginny nodded in agreement. "I like his folks, too—nice people."

"You know his parents?" Mia asked curiously.

"This town ain't that big; his folks live 'cross the

road from me." Ginny nodded at the spread and turned to go back inside. "Now, Mia, I'm gonna be around here, so don't think about doing nothing sneaky." Ginny winked.

Mia could hear the sound of a car pulling up the drive and tugged anxiously on the hem of her black cashmere sweater. Glancing in the mirror before going to the door, she looked herself over. Her unruly, wavy hair was neatly pulled back into a low tied ponytail, and her sweater hung casually from her thin frame. Her dark wash jeans were soft and worn, and a hint of pink balm brushed her lips, a wisp of mascara on her long lashes rimming her emerald eyes. She looked fine, she decided.

Sarah burst through the door first, dropping her book bag beside the hall-tree. "It smells so good in here! You look pretty." Sarah's eyes looked over Mia, before she nodded her approval.

"Everything is set up out back, so help yourself, you know the drill."

Griff and few others ambled in the door, looking around the expansive Chamberland home. Mia knew what they saw, but the luxury for her had long since worn off. The house was one of the largest in town; Jenna had managed to hammer down 'timeless' when it was built.

Mia watched Bryan walked slowly up the plank and stone steps towards the warmth of the home. He looked shy and handsome—an exciting blend. His blue polo shirt was tucked neatly into his jeans and a worn brown leather belt hugged his hips; his hair was messy from gym, and his cheeks were flushed with the afterglow of laughter.

"Nice place." Bryan smiled, a deep dimple piercing his cheek.

"Thanks." Mia smiled back, "Everyone's out back; Ginny put out food—figured you'd be starved after school."

"She's right." Bryan pulling the door closed behind himself.

Laughter filtered through the open door out back, guiding them toward the gathering. The fire pit raged, and the chairs were filled with lounging teenagers snacking and slurping on icy soda.

"Great backyard, Chamberland." Griff raised his soda in approval as Mia and Bryan slipped through the door. Sarah had settled onto his lap, her arm casually draped across his shoulder. They looked comfortable, and a flutter of envy filled Mia's stomach.

"Oh, thanks. Yeah, my parents really wanted to make this, like, an outdoor living room." Mia shrugged, helping herself to a Diet Pepsi floating at the top of the nearly empty basin.

"Very cool," Griff agreed before he planted a kissed Sarah on her cheek

"So how was school?" Mia asked Sarah, glancing at Bryan as he walked towards the cliff edge.

"Same old, same old. You missed nothing!" Sarah took a small sip of her soda before heaving herself up from the chair to join Mia. "Go talk to him." Sarah jerked her head in the direction of Bryan, who was haloed in the light of the fading sun.

"What do I say?" Mia asked, wide eyed, horrified by the thought of approaching him, talking to him.

"I don't know, just talk. It's really not that hard," Sarah sighed, as if what she were saying was common sense and Mia was just slow.

Sarah reached her hand into the tub and pulled out a Sprite, thrusting it into Mia's hand. "Give him that, it's an excuse, then just ask him stuff about sports or work...who cares...just talk to him."

Mia felt the can dampen her hand as she padded across the yard. The thick, plush grass giving beneath the soles of her shoes. "Bryan?"

Bryan spun around quickly and smiled at her approach, his eyes tracing the length of her body in the darkening light. "Hi," he said softly.

"I thought maybe you'd want this." Mia held the can out away from her, offering it to him.

"Thanks, that was real nice of you." Bryan took the can, poping the top open and taking a long swallow of the bubbly, syrupy soda.

"So, um, how was school?" Mia asked quietly, keeping her eyes on the horizon.

"It was okay. I was looking for you, thought maybe you were sick." Bryan tilted his head to the side, shrugging his shoulders in nonchalance.

"No, I'm fine, not sick...just played hooky, mental health day," Mia said with a half-smile, mimicking his casual shrug.

Bryan took another long sip and nodded in agreement, "Mental health?" His tone turned to one of teasing speculation.

"Oh, no, not like crazy-mental-health!" Mia fumbled her words..

"I'm joking," Bryan laughed easily and it was a full-bodied sound, deep and thick and manly.

"Oh." Mia shuffled her feet, feeling the soft grass give, digging her toes into the earth.

"No, really. I think it's cool. Everyone needs a break sometimes."

Mia paced towards the cliff edge, allowing the heavy breeze off the bay to wash over her; it felt good on her warm skin.

"So, a break... What for? Boy troubles?" Bryan pressed, keeping the conversation rolling.

"Nothing like that." Mia shook her head, studying the open sea.

"So what then? I'm curious... Maybe you've got something I could use with my folks."

"My mom died nine years ago today."

"Oh," Bryan mumbled. "I didn't know...well, I knew...but I didn't..." His words caught and failed as he slipped into an awkward silence.

"It's okay." Mia nodded. "Guess that doesn't help you with your parents, though," Mia added lightly.

"No. Not really," Bryan allowed. "I'm sorry." He turned to Mia, lowering his gaze to meet her eyes, and his warm breath, minty and sweet with soda, washed over her face.

"It's okay," Mia repeated, unsure of what else to say. She wasn't good at talking about her mom—not with strangers; tears always threatened just below the surface.

"If you want to talk about it, I'll listen."

Mia's heart swelled. She only talked about her mother with a few people: her father, Ginny, Aunt Sophia, Sarah, and her therapist. But generally, her mother was an off-limits topic; it was still too raw and sensitive. Jenna was soft and raw, like an wound incapable of healing, always threatening to rip away her composure and calm, leaving her vulnerable and emotional.

"Mia!" Ginny hollered from the open doorway, her thick build framed in the buttery light of the kitchen.

Mia glanced woefully at Bryan. "I'll be right back," she said before she took off jogging towards the house.

"Come on inside for a minute." Ginny held the door for Mia, who slipped under her arm and into the overly warm kitchen.

"What's up? Am I in trouble?" Mia asked, concerned.

"Just got off the phone with your dad. He's not going to make it home for dinner." Ginny's eyes pinched, awaiting the disappointment to crush Mia.

"Oh! Is that all?" Mia asked, relief washing over her.

"I figured you'd be upset." Ginny tilted her head, confused.

"It's okay...I kind of overheard your conversation this morning..." Mia admitted.

"This newfound understanding doesn't have anything to do with that handsome young man out there waiting for you?" Ginny smiled suggestively.

"A little bit," Mia answered honestly, her eyes drifting back to the cliff edge. The night was blackening, but she could still see Bryan waiting.

Ginny wrapped Mia in a strong hug, the kind she usually reserved for moments like this; it reminded Mia of when she was a little girl.

"You'll stay the night?" Mia asked hopefully.

"As always." Ginny released her and hustled her back towards the door. "You enjoy your night. And don't worry, I'll fix some pizza and put out more soda for your friends."

"Ginny's making pizza for dinner—can you stay? I think everyone else is," she asked as she reached Bryan again.

"Sure, that sounds good. Thanks." He looped his arm over her shoulder lightly.

"So, you really want to hear about my mom?" Mia asked, raising her face to his.

She was unsure if she could go there with him, but she wanted to. She liked him a lot. It wasn't just his handsome face or his good-hearted nature; she wanted to trust him, to reveal herself to him, to open herself up in a new way.

"I'll listen if you want to talk, but I don't want to...you know...pressure you." Bryan tightened his arm around her; it felt good, strong, and reassuring.

"She had breast cancer. I was only seven when she died, and she was sick for most of my life," Mia began, trying to figure out the right words that would tell the story and keep her safe from an emotional breakdown.

"Wow," Bryan answered softly.

"I remember a lot of things about her—she was amazing. A really great mom; I was lucky. She was an author, a really good one, too...popular." Mia smiled, it wasn't painful to talk about the great things her mom was.

"I'll look up her books—what did she write?" Bryan asked, genuinely interested.

Mia laughed. "Books for women. Women's fiction. Probably not the sort of thing you read."

"Don't be so sure, I'd like to read one—you know, get a feel for who she was."

"She was a great writer. I could lend you one, if you'd like."

"That would be great, thanks."

"So, yeah, today my dad gave me this box—a hope chest—do you know what that is?" Mia asked.

"Kind of."

"Yeah, well, my mom recorded these tapes for me. She called them *milestone tapes.*"

"Really? That's pretty cool."

"I miss her all the time," Mia admitted quietly. "And it's weird, you know, the things you miss."

"Like what?" Bryan asked.

"Normal mother daughter stuff, mostly. But the weirdest one? I kind of wish she was around to ground me. Crazy, I know. Who wants to be grounded?"

"That is crazy..." Bryan laughed loudly. "But you've got your dad."

"Yeah, I do. He's cool, very laid back. He works all the time, which sucks, but I understand it."

"Well, it looks like you live pretty large," Bryan justified.

Mia thought about her life, her comfortable, tended to home, the shiny new Jeep in the driveway—her birthday present—her closet full of expensive clothes, her summer trips to various islands, and her generous allowance, thanks to her padded bank account. Her father provided a very plush life for her with the hours he dutifully put into his work.

"Yeah, all of this is nice, but I wish he was around more."

"He's a single parent, that can't be easy."

"He's a great dad. But when my mom died, he changed. He used to build homes here in town. He wanted to be with my mom and me all the time. But when she died, he was unhappy here, doing that here. I think it reminded him of my mom, like it was pretending that nothing had changed but everything changed. He took a job in Seattle, a few years ago. Now, he shuttles into the city every day...and like tonight...he's not even coming home."

"And you've got Ginny."

"And my Aunt Soph," Mia added. "But if I had my mom, things would be different. So knowing that makes accepting all of this, for what it is, harder."

Mia didn't expect Bryan to understand, she wanted him to, but the understanding was something bigger than an eighteen year old could grasp without real life experience. His life was perfectly normal after all. A mom who was involved and around, a dad who worked fifteen minutes away, a handful of brothers and sisters to love. Mia's life was different.

"So, that's basically it," Mia shrugged away from Bryan and walked closer to the cliff edge, wrapping her arms around herself.

"Mia," Bryan whispered, walking softly towards her. She turned slowly to face him. His eyes blazed warm with something she had never seen before. He lowered his face to hers and brushed his lips lightly against hers. They felt both firm and soft as they moved against hers. He slipped his arms around her lower back, pulling her in closer, the heat of his skin scorching her back through her thin sweater. His breath tasted sweet, he smelt clean and fresh, he felt warm and solid under her light touch.

He pulled back slowly, searching her face for something. Mia's heart fluttered hard in her chest, her eyes closed and a small smile tugged on the corners of her lips.

"Wow," Bryan whispered. "I would love to take you out sometime—just the two of us, not a group thing."

"I'd like that a lot."

Bryan lowered his face again, kissing Mia deeply, weaving his fingers through her ponytail, pulling her face against his and taking her breath away.

"He asked me out!" Mia gushed as she helped Ginny gather the discarded plates and cups that were littered across the patio. The steady hum of nocturnal life droned beside them, the fire pit smoldering itself out.

"He did?" Ginny asked excitedly, plunking an empty cup in the waiting trashcan.

"Yes!" Mia all but screamed into the quiet night.

"That's wonderful."

"Tomorrow night! Can you believe it?"

"Oh, I can believe it, all right. You're a beautiful girl, no reason for boys not to be banging down this door to get a date with you," Ginny laughed lightly.

"Doubtful, but thanks," Mia laughed.

"You never see yourself the way others do. Used to tell my girls that all the time. You see your flaws, others see your perfections," Ginny reasoned.

"We're going to Cafe Garden."

"Oh, very nice."

"What do I wear? Should I get something new?" Mia considered the possibilities in her closet: the little black wrap dress and kitten heels, or the wool sweater dress with black tights and Mary Janes, or the slacks with the pumpkin silk blouse and sweater wrap she'd seen hanging in the boutique the other day. She wanted to look beautiful, mature, and grown-up.

"You'll be beautiful in whatever you choose, sweetness," Ginny said, cinching the bag closed and lifting its weight into her arms.

"I'm nervous," Mia admitted bashfully. She'd been on dates before—that much was true. But the boys she'd humored had never held her interest the way Bryan did. They were sweet and kind and cute, but Bryan stirred her.

"First love is always that way," Ginny dropped the last bag to the trashcan and surveyed the tidy yard.

"'Love?'" Mia asked, surprised to hear the word pass Ginny's lips.

"Of course."

"I don't...love...him."

"Have you ever been in love before?" Ginny asked as she settled into a wrought iron chair and looked into the dying embers of the fire pit.

"No!"

"Well, I can just tell you what I know. I've seen you with this boy, Bryan is a good young man, and you're different with him. Maybe it's not love, not yet, at least for you, but the way he looks at you? He feels something and I think, you're starting to feel the same."

"You can't possibly know that! I hardly know him, we've hung out, sure, but I don't think I love him—doesn't that take, like, I don't know...time?" Mia countered, sitting down beside Ginny, resting her head on Ginny's shoulder.

"I've raised you since you were a little girl, Mia. I know you—everything about you. So, yes, I can see changes in you—even the small ones—I see them all."

Ginny wrapped her arm around Mia, holding her close.

"So what do I wear?"

"Oh, Mia," Ginny laughed loudly, squeezing Mia tightly.

CHAPTER FIFTEEN

NOVEMBER 4, 2011

MIA HEARD HIS CAR PULL the drive and she chewed nervously on the soft inside of her cheek. The sweater dress itched against her back and she wanted to change again, but her time was up.

Bryan knocked carefully on the glass door and waited, then turned his back to the window as he looked out across the yard.

Gabe pulled the door open and appraised the young man bouncing nervously on the step.

"Good evening Mr. Chamberland. I'm here to pick up Mia." Bryan thrust his hand out formally.

"Call me Gabe. Come in for a minute, she's almost ready...I think." Gabe smiled, taking the boy's hand in his own, giving it a solid pump before he pulled the door open wider, allowing Bryan to pass.

Mia had spent the better part of the early evening disassembling her closet. Clothes lay scattered like dead bodies across the floor of her room. She smudged another coat of berry lipstick on her full lips and closed her eyes hard. She was nervous. Sarah had come over earlier to help her pick the right outfit, but quickly gave up when Mia hemmed and hawed over the finer points of black versus grey.

"So, Bryan." Gabe offered Bryan a seat in front of the television. "Tell me about yourself." He muted the volume.

"Well, sir, I'm a senior. I go to school with Mia. I work at the YMCA."

"Any plans for after graduation?" Gabe leaned over, taking his beer from the coaster and crossing one leg casually over the other.

"Seattle University. Early acceptance." Bryan wiped his palms against the pressed front of his khaki pants.

"Impressive. I work in the city, great place." Gabe pushed the bottle to his lips, taking a healthy swallow.

"I've heard that." Bryan scratched lightly at his head, running his fingers through his hair.

"And what are your plans for tonight?" Gabe asked as he replaced his beer.

"I'm taking Mia to Cafe Garden. Then a bunch of our friends are meeting up with us to go to the movies, so, if she wants to, I might take her there, too."

"Just make sure she's home by eleven o'clock." Gabe nodded.

"Of course," Bryan agreed.

"Well, let me go see what's keeping Mia." Gabe shoved off the couch.

"Come in," Mia answered the knock and turned towards the door.

"Mia, honey...wow." Gabe pushed the door open and stopped.

"Do I look okay?" Mia asked, pulling the sleeve of her dress down an inch.

"You look...lovely...just like your mother." The words caught in Gabe's throat as he looked at his little girl, who was not so little anymore. Her long, dark hair fell down her back in waves, her eyes were smoky with rims of mascara, her cheeks were a rosy hue, and her olive skin glowed.

"Thanks, Dad." Mia crossed the room and kissed him lightly on his cheek.

"Your date's waiting." Gabe cleared his throat quietly, blinking hard against the tears.

"I think I'm ready now." Mia laced her arms around Gabe's middle, giving him a light hug.

"Not too late, okay?" Gabe added, looking up at the ceiling, wondering when all of this had happened.

"Dad." Mia rolled her eyes playfully and patted his back as she passed by.

"Have fun," he called after her quietly.

"I had a good time tonight." Bryan leaned on the armrest of the driver's seat, looking intently at Mia.

"Me, too." She smiled.

It had been wonderful. They'd eaten their meal and laughed about school, talked about Bryan's worries over college, Mia's excitement for Sophia's visit. They'd caught a movie with friends and had walked hand in hand down Hollywood Beach with the others. Their rhythm together was simple and Mia had wondered, feeling the warmth of skin against her own if Ginny hadn't been right.

"Can I take you out again?" Bryan leaned over further, fixing Mia with his deep eyes.

"I'd like that," Mia blushed and thanked goodness

that the light in the car was low.

"Actually, no, what I meant was, will you be, like...my girlfriend?"

"Bryan..." Mia's eyes popped open wide with surprise.

"I know that sounds, like, I don't know...dumb. But I like you, Mia, and I just figured we could give this thing a...label." He shrugged, pulling back slightly.

"So, boyfriend and girlfriend?" Mia chewed her lip.

"Yes."

Mia leaned across her seat, across the armrest, and kissed him lightly on the cheek. "Yes."

She opened the car door and slipped out into the driveway, waving once as she ran up the stairs and into the house.

CHAPTER SIXTEEN

DECEMBER 8, 2011

"Kris?" Mia asked, sliding her pasta around the big oversized bowl at Bella Italia.

"Kris." Gabe took a sip of wine.

"And she's like, what? Your girlfriend?" Mia asked again, her eyes lowering in speculation. She had heard Gabe and Ginny discussing this; she knew exactly what Kris was, but played coy.

"She's a friend, an important friend, and I'd like for you to meet her…if you're willing." *Her choice*, Gabe thought, *it must be her choice*—that's how it had to be, at least for now, if he was going to push this on her.

Mia knew what this was.

"Sure, yeah, that's cool. I'll meet your friend." Mia enunciated *friend*, letting Gabe know there was a boundary line to her willingness, but nodded in agreement anyway.

"Okay, good." Gabe smiled at his daughter, taking in the way the light reflected off her dark hair, reminding him so much of Jenna. The thought pinched at his heart.

"Aunt Sophia is coming for a visit, you know, for Christmas...so maybe we could all have dinner or something. Kris could come to the house, and Ginny could cook something before she leaves," Mia suggested, swirling her fork around a cluster of noodles drenched in meat sauce.

"Actually, I was thinking we'd do a weekend in Seattle, take in some culture. And if that goes well, then, yeah, maybe we could do a dinner, but probably not over Soph's Christmas visit." Gabe looked meaningfully at Mia. Gabe knew Sophia would understand. She would probably enjoy meeting Kris, but he wanted Mia to know Kris first.

"Like Pike Place and stuff?" Mia asked hopefully, visibly brightening. She'd been only a few times, despite living so close to Seattle and being old enough to drive herself. But it had worked out that Gabe spent so much time in the city for work that when they had free time he coaxed Mia to the coast or the rainforest or just preferred the comforts of home. She imagined picking up a few small Christmas gifts for her friends and Ginny and Aunt Sophia and the boys and Bryan while she was there.

"Sure, we could get some of that golden raspberry jam you and Ginny like so much," Gabe suggested, relief washing over him like salve. Mia was willing, maybe excited even. He couldn't have hoped for more, didn't have the right to hope for more, and yet the joy bubbled up. Kris and Mia were going to meet each other.

"Can Ginny come?"

"Maybe next time." Gabe could understand Mia wanting reinforcements, someone to lean on if things got awkward—he could even respect that—but Mia had him, and he'd be her ally.

He'd known Ginny was right. Mia was almost an adult, a smart, well-adjusted teenager who wouldn't want her father to be lonely for the rest of his life; she was smart enough to understand the concept of balance. He couldn't run away from relationships just because he was scared; he was in love with Kris, and he wanted to her in his life, his whole life, not just particular parts of it.

Kris, for her part, had been thrilled, and was so excited to meet Mia. She had offered the guest room in her apartment and suggested different plays at the local theater they could take in, offering to make reservations and buy tickets. She mentioned a shopping trip to a local boutique that offered handmade wears and a trip to the spa below her building for manicures. She was trying.

Kris was a beautiful, smart, successful woman, and he had been attracted to her immediately— for all the wrong reasons in the beginning, he had to admit: she was drop dead sexy. A photographer working and living in Seattle, Kris was divorced with no children of her own, but she was warm and inviting and soft and creative. Gabe had met her while finishing up the design of a hotel; she had been photographing the promotional campaign. They had spent months getting to know each other as friends before their relationship became tangled up and turned into a romance.

"So when are we going?" Mia pressed, sipping an icy Coke and wiping her mouth with a pressed cloth napkin.

"Are you free this weekend?"

"Yeah, sure." Mia shrugged indifferently.

"Great. I'll book your charter flight out of the airport for after school on Friday. Ginny can drop you off and I'll meet you at SeaTac when you land."

"Or I could drive myself," Mia suggested.

"To the airport?"

"To Seattle. Then we can just drive back home together on Sunday."

"I don't know, Mia, Seattle's not a short drive, and there are lots of highways and bridges." Gabe shuddered lightly, imagining his little girl sailing along the wet, winding roads.

"I'll be fine, Dad. I'll take the ferry, skip the bridge, and be in Seattle by dinnertime." Mia smiled, liking her plan.

Gabe balled his napkin underneath the table, leaning back in his chair and stretching his legs out. "If you can promise me that you'll go straight there— no stops, no messing around. Fill up with gas in town, and call me along the way."

"Yeah, straight there, I promise." Mia held up her hand in a visible oath before continuing, "So, since I'm going to meet this Kris lady, tell me about her..."

Gabe sighed deeply before starting, "Well, let's see, she's a photographer. Really talented, does a lot of work in Seattle, but she also travels all over. She actually does a lot of freelance work for a travel magazine—man, the places she's been." Gabe said, shaking his head with an impressed smile.

"So she travels a lot. That's cool. Maybe she could recommend somewhere for us to go over spring break?" Mia suggested, raising her eyebrow. She was always up for somewhere warm that offered beaches with sand instead of rocks. Gabe pursed his lips and nodded in agreement; he liked to treat Mia to good travel and nice vacations.

"She's very nice. About my age—"

"So old?" Mia smirked across the table, cutting her father off.

"She is forty-three—she is not old! Do you think I'm old? I'm not old!" Gabe feigned horror. It was true, he was fifty-nine—almost sixty—but he didn't feel old; Mia had kept him young.

"You're old*er*...and way older than her," Mia corrected teasingly, still laughing, mentally calculating the difference of sixteen years—her whole life.

"Fine, I'm old*er*. But really, she's a wonderful person—I think you're going to like her," Gabe consented.

"I don't have to like her, Dad, she's your friend," Mia corrected. "You don't like all of my friends."

"That's not true; your friends are fine."

"Oh, really? Is that why you always get uppity when I ask if Bryan can come over?" Mia challenged, lowering her eyes and fixing them on Gabe.

"Believe me, Mia, Bryan isn't interested in just hanging out and being good buddies."

"Okay—ew. No. We're not talking about this, and, for the record, Bryan is a good friend." Mia shuddered. She worked very hard at keeping all things of that nature off the radar with Gabe.

"But, more to the point, I'd like it if you liked Kris."

"We'll see," Mia amended. "Tell me more about her, so it's not weird. Since obviously you know a lot about her and this is the first I'm hearing of her."

"I told you she's a photographer, lives in Seattle...

what else would you like to know?" Gabe offered, suspecting Mia had questions of her own.

"Husband?"

"She's divorced."

"Kids?" Mia looked up for that one making unreadable eye contact.

"No, none." Gabe shook his head.

"Is she pretty?" Mia tilted her head and narrowed her eyes.

Gabe wasn't sure how to elaborate on that. Kris was different than Jenna—not the typical type that attracted him. "She's pretty," Gabe nodded, taking a tip of water.

"Okay." Mia nodded, "What color eyes, hair? Come on, you have to give me something..."

"Blonde hair, green eyes..."

"So why'd she get divorced?"

"That's very personal," Gabe answered quickly, feeling that they were entering dangerous territory.

He'd be happy to answer questions about her art, her easy laugh, even her way of making everything funny or how she was never without her camera strung around her neck. But he felt he owed her her privacy. Mia was a stranger to her, and that question—why her marriage failed—was shockingly personal. It was an uncomfortable balance, keeping her secrets from his daughter when he wanted Mia to know Kris, really know her, to understand why he loved her and why he was now breaking his rules to bring her into the fold with them. He knew that Kris had to make the choices about what Mia knew and when, just as Mia would have to make the choice to open herself up to Kris.

"Bad, huh?" Mia nodded stoically, swirling her

straw around the melting ice in her Coke.

"Not bad, but definitely private. It's a personal thing...relationships, I mean...sometimes they work and sometimes they don't, but that isn't my story to tell you," Gabe tried to explain. It was similar to the answer he'd given Kris when she'd questioned him about Mia: the personal stuff belonged to Mia.

"But she's cool, right?"

"Absolutely. Very, very cool. Smart, you'll think she's funny, and she takes amazing pictures; her eye for that stuff is pretty incredible. Oh, and she likes to shop...just like someone else I know." Gabe raised his brows, finding the common ground.

"You really like her?"

"Yes, I really do. She means a lot to me, and you two should get to know each other."

"Don't you think she's too...you know...young?" Mia asked.

"When you get older, honey, age doesn't mean as much as it does when you're younger and just starting out. Eventually you become an adult, and then you meet another adult, and you're both established and suddenly the difference in age isn't so...so...glaring. You're both kind of in the same place, working, living, paying bills...it's a wash, everybody is sort of equal."

"But she's like...way, way younger." Mia squished her nose up. The sixteen-year age difference was hard for a sixteen-year-old to understand— it was, after all, the sum of her entire life.

"It sounds bigger than it is." Gabe nodded, signaling for the check over Mia's shoulder.

"Can I ask you something and you can't blow it off?" Mia asked quietly.

"Of course, honey, you can ask me whatever you'd like." Gabe took the final swallow of his wine and waited.

"Are you two serious?"

"We're friends," Gabe allowed.

"Dad, you promised..." Mia folded her napkin and fixed her eyes on him.

"Yes, I guess we are serious."

"How serious?"

"Serious enough that I want you to meet her, that you liking her is very important to me..."

"And if I like her, would we move Seattle or something?" Worry creased the spot between Mia's brows into a tight furrow.

"I don't plan to do anything like that." Gabe didn't even have to think about the answer; he'd never considered leaving Port Angeles, had never considered uprooting Mia and taking her to the city. That ship had sailed. If it had ever been a possibility, that time had long since passed. When Mia left Port Angeles, it would be because it was her time to go. She could leave for college, or to chase a dream, but Gabe could not imagine being the one to make the decision to leave this place.

"Are you sure?" Mia asked, suddenly feeling like things were spinning out of her control, imagining a moving truck and cardboard boxes and hugging Ginny for the last time. Tears stung behind her eyes.

Gabe laid a small stack of bills inside a leather folio and locked eyes with Mia. "Why don't we talk about this in the car, okay?" Gabe gathered his coat and helped Mia shrug into hers.

The rain pelted their faces as they walked quickly

towards the sleek black Mercedes parked on the street.

"Is Kris moving here?" Mia implored before Gabe had even turned the engine over.

"You're putting the cart before the horse. This is just the start. If things get to that point, we'll all make that choice together, and you'll have your say, same as always."

"I want you tell me the truth, Dad." Mia snuggled down into the warm, dry leather. "You're telling me she's a friend, but it's obviously something more."

"Oh, Mia, it's complicated, and I want to ease you into it. This is...new...for both of us—for all three of us, actually." Gabe pulled the car out onto the road and concentrated on navigating the slick black pavement.

"The truth, Dad, come on. I'm not some little kid."

"I've told you the truth, honey," Gabe reminded her. "I like her a lot, and I want you to get to know her, as well. That's all this is right now."

Mia glared hard out the windshield as the small town whipped by.

"Dad?"

"Yeah?"

"Have you always dated a lot?" Mia was suddenly curious.

"Off and on over the years, honestly. Nothing serious." Gabe nodded, squeezing the steering wheel.

"Oh."

"Does that bother you?"

"I don't know. Yes and no. I guess I always suspected as much; I just wish you had told me," Mia answered honestly, the words catching in her throat.

"I'm sorry." It was all Gabe could think of to say. He wasn't sure how to explain the balance he'd tried to construct for them all, how he'd felt like for a long time that he was being an unfaithful husband, an unfaithful father. How he'd wanted to move on with his life, but he wanted Mia's life to stay the same. It was the balance of polar fields, magnets of the same charge being forced together.

"Are you going to marry Kris? Is that why I'm meeting her now?"

"I don't know, Mia—that's the truth. It's was more about this being the right time than anything else, hon. Now, is it my turn for questions?" Gabe asked, pulled the car under the sweeping carport and turning the engine off.

"Sure, what do you want to know?" Mia slid out the door and walked towards the side entrance of the house and into the mudroom.

"Tell me about your friend...?" Gabe asked, hanging his coat up on a peg and wandering into the kitchen.

"Bryan? Well, let's see," Mia slipped onto a bar stool and rested her chin in her hands. "He's very nice," she said.

"Nice?" Gabe raised his eyebrows as he filled a glass with water and leaned against the kitchen counter.

"Very. He's popular. Oh, and his best friend is Sarah's boyfriend, so that's fun. But you've met him; you know all of that stuff." Mia shrugged and plucked a grape from the bunch in the fruit bowl.

He already knew as much, in a small town, it was impossible not to know nearly everyone, and he approved of Bryan—in theory—he approved of him, but Mia was only sixteen, his baby girl, and their budding relationship gave him pause. Kris had laughed at him when he'd voiced his concern over tuna steak the other night, she'd used words like "normal" and "expected."

"I just don't want you rushing into anything—"

"Rushing into what?" Mia furrowed her brows and blinked at Gabe who adverted his eyes.

"Boys are... well, boys. And you're a beautiful girl..."

"Please don't!" Mia felt heat turn her cheeks pink and she held her hand up to stop him.

Gabe nodded and set his glass in the sink.

"He's a good guy, Dad. So you kind of need to back off a little." Mia hinted at the idea of a little more freedom. "I'm sixteen, and I'm not dumb, I am actually a pretty good judge of character—thank you for that trait, by the way—so just let it be, okay?"

"Mia..."

"No, Dad, don't *Mia* me."

Gabe pursed his lips, watching Mia cautiously. "I was just going to say you sound a lot like your mom. She was always for letting it be."

Mia smiled at Gabe, plopping another grape into her mouth.

"All right, I'm beat." Gabe yawned loudly. "I'm gonna get some sleep. Don't say up too late, Mia, you have school tomorrow." He wandered over and kissed her on the crown of her head. "Love you, girl."

"Love you, too, Dad." Mia wrapped her arm around his side and squeezed him tightly.

Mia watched her father amble towards his bedroom. It suddenly dawned on her that she was happy for him. She'd watched her father go to bed alone every night, eat meals alone, worry about life alone. She had never considered that he might be lonely, but being with Bryan had awakened her to another side of things, the side that was better with someone else. Someone you connected to, someone who understood what you were saying, and someone who got you.

Suddenly, Mia knew she wanted to talk to Bryan, to tell him all about her dinner with her dad, to tell him about her realization. She flitted into her room, grabbing her cell, which was charging beside her bed. She scrolled down her saved favorites and found his number, hitting the 'send' button. She listened to trilling on the other end.

"Mia?" Bryan's voice broke off the ring; it was breathy and sexy, and she felt her stomach pinch with desire. She wanted to kiss him.

"Hi! I'm just calling to say...hi." She laughed at how silly that sounded. "How's everything?"

"Can you meet me?" Bryan's voice sounded strange, an urgent tone she'd never heard before.

"My dad's home—" Mia began.

"It's important, we need to talk, please...meet me."

Mia's blood ran cold. He sounded distant, distracted—and she watched enough television to know what talks usually meant. "Oh, Bry, I can't..." She didn't want to go there with him now; she was happy, and she wanted just a few more minutes of happiness.

"Please, Mia...ten minutes, you'll be back in bed by midnight, I promise." His tone was pleading, and rang of importantance.

"Okay, can you come here? Meet me on the trailhead?" Mia offered. If this was bad—and she thought it was going to be bad—the closer to home she was, the better.

"Sure, of course, I'll be there in five. Wait for me."

The line went dead. Mia clicked the 'end' button and slid off her bed onto the floor, pulling her knees up to her chest.

She slipped on her leather loafers and tiptoed out the door towards the edge of the woods. This was their place, where they snuck off to be alone. She heard him trudge up the path before he called her name.

"Mia?" he whispered, reaching for her, pulling her close and pressing his lips to hers hard. Her head swam, light sparks flashed behind her eyes, and she melted into him easily.

"You sounded...bad...what's going on?" She forced herself to concentrate, pulling her fear back to the surface.

"Mia...I...I love you." Bryan took her face in his hands, looking deeply into her eyes.

"You...love...me?" Mia spaced the words out slowly, making room for them in her head, wrapping her mind around what that meant and how it made her feel.

"I do, I love you. I was thinking about it all day, and I realized it, I love you. I can't stop thinking about you, I always want to be with you, you're everything to me—I love you." He kissed her again, softer this time, letting the kisses trail from her lips to her neck, up the path to her ears, to the tender spot behind them, across the planes of her cheeks, and touching on her eyes, her forehead.

"Bryan..." Mia wrapped her arms around his waist, burrowing her face into his chest. "I love you, too." The words slipped from her lips, sweetly and softly without her even consciously thinking them, as natural as breathing. "Very much."

"Oh, Mia!" Bryan kissed her again.

"I thought you were going to end things between us."

"What? No! No way. Why? Why would you think that?" Bryan took a step back.

"Well, there was that phone call...you were pretty urgent..." Mia explained. The fear she had felt seemed almost comical now, silly; she was so excited, so in love, she wanted to dance. Suddenly all the musicals and love songs and stories made sense.

"I was just nervous, I didn't want to lose my nerve. I kept telling myself, if she calls me tonight—no matter what—I'm just gonna tell her...and then you called, and I knew I had to say it to your face, 'cause I love you and that's a big deal!" Bryan's face broke into a triumphant smile.

"I should probably get back home—no telling what my dad will do if he finds out I left." Mia stifled a yawn with her hand.

"Definitely," Bryan agreed, kissing Mia again. "I'll walk you." He took her hand in his, pulling her back towards her yards.

"So tell me..." Mia dragged her feet as they approached the house, which was dark against the night sky. "How did you know that you loved me?"

"It wasn't one thing, honestly, it was everything. It was you. Just you." Bryan fumbled with the words, holding tight to Mia's hand. "How did you know?"

"I don't know, really. I just kissed you and I was so scared you were over this, and I was like, if he says we're done, I'll break into a million little pieces. It wasn't like a conscious decision, you know? I didn't decide to love you. It was just a feeling." She pulled his hand to her mouth and kissed it softly.

"I've never felt like this before, Mia—ever. Thank you for this." He kissed her softly, depositing her on the doorstep. "I'll see you at school?"

"Yes, I'll be there." Mia smiled

"I love you, Mia."

"Love you, too."

Mia floated inside, weightless with wonder. She felt good—better than good, she felt alive and centered and changed, like suddenly all the feelings she had for Bryan were summed up in a single word: love. She loved him, everything about him.

The house was still dark; Gabe was sleeping undisturbed. Mia knew she needed to sleep, too, that the morning would creep up soon and she'd be expected to be present and awake and ready to learn. She'd walk down the bland hallway that was papered with posters and flyers and everything that colored her ordinary day, only now she'd be holding Bryan's hand, knowing that everything about their relationship had shifted: they were in love.

But she was wired, restless—excitement and joy gave her energy. She knew what she wanted to do. Creeping silently towards her bedroom, her anticipation mounted with each step. The pretty box sat atop her desk.

The first time I fell in love, Mia, I was eighteen. It was the summer between high school and college, and I was counting down the days until I left for school, writing notes to my future roommate, Diane, dragging my mom to Marshall Fields to pick out my dorm bedding and wardrobe. I worked nights at the neighborhood Dairy Queen and spent the days slathered in baby oil, working on my tan. It was pretty great.

That's where I met this boy, David Greene—at the local swimming pool. He was handsome and funny, and he had this very, very cool car—a midnight blue Mustang.

All the girls liked him. And it's funny, because I was definitely not the type to fall for the popular boy...but David was different. I knew that almost immediately. He had enlisted in the Army a few weeks before we met and was shipping off at the end of summer for boot camp, so we were both kind of in the same place, more or less...both moving forward, getting out, going on, and just trying to have fun, counting down the days to real freedom. It's an exciting time, being in that precarious balance between childhood and adulthood.

We spent the summer just hanging out. We would go bowling and dancing, lay out at the pool, and sometimes go to downtown Chicago or to the lake beaches. It was fun; he was fun. Slowly, I started to feel this pull. It wasn't an instant thing, like love can sometimes be, but rather it was like this gradual building of something I couldn't explain. And then, one day, I just realized that what I was feeling was love and that yes, I loved him.

I knew I loved him because, suddenly, all the things that were changing for him were more important than the things that were changing for me. I worried about everything he'd see and be a part of, things that were so far beyond my control, and those things kept me up at night. I wanted to make sure he'd be safe, and comfortable...even though I knew he'd never be safe—he was going into the Army, and being comfortable was very subjective. I just wanted to protect him from all the bad stuff—so much it hurt. That was the way my love for David Greene came out, the way it manifested itself. I can only tell you this: when you know, you just know.

Once I knew I loved him, I wanted to keep him with me. Suddenly all the things that were so important not that long ago shifted; he had become what was important. When we started seeing each other, we had both had these big plans, and now it was like I was trying to figure out ways to make Dave and me work against these impossible odds. I told him how I felt, I told him I loved him...and you know what? He told me he loved me, too. It is amazing, like nothing else in this world...to love and be loved...it's wonderful, Mia.

Being in love means a different sort of responsibility than you've probably ever had before. It means putting another person before yourself, and taking care of their heart the same as you take care of your own. It's a tremendous responsibility. Even if you're young, love and all that comes with it can be very, very real and very, very strong.

Love will never be sweeter than the first time. You have no emotional baggage, no prior disappointments, and no emotional scars. You will learn so much about yourself as you give away a part of yourself to another person.

Mia, I am so happy you have met someone who inspires you to love them—I am sure whoever you've chosen is an amazing person. You are an incredibly lovable person, so I'm not surprised that love has found you. But I just want you to be safe and smart about it. I want you to remember, no matter what, that you have to still keep your priorities in line ... that means making time for school, friends, extracurricular activities, your family. Find balance, a healthy balance. Love can fit into your life, and you don't have to give up anything to have it.

This is a very exciting time. Enjoy it, learn from it, and grow. I love you.

The tape clicked to an audible end. Mia sat quietly, wiping tears away with the back of her hands. Her mother's voice—she missed the words, the meaning, and only heard the voice. Her soft, sweet voice. She was lost in the way the midwestern hitch caught some words and flattened others. The pitch and tone—so familiar and foreign to her. She rewound the tape, playing it again, this time taking in the words. Listening, just listening.

Mia crawled into her bed that night, beneath the soft

sheets, and laid her head on the fluffed down pillow. She closed her eyes and imagined her mom—young and tan and very much alive—feeling just as she did right now. She felt linked to her in that moment; she could see her mother's world—before cancer, before her father, before Seattle and college—when she was young and just starting out, in love with a boy who had deployment papers and a blue Mustang.

CHAPTER SEVENTEEN

DECEMBER 9, 2011

"I LISTENED TO A TAPE LAST night." Mia chewed her cereal slowly, carefully. The morning was surprisingly bright, rising to meet her mood.

"Which one?" Ginny asked, lowering her glasses and pushing the morning paper aside, deciding whatever Mia was about to say was far more interesting than the latest news from the West End.

"The 'first love' tape." Mia focused on nonchalance, sipping her glass of freshly squeezed juice.

"Whoa, back up just one minute, sweetness…love?"

"Yes, love. I love him, Ginny." Mia allowed a small smile before going back full force to the bowl.

"Wow. I take a week to go visit my son, and *bam*… you're in love." Ginny let out a long, low whistle and settled back in her chair.

"Do you think it's too soon?" Mia asked, concerned. She wasn't sure how this love thing was supposed to work.

"Everyone moves at their own pace, Mia. Sometimes it's fast, and sometimes it's slow." Ginny waved her hand in the air, dismissing Mia's concerns.

"Oh," Mia nodded, it sounded very much like what her mother said on the tapes.

"I think you're young..." Ginny allowed. "So I want you to be safe and responsible with your feelings and where they may...go..." Ginny smiled as she trailed off, adding a subtle wink for good measure.

"Ginny, are you talking about sex?" Mia laughed at the thought. Aunt Sophia had beat her to the punch years ago—the bees and birds weren't strangers to Mia.

"More or less," Ginny admitted, running her finger along he lip of her coffee cup.

"Aunt Soph already told me about it, don't worry." Mia felt the all-too-familiar blush creep up her neck, threatening her cheeks.

"All the same, if you need to go to a doctor, you let me know, okay? No need to be embarrassed about these things, I raised four kids. I know a thing or two. Now, tell me about the tape."

Mia shook her head, trying to empty her mind of the almost sex talk.

"Mom told me about her first love." Mia gathered her bowl and spoon and made her way to the sink. "She told me how love is about balance, and how my first love will be the sweetest."

Ginny nodded. "Your mom was a very smart woman."

"I listened to tape like ten times, just to hear her voice," Mia admitted. Hearing her mother's laugh, hearing her tell a story—it was addictive. "I felt like I got to know her a little, like she was real again, like she was there, in my room, and understood exactly how I was feeling and said exactly what I needed to hear."

"I believe that was the point, honey. She wanted to

stay with you in whatever way she could, and I think she'd be so happy to know that you feel like she's still here when you listen to the tapes."

"I really did, it was weird. I fell asleep seeing her— she was young and carefree, with this boy who she loved." Mia smiled. "I pictured her licking the side of a ice cream cone under the Chicago sun, perched atop a glittery blue Mustang, dreaming about becoming a writer and being madly in love with a boy who would soon be off to fight for his country."

"That's probably very close to how it was," Ginny mused, loading the mess from the sink into the dishwasher.

"So guess what?" Mia changed the topic.

"Hmm?"

"Dad has a girlfriend." Mia hopped on top of the counter, calculating how long she had before she'd officially be running late.

"Mmhmm."

"And I'm going to meet her."

That got Ginny's attention. "Really? When?"

"We're going to Seattle on Friday. I'm driving down after school." Mia pulled a loose thread on her jeans.

"That'll be nice. Are you excited?"

"Kind of. Interested, curious. This Kris lady is apparently *very important* to Dad." Mia mimicked her dad's tone.

"Is that so?"

"Yeah, that's what he said. He tried to do the whole 'she's my friend' thing, but I saw through that real quick." Mia added the quotation for good measure.

"And you'll remember to be nice? Even if you don't take to her right away?" Ginny adjusted her glasses and pulled a bunch of tomatoes from the fridge.

"Of course! At least, I'll try," Mia amended, wondering for the first time how she'd feel if it turned out Kris wasn't what she was imagining.

"Good. You can't go runnin' around with bad manners." Ginny pulled a knife from the carving block and turned the faucet on ice cold.

"But what if I don't like her, or what if she doesn't like me?" Mia worried.

"Honey, you are who you are...she is who she is, and if your father picked her, I'm sure she's a good person. You'll take it as it comes, that's all anyone can ask of you."

Mia nodded in agreement, hoping off the counter. "I've gotta go to school."

"Okay, sweetness, your lunch is in the fridge." Ginny gestured the knife toward the fridge.

"Thanks, Ginny, see you later." Mia kissed her quickly on the cheek, gathered her things, and made her way towards the front door.

The drive into Seattle was easy. Mia had enjoyed the way the Jeep took the curves and rolled over the empty, winding roads. Her nerves jangled hard; she wasn't sure how this was supposed to go. Was she supposed to hug Kris or could she just shake her hand?

As she pulled into the restaurant, she mentally stecled herself for whatever was waiting for her.

"You made it in one piece." Gabe walked across the damp parking lot towards her, and Mia's eyes darted around the parking lot, looking for any hint of Kris.

"Hey, Dad." Mia gave him a quick hug, looking

over his shoulder.

"How was the drive? Okay?"

"Super easy. Am I late?" Mia glanced at her watch.

"No, not at all. Kris is over there." Gabe gestured towards the sloping green canvas awning illuminated by soft spots of light bleeding from the restaurant's entryway.

Mia spotted her. She wasn't what she had been expecting. Beneath the awning stood an average looking blonde clutching a small leather bag, gnawing nervously on her lip. Mia caught her eye and raised an arm meekly in greeting.

"Ready?" Gabe draped his arm over Mia's shoulder, guiding her toward the door of the restaurant.

"Sure." Mia inhaled through her nose.

Soft music pooled out the door, greeting them as they walked towards the restaurant.

"Mia?" Kris smiled.

Mia took her in. She had thick, buttery blonde hair that snaked over her shoulders, heavily fringed bangs, hauntingly bright green eyes—like backlit emeralds, silky tan skin, and full lips that spread into the most glorious smile. She wasn't thin; she was curvy and full, dressed in an amethyst silk sheath that hugged and flowed in all the right places. Bangles of raw-cut stones clattered on her wrists when she waved hello and matched the necklace strung around her neck, and a tiny diamond glinted from one exposed earlobe. Her nails were cut short and buffed to a high shine. She was manicured and feminine and pretty, but just short of beautiful. Her eyes were close set and her button nose was just a tad too large for her face.

"Hi." Mia walked over and extended her hand.

"It's so nice to finally meet you! Thank you for coming to Seattle." Kris grasped her hand; her skin was warm and soft.

"No problem." Mia hesitantly smiled.

"Shall we go in?" Gabe tugged open the door and held it while they passed through.

"This is my favorite place, the seafood is delicious. Do you like seafood?" Kris conversationally inquired as Gabe wandered to the hostess podium to give their name.

"Sure." Mia shrugged, feeling awkward and out of place alone with Kris, wishing she'd insisted that Ginny come. She realized that this place must be somewhere they go often, feeling for the first time that her father had a whole separate life she knew so little about. That truth smacked like an ugly secret, but she also supposed to same could be true for anyone. Wasn't she different with her friends than with she was with her father? Didn't she keep things to herself until the time came to share. That was human nature.

"Your dad says the crab cakes are the best here, but I'm not so sure—too much cake, not enough crab. I like the salmon, or the tuna steak...those are both really good." Kris smiled brightly.

"Okay." Mia shrugged indifferently.

"Our table's ready." Gabe made his way back to Kris and Mia, holding his hand out for Kris's.

"Great," Mia followed behind slowly, feeling slightly sick at the easy way they moved with the practiced poise of a couple, with a subtle familiarity. She watched as he dropped Kris' hand to pull out a chair for her, and then one for Mia.

"So, Mia, how was school?" Kris asked, opening

the thick leather folder, letting her eyes slide down, reading the specials.

"Good, happy it's Friday." Mia opened her own menu, wishing she were at home in the comfort of her bed with a pizza box and a stack of movies.

"I remember that feeling." Kris laughed, closing the menu, reaching over to brush Gabe's arm, meeting his eyes. "Tuna steak tonight for me." She smiled.

"How's Bryan?" Gabe interjected, closing his menu and turning his attention to Mia.

"He's good. Camping and hiking this weekend, so that should be fun." Mia chewed her lip, trying to decide between a seafood salad and a simple lobster bisque.

"How fun!" Kris seemed genuinely enthused. "Whereabouts?"

"Just the rainforest, they go there all the time." Mia decided on her meal and placed her menu on top of the others on the table.

"Wow, it's cold this time of year," Gabe chimed in.

"I think that's part of the fun." Kris smiled and winked at Mia. "I know, when I'm traveling the elements always make it that much more exciting. They add to the unknown. You can plan, but not for everything, somethings you just have to wing."

The waiter wandered over, offering a bottle of wine, which Gabe approved. Mia ordered a soda.

"Speaking of which, I'm going on assignment over the holidays," Kris announced, sipping her wine.

"Really?" Gabe's eyes narrowed.

"Yes, I was hired on to take the photos for a Best Holiday Getaways piece, and they want photos from the actual holiday celebrations there." Kris shrugged.

"Well, that's great. Where are you going?" Gabe asked, picking at salad of leafy greens and cherry tomatoes drizzled heavy with blue cheese dressing.

"St. Kitts." Kris spooned a little soup into her mouth, dabbing at the corners with a cloth napkin.

"That should be fun," Mia interjected, imagining the sky blue surf and sun-warmed sand.

"Have you ever been?" Kris asked, fixing her eyes on Mia.

"No, we usually do Hawaii or California, sometimes Cabo."

"You should absolutely go sometime, it's wonderful." Kris smiled again and dipped a piece of crusty table bread into her soup.

Gabe and Kris dissolved into conversation and Mia watched them, the way Kris would rest her hand lightly and affectionately on Gabe's arm when she spoke, or how Gabe would casually rest his arm across the back of Kris's chair. She noted the way Kris's eyes would flash when she smiled, and the way her father would work hard to make that happen, as though her happiness was his reward.

"So, Mia. Your dad has a meeting tomorrow, which shouldn't be long—so he says—but I was thinking we'd take advantage of that and go get pedicures or manicures or, oh, maybe facials?" She was excited, Mia could tell; it didn't seem forced or put on for the benefit of Gabe. It was genuine anticipation.

"I've never had a facial," Mia replied, glancing down at her nails. She had painstakingly painted them last night under the light of her desk lamp; the sparkly red was the latest OPI color from their holiday collection, but it looked sloppy and undone to her now, under the romantic lights of the restaurant.

"Then facials it is! I think I have the spa menu at home somewhere, you can pick whatever you'd like—my treat." The smile again, winning and endearing and sweet; it was hard to look into something so warm and not smile back.

"Can we go to Pike Place?" Mia asked, remembering her list of Christmas gifts to buy.

"Of course! Your dad told me that you needed to do some Christmas shopping. We can do whatever you want, we don't have to do the spa—"

"No, the spa sounds great. I just thinking in addition to, not instead of," Mia shook her head, not wanting hurt Kris' feelings.

"Excellent, then it's set...Pike Place and the spa. We're going to have so much fun." Kris reached across the table and grabbed Mia's hand in her own, squeezing it.

CHAPTER EIGHTEEN

DECEMBER 10, 2011

"So, Mia, did you decide what you want?" Kris asked, munching on a pineapple slice at her white washed kitchen table.

Mia had hovered over the menu for a solid ten minutes. Each facial description was better than the last, making it hard to decide. Words like *honey blossom, chocolate, seaweed, and twenty-four-karat gold* bounced off the page, offering pure luxury and total indulgence.

"What do you normally get?" Mia asked, looking up.

"Um, let's see...last time I did the Chocolate Lover's, it was nice, but I left smelling like a Hershey's bar," Kris broke into carefree laughter, her head tilting back, flashing her perfect teeth with abandon, and Mia couldn't help but laugh along. "The twenty-four-karat is pretty awesome, my skin was literally glistening. Can you believe they actually massage gold paste into your skin? It's unreal, all the rage in India."

Mia glanced down at the price and immediately disregarded the three-figure facial. The cheapest on the page was a teen facial, simple and to the point—

wash, scrub, mask, polish—and that was still pricey.

"Maybe the teen one?" Mia closed the pamphlet and slid it away, back towards Kris.

"Mia, this is my treat. Something I want to do." Kris laughed. "A little splurge. You're getting the gold facial and so am I! That teen stuff isn't worth it, and you know what? We deserve the good stuff." She pushed her chair away, reaching for the phone that sat on the counter.

Mia listened while Kris made the appointment for late in the afternoon, adding on two pedicures at the last minute.

"We're all set! Why don't you go and get changed, and then we can head over to the market?" Kris suggested, gathering the tray of fruit and depositing it back in the fridge.

Kris's apartment was an amazing pre-war, with wood-clad ceilings and thick moldings, heavily knotted scuffed plank floors—everything was clean and soft and eclectic, with framed photos cluttering most of the white walls and built-in bookcases dotted with treasures from faraway places. Kris had explained that her art was her focus, which, she reasoned, explained the lack of color elsewhere. The guest room was small and filled with comfortable things. Kris had put a mini fridge beside her bed and stuffed it with soda and water. The bed was made up with a bright pink quilt that Kris had probably found in some secluded beach town, Mia figured. There was a phone, which Kris encouraged her to use if she needed to call anyone, and a closet with extra pillows and towels. An en suite bathroom was an unexpected surprise, and was nicely finished with a huge claw foot soaking tub and marble surfaces of heavily veined white and grey.

Gabe had left earlier, kissing them both goodbye before slipping away to work. Kris had fixed a small breakfast of fresh fruit and muffins, laughing about her lackluster cooking abilities and apologizing.

"Okay, thanks." Mia stood up and pushed her chair in carefully.

Kris settled back down with a thick manila folder and the portable phone, giving Mia a small wave as she padded out of the room down the long, narrow hallway towards the guest room.

Rain pelted the thin panes of the old windows, the sky was smothered with thick, low clouds, and Mia suddenly lost all motivation to get changed, spying the plush bed with its disheveled warm quilt and well-washed flannel sheets. It was comfortable. Lying down in the warm bed, Mia reached for her cell phone, punching in Ginny's familiar number.

"'Ello?" Ginny's voice burst on the line.

"Ginny, it's Mia,"

"Oh hiya, sweetness, how's Seattle?"

"Good, not bad. We're going to the spa today and Pike Place, and I'm going to grab us some of that jam." Mia settled back against the pillows in the unfamiliar room, suddenly feeling homesick.

"Golden raspberry, and I'll bake us some corn muffins" Ginny enthused over the line. "And Kris—she's nice?"

"She's nice." Mia bit her lip, holding back the tears that threatened, burning behind her eyes.

Hearing Ginny's voice reminded her of home. Her bed, her things, her mother. This walk-up apartment was lovely and Kris was lovely and the weekend she'd planned was lovely, but it all felt bittersweet, and she longed for what was hers.

"What's wrong, honey?" Ginny voice lulled with concern.

"I don't know. I was fine—I was, really. I guess I just feel kind of thrown." Mia gritted her teeth, willing herself not to cry.

"Where's your dad, honey?" Ginny asked.

"Working. He had a meeting, last minute I guess, I don't know." Mia rubbed her eyes.

"And you're with Kris, alone?" Ginny's voice sounded oddly judgmental, a tone she rarely used.

"Yeah." Mia felt like a little girl again, away at sleepover camp, calling home to feel a connection.

"You're gonna be fine, Mia, just fine. Let me guess: you're still in your jammies, snuggled up in bed?"

"Mmhmm." Mia smiled, Ginny knew her so well.

"All right, that's the problem. You're trapping yourself. Go get in the shower, wash your face, put on something comfortable, and go shopping. You'll feel better in neutral territory."

"Okay…" Mia sighed, knowing Ginny was probably very close to the truth.

"I'll be around all day, doin' nothing but watchin' TV, so you call me if you need me, 'kay, sweetness?"

"Okay."

"Good girl, now go get cleaned up and try to be optimistic—you promised me," Ginny reminded her.

Mia hung up the phone and wandered into the bathroom, turning on the water as hot as it would go. Testing it with her fingertips, she stripped off her nightshirt and bottoms and stepped into the stall. The water was soothing and healing as it ran rivers through her hair and down her back and arms and legs. She lathered and conditioned, brushed her teeth, and shaved her legs. She felt better as she wrapped herself in one of the bright, overly fluffed white towels that were hanging on a chrome hook.

Mia slipped into a pair of worn out jeans and a soft jersey knit long sleeve shirt, pulling her damp hair back into a knot. Padding back down the hall, she found Kris sitting at the table still, putting her folder away in a worn leather messenger bag.

"You look cute." Kris smiled and tucked the bag under her built-in desk. "Ready to go shopping?"

"Sure." Mia smiled, stepping into her shoes and pulling on her raincoat.

"Great." Kris looped her arm through Mia's and pulled her towards the door.

Kris pressed the button on her key-fob and the lights of a silver Escalade in the parking garage blinked.

"Nice car." Mia settled into the waxy black leather seats, looking around the massive cabin.

"Thanks." Kris laughed as she started it up and pulled skillfully out of the tight spot. "So you probably have a lot of questions for me, huh?" Kris smiled as she flipped the wipers on, heading out onto the main street.

"Yeah, kind of," Mia admitted.

"Okay, the floor's yours…ask anything you'd like."

"How long have you been seeing my dad?" The question slipped past Mia's lips before she could stop it. She'd been wondering since last night after watching their obvious comfort with each other.

"About nine months, maybe a little bit longer. We were friends first." Kris glanced over at Mia, waiting for her reaction.

"Wow," was all Mia could say. She felt like a visitor to another planet where there was a whole other world of people she thought she knew.

"That feels weird, right?" Kris offered.

"Honestly? Yeah, it does. It's like my dad, the guy who lives in my house with me, who hangs out and eats dinner with me, who I should know better than anyone in this world, has this whole double life three hours away..." Mia looked out the window, studying the buildings as they slid past.

"I can understand that." Kris nodded her head, biting down on her lower lip before continuing, "But I think he's keeping me private came from a place of love. I felt kind of the same way, you know? Here's this guy, who I was starting to love, and he had this whole other life that I couldn't be a part of—I mean, of course I knew about you, and Ginny, but it was off-limits to me. But honestly, it was only to protect you. He loves you so much and he didn't want to give you more than you could handle."

Mia sat quietly, thinking about Kris's words. "Protecting me from what?" Mia asked.

"Well, I think he didn't want you to get tangled up in a relationship that wasn't a sure thing." Kris tried to explain. "I think your dad wanted to know me first, make sure I was a good, solid person, someone you should get to know...and also to figure out how he felt about me...before bringing you into our relationship—before you and I could build a relationship. He doesn't want to take people away from you."

Mia had to admit that her logic made sense.

"So you and my dad are serious, then?"

Kris nodded. "We are. I'm not going to confuse you with double talk...I love your dad very much. He's a good man, he makes me laugh, and we have fun together."

"Can I ask you something kind of personal?" Mia couldn't stop herself now; Kris was so candid and forthcoming that she wanted to press a little more.

"Of course..." Kris replied, climbing out of the car.

"You were married before, right?"

"Yes, I was."

"Why didn't that...work out?" Mia felt her face burn with a fresh blush.

"I was very young when I got married, not much older than you, if you can imagine that." Kris chirped the locks and kept pace with Mia as they walked across the empty parking lot. "We were high school sweethearts, and he asked me to marry him on our graduation day." Kris smiled at the memory. "We went off to college together and were married the summer after our freshman year. We worked our way through school, graduated, bought a small home not too far from where you live now—Gig Harbor. He went into law school immediately, and I started working as a photographer.

"We were like ships passing in the night: he was always at school, and I was on the road, building my portfolio and taking any job that came my way. But we made it work—we really, really loved each other. So, after he graduated law school and went into a well-established practice, he figured we should start a family. He was settled, he'd reached his goals, he was working at a job he loved, making solid money...he felt finished—if that makes sense.

"For my part, I wasn't sure what I wanted, but my career was just taking off. I was starting to get the sorts of jobs that paid a lot of money, and I was starting to get noticed, doing what I loved to do—it was bliss for me, I loved it. But that sort of success requires a lot from the someone. I traveled all the time, I worked crazy hours editing and developing, I was always involved in something...it just felt to me like having a baby right then would be unfair to the child. Honestly, I wasn't ready to settle down and do the whole 'Mom' thing. But he was. He wanted kids and all that went along with them; he didn't want to wait, and I felt it was unfair to ask him to...so we went our separate ways—it wasn't because we hated each other, or because our relationship was bad, but I loved him enough to let him go find the things that he really wanted—and in turn, he did the same for me." Kris pulled her wool sweater tighter across her middle.

"Did you ever get remarried?" Mia knew she hadn't—her father had only mentioned one divorce—but she couldn't think of anything else to say.

"No." Kris shook her head.

"Do you wish you had, you know, done the kid thing?" Mia asked, painfully curious now.

"Wow, these are heavy questions," Kris laughed before continuing. "Yes, of course, I wish I had a child or two or ten. Kids are great; I have nieces and nephews and when I'm with them, I see what I missed out on. Like now, with you, I see what I missed." She gestured to the space between them.

"But I made a choice. I can't say it was the wrong one, but with every choice—even the right choice—there is always a sacrifice. Even when it's something as simple as ordering dinner, if you choose one entree, you miss out on all the others. But I never really thought when I decided to leave my marriage that having children that the dream of that was over for me. I figured I'd meet someone later, when the time was right, and I'd do the whole parenting thing...but that obviously didn't happen."

Kris read like an open book, and Mia found it hard not to be drawn into her. She was warm, and honest and friendly. She was easy to be with.

"Thanks for being honest with me," Mia added. She wanted to tell Kris she would have been a great mom, but wasn't sure what it would mean to say that to her now.

"Anytime."

They walked in companionable silence for a while, passing stalls of fresh seafood and produce, weaving their way towards the artist booths.

"So what is it you're looking for?" Kris chimed in.

"I need stuff for Dad, Ginny, my Aunt Soph and her three boys, Bryan, my friend Sarah..." Mia rattled off, mentally adding Kris to that list.

"I know this great artist...here, follow me." Kris grabbed her hand and tugged her through the masses of people toward a small stand.

The small shop was perfect. Hand knit scarves hung lightly from rods, colorful hats were strewn across tabletops, and glass bowls overflowed with mittens. It was a beautiful and colorful assortment of winter odds and ends. Mia gravitated towards an emerald green chunky knit scarf with shots of copper thread through it. She gently lifted it off the rod and knew this was perfect for Kris. She grabbed another in pumpkin for

Aunt Sophia, a cheerful red one for Ginny, and a hot pink one for Sarah. She found matching mittens and hats and added those to her basket, as well.

"That was successful." Kris noted the overstuffed brown bag Mia carried.

"That place was awesome!" Mia agreed.

"The boys, now?"

"Yeah..." Mia chewed her lip, looking around for inspiration and finding none.

"Oh! You know what? There is this store right by my house—tons of video games and music and books. Want to go there after the spa?" Kris suggested.

"That'd be great," Mia agreed, thinking she'd snag the boys something along those lines.

They travelled through the rest of the market. Mia picked up a piece of pottery for Aunt Sophia, a hand-thrown bowl for Ginny, a silver and sea glass bracelet for Kris, a vintage watch for her father, and a jar of preserves for everyone to share on Christmas morning. For Bryan, she found a hand-stamped wallet with the Seattle University logo pressed into the tanned leather.

"Mia, do you like crab?" Kris asked as they made their way to the exit, their arms loaded down with Mia's scores for the day.

"Sure." Mia nodded.

"This booth has the best crab; why don't I grab us some for dinner?" Kris fished around her purse and handed Mia a wad of bills. "You can run over there and grab some stuff for a salad—would you mind?"

"No problem."

"Great! Your dad will be happy we're not eating out every night. Meet me by the exit?"

"Yep." Mia turned towards a booth overflowing

with local produce.

She gathered a head of lettuce, a few heirloom tomatoes, a burpless cucumber, a few green peppers, and a bag of homemade croutons. She spotted a bottle of apple dressing and added that to her haul, as well. She also grabbed a couple pints of blackberries, figuring she'd make dessert and hoping Kris wouldn't mind.

"Ready?" Kris smiled as she spotted Mia walking towards her.

"I hope you don't mind," Mia said, holding up the thin plastic bag. "I bought some blackberries, I was going to make dessert..."

"Mind? Of course not! I'm excited—thank you for thinking of it!" Kris gave a wide, perfect smile and started through the door. "What are you making?"

"My mom's blackberry cobbler," Mia swallowed, caught in the sudden onslaught of thinking of her mother.

"Oh." Something Mia couldn't read crossed Kris's face, but she recovered smoothly, smiling brightly. "Sounds great."

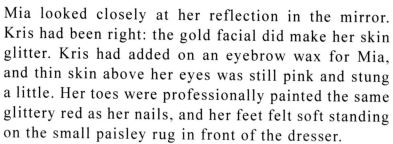

Mia looked closely at her reflection in the mirror. Kris had been right: the gold facial did make her skin glitter. Kris had added on an eyebrow wax for Mia, and thin skin above her eyes was still pink and stung a little. Her toes were professionally painted the same glittery red as her nails, and her feet felt soft standing on the small paisley rug in front of the dresser.

Mia could hear Gabe and Kris laughing in the kitchen. Crab was steaming in a pot and the salad was already laid out on the table in a large terra-cotta bowl that had obvious Indian roots. Mia's cobbler was bubbling in the oven, and she had excused herself to freshen up.

She thought a lot about that day as she appraised her freshly-scrubbed skin and manicured brows. She liked Kris, she decided. She was an interesting enough person, and her dad seemed happy, almost like he was lighter with her around. They bantered back and forth teasingly, laughed at all the same things—even the stuff Mia didn't find remotely funny. The atmosphere around them when they were together was warm and swimming with affection.

Her phone vibrated loudly on the nightstand.

Mia grabbed it quickly and punched the answer button.

"Hello?"

"Hey babe, what's up?" Bryan said on the other end. His voice was smooth and sweet.

"Not much, just hanging out before dinner. How's camping?" Mia asked, twirling a fine strand of hair around her finger, watching the curl stretch and recoil.

"We didn't go. Griff has some sort of flu," Bryan answered, and disappointment edged his tone.

"That sucks, is Sarah sick, too?" Mia made the mental note to call and check on her later.

"I don't think so...but who knows. So tell me, how's Kris?" Bryan sounded genuinely interested.

"So far so good; she's actually pretty nice. We went shopping today and got facials at the spa. It was really fun."

"That's great, babe."

"Yeah. And I can tell my dad is super happy with

her, so that's nice."

"I'm happy it's going well. Are you coming home tomorrow?"

"That's the plan, but probably not until late—but I have my car, so I can leave whenever." Mia knotted her hair at the nape of her neck in a tight coil and wiggled her toes, admiring the precision paint job.

"Cool. Well, call me if you get in early; we can go to a movie or grab dinner or whatever, okay?" Bryan offered.

"I'll call you." Mia stretched.

"Have a good time, babe, love you."

"You, too." Mia disconnected the call and replaced the phone.

In the kitchen, Gabe was stirring rice on the stove and Kris was sprinkling freshly grated cheese on a salad. Red, steaming crab legs sat on a large oval platter beside small dishes of melted butter and cocktail sauce, juicy wedges of lemon filled a bowl. A cobbler sat neatly on a cooling rack beside the stove, and Kris had thoughtfully set out cinnamon and sugar. The kitchen smelled savory and sweet, and was warm, despite the heavy rain and the wind howling against the building.

"This looks...amazing." Mia looked around the kitchen, taking in the delicious bounty that flooded the room. "I thought you said you couldn't cook?"

"I can do some things. And thanks." Kris grinned as she helped Gabe transfer the rice into a serving bowl. "I hope you're hungry; we have enough to feed an army!" Her laugh rang out like bells.

"Starved. Who knew a day of complete relaxation

could totally exhaust you?" Mia joked as she slipped into her chair at the table.

"So you girls had a good time?" Gabe asked, placing the rice on the table.

"It was great, but you better watch out, Dad—I think this was the first of many facial treatments. Thanks again, Kris, that was really nice," Mia teased lightly.

"It was my pleasure. I'm so glad you liked it. Do you have many spas in Port Angeles?" Kris asked.

"Some, not a ton, and nothing as nice as that place we went today." Mia took a heaping helping of salad and drizzled it with the fancy dressing she had picked out today.

"Well, maybe next time I'll come to you—I haven't been to Port Angeles in years." Kris speared a crab leg and dropped it onto her plate, splashing some lemon juice on the white meat.

"You should come out when you get back from St. Kitts," Gabe offered, forking a mound of rice onto his plate.

Kris glanced at Mia, awaiting a reaction. "You should totally come out," Mia agreed, nodding.

"Really? That would be...nice. Thank you, Mia, Gabe." Kris seemed touched by the invitation, and dabbed her eyes quickly with the corner of her napkin.

"Can I just say that I'm happy you two had fun while I had to work all day." Gabe laughed, but there was something deep and real in his eyes—a genuine contentment.

"I got that jam, so Ginny is going to be thrilled." Mia took a small bite of the crab, savoring the way the flavor of the salty and sweet meat exploded over her tongue. "Oh my God."

"What? Is it okay?" Kris asked quickly, a concerned look furrowing her brows.

"It's amazing. Dad, this is seriously amazing." Mia gestured to the leg, giving Kris a thumbs-up.

CHAPTER NINETEEN

DECEMBER 20, 2011

MIA PULLED THE HEAVY CARDBOARD boxes out of storage one by one, carefully hauling them up the steep stairs to the kitchen. Ginny unpacked each ornament, stocking, and decoration with dedicated care.

"It looks good." Mia stood back, her hands raw from the pine needles and balled into fists on her hips.

They'd spent the morning decorating the house, tying bows and sprinkling fake snow across the mantel, righting the tree and icing it with hundreds of blown glass balls in every shade of the rainbow. It was a real winter wonderland, one that even Sophia would approve of. It felt festive and bright, like an air of cheer had blown through the house. A pair of wreaths hung from the door, and Mia wrapped thousands of twinkling lights around the pillars. Ginny had changed the linens in the guest room to festive soft flannel sheets with fat snowmen and jolly Santas dancing across them.

"Real beautiful, Mia." Ginny nodded in agreement.

Ginny was busy melting chocolate on the stove for her famous hot cocoa when headlights swept across the yard.

"Aunt Soph is here!" Mia screamed, launching herself through the door and out onto the porch.

"I always forget how long it takes to get here," Aunt Sophia laughed, half-running to Mia and smothering her in a huge hug, rocking her from left to right. "Look at you—so much like Jenna!" She kissed her cheeks and hugged her again.

In all the years Mia had known Sophia, she had never changed. She still had a sleek, freshly cut blond bob to frame her round face and heavy dollops of pink on her full cheeks, hopeful eyes, and her heavily-lipsticked pout. She was heavier now, rounder and softer, beneath a huge down parka with real mink cuffs.

"You look good." Mia smiled, hugging her back.

Caleb dutifully unpacked the trunk while Harlen and Thomas lugged the expensive luggage and dozens of perfectly wrapped presents to the shelter of the porch.

Sophia still owned her boutique, which had gone all but global, written up in decorating magazines as the place to go for hidden treasures in the South, she was wildly successful and each bit was hard earned and well deserved.

"Guys, put the luggage in the guest rooms and the presents under the tree, then you can go into the basement and play those damn video games," Sophia instructed, linking her arm though Mia's and starting up the porch towards the brightly-lit house. "That's the good thing about having all those boys: built-in helpers," she giggled, resting her head on Mia's shoulder, "I have missed you so much."

Ginny and Sophia hugged for a long time, and then lapsed into chatter about Sophia's flight, the store,

Ginny's family, and her holiday plans, which included two long weeks of travel, visiting her children, who were spread coast to coast.

"That'll be wonderful!" Sophia enthused.

"I'm lookin' forward to all them grandbabies." Ginny's eyes seemed to light up behind her glasses at the mention of her grandchildren, "They are growin' up so darn quick."

"Believe me...I know how that feels. Even when you see them every day, it's like, wow, they're getting so big, so grown up," Sophia agreed, looking towards the basement door, through which the sounds of rapid machine gun fire and screams of dying men filtered.

"So, Mia." Sophia sat down beside her on a bar stool, a cup of hot cocoa in her hand. "Tell me, how is life?"

"It's good," Mia answered quickly.

"And how's the boyfriend?" Sophia nudged Mia lightly, encouraging her, winking at Ginny.

Mia blushed almost painfully, knowing her relationship with Bryan had become the fodder of cross-country gossip. "He's wonderful. He's with his family in Oregon for the holidays."

"So I won't be meeting him?" Sophia took a long swallow of hot cocoa.

"No. He left this morning—he's gone for two weeks."

"That's too bad. I was looking forward to getting to know this Bryan character." She frowned.

"He's great. Isn't he great, Ginny?"

"He's a good young man, comes from a good family," Ginny agreed, loaded down with three mugs of cocoa for the boys.

"I'm very happy for you, honey." Sophia patted Mia's back tenderly. "And you're taking things...slow?"

"Aunt Sophia!" Mia blushed again, hotter than before, flustered.

"Well, are you? I'm not here to be the heavy, honey—really, I'm not. And I'm not trying to embarrass you or put you on the spot or make you uncomfortable. But I'm your aunt and I'm trying to make sure you're doing what's in your best interests. I'm also the mother of three boys and God knows I have a handle on where their minds are...I'm guessing this Bryan fellow is even beyond that," Sophia explained, leveling Mia with a no-nonsense stare.

"Yeah, we're taking things slow." Mia lowered her head, concentrating on her fingernails, avoiding eye contact.

"So no need for a refresher course on the basics and how to be...mature...about things?"

"Oh my God, I am not talking about this. We're not...doing...that, we're not doing anything!" Mia's face felt feverish and she wiped her clammy hands on the legs of her jeans.

"Okay, okay." Sophia held her hands up in surrender. "So, tell me, how's your dad?"

"Oh, oh, oh! I met Kris!" Mia announced, looking up, her lips pulled into a small smile.

"You did? When?" Sophia asked. Her lack of surprise let Mia know that Sophia probably already knew.

"Last weekend. We went into Seattle and I spent the weekend with them there," Mia explained.

"How was it? Did you like her? Tell me everything!" Sophia beamed, clasping her hands together, resting her chin on them, fully engaged.

"She was really nice. She took me to the spa and we got facials and pedicures and I had my eyebrows waxed. She helped me with my Christmas shopping. Dad's different with her. Happier. He laughs all the time, and I can tell she really cares about him, too—which makes me feel better about things," Mia gushed.

"Oh, honey, that's wonderful!" Sophia smiled, taking a small sip of her cooling cocoa.

"I know, right? I was really hesitant. I kept having these visions of her being like some Wicked Witch of the West—literally—but she wasn't...she was really very cool."

"That's great. Really great. Your dad deserves that," Sophia nodded.

"Hey, Aunt Soph, did you ever...you know...date... after your divorce?" Mia asked hesitantly.

"A little. Nothing ever became serious," Sophia answered thoughtfully, running her finger over the rim of the mug. "I am married to my business, and my boys take up a lot of time—those two halves equal my whole—I don't need more than that. I dated...still date...casually, of course, and I enjoy that for what it is—the fun of it, the novelty of it. But the relationship part of my life—that serious, love of my life, marriage and children and death do us part—that was over for me when Alex left."

Mia understood; she had always figured her father had felt much the same way after her mother had died—until he mentioned Kris and brought her into Mia's life.

"Did the boys ever meet any of your boyfriends?" Mia asked curiously, wondering how it worked for other people.

"Oh, sure. Sometimes. When the guy would come to pick me up, the boys would be home with a babysitter." Sophia grinned wistfully.

"And they were just cool with it? It never bothered them?"

"You have to remember, Mia, Alex remarried right away. The boys were young; it seemed very normal to them for Alex and I to have other...relationships, other people in our separate lives. It took some adjustments at the start, but by the time I got back out there, the boys were pretty comfortable with the fact that they were loved no matter what." Sophia nodded.

"Do you think Mom would want him to fall in love and get remarried?" Mia asked, curiously.

"I think she would." Her lips turning down into a thoughtful frown. "She loved your father very, very much—they were best friends above and beyond all else. She wouldn't want him to be alone for the rest of his life. She worried about him and hoped he'd be happy again someday."

Mia bobbed her head in agreement. "Did you know about Kris?"

"I knew a little about her." Sophia raised her cup to her lips slowly.

Gabe and Sophia spoke often about Mia and life and sometimes Jenna. Their once-cool relationship had warmed up significantly, and they had learned to lean on each other. They counted themselves as family, closely bound family, just as Jenna had wished.

"And you didn't tell me?" Mia felt outrage bubbling in her chest; she had always believed that Sophia was honest with her and would tell her anything. This felt very much like a cruel deception.

"It wasn't my place to tell you, sweetheart. Don't be angry with me. He wanted to be sure Kris was... the right person...before he brought her into your life. And, not to mention, when they met, you were only, like, what? Thirteen?"

Mia drummed her fingers against the cool, dense stone.

Sophia shrugged, tucking a strand of hair behind her ear, where a fat diamond stud sparkled in the low light of the kitchen. "He's been very careful with you, Mia."

"I think they're going to get married," Mia concluded, looking at her aunt for a reaction, but she sat motionless.

"And how would that make you feel?"

"I don't know. I mean, yeah, I like her. She's cool enough and she makes my dad happy. But I like this life, too—as it is, right here, in this home. I don't want this to change." Mia gestured wildly, grandly swooping her arms.

"And you think any of this—all of this—would change?" Sophia asked quizzically.

"How could it not?" Mia asked, resting her chin hopelessly in her hands.

"Well, for starters, your dad likes this place." Sophia pointed out.

"But he loves her!"

"I think you're jumping to conclusions. You need to talk to him about this before you go making yourself crazy over this, honey." Sophia shook her head slowly, patting Mia's arm softly.

Sophia heaved herself off the stool. "I'm going to get changed. If the boys get too loud, just yell at them." She winked, walking slowly from the room.

CHAPTER TWENTY

DECEMBER 25, 2011

Port Angeles was covered with a dusting of dazzlingly white snow as Christmas morning dawned. Gabe stood over the stove, bacon sizzling and popping under his watchful eye, and a felted Santa hat sat on his head. Mia popped several sugar-crusted muffins out of their pan and onto the special holiday platter they only used at this time of year. Sliced fruit was set out on the good silver servers beside a tray of bagels and tubs of cream cheese.

The boys were busy separating gifts, and Sophia was stirring a spoonful of sugar around in her coffee while waiting, laughing gamely at Gabe's Christmas getup.

"A Santa hat?" she snickered, dribbling cream into her steaming cup.

"It's tradition, have some respect," Gabe laughed.

"Dad, the table's all set." Mia washed her hands in the sink and helped herself to a cup of coffee.

"Since when are you a coffee drinker?" Gabe asked, eyeing Mia as she poured a bucket of sugar into her mug.

"For a while now." she announced, sipping it.

"Just like Jenna," Sophia observed.

The room fell silent. Holidays were still hard without Jenna flitting around the house, singing Christmas carols off-key and spiking the eggnog. She had loved Christmas, the rare type who enjoyed the crowds, the hustle and bustle, the wrapping and baking and celebrating. It was hard not to feel her absence on this day of all days.

Even when she had been sick, she still put together wonderful holidays. She'd deck the house with fluffs of white manufactured snow; she'd hang beautiful blown glass globes from the tree in festive colors. And, of course, she'd always place the red felted hat on Gabe's head for good measure. It was harder as the disease progressed, but she never let the importance and wonder of the season slip by uncelebrated.

"Should we eat?" Mia offered, breaking the uncomfortable silence by reaching for a fat muffin.

"Sure." Gabe smiled weakly, moving the platter of crispy bacon to the center of the table, pulling out a chair and settling in.

"Have you heard from Kris?" Mia asked conversationally, taking a healthy bite of the white chocolate blackberry muffin, which was still piping hot in the middle.

"I did—she landed late last night. She said it's warm there and not very Christmas-y. I think she's the sort of person who needs snow to set the scene." Gabe piled his plate with bacon and bagels smeared with cream cheese and golden raspberry jam.

"She have a safe flight?" Sophia asked, biting down on her own bagel.

"Yes, a little snow delay in Chicago, but it was no

big deal."

"Hey...hey boys? We're going to be opening presents after breakfast...so don't get sucked into those games, okay?" Sophia grabbed the back of Caleb's shirt midstride as he headed towards the basement, carrying a plate loaded down with food, and rolled her eyes.

"Mom," Caleb whined, twisting away from her hold.

"I'm just saying...I don't want to hear any of that 'one minute, Mom' stuff this morning...no 'let us just finish this level.' It's Christmas, okay?"

"Got it," he called back, trudging down the stairs. The TV was already blasting the start-up song for whatever mass murder, hunt, and destroy game they were playing.

"Boys." Sophia rolled her eyes again, shrugging her shoulders.

The family room had dissolved into a mess of torn wrapping paper and piles of boxes. Laughter bounced off the walls as everyone was trying on clothes, holding up gifts, and smiling for posed pictures.

"Honey, this is for you...from Kris." Gabe held out a large, square box for Mia.

"Really?" Mia asked, taking the heavy present in her hands, carefully pulling back the paper. "Oh my God, really? Wow! This is so cool!" Mia held up the expensive, obviously professional camera for everyone to see. "Dad, this is great! I should call Kris and thank her...Wow!"

"She thought you'd enjoy it," Gabe said smiling, gathering wads of discarded paper and shoving them deep in a trash bag.

"I can't wait to use it!" Mia beamed, opening the box and looking at the thick, confusing manual.

"Kris said she'd show you all the tricks and stuff when she comes up next weekend."

"She's coming? Next weekend?" Mia asked, still distracted by the tiny print.

"She figured you'd want to show her the ropes here," Gabe gently reminded her.

"Sure, cool." Mia replaced the manual, latching the box. She reached for the last present, her gift from Bryan.

"What's that?" Sophia asked.

"It's from Bryan, he left it for me before he went to see his grandparents."

"That was very thoughtful of him," Sophia commented, glancing at Gabe.

Mia carefully undid the wrapping and lifted the lid on the tiny red velvet jewelry box. Inside, nestled on a bed of cream-colored silk, lay a beautiful necklace. Emerald green and ocean blue stones beveled in hammered silver twinkled under the light of the Christmas tree. A knotted silver chain traced its way behind the bedding, coiled at the bottom of the box.

"Wow." Mia undid the bindings and lifted the necklace up to look at it more closely. The stones were cut in all shapes and sizes; pears and cushions, princesses and ovals all danced together, creating an intricate web.

"That's beautiful," Sophia gasped, letting a low whistle of appreciation escape.

"That's very nice." Gabe admired the pretty pendant that swung from Mia's hand, catching the light.

"He must really like you," Sophia observed.

"Yeah." Mia felt the heavy, observant eyes on her and she flushed instantly.

"Oh honey, don't blush!" Sophia laughed. "That's a great thing, and that's a lovely necklace."

CHAPTER TWENTY-ONE

JANUARY 5, 2012

"MIA?" GABE CALLED TO HER as he walked towards the kitchen. "Can you meet me in my office for a minute? I want to talk to you."

Mia paused her movie and followed him into the office.

The room glowed from the light of two drafting lamps, and Gabe had a beer sitting on the lacquered top of his desk. His legs were stretched out, his hands casually resting behind his head.

"Hey Dad, what's up?" Mia crossed the distance and sat, folding her legs under herself in the overstuffed leather wing chair across from him.

"I wanted to talk you about Kris...and about us—as in, you and I." He paused briefly before continuing.

"I promised you that if anything changed, I would talk to you first, and that's why I called you in here. I want to ask Kris to marry me."

Mia's mouth popped open in an audible "oh" and she felt the wind rush from her lungs.

"I know this feels sudden to you, kiddo, but for Kris and I...it's the natural progression of things. I love her, Mia, and I want her to be my wife."

"Dad..." Mia began, but Gabe held up his hand, stopping her.

"I need you to know that I still love your mom and I always will. Nothing could ever change the way I felt about her. She was two things: She was the love of my life and she was my best friend. For a long time I thought I would never feel for someone else what I felt for her. I didn't think it was possible that twice in life I could be that lucky. But Kris...she's an amazing woman, too. Loving her doesn't diminish what I felt for your mom, if anything, I've found that it makes it stronger and makes me appreciate what she and I had. But the thing about love, Mia, is that you can love two people at the same time, in exactly the same way." He leaned back again, giving Mia the floor.

"I don't know what to say, I have to think about this..." Mia began slowly, thinking of all the fears and questions and concerns she'd calculated over the past few weeks.

"Mia, honey, this isn't a committee vote...I'm asking her to marry me," Gabe leveled with her. "I would like your blessing, but if not that, then at least your understanding."

Mia nodded, climbing out of the chair and walking across the room towards the door. Sophia was in the kitchen battering chicken cutlets.

"Hiya honey, everything okay?" she asked over her shoulder, dipping another tender in her buttermilk before pressing it into the breadcrumbs.

"Dad's marrying Kris," Mia answered numbly.

"What?" Sophia spun on her heels to face Mia, her face creased with confusion.

"Yep, just told me." Mia glanced over her shoulder towards the office door that was now closed, tucking her father away.

"Wow." Sophia tried to force a smile, wiping her hands on the front of her apron.

"Everything is going to change."

Sophia came around the counter and brushed a piece of Mia's hair behind her ear. "Some things are going to change, you're right about that...but not everything."

"I don't want anything to change; I like my life." Mia pulled a face, grumbling.

"Life is full of change. You don't have to like it exactly, but that's how things work. Look at all the changes that—regardless of your Dad and Kris—are coming for you: college, a career, maybe marriage... You can't stand still just because it's comfortable."

"Yeah, but—"

"No buts. Life changes all the time. You have to roll with it, girlfriend." Sophia kissed the top of Mia's head and pulled her in close. "It's terrifying, but certain."

"I'm not scared!" Mia pulled back, stung.

"Of course you are. But think about it...In another couple of years, it will be *you* making the changes. You'll be the one to sit your father down and tell him where you want to go to college, where you see your future heading, and let me tell you this about that: Your decisions will terrify him. He will want to keep you his little girl because that's what all fathers want. But, let me ask you something...what will you want from him when that time comes? Will you want him to mope around and make you feel like you're making a mistake, or, will you want him to give you his blessing to make your life the way you want it to be?"

"I don't know," Mia shook her head.

"I think you do know." Sophia tilted her head and smiled.

Sophia gave Mia another gentle squeeze and went back to fixing dinner while Mia wandered off towards her room. She put away the jacket Sophia had given her, the books and sweaters and jeans and the rest of her Christmas haul, which had been left on the floor for the past few days. She yanked back the covers on her bed and crawled beneath the familiar sheets in her familiar bed in her forever room. It hadn't changed in all the years she'd lived there: she still had the bed her mother had picked out, the same overly washed, soft lavender sheets. The same child-sized white wooden desk. Her built-in bookcases still displayed the piggy bank her mother had painted and the books her mother had read to her. Even the pictures—childish scenes of simple sailboats and wildflowers—hung on the wall; they had survived, despite being sorely outdated.

She didn't want to move to Seattle, she couldn't bear the thought of leaving Ginny or her friends or her school or her house, with its familiar rooms and nooks. But, at the same time, she couldn't imagine Kris living there, either. Mia couldn't envision Kris's clothes hanging in her mother's closet, or Kris taking down her mother's art to hang her photos. She couldn't conceive of a balance between these two worlds, and yet she knew that they would somehow have to blend now, swirl together and change everything.

CHAPTER TWENTY-TWO

FEBRUARY 14, 2012

But change comes.

CHAPTER TWENTY-THREE

MARCH 24, 2012

K RIS AND GABE SAT ACROSS from Mia at the kitchen table, looking serious and thoughtful. A large diamond set low in a thick gold band twinkled on Kris's finger.

"Mia, we want to discuss...changes," Gabe launched, taking Kris's hand in his own. "We both work in Seattle, and we think that it would make more sense to consider...relocating...there."

"That's not what my mom wanted, she wanted me to be raised here, in this home—not in Seattle," Mia challenged, glaring at her father.

"Mia, you'll be leaving for college in another year. And I wouldn't have kept this house when you left; it's way too big for me by myself with you gone." Gabe released Kris's hand and refolded his neatly in front of himself.

"So stay until I go to college!" Mia threw her hands up, shaking her head. It seemed reasonable; Gabe had been commuting to Seattle for years without complaint. Now, in the home stretch, he wanted to move.

"I think it would be easier if we at least entertained

the thought of moving to Seattle—for everyone," Gabe added for good measure.

"This is my home, Dad," Mia pleaded, glancing at Kris who was looking down, not meeting her eyes.

Kris and Gabe had gotten engaged shortly after New Years. They had celebrated with champagne and passed Mia a glass, toasting to love and life and the future. Mia had hugged Kris and congratulated them both, grappling with a feeling of dread.

Kris had become a regular at the Chamberland home. Flitting in and out, flying away for business and coming back tanned and exhausted. She was busy planning their wedding, somewhere warm and tropical where they served drinks with umbrellas and skewers of cherries, a place Mia couldn't pronounce and couldn't find on her desk globe.

And yet, all of that was fine. Mia wasn't so much bothered by the remarriage, or Kris, or Kris's things— she just didn't want to leave her home.

"What about school?" she asked.

"You can finish out your junior year. We won't ask you to leave now. But we can start to process you know, start moving some things to the city on the weekend..."

"And what about Ginny?" Mia glared at her father.

Ginny. Her Ginny. The closest thing she had to a mother, her true best friend in the world, the woman who considered her her own.

"I never planned on letting Ginny go." Gabe sighed. "I figured we'd get a bigger place in the city, she'd have her own space and a plane ticket home for her weekend if she felt like going."

"And what if she doesn't? What if she doesn't want

to leave Port Angeles and move to accommodate you two?" Mia lowered her eyes.

"You're old enough to take care of yourself. Besides, if you're in the city, I'll be around more—no more commuting," Gabe offered, as if that solved all their problems.

"And what about you, Kris?" Mia squared her glare on her. "What's your take on this?"

Kris just shook her head slowly back and forth, her long blond hair swishing softly around her face. Unreadable. Mia wondered idly if it was in disagreement or resignation or something more—disappointment, maybe.

"Mia!" Gabe boomed, half standing up, his hands pressing into the table, leaning forward.

"What, Dad? She's part of this, right?" Mia flung her hand at Kris, challenging her father to declare otherwise.

"You will not be disrespectful. Do you understand me?" he continued, his voice raised just below officially yelling.

"How am I being disrespectful? I only asked her a question...and I'm not the one yelling." Mia sat back, crossing her arms across her chest.

"You know what I mean, Mia, it's not nice—and, more to the point, that's not how I raised you." His tone was still threatening and his eyes flashed with anger.

"Okay, how's this, Dad: Kris, pray tell, what are your feelings on this matter?" Mia asked in a tone dripping with sarcasm and saccharine.

"I can see both sides. But yes, I agree with your father, I think, logistically, it makes more sense for us all to be in the same city instead of jetting all over the place." Kris finally spoke softly.

"Oh surprise, surprise." Mia slumped further into her chair.

"That's it, Mia, go to your room!" Gabe leapt to his feet, smashing his fist on the table. "Go! Now! Out of my sight—and when you can be decent, we'll finish this discussion."

Mia rolled her eyes dramatically and stalked from the room. Mia knew the discussion was over before it started; the decision was made. Two against one never really worked out for the underdog.

Mia pressed her ear against the door, listening to what was being said in her absence.

"I don't want her to hate me." Kris sounded like she was crying.

"She's a teenager, Kris, she's going to hate you— and the rules. I used to called her Tropical Storm Mia, she comes in quick, blows over fast. Let her cool down and think about this without the hysterics." Gabe sounded calm again, rational and smooth—unfazed, which bothered Mia.

Mia could hear chairs being pushed in, and the sound of footfalls as they passed by her door, off to their shared bedroom.

"Fuck you, Dad," Mia whispered. Her feelings weren't some worthless storm; this wasn't something that blew over. This was her life, her whole life.

Frantically, Mia grabbed for her cell phone, and scrolling through her contacts she found Sophia's number and hit 'send.' It was late in North Carolina, but Mia knew Sophia would still be tending to her store.

"Hello?"

"Aunt Soph?"

"Oh, Mia, hi honey, what's up?"

"We're moving," Mia breathed.

"What?" Sophia's voice pitched up an octave.

"Yeah, to Seattle...this summer," Mia spat the words like a curse, dirty and disgusting.

"No!" Sophia's tone sounded disbelieving.

"This summer, Aunt Soph. So we can all 'be together, logistically speaking,'" Mia imitated Kris's voice perfectly.

"That's not very nice, Mia. You shouldn't mock her." Sophia tsked her quietly.

"What am I going to do?" Mia felt like crying, the unspent tears burning behind her eyes.

"You're going to be fine, sweetheart, no matter what, no matter where you live." Sophia was still quiet, her voice calm and reflective.

"I don't want this," Mia whispered.

"I know, honey. You know what I think you should do? You should listen to your mom's tape," Sophia urged.

Mia looked towards the box; she hadn't wanted to listen to that tape. She hadn't wanted any of this. A girlfriend was one thing; a wife was another. But her mother wanted her to be prepared for this.

"Okay." Mia wiped away a stray tear.

"You call me if you need anything, okay, honey?"

"Okay, thanks, Aunt Soph."

"Remember, you're a good girl... Be respectful, none of that snarky mocking stuff—okay?"

"Got it," Mia clicked the 'off' button.

Mia, this is probably the hardest tape for
me. To think about your father meeting and

marrying another woman—that's very hard for me. But the truth is, I love him enough to want that for him. Your father has been an amazing husband, a good, solid partner—he was my very best friend, and the person I was closest to in this world. And for those reasons, I want him to be happy, I want him to have a full life surrounded by people who love him. And that may seem strange to you, but I know, had things been different, he would have wanted the same for me.

When I met your dad, from that first night, I knew he was it for me. The One. He was my future, where my life was going. And we had the most amazing life together. We had the years of being just Gabe and Jenna, living in the city—he was designing, I was writing—and those days were good. Then we moved to Port Angeles and we had you. And, as much as I loved him before—which was a lot—that was multiplied by a thousand. I watched him love you and I knew, without a shadow of a doubt, that I was the luckiest woman in the whole world. Not only was he a good man, but he was a good husband; not only was he a good husband, but he was a good father. And I know he felt the same way about me, that he loved me, and that he cherished our marriage and our family and our time together.

If you're listening to this tape, that means your father has met someone. It means he's going to get married and start a life with someone new, someone whom he loves. And to me, that's a wonderful thing. When I learned that I was dying, I worried about you, naturally. You were just a little girl and you needed so much guidance—but I also worried about your father. I didn't want him to shoulder the responsibility of raising you alone; I didn't want him to be alone, period. I wanted your dad to be happy again, even if that meant with someone else. I wanted him to have a partner, someone to experience life with, someone who will love him—someone he can love in return. And that wish was as much for you as it was for him. I want you to have a mother figure. I know you have Ginny and Aunt Sophia, but I want something more for you. Someone you can go to with questions, someone who will always be in your corner, someone to help you plan your wedding and decorate your first place, someone you'll count among your best friends. A good rule of thumb is to know that you can never be loved by too many people.

I don't want you to feel like, with your father getting married, that she's taking my place. I'm your mother. No one, no matter what, can take that away. But she can be your friend. I don't want you to feel like you're being disloyal to me by welcoming her into our family. And if you love her, you shouldn't feel guilty about that. If you don't always see eye to eye, try. If it's hard, try harder. Remember to always be respectful and kind, no matter what. Remember that this woman means a lot to your dad, so try. And if you just don't like her—which I hope is only a worst case scenario and not the truth—keep in mind, there is good in everyone; sometimes you have to look harder for it, but it's there.

This may be the hardest relationship of your life. It might require compromise on your part; it may require you to dig deep. But like with everything in life, if you're open to the experience, you may take away something precious from it.

I'm sure having a stepmom isn't the easiest thing in the world, no matter how you feel about her, but I'd like to believe that it means that there's just one more person loving you.

I love you.

CHAPTER TWENTY-FOUR

MARCH 25, 2012

"KRIS?" MIA WALKED INTO THE kitchen where she found Kris, sitting with a newspaper laid out in front of her.

"Yes?" Kris lifted her eyes. They looked slightly raw around the edges, and Mia felt a sick pit of guilt opening up in her stomach.

"Do you have a minute?" Mia clasped her hands in front of her, feeling embarrassed by her outburst in the morning light.

"Sure." Kris motioned to the chair across from her.

"I just wanted to apologize. I was a real bitch last night, and you didn't deserve that. I'm sorry."

"It's okay. No harm done," Kris half-smiled, but her expression betrayed her words.

"I was just upset, but not with you," Mia offered, trying to figure out how to explain her emotions. Usually it was easy, but the words weren't coming.

Kris just nodded, saying nothing more.

"This is...new for me. A stepmom, moving...it's a lot."

"I know that, I understand that. I'm really trying

not to be the bad guy here, Mia. But the thing is, this is new for me, too. I don't know what I'm doing. I've never been a parent, and now I have a teenager. I know your life here is stable, but my life is stable, too. None of us—not even your dad—is in familiar territory. And things can't stay the same now—not if this is going to work."

Mia nodded, feeling that Kris had more to say.

"It's not that I want to take away everything from you. And, I guess—well, the first year of marriage is the hardest and maybe it would be easier to keep things the way they are, and maybe it's still worth considering. But the truth is? I don't want to put off the transition. I want us to figure this new life out, and I want to do it together."

"This is all I know." Mia looked around her house, with its familiarity.

"So how can we make this work without you feeling like you're losing everything?" Kris shut her paper and folded her hands on the table.

"Where are we going to live in Seattle?"

"My first thought was my condo," Kris answered. "I already have a darkroom built in, and to find another place with that much room would be hard, but if you want Ginny to come with us, then we can find another place big enough for us all."

"And you can't do that here?" Mia asked, wondering how, for so many years, her father had managed, but Kris couldn't.

"I need to be able to work in the city; my job may seem flexible, but everyone I work with—editors, my agent, everyone—they're all in the city. Your dad—his job is in the city. It just makes more sense to be there where we can work and still be with you."

"But my dad has done the commuting thing for years..."

"And how many hours a week do you think he dedicates to that? It's somewhere around another twenty hours...and the price of those tickets? And the worst part of it is, the time he spends coming and going, that's time he misses with you."

"Can I paint my room?" Mia wondered, thinking of the bland walls.

Kris laughed before giving Mia a wide grin. "Of course you can!"

"Thanks." Mia smiled lightly.

"Do you have any color ideas?" Kris asked.

"I think green—like the forest. I'm going to miss seeing this every morning."

"That would be pretty," Kris agreed. "It's beautiful here. Your mom had amazing taste."

"Thanks. She built this place for me. She wanted us to have a family home—like one of those generational things, some place that would always be ours." Mia looked around the room.

"Really? I didn't know that." Kris followed Mia's eyes around the room, seeing it through the eyes of a daughter who had lost her mother much too soon.

"Yeah. This was her dream." Mia ran her hand over the smooth wood table. Like everything else in the house, her mother had decided on this. It would all be hard to leave behind.

"It was a beautiful dream," Kris agreed.

"Thanks, Kris, for talking to me. I'm really sorry about last night."

"Don't worry about it. I'm just sorry this is so

hard on you. I promise I'll try to remember that." Kris patted her hand softly.

"I think I'm going to go down to the beach—would you like to come with me?" Mia asked, scooting her chair away from the table.

"I'm going to hang around here for a while. I wanted to square up some things with your dad. Maybe later?" Kris stood up, too, heading towards the master bedroom.

"Sure, see you."

"Be careful!" Kris called after her.

———————❦———————

Hollywood Beach always reminded Mia of her mother. As she walked across the small dash of beach with its lazy, lapping waves and black sand, she remembered their family trip to the wild coast, so different than this beach, but she still felt a nostalgic pull. She remembered her mom, on her knees in the rocks with the wind turning the tip of her nose red, telling her about the glass float that she had found bumped up against the bleached driftwood trees washed ashore, and how that had been one of Mia's happiest days.

She wondered what her life would have been like if her mother had lived. Would she be dying to escape this little pass-through town rather than fighting to stay? Would she be like her friends, at constant odds with their own mothers over everything from eye shadow to boys and curfews?

She wanted to remember what her mother had smelled like, and maybe that was what drew her to the beach. In her memories, her mom had always smelt of salt and brine and fresh air. All she had of her mother was this—her house, her room, her things. She'd been too young to remember details, times, and places, and once all of that was gone, would her few memories of her mother slip away, too? If she couldn't touch them anymore, would they fail to remain real? She couldn't be sure, but the thought terrified her.

"Mia?" Gabe's voice shook her from her thoughts. His heavy steps rang like castanets knocking the rocks on the beach together.

"Dad?" Mia started towards him.

"Kris told me you came here. I wanted to talk to you." Gabe motioned for Mia to sit on the damp log tucked into a small inlet.

"I'm sorry about last night, I was out of line." Mia wrapped her thin spring scarf tighter around her neck.

"I know. Me, too. I hate that it got to that place, that's not what I wanted." Gabe sighed, resting his elbows on his knees, looking out across the bay. "You know, your mom loved this place. It's what sold her on Port Angeles."

"Really?" Mia followed his gaze out over the bay.

"Yeah. We drove all over this state looking for the right place to raise a family. This spot fit. She used to say you'd have the best of all worlds here...the city, the coast, the rainforest...she said it was the perfect place for a child to grow up, and she was right." Gabe was far away then, seventeen years in the past, in a place where his wife was still alive and their whole lives stretched out before them.

"I didn't know that," Mia murmured softly.

"Kris had an idea. And I think it could work, but you'd have to agree," Gabe began. "This house was for you...well, for us...but mostly, it was for you. Your mom said to me *build me a house and I'll write us a happy ending.* Your mom paid for this house when she started making money from her books—so, really, that money is yours, because of your trust."

Mia wasn't really following, but nodded, willing him to continue.

"I can save this house for you. We can take care of it as needed, come up on the weekends or once a month or whatever—like a vacation property. It won't be yours until you finish college, but if you still want it then, you can have it—or you can sell it and take the money—but the choice will be there no matter what you decide."

"Really?"

"Yeah. This house is free and clear now. It costs money to run and maintain, of course, but...this house was built to be a family home, and Kris was right: it should be a family house. But for right now, kiddo, we need to move on." Gabe nodded into the light breeze. "I don't know if I did right by you, Mia, keeping you here all these years after Mom was gone. Leaving you, flying to Seattle every morning and back every night, depending so much on Ginny...part of me wonders if, maybe, I don't know—if I should have done things differently."

"Dad..." Mia word drifted.

"I don't want this to be hard on you, hon. I want you to be happy, and it kills me to know that you're not."

"I'm okay, Dad, really, and I promise I'll keep trying." Mia scooted over and looped her arm through her dad's, resting her head on his shoulder. "There are just a lot of changes...but you deserve to be happy, and I understand that."

Gabe and Mia sat like that until the sun fell out of the sky and the darkness swallowed them.

Kris was fixing a light dinner of Greek salad and crusty bread, working her way around the kitchen when Gabe and Mia walked through the front door.

"Hi guys, dinner's almost ready." She placed the large bowl down on the table. "Did you two have a nice afternoon?"

"Yeah, we talked about the house." Gabe smiled, walking over to the sink to wash up.

"Kris...thanks." Mia ambled over to Kris and wrapped her arms around her.

"Oh." She laughed lightly in surprise before winding her arms around Mia. "You're very, very welcome."

CHAPTER TWENTY-FIVE

MAY 8, 2012

M IA FINISHED BUILDING THE LAST box left, taping
down the flap and then neatly filling it with her
fall and winter clothes. Her room looked almost the
same: the book shelves were still adorned with all
of her knickknacks, the old desk was cluttered with
stationery, pencils, paperclips, and her old computer.
Her dresser was still in the same nook, only emptied
of all of her clothes.

"Keep everything you'll need for the weekends
here; it'll make it easier for us to come and go," Kris
called from down the hall, where she was dutifully
packing Gabe's work clothes, sorting them from his
casual stuff she would later supplement in the city.

Mia tucked her glass float safely between two
sweaters, figuring a bit of home in her new room
would be nice.

"The movers will be here around ten in the morning
tomorrow, so make sure you're totally packed!" Kris
hollered again.

"I'm almost done," Mia answered and snapped a
roll of tape against the top of the box, smoothing it

closed, then sliding it across the floor to where all the others sat.

Mia found Ginny lounging in the family room.

"Hey Ginny, what's up?"

"Just relaxing, sugar."

Ginny wasn't joining Mia in her life in Seattle, and in many ways that was harder than leaving the house. But Mia knew the truth: Ginny was older now, slowing down. Ginny had started a second life when she was hired on by the Chamberlands to care for Mia while her mother underwent to treatment. It was supposed to be only temporary. At that time, Ginny had already been a sixty-year-old widow. She had already raised her children and sent them off into the world, and had somehow gotten snagged into raising another child. Now, she was seventy-six. Her hair was a puff of grey, her skin slack with webs of wrinkles. She was still strong and smart and no-nonsense, but she wasn't moving to Seattle with them.

Mia had cried hard when Ginny had told her that. Begged and pleaded and promised she'd be good, easy to look after. But Ginny had just hugged her tight and tried to explain that the time had come and her life was here.

"So are you all packed up and ready to go?" Ginny patted the cushion beside her for Mia to join her.

"Pretty much." Mia collapsed down beside her.

"Are you gettin' excited?" Ginny had tried to convince Mia that the big city would woo her and win her over with its eclectic shopping, delicious restaurants, and boundless energy, but Mia wasn't sold.

"Eh." Mia shrugged, laying her head back.

"This is gonna be a good move for you, change

of scenery."

"I love you, Ginny, and I'm going to miss you a lot."

"I love you, too, honey. And I'm going to miss you a lot more than you'll miss me." Ginny patted Mia's knee.

"I just feel like everything has changed so much. And it's not that I'm not happy...I'm trying..." Mia trailed off.

"Find the good—'cause there's lots of good about this."

"What do you mean?"

"Well, for starters, you're gettin' yourself a wonderful stepmom. Kris is a nice lady, and I can tell she cares about you a great deal. You're gonna be livin' in Seattle, and you're gonna get to do big city things—like museums and taking in all kinds of culture. You're not sellin' this house, and when you come back on weekends, I'll be beatin' down this door to spend time with you." Ginny made a short list.

"I just...don't...want to leave you," Mia admitted, and she dabbed at her eyes with the cuff of her sweatshirt. The thought of saying goodbye to Ginny crushed her.

"Do you know something I don't? 'Cause from the way I see it, you're not leaving me, I'm a phone call away, and I'll be seeing you every few weekends or so. Besides, in another year you'd be goin' off to college, and I'd be staying here in Port Angeles anyway—you wouldn't want me where you're going to off to college with you." She laughed loudly at the last part.

"I know...it's just...hard."

"Life is sometimes hard, but you can't give yourself

permission to wallow in it. That isn't how I raised you; that's not what I taught you to do. You have been like a daughter to me in many, many ways—and I will always count you among my kids. And you moving? Hurts like hell for me, too. But that's how this goes, this whole childrearing thing. You give 'em roots and then you give 'em wings."

Mia wandered over to the windows and thought about what Ginny had said. This home—it was her root system. Stable, healthy, nourished, and loved. She didn't need to stay here to keep that with her. But her wings, she wanted to try them now.

"I'm gonna go, sugar." Ginny hefted herself from the couch and started towards the door.

"You're leaving?" Mia spun around, panicked. She wasn't ready.

"Relax, I'll be back in the morning. I'm just tired, need a good nap." Ginny winked and called out a goodbye to Kris.

"Ginny?" Mia called out.

"Yes, hon?" Ginny replied, pulling on her shoes by the door.

"I love you," Mia almost whispered, her voice carrying over the empty space of the house.

"I'll always loved you, too. Always."

———————❧———————

Kris had ordered pizza from a local shop, and the greasy cardboard box laid across the table, paper plates smeared with forgotten toppings shoved into the garbage can. Gabe had grabbed a beer from the fridge before shutting himself in his office to finish packing. Kris was mulling around the house, moving from one task to another.

Mia grabbed her phone and strayed into the family room, punching in the familiar set of numbers.

"Bryan! Oh, hey, I've been trying to reach you! Where have you been?" Mia breathed a sigh of relief into her phone, laying down on the couch.

"Oh, hi, Mia. I've been...busy. What's up?" he asked, his voiced sounding faintly of disinterest.

"I was just calling to say hi—we're leaving in the morning and I just wanted to..." She sat up, resting her elbows on her knees, feeling slightly off kilter.

"Can I come over? " Bryan cut her off casually..

"Oh—sure, yeah." Mia brightened. She wanted to feel her hand in his; she wanted to talk about how things in Seattle might be good and exciting for them.

"Okay, cool. See you." The phone clicked off quickly.

Mia pulled on a light summer-weight sweater and her hiking shoes. Boxes held most of her belongings now, and they were stacked high along the walls boarding the hallways.

"Dad? Kris? Bryan is going to stop by, we'll be in the yard!" She slid the slider closed and settled into a chair to wait for him.

The woods beyond her yard smelled mossy and fresh. Mia wished she had brought her camera, wished she could document the wonder and beauty and grace of her childhood home, knowing that soon the wide open spaces and towering trees would be replaced with gritty concrete, chrome, and glass buildings. She wanted to somehow keep all of this with her when they left.

"Hi." Bryan had come up behind her silently.

"Oh, Jesus, you scared me." Mia laughed, clutching her chest.

"Sorry." Bryan shuffled his feet, looking down.

"I've been trying to call you all day...Kris wanted to know if you wanted to join us for dinner. We're leaving tomorrow—"

"I know."

"And you what? Just didn't answer?" Mia felt the prickle of outrage.

"I was busy."

"Oh, that's okay, would you like to—"

"Mia—" Bryan cut her off.

"What's wrong?" Mia blurted out.

"What do you mean?" Bryan asked innocently, his eyes going wide with surprise at her question.

Mia fingered the necklace he had given her for Christmas, the rough stones under her fingers, distracting her from the panic rapidly building in her chest. "You're acting...weird, Bryan, what's going on?"

"Mia..." Bryan began, kicking at a clump of wood chips. "This isn't working anymore." He avoided her eyes. "I think we should, you know, just be friends."

"Are you breaking up with me?" The words jumbled in her mouth and she watched as he lifted his head and looked at her.

"What? You want to—why?" Mia asked incredulously, gasping.

"I've been thinking about this for a while now, trying to figure out a way to—be fair to you," he stuttered over his words.

"You've been...thinking about this?" Mia felt a pain rip into her chest. She wanted to fall to the ground. She loved him, trusted him, and he had been planning on leaving her, plotting to hurt her.

"I don't know, Mia, it's just that...I'm going to college, it's a different world than you're going to be living in." Bryan raised his hand as if to cup her face, but let his hand fall back to his side, looking into her eyes. "It's not that I don't...love you anymore, I do... but things are going to be ... different now, and I think it would just be easier for both of us if—"

"But..." Mia began, biting her tongue, cutting him off. His words were empty shells, devoid of meaning and sincerity. She tasted blood. She wanted to yell at him, scream that she hated him and that he was ruining her life, taking away the last bit of her familiar happiness, her normalcy. But she couldn't. She wouldn't give him the satisfaction of that.

Her words failed her, fell away into black nothingness, and she let them go. She felt hollow and broken, standing in the same place where he'd once professed his love for her.

"I'm sorry, Mia...really. I hate myself for doing this, and I should have realized before how hard it would be, you in high school, me in college, but I can't—I won't—lead you on anymore. I hope you can understand."

"I'll be fine," she lied, willing herself not to cry, gnawing on her lip, swallowing down the thickness in her throat.

"I know you will." Bryan pulled her in close, pressing her against him.

She breathed in deeply. He smelled like he always did, also of something sweet, something she didn't recognize, something delicate and floral. And then she knew. Mia tugged herself out of his embrace; she spun around and headed back towards the safety of her home.

"Goodbye, Bryan," she called over her shoulder, quickening her pace, pleading with herself to save the tears until she was in the privacy of her room.

"Mia, wait..." he called after her. She could hear him start after her and quickly give up, but she didn't slow down or turn around or speak another word. She left him standing there, not caring whether he stayed or left, lived or died. He wasn't her Bryan anymore, she didn't know the boy standing there, calling after her; her Bryan was gone, and for how long, she didn't really know.

Mia breezed by Kris, who stood frozen, watching with a fearful expression that mimicked Mia's, her hand half-extended, unsure.

She slammed the door to her room with enough force to shake the frame.

And she let herself go.

The tears were silent and vicious, wracking her body, shaking her, spilling down her cheeks, pooling at the hollow of her throat. Everything hurt and her eyes burned, her stomach heaved with violent, empty retches, and she couldn't breathe. She wrapped her arms around herself until the emotional onslaught passed.

Mia knew Kris was outside her door, and that comforted her, but she didn't want her—or Gabe or Sophia or even Ginny—she only wanted her mom.

Scrambling to her feet, she opened the small box on her desk, shuffling the tapes noisily until she found the one she needed. Snapping open the compact plastic sleeve, she wrestled the tape inside the small recorder, clamped it shut, stomped her finger down on the play button, exhaled, and listened. Her mother's voice filled her room.

Right now, you probably feel like the world has ended and you're the sole survivor; alone and scared and confused...and most of all—worst of all—hurt.

When I started recording these tapes for you, sweetheart, there were some I hoped you would never listen to...this was just one of them. But a broken heart—that's part of life. It's one of the cruel, unfair parts of being sensitive and giving and emotional.

When you fall in love with someone, you always go in with the best of intentions. You go in believing this could be the One, that the way you feel for him in the beginning will be the way you always feel, but oftentimes, that's not how it ends—especially when you're young. And you know what? What you're feeling right now, that's just another part of being in love...the end of it. You're not crying for all the things you had, the memories you made, the way you felt...you're crying for all the things you'll never have, the memories you won't make, the way you won't feel—about that person—anymore.

I wish I had the words to take away your pain...but I don't. Truthfully, honey, no one does. Time is the only thing that will ease the hurt. It won't happen overnight, unfortunately, and it may get worse before it gets better. But someday you'll wake up and feel better, marginally at first, and then over time you'll notice that the tears and ache have faded, and one day you're just okay again. Broken hearts do heal, but not with words or a magic pill or a Band-Aid, only with time, and that's what you'll find out. This pain, it's not forever.

Do you remember when I told you about David Greene? Well, the story, as you may have guessed, didn't end with us driving off in his blue Mustang to live our happily ever after. And, by the way, thank goodness we didn't...otherwise I would have missed out on your daddy and, most of all, I would have missed out on you.

David left for boot camp at the start of August, as planned. And in the beginning, we wrote each other often. I was the girl who sprayed the notebook paper with perfume and wrote the word 'love' with a heart instead of a 'v.' At first, it was great. When the mailman came, I could almost count on a letter in David's block handwriting to be waiting for me. I went off to Seattle for school and things changed then, the letters trickled off and eventually completely stopped. I made excuses and figured he was busy, but the truth was, he was ending our relationship the only way he knew how, which was to stop being an active participant in it.

I spent the first half of my freshman year—the time I should have been making friends and studying and living it up—mourning the loss of my relationship. Do I regret that? Now that I've had you, and your father, and our life together...yes. But at the time, I was so hurt and confused, there was no other way for me to feel—I didn't know that all wonderful things that lay ahead of me, so I let the pain hold me in one place.

And, just like I told you, I hurt over that for a long time...but it got better. I met new people and surrounded myself with the things I enjoyed, and one day I woke up and I was okay—I was changed, definitely not the same, but I'd like to think David Greene made me a better person. I learned from him and our relationship. I learned to treat people with respect, to own my decisions and hold myself accountable for my choices. That's how you make the most of this: you take the good things you can learn from, and you leave the rest behind.

So, Mia, I know right now you're feeling like this just the end of everything that matters. But it's not, I promise you. You'll cry your tears, and that's okay...but you pick yourself up and put yourself back together. When you're dating someone, when you're in love with someone, and even when you're married to someone, heartbreak is a risk you take. Not everyone you meet is the one you're meant to be with. It doesn't matter how many times you're wrong about someone or how many times you fall in and out of love, it only matters that, just once, you're right—and that one time, that's the time that really counts.

I'm sorry you're hurting, honey, and I wish I could undo your pain...but be strong and be brave. I love you.

Mia listened for the familiar recorder click off, and pressed the rewind button. Her throat ached around her empty sobs, she felt exhausted and wired all at the same time, and her chest hurt like someone had run through her. Someone had. She wanted her mom, not some recording on a tape, but her real flesh-and-blood mother with warm arms and a soft touch and the patience to weather this devastation with her.

Kris opened the door slowly, crossed the room, and slunk onto the floor where Mia had curled into a tight ball. Kris gently pulled Mia into her arms, onto her lap, rocking her softly as though Mia were just a little girl.

"He—" Mia hiccupped, trying to put the words in the right order, trying to force them out, but she couldn't, she couldn't say the words out loud or to herself. The pain reeled, licking against her like flames.

"Shh," Kris cooed softly in her ear, hugging her closer, holding her broken pieces together.

Mia's eyes slid shut without effort, and that was the last thing she remembered.

CHAPTER TWENTY-SIX

MAY 9, 2012

MIA FELT TIRED, HER EYES burned, and her throat felt like sandpaper. Someone had put her in bed, pulled her sodden sweater and ruined jeans off, and replaced them with a soft night shirt. It crashed down on her; she remembered everything, the blissful moment of disillusionment sweeping away when she remembered. It hadn't been a dream; she was broken, nothing had changed while she slept.

"Oh, you're awake," Kris said as she pushed open the door into Mia's room. She was still dressed in her moving clothes from yesterday and looked tattered. Her hair was knotted in a low, messy ponytail, her eyes looked bleary with exhaustion. Mia wondered if she had slept that night.

"I'm up." Mia rolled over, pulling her knees to her chest and tucking the quilt under her chin.

"Can I get you anything? Tea or juice, water?" Kris offered, her hand still on the knob of the door, hesitant.

"No—thanks, though." Mia just wanted to fall asleep again, a peaceful sleep where there were no broken hearts or empty promises.

"Okay, honey—well, I'm just outside the door if you need anything." Kris nodded slowly, starting to pull back.

"He dumped me," Mia blurted out, feeling a fresh wash of tears spring to her eyes.

Kris crossed the room and sat carefully on the edge of the bed beside Mia, lightly stroking her back and her hair.

"He said that he—" Mia couldn't finish, her words and thoughts pinned down by tears. "I just want it to stop hurting," she managed to force out between heavy sobs.

"And it will, honey, in time," Kris lulled.

"I love him," Mia simpered into her pillow.

"And you'll feel like that for a while, but just like the pain, that feeling doesn't go on indefinitely, either."

"When does it stop?"

"When you realize that this wasn't your great love. When you realize that there is someone else out there, someone who is better for you."

Mia imagined feeling that way, putting Bryan behind her and moving on, but she couldn't. "I don't think there is anyone else."

Kris gave a short laugh. "Everyone feels that way. But there is someone else, someone amazing—I'm sure of that. You're still so young, Mia."

"It just hurts so bad," Mia gasped.

"Hurt hurts," Kris reasoned, still brushing her fingers down Mia's spine comfortingly.

"I don't understand...what did I do wrong?"

"Probably nothing. That's the kicker. You probably had absolutely nothing to do with his decision."

"He told me he still loved me still...so how could

he do this? Why would he want this if he loved me?"

"That's something very hard to understand...believe me, I know. When I asked my ex-husband for a divorce, it wasn't because I didn't love him anymore—I did, we'd spent more than half our lives together, that's a very, very deep love, a companionship.

"And I felt like a huge failure, I wanted to just crawl under the covers and die. Truthfully, I was terrified that I had just made the biggest mistake of my life, and I hated myself by inches for what I'd done to him and our marriage because I was being selfish, putting myself first.

"I wished that I had been able to push my own wants aside and meet his expectations. But the real issue was that we had to realize that we were in different places now, even after being on exactly the same page for so long. Our relationship had changed, and accepting that, while hard, was the best thing for us both."

"But you left him," Mia reasoned, wiping her tears away with the back of her hand.

"Those are the semantics. When a relationship ends, no one gets out without regret and pain."

"Do you think Bryan is sad?" Mia asked, sitting up, hugging her knees to her chest.

Kris nodded slowly. "I'm sure he's feeling very bad about this—mostly about having hurt you."

"He said..." Mia gathered her words. "That we were going to be in different worlds, and that was why it wasn't going to work."

Kris pursed her lips thoughtfully before continuing. "A year from now, Mia, I'm going to ask you how you're feeling about your future. And you're probably going to tell me you're excited, nervous, scared, apprehensive—because all of those feelings, they are absurdly normal, exactly how you're supposed to feel. College will mean big life changes. I'm betting that's how Bryan feels. Like he's standing on the edge of everything and he just needs to jump in. Sometimes that leap is easier to take alone. That doesn't mean he didn't love you, or regrets the time he spent with you...it only means that he's on his own journey."

"I'm going to miss him," Mia sniffed.

"You could always consider being friends," Kris suggested lightly.

"I couldn't! What if he gets a new girlfriend—?"

"And what if you have a new boyfriend? Listen, the last time your dad and I were in the city, we had dinner with my ex-husband and his new wife...and we looked at pictures of his children. You don't get to the place where you can do that overnight, but don't count it out entirely."

"Thanks, Kris. I'm going to get up now, get moving. The truck will be here any minute." Mia leaned over, hugging her close.

"Honey, any time you want talk, I'm here, and I promise, I'll listen."

"You would have been a good mom," Mia thought out loud, knowing the words were true. Whatever it was she had felt Kris was taking away from her, she was giving her more in exchange.

"I hope I can be a good mom to you." Kris kissed the top of Mia's head lightly, walking back towards the door.

———————————⟨≈⟩———————————

Mia held the tape recorder open and slipped the tape into the slot.

The moving truck had just pulled away from the drive, full of her life and her things, off to her future in the big city, her new home. Kris had convinced Gabe to let Mia linger. She needed time, just her and the house.

Mia, I'm sure today is a very scary and probably exciting day for you. Leaving home always is. I don't know if you're ten or eighteen, I don't know if you're moving for a change of scenery or simply moving on with your life. But that doesn't so much matter. Change, however it comes, is scary. It's the realization that everything comfortable and familiar is gone, and that you have to adjust to the new and learn to be happy with where you land. It's a big thing—and yes, a tremendous milestone.

I loved the city, but I wanted Port Angeles for you. I wanted you to grow up with grass under your feet and the sound of the ocean in your ears. I wanted you to appreciate the majesty of the natural world—not just the things man can create. I wanted you to live in a neighborhood, with sidewalks safe for riding bikes and friends no matter which way you rode. The city offers you a sort of life that is fast and exciting and full; it gives you culture and education and brilliance, and I always knew someday you'd chase those things all on your own. But childhood is short, and I wanted you to take those years to really live a simpler sort of life where time was measured by the tides, not by rush hour.

I left home at eighteen. I was going to college. Moving across the country where I didn't know a soul. I was going to have a roommate for the first time in my life, I was going to have a bank account and responsibility and what I did with my life from that moment on—it all mattered. The night before I left for Seattle, I sat outside with my mother. We talked about all sorts of things, serious and silly, all of them important—things I still remember to this day. That was the last time I saw my mom healthy. The next time I was with her, over the holidays, she was sick, and everything was different. But now, when I close my eyes and think of your grandmother, I remember her as the vibrant, funny, smart lady sitting beside me on a summer night in Chicago, sipping a Long Island ice tea, reminding me to wash my sheets at least twice a week.

I don't know how to prepare you to leave our home. I don't know how much or how little to tell you, and I wish I did. So, instead, I've left you something. It's in the hall closet, on the top shelf, you'll know it when you see it. You can go get it now, read it—we'll talk about it when you get back.

Mia clicked the tape off, and wandered through the

nearly empty kitchen to the hall coat closet.

There, on the high shelf, rested the present, just as her mother had promised. A sprig of dried lavender was woven into the raffia bow.

"Mom," Mia whispered, pushing the package to her chest, breathing in deeply.

Mia carried the present into her room, sitting softly on the edge of her bed. She undid the wrapping slowly, pulling the edges of the bow and slipping her fingers beneath the thick material and setting it all beside her. A card was taped to the cover of the colorful book, and she brushed a tear away and slipped her finger under the seal, opening it slowly.

> *Dear Mia,*
> *The lavender flower was what I carried down the aisle when I married your father. We stopped at a U-pick lavender farm in Sequim and gathered a bouquet. This stem is one of the many that I carried, and the only one that I saved. The lavender flower is symbol of devotion. It was perfect for my wedding, and it's perfect for you now. We've always been a family of devotion. Nothing changes that.*
> *Love you.*
> *Love, Mom*

Mia flipped the cover of the book open and began to read *Oh, the Places You'll Go.*

She absorbed the rhythmic flow of the words and message, blinking back the tears that welled up in her eyes and dribbled down her cheeks. Her hands shook with emotion as she turned the thin pages. Closing the cover, she reached for the recorder and pressed 'Play.' Her mother's voice filled the room.

This book, it's important, not simply because the message is wise and meaningful and will become more so over time, but because it's the truth. Mia—Dr. Seuss is a genius and he said it better than I ever could. This life you've had here, the security of this home, the comfortable spaces and familiar rooms—that's only part of your journey. It's the facing of new experiences— new challenges and even the letdowns that sometimes come along with them—that is part of the adventure. Have an adventure.

Mia, I'll be with you everywhere. It may feel different somewhere new, but still, I'm there with you. Don't be afraid or worried that when you leave this place, you're leaving me...because that isn't true, I'm always, always with you—no matter where your adventure takes you. Your grandmother used to say that a mother's job was to help her child find her wings. It's time for you to fly.

I love you.

It would never be the same, Mia realized. She might come back someday to start her own life, her own family, have her own things and children, but maybe she wouldn't. She might even come back often, but things would always be different. This would always be the place where she had had her mother, the place where they had baked and colored and laughed and celebrated and kissed goodbye, the place where she had been real. It would be her forever home, no matter where she landed. Her mother wasn't drywall and nails and furniture and things; she was alive in her stories and lessons and love and memories, things easily carried and never put down, no matter how far away she traveled. All the places she'd go, her mother would be there with her.

THE
BEGINNING - EPILOGUE

SOMEDAY

S HE STOOD ON THE EDGE of the cliff, her long dress brushing against her ankles, moved by the strong summer wind. She ran her fingers thoughtfully over her wide, full belly, the light butterfly kicks inside making her heart skip.

Walking back towards the expansive house, she delicately pondered on all the ways her life had been blessed. Her husband waved, flashing a devastatingly handsome smile from the patio, hanging a string of Chinese lanterns. She raised her hand in return, smiling brightly, taking in the way the morning sun danced off his bare chest while he worked. Her life was good, she mused, knowing it had become something that was full and beautiful and meaningful. She had more than she had ever dared to hope for.

The nursery was perfect now. It was the last room they changed when they moved back here, to this home high above the Sound, nestled in the clearing, surrounded on either side by the same aged, mossy trees she'd played amongst as a child.

Walking into the space just off the kitchen, the onslaught of feelings she had still caught in her chest. The room was enchanting. The walls were painted a soft pearl lavender, complimented by shades of grey, dove, and charcoal and silver—a complete, distinctly feminine feel. The windows were draped with heavy raw silk panels in a smoky shade, and lighter linen sheers cascaded to the floor behind them. The dark plank floor was dotted with thick shag area rugs that felt like clouds under her feet. A tiny crystal chandelier hung in the center of the room and the glass globes glinted in the late morning sun. Stuffed animals and books, a spring of dried lavender in a vintage glass bud vase, and a single Japanese glass float adorned the built-in bookcases, which were freshly painted a happy shade of bright white. A mobile hung over her old crib; a collection of tiny silver rabbits suspended in mid-leap hung in the air by thin slices of wire. It was perfect, exactly what she wanted: a nest for her baby girl. Somewhere safe, inviting, and exclusively hers.

She settled into the old rocker—her rocker—and fished the recorder out of the pocket of her dress. She had put the tape in earlier that day, now that the nursery was finished, she could listen.

Oh, Mia, you're going to be a mother! I cannot tell you how happy that makes me and how badly I wish I could be there to help you. This is truly a time that I was looking forward to. I know that sounds funny, since you are only seven right now as I record this, but even better than being a mother is being a grandmother—all the love and spoiling without any of frustration!

Being a mother, Mia, is not easy. It will bring you joy and pleasure and laughter, as well as tears and hurt and aggravation. And no matter how prepared you are, or how badly you want it...it's always a labor of love. Honestly, it's the best thing in this whole world. It's everything, and you'll see that. When they put that little life in your arms for the first time and you have that moment of clarity, when you understand that you are the one responsible for this baby's—your baby's—happiness, you'll be overwhelmed by your capacity to love, and how ferociously protective you'll be. It will feel like your heart has grown, doubled itself in one single moment. The love you feel for your child will be different than any other love, and when you feel that, you'll understand how I felt for you.

I think now is the right time to tell you the story of you. I'm sure your father's had his say, but, mother to mother, I want you to know how deeply loved you are.

You were born very early on a beautiful sunny morning. I labored with you, for, oh, thirteen hours? And then suddenly, after all of that pain and pushing, it was over, you were out and here finally, and crying wildly. Then the nurse came around and handed me this beautiful little baby girl swaddled in pink. You had the tiniest little hands and feet, and I must have counted your fingers and toes fifty times before I trusted my math, but, yes, you were perfect. Perfectly healthy, with an amazing set of lungs.

I looked at you and thought, Mine. You were mine. My baby girl, after years of wanting you, you were finally here. In the Italian language, cara mia means 'My Dear'—which I felt fit you. You were my dear. Elizabeth was my mother's name, and I wanted to honor her with that. Mia Elizabeth Chamberland, my daughter.

We had three years of bliss. I took to being a mother easily, and you were such a sweet baby. So pleasant and good-natured. You won't remember, but I used to have a bassinet in my office where you'd nap while I wrote, and it was as if we had this unspoken rhythm. Just as I needed a break, you'd wake up and want my attention. We'd go into your nursery and rock in the chair by the window for hours, I'd sing to you and read you stories, I'd make faces and you'd collapse into a fit of giggles. I'd nurse you, and the weight of you in my arms was the most peaceful feeling in the world.

I'll be honest with you, Mia: it's the most rewarding job, raising a little one, but it's far from the easiest. A child will test your patience and you'll develop broken record syndrome—repeating yourself over and over just to get the small things accomplished. There will be moments where you will honestly believe you can't take a minute more of the backtalk and sass and bad behavior and the not listening...but that's never truly the case. Kids will be kids, and your child will test your boundaries, just as you tested mine. But those moments never last. They are tough and exhausting, but it's all part of it.

Pick your battles, but always remember: what you do and what you say will shape your child—for the better and for the worse. Sometimes letting things slide because it's easier than holding your ground isn't the best thing. Knowing when and why to fight the good fight is a talent—but you'll just know.

Be a parent first and friend second. It's the natural inclination to want to be the cool mom, the mom that is fun all the time and has no rules and goes with the flow. But that's not the reality of parenthood— you're not their friend. Parenting comes first; you can be your child's friend later. You might think, as a first time mother, that if you're not cool enough, your child will resent you and because of that, you'll grow distant. That's absolutely not the case. When you can balance the two—the parenting and friendship—your relationship will be stronger for it.

Take time for you. I remember, back before I was sick, when we would go to Mommy-and-me classes, and the playground and preschool, there were mothers whose whole lives would revolve around their kids. They'd be worn thin, irritable, cranky, no fun at all. I think everyone needs a break— it's good for your marriage and it's good for the baby. Motherhood is a part of who you are—but it's not all that you are. Sure, there will be times when every waking minute is devoted to childcare...but go to the salon, get a pedicure or manicure, go on a date with your husband, or have a girls' day with your friends. Don't lose yourself, because once you do, I think it's very hard to get that part back.

Have more than one. Okay, now that sounds like pressure, and I don't want it to be. But that's my advice. When we had you, I believed that was it for us. Our one little beautiful baby girl. I was older, and so was your father...it didn't feel like there was enough time to do it again. But when you turned three, I got the itch to do it again. Had I been younger, I probably would have had a gaggle of babies. I loved being a mother; I loved you, and the toys, the chaos, and everything. So your father and I talked for a while and decided to try just one more time. We were going to give you a sibling. It never happened, and if I have any strong regrets about this life I've led and the choices I've made, that well could be the strongest of them all. Those dreams ended then, but I wish I could have given you a built-in best friend.

Being a mother—your mother—that was the best thing I ever did in my life. And I know our relationship ended too soon. But always know that you were my greatest joy, my deepest love. I hope your life is happy and teeming with love, that the things you need you have, and that you give more than you take, and, in turn, that you'll teach your child those things. I know, even now, that you'll be an incredible mom.

I love you.

She listened as the tape whirred to an end and the recording clicked to a close. Mia slowly ran her hand lightly over the rise of her stomach, and a firm nudge responded.

"Jenna Virginia Kristine…my baby," Mia whispered.

FOR MY READERS

Over the past two years, since the release of The Milestone Tapes, I have received so many wonderful e-mails and letters from readers and the one question that everyone seems to ask is: *Where are the rest of the tapes!*

I'm what is called a *pantser,* meaning I very, very loosely plot my novels and I allow my characters complete creative control over where their story is going. But, the tapes not featured in the novel do exist. Between writing Jenna's story and Mia's, I wrote all ten that Jenna left for Mia *just incase*. I did so because, just like Jenna, I had no idea who Mia would become and I wanted to be prepared for whatever she may encounter.

In the final version of The Milestone Tapes, we spend just a few months with Mia and, sadly, some of Jenna's tapes go unheard. I wasn't sure that I was going to release the five additional tapes, or, if I did, how I'd go about doing so, but when I decided publish a second edition for the book's anniversary, I thought it might be nice to include them. I hope you enjoy what I call "the deleted tapes." They are unedited and very rough and in no particular order, but I hope those of you who have asked for them will enjoy Jenna's take on marriage, college, graduation, cancer and, yes, sex, too.

Love Always,
Ashley

The deleted tapes

HIGH SCHOOL GRADUATION

High school graduation. Wow, where has the time had gone? Not so long ago you were my little girl, and your life revolved around pig-tails and climbing trees and coloring books. Now, in just a few short months, you'll be off to college. I can only imagine how your dad must feel watching you walk across the stage, seeing you accept your diploma. He must be so proud of you and I know I certainly am.

The year I turned 31, I had this moment where I realized that I'd been out of school for as long as I ever was in it. Kindergarten through high-school, those years felt like the longest of my life and then I woke up one day and the same amount of time had passed and it had gone so quickly. Someday, I suspect, you'll feel much the same looking back on your life, your friendships, the home you grew up in and the people who've loved you. I hope when you do, you'll feel good about the places you've gone and the things you've done but right now, this is the time to say goodbye, the time to realize that you can't take it all with you and some things are better left in the past. It's bitter and it's sweet, it's sad and it's exciting. It's the way it should be. From this moment forward, you're working towards becoming the woman you were always meant to be.

Take college seriously. Go to class, not because you have someone breathing down your neck and telling you to go, but because it's what you're supposed to do and what you're there for and it's your job. Learn everything you can — take the obscure classes that fascinate you and the ones that will help you in the long run. Drink it all in. Enjoy it all, because it goes fast and what comes afterwards will be very serious.

Congratulations, baby. I love you.

YOUR FIRST TIME

Sex. Are you blushing? Because goodness knows I am. But, I'm your mother and this is my job, so here's the deal...I'm not going to tell you how it works, I'm sure Aunt Sophia and Ginny have filled you in on the basics of the birds and bees and any question you have, you know you can go to them. Instead, I want to talk to you about what it means now that you're here in this place, because that is as important as knowing anything else...

Giving yourself to another person, Mia, is a gift. It is a privilege to share your heart and body with another, and, in a perfect world, it means something incredibly important. That's not say every time will be with someone you love and not every time will be with someone who is important to you, I'm not a prude enough to believe that, and I know that sex and love aren't always mutually exclusive...but just that, in a perfect world, every time you give yourself away, the person you're giving yourself to should be someone deserving of you. They should be someone you care for, and someone who cares for you return. And if they aren't...think about how you feel afterwards. Consider it. That's all I'm asking.

Safety. Oh what *can't* I say about that? There is safe-sex and that's important. You need to use some sort of birth-control, but there is more to be safe than just the contraceptives you use.. There is being safe with your choices. What does that mean? It means knowing how to protect yourself and not feel pressured into anything you're not ready for just because it's what *everyone else is doing it.* You're your own woman, make your own choices. And if a time should come when you feel differently, when, maybe you thought you were ready, and maybe afterwards you feel less certain, know that you can stop. Just because you started doesn't mean you have to continue. You can decide that, you know what, you're not ready and you want to wait a bit longer and there is nothing wrong with that. Anyone worth anything will hear you when you speak and understand what you say.

Mia, you've made an incredibly adult decision and I hope you understand all the things that come with making it. I wish I could take you out for a cup coffee, or, if you're over twenty-one, a strong drink, and look into your eyes and see who you are at this exact moment and gage whether or not I think you're ready for this, but I can't...so I want you to know... this milestone, Mia, more than any other, is the one that the power to change your life before you're ready for your life to change. Mistakes here don't just effect you, but everything. They're easy to make and the consequences of them are huge. Think with your head, feel with your heart.

I love you.

COLLEGE GRADUATION

Today is the first day of the rest of your life. Up until this moment, you've been my little girl, but tomorrow when you wake up, you're a grown woman, an adult, ready to plough into the world and make your own way. I'm so proud of you.

Being an adult is hard. You wait your whole childhood to grow up, and nearly the minute after you have, you'll find yourself wishing life could be as easy as it once was again. Suddenly you're faced with things like finding a job and making rent, punching a clock and trying to please a boss who may be unappeasable. You might even be tempted to measure your successes by those of others, but please, try to resist that.

Here is what I want you to do for me...I want you to find a job you love. Something that makes you happy. Don't settle for less than you deserve because it's the easier way. What's easy today will always be easy, but what's hard today gets easier tomorrow. Have you ever dreamed of seeing the world? Go do it. Have you ever wanted to be your own boss, thought of opening a small business and watching it grow?

Start that journey now. Whatever it is you want, build the sort of life you imagine for yourself. Take all the chances you can. Know that mistakes are okay, we all make them, but the secret is learning from them, and not allowing them define you. Fail, but fail trying.

I love you more than you'll ever know, and no matter where you land, I'll continue to be just as proud of you as I am today.

I love you.

YOUR WEDDING DAY

Oh, Mia! This is your wedding day. I'm sure you're the most beautiful bride. Of all the moments of your life I'll missed, this is the one I would given anything to see.

All day long and for a while now, I'm certain people have been telling you this is the most important day of your life. A wedding, it's a threshold into a new existence. It's important, please don't get me wrong, but it's not the *most* important one. There is no single *most* important day of your life. Every day is important. Everyday offers you something you didn't have or know before. You're going to have so many important days—like today, when you marry the man you love, but also when you have your children. The day you buy your first house and then, the day you sell that home because you've outgrown it. The day you get the job you've always dreamed of, and the day that job leads to a bigger job with more responsibility. I believe, in a life well lived, you'd never be able to pick just one from them all. I know I never could.

I hope as you've approached this milestone you

took time to realize that the wedding, it's only a party. A big party and maybe the best one of your life...but still, just a party. If things go off-script, if accidents happen, if mistakes are made...remember to tell yourself: It's just a party. More importantly, I hope you've spent the quiet moments leading you to this day focusing on the marriage that lies ahead. And what can I tell you about that? I guess the one thing you need to know is this: Marriage is complex.

It's a living, breathing thing with wants and needs. It's beauty and heartbreak. It's rewarding and it's hard. It's full of compromises and concessions. There is no room for pride or hubris. It's forgiveness and understanding when those things are hard to come by. There are mountains in need of climbing and milestones in need of passing. It's trying harder when you've tried as hard as you know how to. It's romance and practicality. Marriage, Mia, is a balance of all the good and all the bad life can give you and it is a spectacular thing because for all the challenges and triumphs you'll endure, you're doing it with the man you chose to love.

I wish you and your new husband the happiest, most beautiful life. I want for you both all the things you both want for yourselves. I hope that when you two take your vows, you feel them as much as you say them. I hope, in the man you marry, you've found not only a partner, but a best friend and I hope the same things for him as well. And I hope that he knows just how incredibly lucky he is.

I'm so sorry I'm not with you today to straighten your train and fluff your veil. But in all the quiet ways, I am. I'm there in the rain that falls or the sun that shines. I'm in every decision you made. I'm here with you, as you listen to this tape and I'm so incredibly proud of the woman you've become. So go. Go be a beautiful bride. Walk slowly down the aisle, take your time, take it all in. Dance the night away. Make sure you eat, take at least a bite of everything. Do you know the one detail of a wedding a bride misses out on most of all? The food! Too busy greeting guests, and celebrating to remember to eat. More than one bride has been *over served* for that reason alone. Oh, and don't tuck your handkerchief into your bra, it looks awful. Mia, cry happy tears and kiss your husband at the alter for along as you'd like.

Today is a new beginning. I hope you're ready and I hope you're happy and I hope everything from this moment on is all you dream it will be. Congratulations. I love you.

IF YOU'RE EVER IN MY POSITION

The day I was diagnosed, your father and I were in Seattle. We boarded a plane bound for home, and the two of us were just scared. We didn't know what this meant for us, or you. As we sat together on the plane, your dad tried to put cancer into a little box. He wanted us to move back to Seattle for treatment and he focused only on the positive, thinking that's what I needed him to do. Later, he'd tell me we'd have the year from Hell, but after that, we'd have a long life. He saw cancer as something we could climb and overcome. As for me...I sat on that plane and watched the world sail by below. I looked at the mountains and the valleys, the roads and the rivers, and I thought mostly of my mother. Missed her more in that hour long flight than I'd ever missed her before.

In the days following the diagnosis felt like I was standing in a forest at nightfall. Everything was silent, but the silence was so loud. I'd thought I had two options: fight or accept. But there are things in this life you can't outrun, things you can't oversimplify and cancer is just one of them.

You probably don't remember the beginning, and I hope you don't. You were three years old and my little girl and what I going through, it was so beyond what I wanted you to understand. I wanted you to only know the goodness in life, the happiness, the sweet stuff. With cancer comes the fact that you have to face the mortality of your parents. That's a hard thing, even when you're an adult. Mothers and Fathers are supposed to be invincible, to know they aren't changes everything. The truth that they are just human, no more and no less, is a really scary thing. I wanted to shelter you from that and I wanted to fight for my life so I could stay with you.

It felt like a war in the beginning. Almost as if every book I read on the subject and every fact I gathered from the research I studied, were weapons I was arming myself with. Later, as the first year turned into the second year and then the third, only then did I realize acceptance was as big part in the outcome as anything else.

I had to accept the disease to understand it, then I had to accept the help offered to me and admit I couldn't do it all on my own, and then I had to fight when I could and accept that sometimes I couldn't.

If you're listening to this, then you're the one choosing between the fight and the acceptance now, the one in the that forest at night, and I'm sure the world feels quiet and scary. But, I hope for you so many different things. I hope you know that whatever is required of you, you can do.

Chemotherapy, I won't lie to you, isn't easy. I heard

once that every time you go is like being dropped off on death's door step and being asked to walk home barefoot, that journey to and from is uphill both ways. It's a lot like that. Yours day will spent getting sick or getting ready to be sick again. A mastectomy, it can feel like a surrender. The world can make it seem that a woman's breasts are a barometer for her worth. When you grow them, you're growing up. Your cup size can dictate the sort of men interested in you. If you lucky and able, they nourish your children. But they aren't your barometer, and they no more define you then your ten toes do. They are part of you, but they don't decide who you are. If letting them go saves your life...let them go and find a way to be glad their gone. Radiation, it seems like the easiest of it all, but it comes with its challenges all its own. It hurts, but it's a necessary evil. There is specialized care, like oxygen therapy and gel packs...ask for it, advocate for yourself. Get what you need. Don't take no for an answer.

Mia, this is the one tape I hoped you'd never listen to...and if you are, please know, I feel a tremendous amount of guilt. Cancer was something that came with your genes, with your beautiful eyes and long eyelashes, your pretty skin and your lovely smile and your dark hair. I prayed it wouldn't and now, I pray that there will be things available for you that weren't available for me, mostly I pray for a cure and for you to have a long life beyond.

You need to be brave, and you need to be strong. But if you're scared and if you feel weak, know that I'm with you and that I love you.

ACKNOWLEDGEMENTS

To everyone who worked with me on The Milestone Tapes, both the first time around and on the second edition—Renu Sharma, Lauren Dee, Ashley Davis, Scarlett Rugers, Glendon Haddix. Your help to see that the book lived up to its potential is quietly acknowledged in my unwavering gratitude for your time, your talent and your support.

To my immediate family—Sue, Jeff, Michelle, Russ and Judi—and my extended family — the Macklers and Paternostros and Serwinowskis. Thank you seems like such a small word in comparison to all the love and support you've offered throughout the years.

To my husband, Mark, who also doubles as my very best friend: If such a thing as soul-mates exist, I'm certain you are mine. I love you more.

To those who make the writerly world where I work such a blissful place to be: Liz Grace Davis, David Adams, Richard Walls and so many others.

To the friends who have been patient and understanding during my bookish hibernations and have celebrated the last page with me: Gretchen, Abby, and Cyle. There isn't a day that goes by that doesn't find me grateful for the friendship you've given to me.

To the book bloggers who have supported this mission of mine from The Milestone Tapes on. Thank you for sharing screen space with me, and for being so excited about my books you couldn't keep them to yourself! You all are truly the first readers who get to know my characters and that's a very special experience for me.

And, last but never least, to my readers: You have my sincere gratitude. My wish for you all is that each of you find your happily ever after with no compromises...ever.

BIOGRAPHY

Ashley Mackler-Paternostro lives in a suburb of Chicago, Illinois with her husband, Mark, and their three dogs. Ashley considers herself a bit of magpie, picking up inspiration for her novels from the world around her. The Milestone Tapes was Ashley's first full length novel and was first published in the spring of 2011, followed by her sophomore effort, In The After, which went on to become an Amazon Best Seller in the winter of 2012. Her short stories can be found in Holiday Wishes - An Anthology for Charity, and the upcoming One Page Love Story Anthology. More information can on Ashley can be found on her website by visiting: www.ashleymacklerpaternostro.com

SOCIAL MEDIA

Facebook:
https://www.facebook.com/AshleyMacklerPaternostro

Twitter:
https://twitter.com/AshMP

Tumblr:
http://ashleymacklerpaternostro.tumblr.com

CPSIA information can be obtained at www.ICGtesting.com
Printed in the USA
BVOW07s1259280914

368573BV00002B/78/P